A Deceit of
LAPWINGS

PREVIOUS BIRDER MURDER MYSTERIES

A Siege of Bitterns (Book 1)
A Pitying of Doves (Book 2)
A Cast of Falcons (Book 3)
A Shimmer of Hummingbirds (Book 4)
A Tiding of Magpies (Book 5)
A Dance of Cranes (Book 6)
A Foreboding of Petrels (Book 7)
A Nye of Pheasants (Book 8)

ABOUT THE AUTHOR

Steve Burrows has pursued his birdwatching hobby on seven continents. He is a former editor of the *Hong Kong Bird Watching Society* magazine and a contributing field editor for *Asian Geographic*. Steve now lives with his wife and muse, Resa, in Oshawa, Ontario.

A Deceit of
LAPWINGS

STEVE BURROWS

POINT
BLANK

A POINT BLANK BOOK

First published in the United Kingdom, Republic of Ireland and Australia by Point Blank Books, an imprint of Oneworld Publications Ltd, 2025

Copyright © Steve Burrows, 2025

The moral right of Steve Burrows to be identified as the Author of this work has been asserted by him in accordance with the Copyright, Designs and Patents Act 1988

All rights reserved
Copyright under Berne Convention
A CIP record for this title is available from the British Library

ISBN 978-0-86154-179-9
eISBN 978-0-86154-180-5

Printed and bound in Great Britain by Clays Ltd, Elcograf S.p.A.

This book is a work of fiction. Names, characters, businesses, organisations, places and events are either the product of the author's imagination or are used fictitiously. Any resemblance to actual persons, living or dead, events or locales is entirely coincidental.

No part of this publication may be reproduced, stored in a retrieval system, or transmitted, in any form or by any means, electronic, mechanical, photocopying, recording or otherwise, without the prior permission of the publishers.

The authorised representative in the EEA is eucomply OÜ,
Pärnu mnt 139b–14, 11317 Tallinn, Estonia
(email: hello@eucompliancepartner.com / phone: +33757690241)

Oneworld Publications Ltd
10 Bloomsbury Street, London WC1B 3SR, England

Stay up to date with the latest books,
special offers, and exclusive content from
Oneworld with our newsletter

Sign up on our website
oneworld-publications.com/point-blank

For Mackenzie and Harrison:
The world awaits all the wonderful stories
you will have to tell

1

Water is a murderer's friend. It can rinse away blood, wash off fingerprint oils, submerge evidence. If it is dirty enough, water can contaminate wounds and compromise DNA. If it is cold enough, it can falsify the time of death, delaying decomposition and changing lividity, offering up vital hours that may be exploited by clever, pre-planned alibis. But water can do more. It can make moving a body easier so that, when the corpse is gently slid into a river from beneath the darkened archway of a bridge, water can take up the burden and float it along on its surface, leaving the murderer only to hold on and wade alongside, like a pallbearer at a funeral.

With the body supported in this way, the murderer may pause for a moment in the centre of the river and look around, to make sure there are no eyes observing from the darkness beyond the banks. Then, turning, they may locate, through the pale moonlight, the tree limb half-submerged in the water. And move towards it. And when, at last, the body has been guided to its chosen resting place, water can help once more, buoying the corpse, even as it twirls and spins in the current, until the murderer can lift it and hook it onto the gnarled branches, where it may hang suspended like a sad, saturated rag doll, until the coming dawn reveals it to the world.

Afterwards, when the murderer has returned to the bank, soaked and exhausted from their exertions, it is to the water that their eyes turn once more. As they sit and wait to recover the strength to complete the next phase of their task, they look out at the tree limb, bowed down now with the weight of its dreadful new bounty. The fast-flowing waters of the river approach, ready to wash past the new obstacle. But on their surface they carry a tiny object; a feather, caught in the trail of moonlight. It revolves slowly, buffeted by the racing waters but not conquered by them, fighting determinedly to stay afloat. As it reaches the body, the feather becomes caught in an eddy churning in front of the obstruction. Spinning in place, it seems to be trying to decide which side to pass; until some unseen force chooses for it. The water eases the feather around the body on silver ribbons of current; carrying it away into the night.

Because night, too, is a friend of one who chooses to take another's life. It shrouds the act in darkness, shielding the crime from prying eyes and cameras. For the murderer who requires time to complete their task – to drive, to kill, to load a vehicle, and then to drive some more – night provides the necessary cover. And when the driver has made the turn from the narrow road into the field and switched off the headlights to complete the careful approach down to the water's edge, night will be waiting once again, beneath the bridge. It will hide the murderer's movements as they enter the water with their heavy burden, and when they return afterwards to retrieve the body and ease it, too, into the river, and float it to its resting place.

But although the twin allies of night and water can conspire to conceal the act and wash away the evidence, what they cannot do, either of them, is hide the guilt or cleanse the taint of having taken a life. Those feelings will remain as the murderer stands and walks back to their vehicle, and linger as they turn to stare for another long moment at the water, illuminated still only by the palest of moonlight. The feelings will be there as the murderer climbs into the driver's seat and turns the key. And as they reverse back up the slope beside the bridge, turn onto the narrow track leading away from the river, and begin to drive from the scene. They will always be there.

The vehicle lurched slightly as it mounted the grassy verge and returned to the paved road surface. With a flick of the switch, the headlights suffused the surrounding land in a soft, ghostly glow. The scene at the river was set now; the tree limb in place, the body suspended from it. By the time the sun rose on the low, flat landscape, it would reveal the narrative the killer intended. As would the other scene that would be found in the morning. That one already held its story: the victim's laptop still open on the desk where he had been surprised at his work, the chair upturned during the struggle that led to his death, the murder weapon lying on the floor of the office. Everything was in place; the computer cord, the empty file folder, the door. *The door.* That was wrong, the killer realised now. A small oversight, perhaps, but enough? It was too late now to do anything about it. Returning to the office was out of the question. Ever since Dostoyevsky had Raskolnikov do so in *Crime and Punishment*, the myth has existed that killers will return to the scene of the crime. These days, the professionals who investigate murders don't give much credence to the idea. Most murderers, they know, like to give the crime scene as wide a berth as possible. Still, there are some who are compelled to return, out of a sense of remorse, perhaps, or perverse satisfaction, or even in an attempt to come to terms with what they have done. But surely none ever needed to add finishing touches to a story, as this killer must do now. So yes, there would be a return to the scene of the crime. But not the one at the office.

The river was disappearing in the rear-view mirror now. That office lay behind it to the east, where the earliest rays of the sun were already beginning to trace a thin line on the horizon. But the vehicle was heading west, towards a hill overlooking a valley filled with sharp, angular lines. At the very top of the hill, on a wide, flat expanse of grass criss-crossed with walking paths and fringed by an ancient woodland, lay a scene that told a story the killer still needed to change. Timelines had to be blurred, clues disguised, evidence concealed. The killer needed to erase any sign that this was the scene where the victim had been murdered. For the second time.

2

'Resignation!'

The word had ricocheted around the walls of DCS Colleen Shepherd's office and left a gaping, stunned silence in its wake. It had come only a few minutes into Domenic Jejeune's entrance, at Shepherd's invitation.

'Well, that's me done,' she had announced as he entered the room. She had tapped a sheaf of files into a tidy stack and set them in her out-tray.

'Done?' asked Jejeune.

'Finished. I'm out of here.'

Jejeune looked out of the window behind Shepherd. His life seemed to be in a constant state of turmoil these days. There had been the recent tragic incident involving a colleague, and, if blame could not be laid at his feet, it did not alleviate the feeling that he could have done more to prevent it. Then there was his previous sergeant, life coach and support system moving on to pastures new. Even his long-time partner, Lindy, had been expressing some restlessness lately about the direction of her future, and by extension, he supposed, their relationship. And now this.

He fixed his gaze on the view beyond Shepherd's office window, the fields bathed in the bright spring sunshine. This was one of his favourite birding seasons, with its migration spectacles and its courtship displays, but it was a time of great change, too. In contrast, there had always been a reassuring permanence to the slow, measured rise and fall of the fields as they rolled away towards the distant fringe of pine trees marking the far boundary. Despite the ever-changing moods set by the weather, this landscape provided constancy, when all about him seemed to be in flux, as it so frequently did.

'Don't look so down in the mouth, Domenic. If you're concerned about my replacement, it's all been sorted. In fact, that was what I wanted to talk to you about.'

Shepherd's customary briskness appeared to hold no hint of regret. The decision seemed to have come so suddenly, Jejeune wondered if it had been triggered by some specific incident. It was the little things that usually broke the spirit in the end, some tiny, momentary detail that normally would have been processed, but had this time managed to pierce the battle-hardened armour of a career police officer. Perhaps it was a dead child's outstretched arm, as if pleading for help you were unable to give. Or the flicker of terror you remembered from the face of a now murdered woman when her husband's earlier domestic abuse charge had been dismissed. Or the veiled sadness in the eyes of a bereaved elderly person who could no longer find any tears. Any one of these, or a thousand other scenarios, could have been the catalyst that caused Colleen Shepherd to call time on her career. Or perhaps it was something else.

'Is everything okay?' asked Jejeune. 'Health-wise, I mean.'

'With me?' The question seemed to surprise Shepherd. 'Never felt better. That's part of what went into the decision, actually. You know, do it while we still can. And the prices are unlikely to be this good again for a long time, if ever.'

'Prices?'

'For flights, Domenic. We leave for Perth. Tonight. Four glorious weeks in sunny Australia. Where did you think I was going?' There was an awkward pause as the realisation dawned on her. 'You thought I was jacking it all in?' She smiled cruelly. 'No, Domenic, I was talking about the long-deferred holiday Eric and I have been planning. The stars have finally aligned and we're able to do it.'

'Resignation!' Back in the present, Shepherd repeated the word and shook her head in wonder. 'Honestly, Domenic, I can't believe you'd imagine I was even considering such a thing. Whatever gave you that idea?'

He shrugged. 'Nothing, I was just thinking…'

'Yes, well, it would appear that your thinking, wishful or otherwise, is somewhat wide of the mark. Despite the numerous challenges brought by this position' — she paused and offered Jejeune a significant look over the rim of her glasses — 'I still find that the rewards outweigh them. Should that ever change, I'll be sure to let you know.'

Jejeune tried to find a suitable expression from somewhere. For all her testiness and impatience with him, DCS Colleen Shepherd was a superb administrator and he was content being part of her team. He doubted her temporary replacement, whoever it turned out to be, would provide anything like the smooth running the station enjoyed under her watchful eye. Who would it be? And that, he remembered now, was what he had been summoned in here to discuss.

'I suppose it will be Greene coming in?'

Shepherd's eyes found her desktop. 'Under normal circumstances it would have been, but he's off on a compassionate.'

She glanced up. 'It looks like it might be a long one, sadly. So they'll be bringing someone else in. That's what I wanted to talk to you about.'

It was the second time she had used the phrase, which in Jejeune's experience meant that it was almost certainly something she did *not* want to talk to him about, but rather something she felt she *had* to. And now, he had a good idea why. He looked out of the window again, as he composed himself. He recalled once watching a Kestrel from here, earning its epithet of *windhover* as it hawked dragonflies over the fields. It was a similar day to this, weather-wise, though perhaps it was later in the season. He had suspended a report to her in mid-sentence to watch the bird, and Shepherd had waited as she did now, her expression a fine balance between weary indulgence and a barely suppressed irritation.

'King's Landing?' he asked finally.

Shepherd nodded shortly. 'He'll be temporarily overseeing both areas, KL and Saltmarsh. The emphasis here is on *temporarily*, Domenic. Four short weeks is all, and then I'll be back. Besides, from what I'm hearing, Marvin Laraby is a changed man these days. Promotion to DCS seems to agree with him. And whatever you may think about his methods, you can't deny he gets results.'

Jejeune nodded. The same could be said of bombs and bulldozers, but, as with Laraby, cleaning up in their aftermath was not for the faint of heart. 'I can't see his methods aligning with the CC's declared aims of a more humane police service,' he said.

'He seems to have learned the art of compromise. If you have any thoughts about future advancement, it's a lesson you might do well to take on board yourself.' She fell silent for a moment, recalling the many spectacular successes her DCI had achieved precisely because of his refusal to compromise. 'All I'm saying is, despite your past differences, I'm sure the two of you can manage to get along until I come back.'

Sometimes, the blankness of Jejeune's expression was like the most highly silvered mirror, in which you found your inner thoughts reflected back at you even as your words professed the opposite. 'I hardly expect Laraby will be going out of his way to make life difficult for you, Dominic.'

Jejeune doubted he'd pass up an opportunity, either, but he said nothing.

'Certainly Danny Maik is having no trouble working under him,' she added resolutely.

Jejeune gave no response to this comment either. His former sergeant had forged a career by making himself invaluable to his superiors, and, in all the time Jejeune had worked with him, he could never remember Maik voicing open criticism of one. The reference was undoubtedly intended to suggest that perhaps Danny might be a bridge between him and Laraby. But it would be a big ask. Jejeune knew Marvin Laraby had a great deal of respect for Danny Maik, both as a police officer and as a person. The same could not be said of the incoming DCS's views of Domenic Jejeune. In either category.

'I'd like to hand Laraby over as clean a slate as possible. There isn't much on the board at the moment, save that idiot from HR Holdings throwing a high-profile temper tantrum.'

Jejeune looked at her uncomprehendingly. As uncomfortable as it was for him to admit, the lives of Saltmarsh's citizens didn't often cross his radar unless a violent death had clouded their horizon.

'Marius Huebner. It's just been revealed that he was the central figure in that sketchy land deal the government got embroiled in. The fact that he was involved sheds a new and even more unsavoury light on the whole affair. It's no wonder the government went out of its way to hide his identity. They should have known better than to get in bed with the likes of Huebner in the first place. He's always been bad news.'

'Nobody pointed this out at the time?'

'I understand that, even though some objections were raised, the deal was ultimately justified as being in the interest of the greater good.'

'Another compromise?' said Jejeune.

Shepherd acknowledged the point with a tilt of her head. 'It's hard to see the greater good in protecting a vile article like Huebner, I'll grant you,' she said. 'He's a proper old-school villain. Callous, intimidating, and brutal. But he's clever, too, as calculating as they come. Never draws a breath without looking at all the risks. It's why we've never been able to get him on anything. If it was me, I have to say, I'd have been more inclined to pursue the lesser good and nail him once and for all.'

'But the word is out now that he was involved in this deal?'

'It is. Despite the government's best efforts to prevent it. Somebody released his name to a podcaster who, of course, wasted no time in revealing it in his most recent episode. Now Huebner is swearing vengeance on whoever gave up his name. Only he's doing it online, in language that borders on the illegal. And since he has both the means and the disposition to follow through on his threats, we're going to have to get someone out there to have a word with him.' She paused, but Jejeune seemed disinclined to volunteer for the task. 'I feel confident I can get on that plane tonight knowing that this has been taken care of,' she said flatly.

There were lots of ways to ensure something got done in a police station, from direct threats to gentle cajoling, and in his time as a detective, Jejeune had encountered most of them. But Shepherd's way of simply stating her confidence in an outcome was as compelling and effective as any he had come across. 'I'll see to it,' he said.

Shepherd nodded shortly. She knew he would. 'Good. So with that, I shall take my leave of you. I've still got a lot of running around to do before I get on that plane. The Huebner file is there on my desk.' At the doorway, she turned. 'Compromise, Domenic,' she said. 'It's not a word any of us likes, but it's a reality in today's world. Lock the door when you leave, would you?'

He stood for a few minutes in the empty office, looking out of the window again. For a moment he contemplated how different that landscape might appear to him if Shepherd really was leaving. It was inevitable that one day she would. She was closing in on her pension eligibility and, for all her professed love for the job, he knew this trip was merely a foretaste of the travelling she and Eric had planned for the future. But she had assured him that she would be around for some time yet. And Jejeune knew that, among Colleen Shepherd's many other admirable qualities, she could always be taken at her word. With one last long look at the fields, he picked up the file and tucked it under his arm, locking the office door behind him as he left.

3

The rising sun lit the horizon like a distant fire, but its light hadn't fully reached the small group standing on the bridge yet. As he approached, Jejeune could pick out the imposing silhouette of Danny Maik and guess at the identity of two of the others standing beside him. Only one among the group, the smallest shape, was unfamiliar to him.

He walked up to join them, leaning on the wall of the bridge next to a floodlight trained on an object a short distance downriver, in the middle of the water. Even from here, Jejeune could tell it was a human body, snagged against a half-submerged tree limb bleached white by the glare of the floodlight. Marvin Laraby eased himself up from his own position against the wall and extended a hand. 'DCI Jejeune. Nice of you to join us.'

Danny turned and nodded a short greeting towards Jejeune. He knew the history between these two men and appreciated how Laraby's innocuous greeting could have carried a hint of sarcasm. Tony Holland, standing beside him, would recognise it, too. But Jejeune understood how benign it would have sounded to the unknown woman next to them, who had no knowledge of the men's previous involvement.

'This is Lelia Segal,' said Maik. The woman offered a warm smile in place of a handshake. 'I'm the new regional ME,' she said.

Another change. Jejeune had forgotten that Mansfield Jones had retired. He wondered if dealings with this new ME would prove any less fractious. Her friendly expression and breezy greeting suggested they might.

'Lelia? Not a name I've encountered before.' he said.

'Named after an early Christian saint. Can't say I'm exactly crushing that aspect of it, truth be told,' she said, smiling.

'DCS Shepherd got off okay then?' asked Laraby.

'Last night,' said Jejeune. He turned to survey the surroundings. The bridge elevation was not high, but in these parts it didn't need to be for him to see all the way to the horizon. As the morning light began to seep into the landscape, the features were emerging into focus. Flat land stretched out on both sides of the wide, fast-moving river that passed beneath the bridge. Yellow tape fluttered along both sides of the riverbank. To his right was Saltmarsh district, to his left, King's Landing. Jejeune's knowledge of local history didn't extend to which king might have landed here, or when, but he had been in these parts long enough to know that ancient boundaries, even those now invisible to the human eye, still held an almost mystical power. Though many had undoubtedly been redrawn over time, few, he imagined, would have been as bitterly contested as the latest one. Jejeune had heard it said that the measure of a fair negotiation was one where both parties left the table feeling slightly aggrieved. If so, the recent redistribution of police authority between King's Landing and Saltmarsh, now demarked by the river, had been an unqualified success.

Jejeune raised his binoculars to his eyes to watch the activity in the river. Uniformed officers in waders were approaching the body, their silvery slipstreams glinting in the rising light. A short distance away, a photographer manoeuvred for position to capture his shots. But no one was making any move to detach the corpse from its spindly harness. Instead they were standing around uncertainly and looking back towards the bridge.

'We need to clear up the jurisdictional responsibility before we can remove the body,' Laraby told Jejeune without taking his eyes from the officers. 'As I've already told these people, normally in a boundary case one DCS will simply formally cede it to another and we can get on with things.' He turned to fix Jejeune with a look, as the gazes of the others found him as well.

'I don't have the authority to cede this case. In DCS Shepherd's absence, I'd suggest the decision is going to rest with the Assistant Chief Constable. I thought you were overseeing both areas anyway,' said Jejeune.

'I am, but I don't want any later prosecution compromised by suggestions that it was conducted in the wrong jurisdiction. I've got a call in to the ACC, but for now the body stays where it is.'

'Which is not, frankly, an ideal situation from my point of view,' said Segal. 'Every minute that body is in the water, evidence is being washed away and more and more contaminants are being deposited. Can't we just whip it out to one side or the other and sort out the details later?'

Maik and Jejeune exchanged a glance. Superseding the ACC's authority was not an action to be taken lightly. Colleen Shepherd might have considered it, for the good of an investigation, but both men knew Marvin Laraby wouldn't.

'We certainly caught a break,' said Holland. 'Fast-flowing water like this, if the body hadn't snagged on that dead tree, it might have been carried all the way out to the sea. Could have ended up anywhere along the coast or even drifted away altogether.'

Segal extended a hand to Jejeune. 'Mind if I use those bins for a moment?'

Jejeune handed them over and she took a long, careful look at the body, nodding to herself. 'Deep ligature marks round the neck.'

'Cause of death?'

'I would suggest those wounds are not something anyone could survive.'

She left a look on the bins as she handed them back to Jejeune. 'Zeiss. I should have known. Great low light capabilities.'

'Are you a birder?'

'No, but the quality of those tells me you must take it pretty seriously.'

Laraby moved in to intercept the shared smile. 'Can you tell how long the body has been in the water?'

'It normally takes about three days for a submerged body to float to the surface,' she said. 'I would have said the lividity patterns on the neck look fresher than that. Otherwise, though, I'll need to wait until I've had a proper look at the body in the lab.'

'The jogger who reported it didn't run this route yesterday,' said Holland, 'but he claims it definitely wasn't here two days ago.'

Segal nodded. 'I might be able to tighten up the timeline a bit. No guarantees, though. Immersion in water for any length of time is going to make it tricky.'

Laraby stared around at the landscape. 'So what do we think then, killed up here and dumped in off this bridge?'

Maik looked around them. 'No sign of fibres on the wall, No scuff mark in the gravel, no tyre tracks,' he said. 'If he did go in from here, somebody went to a lot of trouble to tidy things up afterwards.'

Jejeune raised the bins again and focused on a section of the bank downstream beyond the body. It could have been a trick of the morning light, but the grass looked slightly flattened. He switched his focus to the body, cradled against the basket-weave of bare branches. He lowered the glasses and looked around. 'I don't see anywhere that tree limb could have come from. There's nothing taller than a bush anywhere in sight.'

'Went in somewhere upstream and drifted down here, no doubt,' said Laraby. 'Must happen all the time.'

'It would have to have come a long way. I'm pretty sure that's a Green Woodpecker hole in the branch just above the victim's head.'

Even Danny Maik recoiled slightly from the comment. If you were looking for a time when a birding observation might be welcome in a Laraby-run investigation, *never* would probably be your safest bet.

'A woodpecker hole?'

Jejeune nodded. 'A Green. Typically, you'd expect to find them around parks and lawns.' He looked out over the marshy fields. There was not a blade of manicured grass anywhere in sight. He let his silence make the point for him. 'You know, the kind of dry environments where they can find ants to eat,' he added helpfully.

Maik suppressed a smile. He would have said Jejeune was as adept at handling people as anyone he had ever met. It was unlikely that his former DCI would be unaware of how his comments were likely to be received by Laraby. Perhaps not trusting himself with a response, the DCS instead called down to the officers examining the muddy ground around the footings of the bridge. 'Anything?'

'Footprints,' an officer called back. 'Too much of a mishmash to get any clear casts, but somebody was definitely down here.'

'Signs of a struggle?'

'More like something has been dragged through here. Something heavy.'

'The wounds suggest the victim was strangled from behind,' said Segal. 'You would need firm footing to generate the amount of force required. It's not likely you could manage it in mud like that.'

Laraby nodded thoughtfully. 'So he was almost certainly already dead when he was taken down there. But if the killer brought the body here to dispose of it, why not throw it from the bridge? Why risk parking up while he unloads the body and manoeuvres it down a steep embankment just so it can end up in the same place it would have done anyway? What sense does that make?'

Laraby's phone pinged and he reached for it immediately. 'ACC,' he said. He listened intently, head bowed, for a few moments, then pointed to the King's Landing bank before moving away to continue the call. The others watched from the bridge as the recovery team waded to the suspended body and began to meticulously detach it from the branches.

'After all this time in the water, I'm going to forgo any further field examination, in an effort to preserve anything that might still be left on the body,' Segal told them. 'As soon as it's lifted out, I'll have the team bag and seal it and transport it straight back to the lab.'

Laraby returned, having concluded his call, and leaned on the wall again, watching as the ME made her way down to supervise the body's arrival on the bank. 'Sergeant Maik,' he said without taking his eyes from the unfolding scene, 'while we are waiting for the ME's findings, I want you to see if any mispers have come in for a male, well-dressed, early thirties, short black hair, about, what, six foot?'

He pushed himself up off the wall and looked squarely at Jejeune. 'If anything pops, we'll run it for a match against our victim and let you know. In the meantime, in the absence of any evidence, ID, or even a murder scene, I'd suggest your skills are not yet required, Inspector. I'll let you know when they are.'

Quite when that might be, Danny Maik wouldn't have liked to say. He was keeping his own focus firmly on the activity in the centre of the river. But also on the tree branch. A thoughtful expression crossed his face. He didn't know what had happened here, but he did know one thing. When it came to birding matters, Domenic Jejeune rarely got it wrong.

4

'Laraby?' Lindy Hey's voice rose in disbelief. 'Marvin bloody Laraby? A DCS?' Frustration never seemed to be far below the surface for Jejeune's partner these days, but in truth the news would probably not have met with any kinder reception even on one of her better days. 'The police promotions board must have no standards at all.' Having tolerated Jejeune's momentary sojourn to watch a Reed Bunting with thinly veiled impatience, Lindy set off again at pace. 'Laraby's an embarrassment to the service.'

Jejeune shrugged as he fell into step beside her. 'Clearly the board don't feel that way.'

'No, they tend to get blinders on when someone is telling them what they want to hear. But giving all the right answers at an interview and having the basic skills to do the job properly are two different things. Marvin Laraby has all the wisdom and insight of a fridge magnet.'

They continued walking along the riverbank at the crisp pace set by Lindy. Behind them was the bridge on which Jejeune had stood earlier in the morning, watching as the team extracted the body of the man snagged on a large tree branch. That, too, was behind them, in the water on the far side of the bridge. Jejeune wasn't sure he'd quite go along with Lindy's views on Laraby's intellectual abilities, but she was never at her most restrained when she was defending him. And it was undeniably true that Laraby had caused Domenic his fair share of grief over the years. Considering Lindy's ability to move on from her own setbacks, it never ceased to amaze him how tenaciously she could hold on to grievances from his. But Jejeune suspected her ire today had deeper roots than Marvin Laraby's undeserved promotion. Until the cause was ready for public airing, though, Lindy would guard it carefully. Past experience had taught him that the best thing to do for now was simply to move on to other matters.

'What are we doing here anyway?' she asked, looking around as if noticing her surroundings for the first time. 'Isn't this your scene of crime? I'd have thought you'd spent enough time here for one day. Besides, wasn't the body found down by the bridge? Why are we walking away from it?'

'There wasn't enough time to get a proper look at the area when I was here earlier. Now that forensics have finished, there's something I want to check.'

Jejeune snapped his bins up at a flicker in the vegetation, but lowered them again quickly. The same Reed Bunting as before was apparently following them along the water's edge. On another day, he might have spent more time watching it, but Lindy's desire to be on the move was obvious, and she was off again as soon as he turned.

'Is there any reason you're in such a hurry today?'

'I'm trying to get in shape,' she said resolutely. 'I'm going to take up hiking.'

'Hiking? Does this mean you're planning to start coming on my birding trips with me?' Even to him his tone sounded somewhere between surprise and alarm. But Lindy just turned her gaze on him.

'To paraphrase Mr Twain, birding is a good hike spoiled. No, I mean serious hiking. I'm joining a club. I'm going to do the Pennine Way. After that I might do the Coast to Coast. Maybe I'll do John o' Groats to Land's End, as well.'

'Unless you're planning to do them all in a day, I'd suggest you could slacken off the pace a little.' Jejeune was puzzled. Lindy was not really a joiner, so he doubted this sudden interest was part of some social activity. 'What's brought this on?'

'I just feel I need to do something significant with my life, that's all.' She seemed poised to continue, but the impulse passed. 'What's Laraby doing on this case anyway? I thought the river was the jurisdictional boundary now.'

'He's the senior officer in charge of both areas. Temporarily.'

Lindy frowned and looked at him. 'What about Shepherd? Oh right.' She nodded to herself. 'She's off on holiday with Eric.'

'Australia. Their long-planned trip,' said Jejeune. He regretted the reference immediately. The continent was the last reported whereabouts of a man who had once held Lindy's fate in his hands, who perhaps still did. Ray Hayes had risen like a spectre from Jejeune's past and come as close to fracturing their relationship as anyone ever had. Even tangential references to the man or his place of residence were still enough to cause Lindy a frisson of unease.

'Australia is a big place, Lindy,' he said gently. 'It's well over thirty times the size of the UK. There's plenty of room for a man like Hayes to hide out and never be heard from again. They won't run into him while they're over there. No one from here ever will. He'll want it that way, and he's clever enough to ensure it.'

Lindy nodded at the reassurance, keen to put the topic behind her. Her current concerns were enough to consign horrors from the past to the shadows. 'So while our bosses are swanning off to exotic locales, I'm stuck here covering stories of no importance whatsoever. Could my life even get any better?' she asked sarcastically. She scrutinised the bunting's behaviour with interest. 'Is there something wrong with that little bird? It looks like it's hurt.'

'Reed Buntings are known for feigning injury. It's trying to distract us. Its nest must be nearby.'

'It should be ashamed of itself,' she said shortly. 'What if it was in real distress? Has it never heard the story of the little bird who chirped *wolf*?'

'A number of species engage in decoy activities like this.' He paused. 'Lindy, you know I'd support you in anything you'd want to do, but hiking… I mean, are you sure it's something you could properly get into?'

'I need to do something I can look back on and be proud of,' she said resuming her high-speed pace. 'Clearly the days of breaking major news stories are a thing of the past.'

Jejeune had fallen into step beside her, but he stopped suddenly now and Lindy followed suit. 'You're talking about this guy who revealed Marius Huebner's name? That was a podcast, Lindy. That isn't real journalism.'

'It is, Dom, it's the new real journalism, where investigative leads are generated and the public interest is engaged. It's how people want to follow stories these days. Have you seen that podcast's numbers? They dwarf ours, they're multiples of the circulation the mag gets on its best day. I'm a dinosaur trapped in a bed of limestone. It's why I'm stuck covering local gossip instead of doing work I can be proud of.'

'There's plenty of other things for you to be proud of. Look at that rockery you've built at home. It looks great, and that's all you. I had no input into that at all.'

Lindy flapped a hand in frustration, sending the Reed Bunting into flight. 'Wow, gardening, and while I've still got my own teeth, too. What an accomplishment!' She softened her tone. 'Sorry, I know you're just trying to make me feel better. It's not your fault you're crap at it.'

The bunting settled in a patch of spindly grasses on the far side of the river and began busily foraging for food among the stems. Apparently it no longer felt the need to distract the sparring couple on the other bank. Lindy gave a deep sigh as she watched the bird. 'Don't mind me, I'm just having a bit of a midlife crisis, I suppose.' She cast a glance Jejeune's way. 'And this is the part where you say *Surely it's much too early for that.*' She shook her head again. 'I should have known Johnno would end up podcasting. He always was good at spotting trends. He was on about podcasts and YouTube channels before I'd even heard about them.'

'You know him?'

She nodded. 'From uni, yeah. Breaking news like this was what he lived for. Even when we did our civics courses on zoning and planning together, his focus was still on where the stories would be. It was all he cared about. Commitment, you see, dedication to your craft. That's what gets you the big stories.'

'You cover big stories, Lindy. You've won awards.'

'Not lately. And look at me now. While Johnno gets to break a major government scandal, you know what my latest assignment is? The local horticultural fair.'

'Well, at least you'd be able to get some tips about your rockery plants.'

Lindy smiled sadly. 'That business about you being crap at making me feel better. I take it all back. It is your fault.'

The river had carved a pronounced curve from the flat landscape and as they rounded it Jejeune stopped and stared. A jumble of dead tree limbs were stacked against the far bank, tangled up with other natural detritus that had been deposited by the water as it curled around the bend.

'A snag the size of the one that poor man was caught on could never have made it past here down to that stretch of river, could it?' asked Lindy.

Jejeune's silence as he stared at the web of branches told her he agreed.

'That must mean somebody threw it in there further down. Off the bridge, perhaps.' She nodded to herself. 'You don't think it was an accident that the body snagged on it, do you?'

'I think somebody wanted to make sure that body was found.'

'And you've probably got some thoughts as to why.'

He stared at the tangled mass of branches, lifting slightly but still holding firm as the water gently churned past. 'Some,' he said.

'But none you'd be prepared to share with Laraby at this point, I presume?' Lindy's phone pinged and she looked at it.

'It's a text from Danny. He wants you to call him. They have something.' She shook her head as she tucked her phone away again. 'You won't get away with it on this case, you know.'

'With what?'

'Going dark when you're off birding, or... like this. It might be all right under Shepherd, but Laraby won't stand for it. And you can't expect Danny to keep covering for you. He doesn't even work for you anymore.'

No, thought Jejeune, he works for Laraby. And Maik's loyalty would always be to his duty. In his own defence, given that the body had already been recovered and SOCO had processed the site, it seemed to Jejeune that being unreachable for a few minutes was unlikely to make much of a difference at this early stage of the investigation. But Lindy had a point. It was one more change, among many, that he was going to have to come to terms with now that Maik had moved on to another police division. He turned on his phone and dialled.

'Sampson Lee,' Maik told him without preamble. 'Lived in one of the cottages off Ambler Drive. I'm heading over there now. Do you want me to pick you up?'

'Lindy can drop me off. I'll meet you there.'

He hung up and looked at Lindy. 'The victim has been identified. I need a lift to his place in Ambler Drive.'

'The one in Saltmarsh?' asked Lindy. 'Well at least you'll be on home turf.'

Jejeune nodded, but he didn't return Lindy's smile. It troubled him slightly to know she probably wasn't the only one thinking in those terms.

5

Danny Maik was sitting in his Mini when Lindy pulled up beside the car. She smiled as she recognised the song he was listening to. '"Mercy Mercy Me", Danny? I thought Marvin Gaye might be a thing of the past, now that there's a new sheriff in town.'

Maik returned her smile of greeting. 'I imagine DCS Laraby has got other things than my Motown to be concerning himself with.'

'Still.' She inclined her head towards the lyrics. '"*Things ain't what they used to be*". Where *did* all those blue skies go, I wonder?'

'It's Norfolk,' he said with a wry grin. 'Weather's changeable.'

She drove off with a wave and Jejeune stood beside the Mini as Maik turned off the song and got out. 'You didn't need to wait for me before going in, Sergeant,' he told him.

Maik shrugged easily, but the message was clear. It was the way they used to do it. The way they'd always done it.

'Do we know anything about our victim?'

'I managed to get a bit of background while I was waiting. Only online stuff.' Maik's expression suggested the provenance might cast a shadow over the information. 'He seems to have been a mathematician, designing software for some avian research programmes they are developing up there at the university? At a place called the Euclid Lab.'

'He's a birder?'

'No evidence of it,' said Maik, who'd spent enough time around the DCI to know working on birding software was a far cry from hunkering down in fierce onshore breezes to watch a tiny group of waders scuttling up and down a beach.

As the men approached the house, Jejeune stopped, stepped aside and opened the low gate. After a moment's hesitation, Maik passed through first. He turned to Jejeune. 'That tree branch, sir, you think the killer took it there with the body and threw them both in the water at the same time?'

'Not threw, Sergeant. Placed.'

Maik waited. The best explanation seemed to be to make sure the body was discovered instead of letting it just drift away on the river currents. But why? To ensure a message was delivered? *I crossed someone, and this was my fate.* 'So I suppose the obvious question then,' continued the sergeant, 'is why not choose a stretch of water that already had branches in it to dump the body?'

Jejeune inclined his head and smiled slightly, as if to suggest perhaps that obvious questions sometimes had less-than-obvious answers.

Maik tested the front door and shook his head. 'Locked.' He indicated a narrow passage along the side of the house. 'I'll have a look round the back.' Jejeune followed him along the passage a moment later. He found the sergeant waiting by the kitchen door when he emerged. 'This one's open,' said Maik.

Jejeune paused before they entered. How many times had they faced this moment together? Preparing to enter into an unknown situation never got any easier, but one thing was for sure. They weren't going to get any answers out here.

Maik eased open the door quietly and the two men entered, listening for movement. The cottage sent back only the hiss of its silence. The kitchen was tidy; not obsessively so, but enough to suggest someone who enjoyed neatness and organisation in his workspaces. They moved on through into the hallway, pausing and checking recesses and open areas with a synchronicity built of many years' practice. At the foot of the stairs, Maik pointed upwards. Jejeune nodded and continued into the first of the two rooms opening off the hallway at the front of the cottage.

He looked around at another tidily arranged room. The furniture was precisely positioned to maximise the space around it. It wasn't a setting that was particularly welcoming, but rather one that was functional and efficient.

Maik appeared in the doorway behind him. 'Clear upstairs,' he said in a normal voice. 'It looks like the action took place across the hall.' This time he stood aside for Jejeune to cross the hallway and enter before him. They advanced only a step or two inside the room before stopping to take in the scene.

They'd walked in on worse. The neat office, as organised and orderly as the rest of the home, showed only one piece of furniture out of place. A computer chair that had been behind the glass-topped desk was now lying on its back, a few feet away. A thin black electrical cord, still plugged in to a wall outlet, snaked across the floor beside it. The desktop itself showed no obvious signs of disturbance. A stack of papers still lay in a neat pile in a tray on the corner of the desk. Beside it was a mug filled with highlighters and markers. A stapler and a tray of paperclips lay in neat alignment on the other side of the desk, along with two pens and two sharpened pencils arranged in a tidy row. Even the open laptop computer was precisely placed, neatly aligned with the edge of the desk. The men looked at each other. Though neither could have expressed the reason for it, they couldn't shake the feeling that something didn't seem right.

Jejeune crossed to the desk and reached to turn on the laptop. The screen flickered to life, a blank cursor pulsing beside a box that requested a password. A couple of yellow Post-it notes had been stuck around the edge of the screen, looking like discarded bunting from a long-past celebration. A name on one of the slips caught Jejeune's eye, and he took out his phone to take a picture of it. 'Do we have a time of death yet?' he asked over his shoulder.

'Nothing further from the ME. It'll be a tough one, being in the water and all. We might have to build a timeline from his known activities.'

Jejeune nodded. 'So he's seated here when his killer enters. He doesn't even stand to greet them because he knows them so well.'

'He feels confident enough to let them come round behind him,' continued Maik, 'and that's when the killer strikes. He snatches the cord from the side of the computer and strangles our victim, pulling him backwards off his chair in the process.' He leaned down to look at the electrical lead but didn't touch it. 'Traces of blood and skin on it.'

'Enough to get a match to Sampson Lee's wounds?'

'I'd say so, yes,' said Maik. 'You want me to call SOCO in, tell them we have a potential murder scene?' But his tone suggested he already knew Jejeune would decline the offer.

'It would have been on top, wouldn't it?' said Jejeune, coming round the desk to look at the cord. 'Last item to drop, after the chair had been tipped. And the victim had stopped struggling, completely subdued now, strangled to death. That's when you'd drop the cord. And it would have landed on top of the chair, not beside it.'

'Perhaps the killer used it to power up the computer after he'd killed Lee. Maybe he was looking for something on there.'

'Why would he need to power it up? The indications are that Lee was working on his computer when the killer entered. With the lead this close it means it was almost certainly plugged in. It's likely the killer wouldn't even have needed a password to get into the computer.'

Maik allowed himself the briefest of half-smiles. When he was working with the DCI, he was never quite sure whether he had already reached the conclusion himself and Jejeune was just more adept at expressing it, or if it was still a jumbled mass of disconnected thoughts rattling around in his mind, and a simple phrase or two from the DCI distilled it all into clarity. All he knew was that, now Jejeune had pinpointed what had been troubling them, it all made sense.

'There's something else, too,' said Maik. 'This door. When I came in, it was closed.' He crossed to the office door now and touched it gently. It swung freely, but stopped in position as soon as it was released. It hadn't drifted shut on its own.

Jejeune nodded thoughtfully. 'You've just killed somebody. There's been a lot of frantic thrashing around, an intense few moments of holding the cord tight, keeping it cinched. Your heart is pounding from all that adrenalin, the blood is pulsing through your veins. And now, you've got a body on your hands. You need to get it out of here. Back door, you think?'

'Makes sense,' said Maik. 'Out of view of the neighbours. You'd park close if you knew what you were coming here to do. And it seems pretty clear this was no spontaneous act. But that office door would need to have been open to get the body out of this room and into the corridor. So you open the door, drag the body out and put it in your car. And then…'

'Then you come all the way back in here, just to close the door?'

And this time, Maik was sure he was right there with Jejeune's thinking. Somebody else had been in here, after the killer had removed the body. It had been long enough afterwards that they needed to plug in the lead to power up the computer that had run out of charge. Whether they had found what they were looking for on that computer, Maik didn't know. But either way, they had been clever enough not to take it away with them. In fact, they had been very careful to hide their presence here at all. But not quite careful enough.

Jejeune had watched in silence as Maik registered it all, and he was still looking at him now. The sergeant returned his gaze and understood the message. Now he could call it in.

6

Though Domenic Jejeune had been in the Incident Room at King's Landing before, this was the first time it was as a part of an investigation team. It caused him to look at his surroundings in a new light. Whereas the Saltmarsh offices still carried the freshness of DCS Shepherd's recent facelift in a moment of downtime, this room bore the patina of its years. It had always been an unfussy, no-nonsense space, but Jejeune remembered its well-worn look as being much more welcoming. Now, with the exception of a couple of coffee mugs, the desks beneath the harsh ceiling lights held few non-essential trinkets, and there was little on the walls that didn't relate to prosaic efficiency and police practices. It had not taken Laraby long to set his stamp on the place.

The DCS was standing before a white smartboard at the front of the room, and waited until Jejeune had taken a place leaning against a side wall before beginning. 'Right, I'm sure you all know DCI Jejeune and DC Holland from Saltmarsh.' He pointed to the constable seated in the front row. 'We're running a joint op, but I don't think it's going to be necessary to assign desk space here. Although KL will be the command centre, I don't see why you two can't work out of Saltmarsh.'

He paused to look at the two men, but it wasn't for consensus.

'It's been decided that the new ME for the region will be working out of this station for the time being, though. And given that collaboration is going to be the name of the game here, we will be asking Constable Holland to act as liaison with Dr Segal for both jurisdictions.'

'No hardship there,' said Holland with a sly smile.

'Glad to hear it. Why don't you get down there now and see if she's got anything for us. Oh and Constable,' he said as Holland rose, 'you will be careful to keep your mind, and all other parts of your anatomy, firmly focused on the task at hand, won't you? We don't want the good doctor getting distracted by the unwanted attentions of some scruffy herbert from the other side of the water, do we, Sergeant Maik? We don't take kindly to people taking liberties with our crew up here in KL.'

Maik's expression remained impassive. There were undoubtedly subtler ways to remind him where his loyalties lay, but then, Laraby had never been one for a velvet glove when a sledgehammer would do. Danny turned from watching Holland's departure to find his DCS staring at him. 'Anything of note from the SOCO findings, Sergeant?'

Maik shifted his big shoulders. 'Not from the house search, sir, no.' He paused, but he had been doing the job too long to hope that Laraby would be prepared to move on. He left his gaze on Danny. 'The branch was from an alder *Alnus glutinosa*. They don't grow in that area. They also recovered some bird feathers,' he said reluctantly, 'from a hole in the branch just above where the victim's body had been snagged. They were confirmed as being from a Green Woodpecker.'

The puzzled silence from those in the room who didn't understand the significance of the comment was matched by the uneasy silence of those who did. It was a moment before Laraby responded, more crisply than he had done so far. 'Well, unless that gets us any closer to finding out why someone strangled Sampson Lee in front of his computer and then transported his body out to the river, I'm not sure it's particularly relevant, is it, Sergeant? Anything else that might be?'

Maik looked at Jejeune but the DCI took a moment before responding. He seemed aware that his answer was going to take them into new territory. Whether he was ready to explore it yet was another question. 'There was a Post-it note on the victim's computer,' said Jejeune finally. 'It had the contact info of the podcaster who announced Marius Huebner's name. Johnno. Full name: Johnson Rory McBride.'

'Huebner?' said Laraby. 'The same bloke who has been setting the internet on fire with his threats? Well, I'm starting to like the way this is going already. So we're thinking Sampson Lee somehow gets hold of the name, and passes it on to this Johnno character so he can announce it on his radio show?'

'Podcast,' corrected Jejeune. 'Only I'm not sure I see a motive for Huebner.'

'You saw those videos he posted. He was pretty adamant about seeking revenge on whoever had leaked his name.'

Jejeune shrugged. 'His anger seemed to be about somebody breaching the confidentiality agreement he had with the government. By all accounts Huebner isn't a man to do anything without a reason, and revenge doesn't really seem to serve any purpose. Preventing the release of his name makes sense as a motive, but the information was already out before Lee was killed.'

'Sometimes it pays not to try to be too clever,' said Laraby impatiently. 'Huebner issues threats over the release of his name, and the bloke responsible turns up dead. Perhaps it's as straightforward as it looks.'

The rest of his point was interrupted by Holland's sudden appearance in the doorway. He was holding a sheet of paper and it was obvious from his breathing that he had run back up the stairs, probably taking them two at a time. His arrival had already caused everybody in the room to look in his direction, so he didn't bother retaking his seat before he delivered his news. 'In addition to the strangulation marks round the throat, sir, the victim suffered catastrophic cranial damage; a massive injury to the back of the head.' He paused for a moment to let the significance of the announcement sink in. 'The ME's initial thoughts are that it came from a heavy, rectangular object, mostly likely a concrete block of some kind.'

Maik was the first to recover. 'And we're only just hearing about this now?'

'To be fair, Sarge, the body was in a bit of a state, being pulled back and forth to free it from that tree branch, and then floated across to the bank on its back and hauled out. Plus, the water had washed away most of the blood around the wound by the time the body was recovered. The injury wasn't visible from the bridge, and, since there was already an apparent cause of the death — strangulation — the body was just bagged and transported as soon as it was recovered from the water.' He looked at Laraby. 'Lelia, that is Dr Segal, only discovered the damage when she started the examination back at the lab.'

'Catastrophic?' said Jejeune. 'As in enough to have killed him?'

Holland hesitated. 'She believes so, yes.'

'There would have been massive blood loss from such traumatic cranial injury, surely,' said Laraby. He turned to

Maik. 'No chance this could have happened at the house, as he was pulled over backwards in that chair? You didn't find any blood?'

'Or evidence that any had been cleaned up,' confirmed Maik. 'And we didn't see any indication that a heavy rectangular object, concrete or otherwise, had been moved or was missing, either.'

'So wherever Lee was when he was struck with this object, it wasn't at the house.'

'There was no blood at the bridge, either,' confirmed Holland, 'so we are definitely looking at a third location.' He hesitated for a second. 'Only the thing is, sir, Dr Segal is certain that the depth of neck lacerations from the strangulation would have been fatal anyway. And forensics have confirmed the blood traces and skin tissue on the cord belonged to Lee. It was definitely the murder weapon.'

'Only now, you're telling us we have a second cause of death. And we're looking for a second murder scene?'

It was the evidence telling them that, but Holland didn't bother making the distinction.

'So why kill him twice?' Laraby asked the room. 'And in two different locations?' He thought for a moment. 'Please tell me at least the time of death matches for both times our victim was killed.'

'As closely as Dr Segal can tell. She did say, though, that there's no way to conclusively determine which injuries would have come first.'

Jejeune looked across at Maik and the sergeant met his gaze, understanding its message. *But we can, can't we, Sergeant?* Danny didn't address his answer to Jejeune, but it took an effort of will. It would take some time for old habits to die. 'It would be next to impossible to have taken a body with a head wound like that into the house and not left any blood trail,' he told the room.

Laraby nodded. 'Fair enough. So the killer strangled Lee at the house and then transported the body to the river, stopping somewhere along the way to stove in his head as well. Danny, let's get some uniforms out along the route between the house and the bridge and see if we can find the site where this second attack took place.'

When Jejeune spoke, it was in the kind of half-musing tone that made you wonder whether he might have been talking to himself. Unless you knew him. 'I thought there might be a patch of flattened grass on the bank further downriver,' he said.

Laraby shook his head contemptuously. 'Further downriver than where the body was snagged? Hardly likely to be relevant, then, is it, since anything happening there is only going to be carried further away from the body in the opposite direction. It's how currents work, see, Inspector. Don't feel bad. Detective work is not for everybody.' He tried to soften the comment with a smile, but Jejeune didn't return it. Laraby paused. 'I suppose we'd better have SOCO out there to have a poke around anyway. Meanwhile, Inspector, get over and have a word with Huebner. Let's see what he has to say for himself.'

With the main suspect and the route to the river already covered, Holland already suspected where his own line of inquiry might fall. 'This work Sampson Lee was doing up at the university,' said Laraby, turning to him. 'Mathematics, higher-level thinking, sounds like it's right up your street, Constable. That said, you can take Sergeant Salter, as I hear she is now, with you if you like. She's about as bright as they come. Pity she couldn't be here herself today, but I'm sure I can rely on you to fill her in on the details.' He straightened and drew a breath. 'Right, we've all got our jobs to do, so let's get to them. But one final thought here, ladies and gentlemen, before we do. There's a lot of talk these days about different versions of the truth, and all that tosh. But there's only one set of truths here. Sampson Lee didn't put himself in that river, and he didn't give himself those injuries. Whoever did this is clever and resourceful and ruthless, so we are going to need to be on top of our game. I encourage you to use your initiative, but there's going to be no room for individual glory-seeking or cowboy tactics here. We all want in on whatever anybody's doing. No going rogue, no haring off to check some wild out-of-the-box theories without authorisation. We all know what lines of inquiry each of us is following at all times on this one, are we clear on that? We share what we have and we follow procedure. Understood?'

Everyone in the room understood. Laraby may have said 'all' a couple of times, but there was really only one person in the room he was speaking to.

7

Sergeant Lauren Salter may have been the senior detective of the two, but she had no qualms about letting Tony Holland drive. She'd always enjoyed the ride in his Audi TT and, for all his flashiness, the constable knew how to handle the car around the narrow country lanes of the district. He'd delivered them to the School of Applied Mathematics and Computer Sciences at North Norfolk University's Fleming Campus more quickly and competently than any other driver in the unit could have done.

'So how was it,' she asked as he drew the Audi into the car park and turned it off. 'Jejeune and Laraby?'

Holland shrugged. 'Not so bad, if you were one of those robot-controlled devices designed to pick its way through a minefield. Otherwise, yeah, pretty much what you'd expect. Danny was fine, though, if that's what you're asking.'

Salter gave a short nod. Her partner had seen enough field combat to know that the best way to avoid getting caught in crossfire was by keeping your head down. Holland had no need to ask why Salter hadn't made the short trip from Saltmarsh herself. Though her earlier relationship with Laraby had ended without incident, the fact that she was now seeing Danny Maik meant that her presence would have introduced a further note of unnecessary tension into a situation already fraught with it.

'What's up with this?' asked Holland as they approached the building. 'Couldn't make up their minds, or what?'

Salter took in the building carefully. The exterior walls of the first block were of simple masonry, punctuated by small square windows, but this modest structure was connected to a second by means of an elevated bridge corridor. Both the corridor and the second block were constructed of a thin steel frame and large rectangular plate glass windows. The two also shared a striking design feature that was absent from the first block: a rigorous observation of proportion.

'The golden ratio,' said Salter. 'In every single feature. Every door, every window, every wall. It's amazing'

'If you say so. What's so "golden" about it?'

'A proportion of approximately one and two thirds to one. It's recognised as a standard of beauty in everything from architecture to human faces and bodies. Don't look at me like that. It's true.'

Holland shook his head. 'I'm officially impressed. Big on this maths business, are you?'

'I didn't mind it at school. Of course when we got to imaginary numbers, I decided I'd reached my limit.'

'Imaginary numbers? Now I know you're having me on.'

'No, really. An imaginary number is a real number multiplied by the imaginary unit known as "i".'

'I should have a word with my bank manager,' said Holland, holding the door open for his sergeant to enter. 'See if imaginary numbers could do anything for my balance.'

Salter laughed. 'Don't forget to remind him that zero is considered to be both real and imaginary.'

The interior of the Euclid Lab continued the slavish observation of the ratio even down to the bright white tiles in the lobby. It made the security booth restricting their entry seem jarringly out of place, in more ways than one.

'Card entry, only,' I'm afraid,' said the guard behind the desk pleasantly. It crossed Holland's mind that, with regard to the part about the ratios for human beauty, the guard seemed to have missed the mark by quite a bit.

'I think you'll find this one will get us through,' said Salter, flashing her warrant card.

The guard tilted his head. 'You'll still have to leave your phones and any other electronic recording devices out here.' He met the detectives' surprised looks with an apologetic smile. 'Orders. Until I get other ones...' He shrugged. 'Or I can have somebody come out to see you.'

Salter supposed the increasing appeal of the path of least resistance was a sign she was getting older. It was not a welcome thought. 'Let's do that, shall we,' she said.

The guard dialled and spoke quietly into his phone. The detectives waited in awkward silence, gazing around at the perfectly-proportioned interior space, until a young man emerged from a doorway behind the guard and came through the booth to greet them. His barrel chest and broad shoulders suggested a lot of time spent on weight machines. 'Amit Chandra,' he said, extending a powerful hand. His exposed forearm showed similar signs of highly developed muscle definition. 'Sorry about all this, but we had a couple of incidents here a short while ago. Since then security has been watertight.'

'I thought this was just a maths lab,' said Salter. 'What kind of research do you do here?'

'Basically, we design predictive algorithms to track different aspects of bird migration.'

'Just for the benefit of my colleague here,' said Holland, 'could you explain in layman's terms what a predictive algorithm is?'

If Chandra was buying Holland's line, he didn't show it. 'An algorithm is a finite sequence of mathematical instructions, used to perform a computation or solve a related group of specific problems known as a class. A predictive algorithm analyses relationships between variables from previous occurrences, and uses them to predict an unknown outcome. It's truly astonishing how accurate some of the prediction models are proving to be these days.' He seemed to remember the reason he had come down to the lobby. 'I imagine you're here about the death of Sampson Lee.'

'He was part of the team here, I take it?' asked Holland.

Chandra nodded. 'Yes, I suppose so.'

'You suppose?'

The man shrugged. 'We didn't really collaborate as such. In fact I rarely saw him. We all work on individual aspects of the project, you see. I am concerned with mass migration events. I analyse satellite images and photographs sent from the International Space Station, and overlay factors like barometric pressure, cloud cover, length of daylight, temperature, wind speed and direction. Sampson's studies involved collating data on available resources for arriving birds: soil quality, shoreline composition, vegetation, et cetera, and looking at the timing of activities that had the potential to be disruptive: construction projects, farm practices like planting and harvesting, that sort of thing. So you see, there really was no overlap at all in our fields.' He paused. 'But, you know, he was still a colleague. And on a personal level, well... it's all so tragic, isn't it?'

He faltered as he seemed to search for something more to say. 'My thoughts go out to those who cared for him.'

Of whom you were clearly not one, thought Salter. 'None of this work sounds like much of a reason for so much security. Having people check their phones and such,' she said.

Chandra shrugged. 'Everything we produce is considered proprietary material of the university, but we occasionally work under contract with certain government agencies. In fact, it was an element of Sampson's research that was the reason for all this security. It was a confidential analysis of shoreline sites for their potential blue carbon rating. An intruder got in and we think that was what he was trying to get hold of.'

'A couple of incidents, you said,' Holland reminded him.

'Ishtara, my colleague here, found an envelope addressed to a science publication in the courier box, ready to be sent out. It contained some of her research data. The material itself wasn't that crucial, but it was a wake-up call. She also designed the system architecture we're using, and having any of that work get out would have been truly damaging. So after those two incidents, the university insisted on all work being air-gapped onto its own internal systems only.' He nodded at the security guard. 'They also initiated this restricted access policy and banned from the lab all personal laptops, phones or anything else that might be used as a recording device.'

Salter nodded. 'Does Mr Lee's death that mean that work on the blue carbon rating project will come to an end?'

Chandra shook his head. 'I can easily pick up the research, possibly even Ishtara could, at a stretch.'

'So his death wouldn't necessarily derail this project?' It seemed important to the sergeant to clarify the point.

'If you're looking at that as a potential motive, I can tell you anyone would realise Sampson's death would have little to no impact on the future of the programme if they had even the most basic understanding of what we do here.' His look seemed to imply that neither of these officers might qualify. Behind him, the security guard offered a wry smile, as if he had long ago accepted his place in the hierarchy of the deep thinkers.

'Are you aware of any problems Mr Lee may have had with anyone?' asked Holland.

'Problems?' Chandra sounded surprised. Perhaps even overly so.

'As in with his colleagues.' Holland's tone slipped a degree or two in friendliness. 'Even supposed ones.'

Chandra shifted slightly. 'The worst things ever got in here was a bit of banter about whose culture had made the most important contributions to the field of mathematics. Sampson liked to remind us all that it was the Chinese who introduced negative numbers. But really, where would the world be without the decimal number system?'

'Which didn't originate in China, I'm guessing.'

'India.' Chandra flashed a short smile. 'First recorded there, anyway.'

'*In here,*' said Salter. '*The worst things ever got in here.* How about elsewhere?'

Chandra turned to look through one of the large windows towards a grassy slope that rose gently from the far side of the car park. 'You might want to talk to his girlfriend, Katie Fairfax. I saw the two of them arguing up by her monitoring station the afternoon he died. It looked quite heated.'

On the crest of the rise, Salter could just see a square white structure about the height of a postbox. 'Any idea what they were arguing about?'

Chandra shook his head. 'All I know is she was very upset when she came in to collect her filters that afternoon.'

'Filters?'

'She uses them to collect air samples, and brings them in for analysis the following morning. Air quality is an important factor in migration, so the data she gathers is built into our programming. Come to think of it, I haven't seen her today.' He turned to the guard. 'Has Katie been in yet?'

The guard shook his head. 'It's not like her to be late, either. Regular as clockwork with collecting those DNA samples, she is.' He dialled a number. In the silence, the detectives could hear the ringing coming from the handset. 'She's not answering,' he said unnecessarily as he returned the phone to its cradle. 'I should go up there and check that she's all right.'

'We'll do that,' said Holland. He pointed to the car park. 'Through there?'

'There's a path up to the monitoring station that leads from the far side. I'll take you,' said Chandra. 'There's a shortcut through the car park, but we'll need my access card.'

The three of them stepped out into the weak sunshine and began to make their way across the car park. It was only now that Holland noticed the entire area was fenced in. As they approached a small gate at the rear, Chandra fished a key card from his pocket and swiped it against the reader.

'We'll be all right on our own from this point,' Salter told him. 'If we need anything further, we'll be in touch.'

Chandra inclined his head. 'As you wish. Just watch out for the Lapwings up there. There's a nest near the station and the chicks have just hatched.'

'We'll be careful not to step on them,' said Holland.

'You won't need to worry about that. The chicks can run almost from the moment of birth, so the adults will lead them off to safety somewhere. But they still won't be happy if you get too close.'

Salter gave him a look. 'I was going to say you know a lot about them,' she said. 'But I suppose you'd all be birders, in this line of work.'

'BINOs these days, unfortunately,' he told her. 'Birders In Name Only. We try not to forget why we became interested in this branch of research in the first place, but it's hard to get out now. Challenging work, long hours. All we want to do at the end of the day is get home and relax.'

'Is that where you were the night Sampson Lee died?'

Chandra nodded. 'And I'm absolutely sure Ishtara would have been home as well. Okay, well, I'll leave you to it, then.'

The detectives began a slow walk along the path that led up the hillside. As they reached the top of the rise, swirling winds blustered around them, buffeting and rocking them. 'Fresh enough up here,' said Holland. He looked around at the wide, flat expanse of grass they had emerged onto. A lone figure of a man was walking a dog over by the fringe of woodland on the far side. But there was no sign of any researcher.

'I suppose this is where she works,' said Salter. The square white box she had noticed from the lab stood nearby. She saw now that it sat atop a metal pole mounted on a concrete plinth. The monitoring station had an air inlet on one side and a series of small dials set behind a perspex screen. On the back side of the box were two flaps, both key-locked. The first was where air filters could be inserted and removed. The second, larger flap sat next to it. Someone had written the words **Filter Trays** on it in black marker, but the weather had faded the words almost to the point of illegibility.

Above the station, the pealing call of a bird cut through the noise of the wind rushing past their ears. Salter looked up and watched the bird as it rode the air currents, swooping in for a low pass before arcing back up into the skies again. She looked down and noticed a group of four fluffy, mottled chicks huddled together near the corner of the concrete base. 'That must be the mother Lapwing up there,' she said. 'But if that call was her way of telling these little ones to run and hide, they don't appear to be paying much attention. At least when Max ignores me, it's not a matter of life or death.'

Holland was about to comment that ignoring his own mom would have been exactly that when something caught his eye. Despite the winds frantically tousling the grasses up on this hilltop, a few tufts around the base of the monitoring station were remaining steadfastly in place. He crossed to them and bent down, peeling back the stuck-together stems. On the corner of the concrete, a dried pool of dark red had stained the masonry.

He looked up at Salter. 'I think we've found our third site,' he said.

'You call it in,' she told him, drawing out her phone. 'I'll put out a regional alert for Katie Fairfax.'

8

London shouldn't be as beguiling as it is, thought Jejeune as he strolled along the riverside towards Southwark. It had all the problems of other big cities: traffic congestion, teeming sidewalks, construction noise. And yet, the personality of the place always seemed to shine through. At least to him. He wondered if the fact that he was not a native contributed to the city's appeal, but he had been here in the UK long enough, even previously lived and worked in London long enough, that any novelty should surely have worn off by now. And yet still there was a charm to certain spots as he turned a corner, vistas that captivated him as he happened upon them, aspects of this vast, pulsating metropolis that brought a particular kind of excitement flooding back every time he returned. As it had today. Despite the purpose of today's journey, he had been glad to be heading back to the place his colleagues up in north Norfolk called *The Smoke*.

As it turned out, the unpalatable reason for his visit hadn't even transpired. Jejeune's appointment with Marius Huebner had been superseded by a summons for the latter to appear before a parliamentary inquiry. It was no doubt a damage control exercise now that Huebner's name had been released to the public, but the postponement had left Jejeune with an afternoon free to stroll the streets of the capital before catching his early evening train back. He stopped and looked around. Whether his subconscious had led him in this direction he couldn't have said, but he found himself now only a few hundred metres from the address of another person with a connection to the case. He arrived at the house just as a man was coming down the street from the opposite direction. A Border collie was walking obediently beside him. Though the dog was on a leash, it really wasn't necessary. Man and beast were in perfect step.

'Are you looking for me?' asked the man as the pair arrived at the front door.

'Johnno McBride?' asked Jejeune, flashing his ID. 'Detective Chief Inspector Jejeune.'

'North Norfolk cops taken to doorstepping innocent folks these days, have they?' Johnno smiled, robbing the words of offence. He removed the collie's leash as he unlocked the door. The dog waited patiently until it swung open and then trotted in quietly and went up a set of stairs leading off the foyer.

'I'm looking into the death of Sampson Lee,' Jejeune told the man.

'And talking to me specifically because I'm the one he released Marius Huebner's name to. Would you like to come in?'

Jejeune followed the man into the house.

'We're on the upper deck,' Johnno told him as they climbed the stairs, 'but the ground floor's been vacant for as long as I can remember, so effectively it's just us.'

'Us?'

'Me and Truth. Best mates, isn't that right, boy?'

The dog was waiting patiently outside the door of the upstairs flat as the men arrived on the landing. He gave his tail a single, laconic wag. Johnno unlocked the door and all three went inside.

Jejeune bent down to pat the dog, whose lustrous coat showed his excellent health. He looked at the black and white pattern and smiled. 'Truth,' he said. 'I wish it was always like you.'

'It is for me,' said Johnno. 'Fancy a builder's?' He smiled at Jejeune's quizzical look and shook his head playfully. 'What on earth are they teaching you up there in north Norfolk? Tea, strong, milk and sugar.'

'No sugar, thanks.'

Johnno disappeared into the doorless kitchen, leaving Jejeune standing on the other side of the opening. Round the doorframe, a winding wreath of leaves and flowers traced its way up and around from the floor on both sides. The quality of the artwork was questionable, but there was no disputing the painter's enthusiasm. Jejeune called round the opening into the sound of the tea-making. 'Did you know Lee well?'

'Not really. He was a source. We talked when he had something to say. Never socially.'

'How did he contact you?'

'Electronically mostly. Who has the time for an in-person interview these days?'

Johnno emerged from the kitchen and handed Jejeune a chipped enamel mug full of umber-coloured liquid before setting down a silver bowl filled with water on the floor in front of the dog. It crossed the detective's mind to wonder whether Truth would mind swapping.

Johnno grabbed his own mug and crossed to the large window at the back of the room, its frame traced by a similar amateurish painted garland to the one round the kitchen doorway. Jejeune joined him and the two men stood, looking out. 'Some view, eh, Inspector. London, in all its glory. There's a story behind every door in this city. All you have to do is uncover it. Much like in your line of work, I imagine.'

Jejeune sipped his tea and suppressed a grimace with an effort of will. The brew was strong enough to stand a spoon up in. 'So you never visited Lee in north Norfolk,' he said.

Johnno shrugged. 'A couple of times, early on. He asked me to meet him at his house. I think he wanted to suss me out before deciding whether to give me the name.'

'How about at his place of work?'

'The Euclid Lab, you mean?' Johnno turned and shook his head. 'No, I never visited him there. He implied it was restricted access. All sounded a bit Area 51 for my liking.' He smiled at another puzzled look from Jejeune. 'Where the US government took those alien bodies? After the crash in Roswell? Not a fan of conspiracy theories, I take it, Inspector. All those cover-ups and lies.'

Jejeune's expression was that of a man who spent his life sifting through cover-ups and lies. 'Did you ever wonder why Lee chose you, when there were so many other podcasters out there?'

'He told me I have a reputation for letting the news tell its own story. No political agenda, he meant. Releasing the name was obviously potentially damaging to the government, but it's not up to me to tell my listeners what to make of the information I give them. Plus, I had some background in the subject matter.'

'Your civics courses on zoning and planning, you mean?' It was Jejeune's turn to smile. 'My partner knows you from your university days together. Lindy Hey.'

Johnno nodded. 'I recognised your name but I thought I'd let you bring it up. I can't imagine it's a particularly comfortable experience, having to interview your partner's ex.'

'Ex?' Even if Jejeune had tried to suppress the surprise in his voice, he doubted he could have managed to keep it from his expression.

Johnno gave another short nod. 'She even lived here for a few months. I'm surprised she didn't mention it. Still, that's Lin for you. She'll have her reasons, no doubt. She always does. How is she?'

'She's well.' An awkward silence fell between the men as Jejeune struggled to find more to say. The other man stepped in with a new topic to help him out.

'I suppose you're looking at Huebner for this, given his online tirades.'

'We're investigating a number of leads,' said Jejeune, recovering into the safety of his professional life.

'Probably none with as much skin in the game as him, though. He had a lot riding on his anonymity in this case.'

'Did he? I'm afraid I haven't had a chance to look into the details yet.'

'Ever hear of blue carbon ecosystems?' asked Johnno. 'They're among the most intensive carbon sinks in the world, removing enormous amounts of greenhouse gases relative to the amount of area they occupy. For that reason, a blue carbon area will have its carbon offsets trade at a premium relative to other sites.'

Jejeune scratched absently behind the dog's ears as he listened, trying to put the news about Lindy aside. Where did omissions fall in the black and white world of Truth, he wondered.

'Salt marshes are among the best blue carbon sites in the world,' continued Johnno. 'And the north Norfolk coastal areas have a lot of them, including some high-value sites on privately held land. The government has been particularly keen to get their hands on these, for obvious reasons; the more blue carbon sites they hold, the better its carbon trading balance sheet looks.'

'I take it the information on which sites the government was targeting was not made public?'

'It was clearly in their best interests to keep that information to themselves, but then, all of a sudden last year, Huebner started approaching these landowners with offers. There was some suggestion that he even represented himself as acting on behalf of the government. If the owners were reluctant to sell, he'd follow up with a warning that the government were considering issuing compulsory purchase orders.'

'Surely there would be no justification for that,' said Jejeune. 'Did the owners believe him?'

'Not all of them, but enough to make it worthwhile. Those who sold got a small increase over the standard land value, but once Huebner owned the properties he sold them on to the government at premium rates; astronomical profits in some cases.'

'And all because he was privy to some inside information. Did they ever identify who had tipped him off?'

'That's what the hearing was meant to establish. But it was all done behind closed doors, citing security considerations. A leak of confidential information, you see. A transcript of the hearings was released after a Freedom of Information appeal was filed, but the document was essentially useless. The IDs of all the participants and properties involved had been redacted. Frankly, we learned less from that transcript than from the general press speculation.'

Jejeune forced down another mouthful of tea and set the mug on the floor at his feet. If he was hoping the dog would finish it off, he was disappointed. Truth had clearly experienced a 'builder's' before and showed no interest whatsoever. 'So how did Lee come by Huebner's name, then?' he asked.

Johnno shrugged. 'He didn't say, but, if you're wondering whether he ID'd the right person, all you have to do is look at Huebner's reaction. In all that online vitriol, did you ever once hear him deny his involvement? Because I didn't. And I paid very close attention. I have a vested interest in getting things like this right. The podcast universe would not be very forgiving if a revelation like this proved to be incorrect.'

'Did Lee provide any other info?'

Johnno shook his head. 'Nothing but the name. I can show you the email.' He reached for his laptop. 'It showed up about an hour before the podcast was scheduled to go out.' He gave a short grin. 'I've never had to work so frantically to re-record something in my life.' He opened his laptop and turned it to show the detective. Only the two words of a name. Marius Hübbner. It was not the way Jejeune had envisioned the spelling of the surname, not least because he had never seen anybody else spell it that way either. He picked up his mug and stood up. 'I should let you get on with your day,' he said. 'We may need your laptop to verify that the message came from Lee's computer.'

'Be my guest.' Johnno took the proffered mug and began to walk the detective to the door. 'Have your tech guys call me. They can come and collect it any time.'

Jejeune stopped with his hand on the door handle. 'I'd like you to find time to make the trip up to Saltmarsh if possible. You said you were at Lee's house a couple of times.'

'Yes, but not for weeks,' Johnno began to protest.

'There still could be fingerprints. It would be helpful to get a set for elimination purposes.'

Johnno looked puzzled. 'Can't I have those taken locally?'

'You could, but you can bring up your laptop when you come. Besides, I imagine Lindy would like to see you again. Unless, of course...' Jejeune indicated the flat with a tilt of his head, 'the way things ended...'

'Not at all. I'm sure we'd still be the best of friends if we hadn't lost touch.' Johnno paused. 'I'd like to see Lin too, but, given that she chose to not to mention our history together, I wonder if a low-key approach might be best, at least at first.' He smiled. 'Listen, I like walks. Why don't we do that, the three of us, and see how it goes. If you'd have no objection to me bringing old Truth here. I know some birders aren't keen.'

'You know I'm a birder?' said Jejeune with surprise.

Johnno smiled again. 'I don't know anybody who isn't going to have a bit of curiosity about their ex's new partner. Just let me know when you want me to come up and I'll be there.'

9

For a man who normally exuded such a pragmatic approach to policing, the energy and enthusiasm coursing through Marvin Laraby when he entered the incident room was all the more notable. His animation brought the low burble of conversation from the seated attendees to an immediate halt. 'Right,' he announced, 'the stakes in this case have just been upped considerably. You need to be aware that eyes are now going to be upon us as we go about our business. Five have been in touch.'

'Five?' asked Holland.

'The Service.'

'Oh, MI5.'

Laraby shot him a disapproving look, as if he might have already breached some code of secrecy by saying the name out loud. 'Yes, Constable. The very same. Apparently, since a redacted name from a transcript of a closed-door government inquiry was somehow made public, this case is now a security matter. Five are requesting ongoing updates on our investigation. I'll be handling liaison with them myself.' He paused and looked around the room. 'Your job is to make sure I have something to tell them.'

Maik wasn't an eye-roller, but he had a particular way of shifting his shoulders that told you, if you had been working with him long enough, exactly how he felt about a development. It was clear from Holland's glance in Jejeune's direction that the DCI hadn't missed Danny's response to this news either.

'It goes without saying that we need to get this right in a hurry,' said Laraby into the silence that had followed his announcement. He paused and took a steadying breath. 'Which means we don't miss evidence like this tyre track that has been discovered at the river.' He glowered at the assembled officers as if looking for someone to blame. 'So who wants to explain this to me in a way that we don't all look like incompetent fools when I brief Five?'

'It wasn't in the original search area,' said Maik in a guarded tone that suggested even he wasn't completely comfortable with where he would have to go next. 'It was further downriver...' Near where Jejeune had observed the flattened grass, he didn't say. He didn't need to.

Laraby sucked in a breath through his teeth, not allowing his eyes to wander anywhere beyond Maik's face. 'No chance it was made later?'

'The access road has been blocked off since the incident. There's no way anybody could have got a vehicle through since we arrived on the scene.'

The DCS nodded slowly. 'Okay, well, I assume a cast has been taken. Let's see if we can find a vehicle to match it to. In the meantime, where are we on the monitoring station evidence? Sergeant Salter, I believe you've been keeping tabs on SOCO on this? Nice to see you here, by the way.'

'It has been confirmed that the blood on the concrete is Lee's,' Salter told the room from her seat in the back row. 'Dr Segal believes the corner of the plinth matches the head wound. SOCO did collect some minute organic particles from the post itself. They've been sent off for analysis but nobody's holding out much hope that they'll get anything from them.'

Maik might not have been the only one listening for telltale signals in Salter's report to her former partner, but he doubted anyone would have detected much beyond a slight extra formality in the crisp, efficient delivery.

'What do we know about the site itself?' asked Laraby. 'It's an air quality monitoring station, have I got that right?'

'The security guard says Katie Fairfax collects DNA samples up there, but that can't be right, can it?' Salter asked the room at large. 'You can't get DNA from the air, surely?'

'To be fair, I don't think that guard is completely up to speed on what goes on up there,' said Holland.

Laraby chose to ignore the point. 'Okay,' he said thoughtfully, 'the first attack is at the house. Lethal injuries, inflicted through strangulation, which is to say no blood splatter. So why transport the body somewhere else and risk getting sprayed with blood mist by bashing his brains in against a concrete block? Especially if the first attack would have been enough to kill him?'

'I can't see Katie Fairfax attacking Lee at his house and then hauling his body all the way up that hill to her own place of work just to finish the job. Perhaps the killer took Lee up to the monitoring station intending to leave him there as a warning to her,' said Salter. She shrugged to show it was just a thought, but Laraby seized on it, snapping his fingers and pointing at her.

'Or maybe even to frame her.' He thought for a second and nodded with satisfaction. 'Okay, this I like. Whoever it was kills Lee and drops the body right where he and his girlfriend had been seen having an argument. Now who do we know who has that kind of cold, ruthless calculation about him?'

For the first time since the meeting began, Laraby turned to Jejeune. 'What did Huebner have to say for himself when you talked to him?'

'I didn't,' said Jejeune flatly. 'By the time I got there, he'd been called back in for another hearing with the Parliamentary Committee.'

'So what did you do down in the Smoke all day, then? Tea at Fortnum's, was it? I'm pretty sure you wouldn't have dropped in at the Met to renew any old acquaintances. I doubt they'd want to see your face around there any more. Or mine, come to that.' Laraby's attempt to take the sting out of the remark by including himself fooled no one. Jejeune simply stared back at him impassively.

'I went to see the podcaster. Johnno McBride. He confirmed it was Lee who gave him Huebner's name. McBride has offered to let us have his computer if we need to verify the email and podcast origins.'

'No need,' said Holland. 'Tech have already confirmed it was sent from Lee's computer via his IP address. And received at Johnno's IP in London at 18:58 p.m. The podcast went out at 20:00 exactly.'

'Remind me again, what did Dr Segal set as TOD?' asked Laraby.

'The body's immersion in water made it more difficult, but she's confident in placing time of death within thirty-six hours prior to discovery.'

'Lee was found just before six a.m. So if he was still alive to send that email at seven p.m. the night before, that tightens our TOD window quite a bit.' Laraby nodded again, more positively this time. 'Good, okay, this is good. Five will be happy with this. So if we accept that our killer, Huebner or whoever, dumped the body at the girlfriend's work site, the next question is, how does it end up in the river? Do we think the girlfriend found it at the monitoring station and moved it? So why do that, then? The proper thing to do would have been to call us up and say, "I've found my boyfriend's body at my workplace. What do I do now?" You don't load it into your car, drive it to the river and dump it in. Have we checked this cast against her vehicle?'

'It's missing,' said Holland simply. 'Like her. The last time anybody saw her was when she went off to check her other monitoring stations further afield. On the evening Lee was killed.'

'Okay.' Laraby rubbed his hands together. 'We're finally starting to make some progress here. Right now, our priority is finding this woman. Even if she didn't kill her boyfriend, she is a person of interest. Danny, I want you on that.' He turned to Jejeune. 'And if you can ever manage to catch up with Huebner, you can have your chat with him. You can take Sergeant Salter with you.'

Jejeune shifted slightly and Laraby flashed a vexed look in his direction. 'Problem, DCI? What am I saying, of course there is.'

'I'll take Constable Holland, if that's okay.'

Laraby's eyes flickered briefly in Salter's direction. 'Up to you.' He offered her an apologetic smile. 'Well, since you find yourself suddenly at a loose end, Sergeant, and you are so comfortable with all this mathematics business by all accounts, perhaps you'd like to do some background on the kind of work they are doing up at that lab. Given that the DCI here is so uneasy with revenge as a motive for Huebner, let's see if Mr Lee got himself mixed up in anything else that might have upset him.'

Holland caught Salter's eye with a look that suggested they might already have some ideas in that direction, but neither of them spoke up. Laraby brought the meeting to a close and strode off purposefully in the direction of his office. He couldn't have signalled his intention to inform Five of their progress any more clearly if he had used a loudspeaker.

Salter was standing in a quiet alcove in the corridor when Maik approached. They didn't stand too close to each other, and they didn't speak in hushed tones, like meeting lovers might. Maik doubted it would do much good. He knew judgements were made not on what people actually saw, but on what their preconceptions led them to believe they had seen. Witnesses could be like that, too, he thought. Only with witnesses, you could sometimes persuade them otherwise.

'Well, it's reassuring to know at least Laraby trusts me,' she said sourly. 'Jejeune doesn't even have enough confidence in me to let me tag along when he's questioning a suspect.'

Maik could understand her anger. It was justified. But he couldn't let it stand. 'The DCI has a lot of respect for you, Lauren. He always has had.'

'Then why deliberately ask Tony to accompany him?'

Maik sighed. 'Because if Laraby is looking to drive a wedge between the inspector and me, somebody I'm involved with who works under Jejeune at Saltmarsh is a good place to start. The DCI's trying to keep you out of the firing line.'

Salter was silent for a moment. 'This can't go on, Danny. I don't mean with me. You can't work in a situation where you are torn between them like this.'

'Not every case out here is going to involve the DCI,' said Maik reasonably. 'Laraby will be fine under any other circumstances. Jejeune is his Achilles heel, that's all. We just have to let him handle this his way. He knows what he's doing.'

'Let's hope so. All that sniping and backbiting, that was hard to watch.'

Maik nodded his agreement. It was going to be a long few weeks. 'How many days until Colleen Shepherd gets back?'

'Twenty-five,' said Salter. 'Not that anyone's counting.' She shook her head. 'It's a bit of a mess this one, isn't it? Three crime scenes, two causes of death, one victim.'

'It's hard to know where to start putting together any sort of a picture,' agreed Danny absently.

'At the house, I suppose,' said Salter. 'After all, it's the one place we actually know what went on.'

Except it wasn't, was it? thought Danny. Somebody had been in the house after the body was moved. Somebody who had gone to a lot of trouble to disguise the fact. Perhaps he understood why Jejeune hadn't mentioned it yet. The Post-it note on the laptop, the connection to the podcaster, these were about the only footholds the DCI had in the investigation at the moment. Lose them, and he would only find himself further marginalised by Laraby. So he was planning to stay silent for now and wait to see what else unfolded. But why had Danny gone along with him, unbidden? Even someone who respected his former DCI as much as Danny did knew better than to suppress information like this. He realised his silence was causing Salter to stare at him. 'Whatever went on,' he said, 'I'm confident Laraby will come to see the value of working closely with the DCI eventually.'

She nodded. 'Good to know.'

One of the things he liked most about her was that, even when he hadn't managed to fool her at all, she sometimes pretended that he had.

10

HR Holdings had chosen a pleasant setting for their corporate headquarters, thought Jejeune as Tony Holland guided the Audi through the open gates onto the property. A dense fringe of native trees and shrubs hugged the low wall surrounding the grounds, and well-manicured lawns stretched towards it in all directions. Holland followed the gentle curve of the tarmacked driveway to the front of the modern office building and brought the Audi to a halt beside a pale blue Porsche with the boot open. A woman in an expensive-looking business suit was hefting a bulky briefcase into the car as the men got out.

'Can I help you with that?' asked Holland.

'You could grab that box on the step if you like.' She nodded towards a cardboard box and Holland moved off to pick it up. She turned her attention to manoeuvring her own burden and Jejeune took in the gardens in silence until Holland returned and squeezed the box into the car's small boot space beside the case. The woman straightened. 'Thank you, Mr...'

'Constable. Holland. And this is DCI Jejeune. We're here to see your boss.'

'I don't have one.' She nodded towards the sign on the door. 'The "R" on there is me. Talia Rowe. HR is alphabetical. It doesn't mean I get second billing. We're partners.'

'Is he here?' asked Jejeune, while the chastened constable recovered his poise.

'He's on his way. He should be here in about ten minutes, if you'd like to wait.' Rowe shook her head. 'I knew you'd be coming for a word with him sooner or later. No matter how upset you are, you can't go around saying things like that. Not even online.'

She fumbled for her car keys and they dropped onto the ground. Holland retrieved them and handed them to her. 'In a hurry to go somewhere, Ms Rowe?' he asked.

'What? No. Just running a bit behind, that's all.' She checked her watch. 'Apologies, Constable. Is there something I can help you with?'

'We're here to see Mr Huebner about someone named Sampson Lee. Have you ever heard him mention anybody by that name?'

'The program developer from the uni?'

'You know him?'

'Only by name. Marius asked me to look into the financial background of an organisation called fLIGHT. It's run out of the Euclid Lab, and Lee's name popped up on their website, that's all.'

'Why would he ask you to research it, if you're a partner?'

'He doesn't do the internet.' She paused beside the car and checked her watch again.

Jejeune made a point of taking in a stand of trees on the far side of the property. 'That's nice bird habitat surrounding the property. It's a pity you don't have any feeders up here. You might attract any number of species. These lawns too. Green Woodpeckers, for example. Ever seen any here?'

'I'm sure I wouldn't know. I mean, I think I'd recognise a woodpecker, but would it be green? I remember once seeing a little bird when I was on holiday in Europe. It had a long grey tail, a completely grey back and a distinct black head and chest. I asked a local birder what it was called, and do you know what he told me: White Wagtail!'

'They're a breed apart, all right, those birders,' agreed Holland, averting his gaze from his DCI.

Jejeune smiled. 'This woodpecker is green.'

'Ah well, in that case I'd have to say I've never noticed one here. Is Lee saying he knows Marius? Is that why you're here?'

'He's not saying much of anything. He's dead.'

The woman leaned a hand against the frame of the car and was silent for a moment. 'That poor boy. Can I ask how he died?'

'I'm afraid we're not at liberty to disclose that,' said Holland. 'But we believe it was him who released Huebner's name to that podcaster. Any reason you can think of that he might do that?'

Rowe shook her head. 'No.' She looked at her watch one more time and got in her car. 'I'm sorry, but I really do have to be going. I'm sure Marius will be here any minute now.'

'He doesn't have anything pressing as well, does he, that might prevent from him having a chat with us when he gets here?'

She shook her head and fired up the car. 'I'm not his secretary, either, but don't worry' — she smiled at the men — 'if it's not a good time, he won't be shy about telling you.' The Porsche disappeared with a throaty growl, leaving the two detectives standing on the driveway looking after it. It was a moment or two before either of them spoke.

'Somebody's in a big hurry to be somewhere,' said Holland.

Jejeune nodded thoughtfully. 'Or away from somewhere.'

'Not a moment too soon, either,' said Holland. He indicated a light grey Bentley just beginning to make the sweep into the driveway from the road. 'I believe our next contestant has just arrived.'

It wasn't often Jejeune found himself staring up at someone, but the man who emerged from the Bentley was an impressive specimen. He had a build to match his height, too, but there was no sense of any excess baggage on the muscular frame. In his youth, with a full head of hair and finely chiselled features, Marius Huebner would have cut an imposing figure. Even now, with his hair retreating to a greying fringe round the back and sides of his head and a mottled complexion peppering the fleshy jowls, he still exuded a formidable presence. He regarded the two men with cold-eyed hostility. 'What do you two want?'

'A change in attitude would be a nice start,' said Holland, producing his warrant card. 'We'd like to ask you about some internet postings that went up recently.'

Huebner nodded. 'Ah, them.'

'They border on uttering threats,' Holland told him.

'Some of 'em even go beyond that, I should say. I'm surprised you lot haven't already done something about it.'

'You're saying you feel the police should bring charges?' Holland looked puzzled, but Jejeune's expression remained impassive as he regarded the man.

Huebner nodded again. 'When you find out who's responsible, I think they should be prosecuted to the fullest extent of the law.'

'Mr Huebner, that's you on there saying those things.'

'Me? No, sorry, son, you're a bit off-base there. It's AI. It's remarkable what they can do with it these days, isn't it?'

'Are you denying that you had anything to do with those messages?'

Huebner shrugged easily. 'I wouldn't even know how to start going about posting something like that. I'm a complete Luddite in that respect, I'm happy to say. I don't even have a smartphone.'

'You have a laptop, though. If we came back with a warrant, I wonder what your browser history would say.'

'Browser's never even been activated. All that distraction, a bloke'd never get any work done. I keep things as simple as possible on there. Word doc, spreadsheet, that's your lot.'

'You've never been online with it? It must be hard to run a business like that,' said Holland. 'How does anybody get in touch with you?'

'My partner's well enough connected for the both of us. I can be reached if necessary. Truth is, though, I tend to like to do business face to face. Up close up and personal, you might say. I find it easier to get your point across.'

'Huebner?' said Jejeune quietly. 'Is that German?'

The man gave a short nod. 'A couple of generations back it was. I'm Yorkshire born and bred,' he confirmed, in case an accent as thick as onion gravy hadn't been enough to make the point. 'Legal name's spelled H.U.B. with an umlaut. Only no bugger up there knew what them little dots were for. Kept calling me Hubbner. I added the "e" to help 'em out. After it became clear a sharp clip round the ear wasn't going to do it.'

'I notice one thing you didn't do in those messages, either you or your alter ego,' Holland paused, 'was deny your involvement in the scheme.'

'Why should I deny it? I made a series of perfectly legitimate deals with the government. I owned property, they wanted it. I sold it to them. They paid me for it. End of.'

'Except for the tip-offs about which properties the government were going to be interested in. The ones you needed to swoop in and purchase first. Those weren't legitimate, were they?'

Huebner shook his head regretfully. 'The findings of the hearing are confidential. I'm not permitted to say anything further on the matter unless you have security clearance.' He looked from one detective to the other. 'I'm taking it you don't? So if that's what you came here to talk about, it looks like you've wasted your time. And mine.'

'Actually, we're here to ask about Sampson Lee,' said Jejeune.

The other man shook his head thoughtfully. 'Can't say I know the name.'

'There's a connection between him and that organisation you had your partner look into: fLIGHT. Have you been in contact with Lee recently?'

'Not recently nor otherwise. I told you, I don't know the bloke. Why?'

'It seems likely he is the person who released your name to the podcaster,' said Holland. 'You know, the one you specifically said you wanted to get up close and personal with.'

'I told you, that wasn't me. It was AI.'

'Sampson Lee is dead, Mr Huebner,' said Jejeune. 'He was killed two nights ago, not far from here.'

There was a beat of silence before Huebner replied. 'I take it you're not just here to deliver the bereavement notice. What would I want to kill him for? If I wanted to make sure my name didn't get out, I left it a bit late, didn't I? The damage is already done. Besides, I have an alibi for that day. Talia will confirm it. If you can find her, that is. I've been trying to reach her for a couple of days now.' He leaned forward, faux confidentially.

'Between you and me, I think she's trying to avoid me. I'm starting to get a complex.'

The detectives didn't look at each other as they received this news. 'Is there any reason she would want to avoid you?' asked Jejeune.

'You'd have to ask her when you find her. Now, if that's all...'

Neither detective made any move to leave.

'Listen,' said Huebner, the irritation beginning to rise in his voice, 'I had nothing to do with that boy's death, d'you hear? But if he's in the habit of releasing names from classified documents, I'm sure he's going to have no shortage of enemies. Some of them in the government, for example. If he had names of others involved in the deal and hadn't got around to releasing them yet, well now, I'd say that's a proper motive. That's how silencing somebody works, see.'

'As appreciative as we are of the public coming up with theories,' said Holland, 'we tend to see that as our job. And at the moment the person we're looking at is you. But since you've obviously given this so much thought, perhaps you could supply us with a list of these people we should be talking to.'

Huebner snorted derisively. 'I don't think so, sunshine. I've told you, everything's classified. Don't you worry, though, the security services won't be comfortable leaving something like this in the hands of the local village coppers for long. They'll relieve you of the burden soon enough and give it to somebody with a bit more nous. Here, maybe they'll even feed it all into one of those AI programs and get that to solve it, eh? Now, if that's all, I've got some work to do.'

He paused as he reached the low step leading to the front door of the office, and turned back to the detectives. 'Oh, and if you do run into Talia, be sure to tell her I'm trying to get in touch with her, would you?'

He turned and entered the building without waiting for an answer. Which was just as well. Neither detective had anything to say.

11

Domenic Jejeune supposed it was a sign of just how settled into his routine he was these days that he noted the absence of the regular barista in his local coffee shop immediately. 'No Ms Tokatlidis today?' he asked as he placed his order with her stand-in.

'Maria had to take off for a couple of hours, so I said I'd cover for her. I'm Kim, by the way.' To Jejeune, the woman looked more like a patron of coffee shops than an employee, a retired teacher or librarian, perhaps, based on the intelligent curiosity that seemed to dance behind the eyes in her pleasantly lined face.

'I trust everything is okay,' he said, absently tapping his credit card against the reader.

'Oh yes. She just had to pop to the bank to wire some money to her kids. They work aboard a cruise ship up in the Arctic. Isn't it wonderful the opportunities young people have these days?' Kim pointed behind Jejeune. 'That corner table is free, if you'd like to grab it. I'll bring your coffee over as soon as it's ready.'

Jejeune settled in at the table and watched the street traffic outside. His morning coffee here was one of the few moments in his day that he could reflect on work without being involved in it. Or distracted from it. If he saw any birds at all it would likely be the family of House Sparrows that were nesting behind the **DAILY GRIND** sign above the door. But mostly it was just a steady stream of human life that provided the backdrop to his thoughts, an indistinct mass passing the window along the high street like a pulsing, multicoloured parade. As he watched now, he thought about the case he was working on; about Huebner and Laraby and the eDNA he had just read about. But mostly, he thought about the house. Even though there had been no discussion between the two men, he had known Danny Maik would back up his decision not to reveal his misgivings while he got his thoughts in order. But Lindy was right, Danny didn't work for him any more and it was wrong to expect him to continue to provide cover. Regardless of his loyalty, Danny's duty lay elsewhere now and he did not deserve to become embroiled in a personal conflict between two superior officers. Jejeune had just resolved to tell him so the next time they spoke when Kim arrived, carrying two cups of coffee.

She set them down on the table and drew out the other chair. 'Mind if I join you? Maria's back now, so I've been relieved of my duties. Frankly, I don't know how she does it, on her feet all day like that. I'm glad I have a desk job. For the most part, anyway. I do still enjoy the field work though.'

'Field work? What is it that you do?' asked Jejeune.

'Intelligence,' said the woman matter-of-factly. 'I'm with GCHQ. Forgive my frankness, Inspector. I do hope you weren't expecting code words or cryptic phrases. We don't really go in for that any more. Disguises, either, thankfully. I never did look good in a false moustache.'

The routine was to give him time to process the initial shock at the woman's revelation, Jejeune realised. It wasn't too late to turn things into a joke if his reaction wasn't what she required.

'Is it still "secret agent", or are you just "operatives" now?' he asked, sipping his coffee. If she'd been expecting surprise, the low-key version in Domenic Jejeune's repertoire might have disappointed her.

'We tend to regard ourselves simply as civil servants these days. We are still fond of the word "spies", though. It does help to remind us of what we are really doing. But generally what you see with an intelligence officer is what you get. Open, unaffected…'

'And trustworthy?'

'That's a decision for others to make. I imagine you're wondering about my reason for telling you all this?'

'It crossed my mind,' said Jejeune drily.

She turned to wave at Maria and the barista waved back, giving her an approving look that might have been related to an older woman sharing a table with a handsome, younger man. 'Maria tells me you were not here yesterday,' said Kim, turning to face him. 'I assume you were off interviewing Marius Huebner. I take it you are not convinced that revenge is enough of a motive for murder?'

Perhaps Jejeune was ready to protest a question about an ongoing line of inquiry, but he realised that, given the very public online threats attributed to Huebner, a visit from the police was an assumption even the average citizen might have been able to make. 'He may be involved in some way but—' He shook his head, 'I very much doubt he killed Lee after the fact for releasing his name.'

'Have you mentioned this to DCS Laraby?'

'I'm not sure he's quite ready to take guidance from me,' said Jejeune with a lopsided grin. 'Besides, he is already getting outside help himself.'

Kim nodded. 'Ah yes, Five! I suspect he won't be getting quite as much input from that side as he thinks. They are in the business of collecting intelligence rather than sharing it. I assume Laraby told you he has been granted jurisdictional oversight of the case. He won't have mentioned that, if it's still open when Shepherd gets back, it will revert to her as senior DCS.' She looked up and locked eyes on him. 'You know what this means.'

'That he'll be in a hurry to close the case before it gets taken away from him.'

'And if he is now to spend precious hours looking in what you believe to be the wrong direction, he'll have to tear around even more frantically when he finds out it's a dead end. And haste, as we both know, is when mistakes get made.'

Kim let her attention fall on the other patrons in the café for a moment. 'The whole world is here in this room, you know: the trusting, the cynical, the innocent, the guilty. It's human life on the micro scale, with all its connections, its motivations, its emotions. Every big picture is made up of countless smaller ones.'

Jejeune waited, sipping his coffee. Outside the window a steady procession of people passed by, others in the pageant of life that Kim was so carefully observing in here. She lifted her coffee cup and continued to gaze around the room. 'The murder of Sampson Lee is not our concern. We're perfectly happy to leave that in the hands of the local police. It is the fact that Lee somehow received the name of one of the principals in an in camera hearing that interests us. Only the redacted document was ever released to the public. Whoever gave Sampson Lee the name of Marius Huebner was in that room, Inspector.' She paused and looked around the coffee shop again. 'Has it also crossed your mind to wonder why I am confiding all this to you?'

'Because the possibility exists that a leak came from within the security services. Perhaps even GCHQ itself. And it might be better to have someone on the outside looking into that possibility.'

'Such an agile mind,' said Kim. 'Your personnel file hardly does you justice.' She nodded. 'If it is one of our people, it would be better for us to hear about it before it became general knowledge in a morning briefing at King's Landing station.'

'And subsequently passed on to Laraby's new contact in MI5, you mean?'

Kim sipped her coffee. 'Laraby has applied for a list of names of the people in the hearing,' she said conversationally. 'He won't get it.'

'Why not?'

'Because at this stage we are not convinced those names would get him any closer to finding out who killed Sampson Lee.'

Jejeune examined the woman's face with renewed interest. 'You don't think it is related to the release of Huebner's name?'

'No, Inspector. I am all but certain that it is not. And it would be reassuring to know at least one officer on this inquiry was keeping that possibility in mind during the course of their investigations.'

'Though I'm assuming you'd prefer I didn't make this an official line of inquiry yet.'

'Surely you have nothing on which to base one, other than the musings of some harmless people-watcher in a coffee shop.'

Though he might have settled on the adjective when they first met, Jejeune was now convinced that the woman sitting opposite him was far from harmless.

'I'd appreciate it if you could keep me up to date with your inquiries. Only insofar as they relate to the source of the leak, you understand. Would you be willing to share those details with me, I wonder?' She looked around the room. 'Though perhaps in a different setting.'

Jejeune understood. Today had taught him that the predictability of an established routine could be a vulnerability.

'Anyway, I should leave you to get on with your day.' As they stood to leave, Kim held up a finger. 'Excuse me for a moment.' He watched her cross to exchange a hug with Maria. Kim smiled and nodded at the other woman's comments, but she was observing the room keenly as she listened, taking in everything.

'More intelligence-gathering?' asked Jejeune as she returned to him.

Kim smiled. 'She wanted to pay me for my time,' she said. 'That's who she is you, see. A model of integrity.' It wasn't necessary to say she had refused Maria's offer. Jejeune suspected Kim felt she'd already received her reward in other ways. 'When you're ready to meet again, Maria will know how to reach me,' she said. 'Just tell her where and when.'

Jejeune nodded. He couldn't say when, but he already had a place in mind. She bade him goodbye outside the shop and made her way along the busy high street. He stood in the doorway for a moment after she'd left, reflecting on all the things he had learned. One very obvious question remained unanswered. Perhaps it was unintentional on Kim's part that all those casual observations about the other patrons, the reflections on the wider world, the fleeting exchanges with

Maria, had combined to distract him from asking it. But he very much doubted it. He suspected Kim wasn't yet ready to tell him just why, exactly, the death of a programmer working on avian tracking software would require one of Britain's intelligence services to keep the other in the dark. But the opportunity to ask that question was now gone. Because when he looked up and down the high street, Kim was no longer in sight.

12

From his living room window, Domenic Jejeune looked out at a sun-painted morning, cradling a cup of coffee to his chest. Thoughts about the previous day's meeting had made for a restless night, but he knew Lindy hadn't slept well, either. From the bedroom, the earlier sighs of exasperation as she got dressed had settled to an ominous silence. It was a difficult one for her, he knew. She wanted to look as good as possible while at the same time disguising the fact that she had gone to any special effort. As far as he was concerned, she could wear jeans, a sweatshirt and no make-up and still stop a clock, but he knew it wasn't his opinion she was concerned about today. She emerged from the bedroom holding her hands out at her sides. 'How's this? For today, I mean. Walking, you know, outside, in this weather.'

'It's fine,' said Jejeune. It was the sort of anodyne response that might have raised her ire at another time, but today it seemed to be just what she needed to hear.

'You're sure you're okay with this?' she asked, giving a frown of genuine concern. 'I mean, I don't know any man who would be exactly comfortable with this situation, but you are pretty secure and trusting, and, and, secure and...'

'Trusting?' he tried. 'Lindy, it's going to be okay. We've already met, remember. He made me tea.'

She smiled. 'Poor you. To be honest, I always wondered if I was being punished for something when he brought me a cup of his builder's.'

Jejeune shook his head at the memory. 'He said it ended well, between you. At least, that's his take.'

'It did. If he's the same guy he was, everything will be okay. But people change, don't they?'

'Not always. I don't think I've changed much since we met, have I?' He had meant it as a joke but she didn't smile. She looked thoughtful for a long moment. 'No, Dom, you really haven't.' She gave him a small smile now, that he assumed was meant to be reassuring. 'Come on, we don't want to be late. Johnno was always big on punctuality. At least you two have that in common. Let's go.'

Lindy had been uncharacteristically quiet in the car on the drive and, even now, on their stroll up to the hilltop, she confined her comments to the views and the weather. Only once, as she paused in the car park to cast an eye over a beat-up jeep with no doors and only a roll-bar for a roof, did she change her focus. 'I can't believe that death trap is still on the road,' she said. As they crested the rise, she stopped suddenly. A short distance ahead, a man was standing with his back to them. He had his hands in his pockets, watching as a Border collie explored a nearby tussock.

'That can't be Truth,' said Lindy.

Johnno spun and turned, his rugged face split by a broad smile. 'He's all grown up now. Same temperament, though. Still as gentle as a lamb.' He bent to ruffle the dog's neck and then straightened, looking at Lindy directly. He held out his arms hesitantly, as if afraid to close the gap between them. 'You look great, Lin. How have you been?'

She moved in for a short, swift hug. Friendship only, it told them all. Nothing more. She backed away to arm's-length and they assessed each other 'I'm good. Really good,' she told him. 'And how about you?'

'Ah, you know. Dodging trouble, or at least trying to provide a moving target.' She had held on to his hands as they'd moved apart, and looked down at them now, taking in the hard, calloused fingertips. 'Still playing the guitar, I see?' She turned to Jejeune. 'Johnno's a fantastic guitarist,' she told him. 'You should hear him play Leonard Cohen songs. They sound amazing.'

'You must be really fantastic if that's the case,' said Jejeune with a smile.

Lindy pursed her lips. 'This is what they like to call humour in the colonies,' she told Johnno. 'We try not to encourage it.'

Johnno raised a set of large binoculars hanging round his neck and looked out over the surrounding countryside. 'Some views from up here,' he said. From overhead, the urgent, recurring call of a bird rang out.

'Lapwing,' Jejeune told them both. 'There must be a nest up here somewhere. She'll settle down as soon as we move on.'

The three of them strolled slowly along the edge of the flat hilltop. Jejeune remained a step behind, listening as the conversation danced like a butterfly between Lindy and Johnno, alighting on old friends, places, events. Neither seemed inclined to dwell on any one topic for long, as if there was some sort of implicit understanding that there might be another time to revisit them in more depth later. Jejeune stopped suddenly and the others instinctively fell silent. From a good way off came the soft drumming of a woodpecker.

'It's somewhere up high in those woods,' he said, indicating the fringe of trees on the far side of the grass.

'Can you tell what kind?' asked Johnno with what seemed like genuine interest.

Jejeune shook his head. 'Probably not a Green, though. They don't typically drum. They make a kind of laughing sound. The old-timers still call them yaffles. That high up, and that soft, it could be a Lesser-spotted.'

'Is that a good bird?'

'Brilliant. It's the fastest-disappearing forest species in Europe.' Jejeune trained his bins up into the canopy while the other two waited patiently.

'This your thing, too, now, Lin?' asked Johnno conversationally.

Jejeune answered for her. 'Lindy's a big fan of the outdoors,' he said, keeping his eyes on the treetops. 'She was just saying the other day she's going to take up hiking.'

'Hiking? That doesn't sound like you.'

'What can I say? I was just having a bit of a midlife crisis, I suppose.'

'Surely it's much too early for that,' said Johnno.

When he had his bins raised to his eyes like this it was hard to read Dom's expression, but she thought she detected a faint clenching of his jaw. 'Find it?' she asked pleasantly.

He shook his head. 'There's a beautiful male Bullfinch lower down, though.'

Johnno raised his own oversized bins. 'It's amazing how you can get on birds so easily. I can't seem to find anything with these.'

'Twelves are too powerful for birding,' Jejeune told him. He tapped his own bins. 'You need 8 x 42s, 10s at most.'

'Here and I thought it was always a good thing to have bigger equipment than the other guy,' said Johnno. The comment received a smile from Jejeune, but it was clear that neither man wanted to take the banter any further.

'So what's the collective noun for woodpeckers?' asked Lindy to relive the awkwardness of the moment.

'A descent,' said Jejeune. 'A descent of woodpeckers.'

She shook her head. 'Typical. I don't know why birders always have to make them so obscure. Tell me, what's wrong with "a drumming"?'

'Ah, same old Lin,' said Johnno with a grin. 'Always questioning the rules.'

Lindy took Dom's arm. 'Oh, I'm okay with rules, when they make sense. Dom knows that, don't you, hon?' It wasn't a term she ever used to address him, and he thought back to the number of times since they'd been up here that she'd looked back at him and smiled or touched his arm or stroked his shoulder. It crossed his mind to wonder just who she was reassuring with this behaviour. Perhaps all of them.

Johnno turned his bins to look out over the valley below. He nodded towards a cluster of rectangular buildings at the base of the slope. 'Is that what I think it is?'

'The place Sampson Lee used to work,' said Jejeune, nodding, 'The Euclid Lab, aka Area 51.'

Lindy shot Jejeune an accusatory glance. Even for a meeting like this, he couldn't avoid choosing somewhere to do with his work. But perhaps that was his price for agreeing to be here. It occurred to her that they had never discussed even the possibility of her coming to the meeting alone and, seeing the two men together now, she realised that the ground rules had been established between them beforehand.

'You can talk shop if you want,' she told him.

'I was just wondering if Lee ever talked to you about his work,' said Jejeune.

'On blue carbon sites?' Johnno shook his head. 'No, I mean maybe we touched on the huge ecological and environmental advantages of them compared to terrestrial forests.' He turned to Lindy. 'Blue carbon sites can store close to ten times the amount a forest can, and, because the carbon is sequestered below water in aquatic forests and wetlands, it's stored for more than ten times longer as well.' He shrugged. 'But Lee never went into any details about the kind of research he was doing, if that's what you're asking. Why would he? It wouldn't have been of any interest to me.'

'Plus it was likely classified. Or at least confidential.'

'There is that,' conceded Johnno.

Their stroll had brought them round to the monitoring station, and Jejeune pointed at it. 'Mind if we just swing over and have a quick look at this?'

As they approached, a Lapwing fluttered to the ground in an ungainly fall and began moving away from them, dragging its wing. Lindy looked at Jejeune in alarm. 'Oh that poor little bird, it's injured, look.'

'She's not really hurt, is she?' asked Johnno. 'That's just their act, leading us away from the nest.'

'She's feigning injury?' asked Lindy. 'You mean like that other one we saw? What was it, the Reed Bunting? Really? Are there any honest birds out there at all?'

'I believe I'm right in saying something like sixty-odd species have been recorded indulging in deception behaviour.' Jejeune looked impressed and Johnno raised his hands. 'When you do an environmental podcast, you pick things up.'

Jejeune nodded. 'A lot of the ground nesting species have developed similar tactics. There's a North American plover called a Killdeer that's particularly well known for it.'

Ahead of them, the bird was still dragging its wing and calling. Jejeune raised his bins and watched as the dog trotted towards the base of the monitoring station. He caught sight of a cluster of downy chicks huddled nearby.

'Young,' he said. 'Recently hatched by the look of it. No wonder the adult's so agitated. I imagine she's concerned about the dog.'

'Ah, they're safe enough with him,' said Johnno, watching as the Border collie nuzzled the chicks with his nose. 'I mean, let's face it, if you can't trust Truth, what can you trust?' He beamed.

'Still, the instinct to protect isn't always rational,' said Jejeune. 'Perhaps we should move off before we cause the adult any more stress.'

They retraced their steps towards the edge of the hilltop and Jejeune looked down again at the buildings in the valley below. He could just make out a yellow flash behind one of the windows. 'Police tape,' he said. 'That must be Sampson Lee's office.' He spent a long moment staring at the building, while the others waited patiently behind him.

'I wonder why he revealed the name,' he said finally.

Lindy was puzzled. 'Sorry?'

'Everybody is concerned with trying to find out how Sampson Lee came up with the name. Regardless of how he did, I was just wondering why he would choose to release it. To you, Johnno, or anybody else. What did he hope to achieve?'

Johnno shrugged. 'That's something I would have liked to ask him myself. But I never got the chance. As soon as the email came in I had get straight to work on revising the podcast. By the time I finished, it was too late to get in touch with him. By the next day, he was dead.'

'Okay,' said Lindy firmly. 'It's too beautiful up here to spoil it with all this talk of that poor man's death.'

'You're right,' said Johnno. 'It is beautiful.' He watched the dog tacking back and forth in pursuit of some invisible scent, head bowed, tail wagging happily. 'Truth certainly seems to enjoy it up here. I might bring him again tomorrow. Listen,' he said, 'this has been great, but I should probably get going. Work, you know.'

There was a moment's hesitation, and Lindy looked at Jejeune. 'Yeah, us too. It's been lovely to see you, Johnno. It really has. Stay in touch.'

He waved as he departed, the dog trotting faithfully by his side. Jejeune stood beside Lindy and watched him leave. Nobody had mentioned the three of them getting together again. But somehow, Jejeune had the feeling they would.

13

'So, Five, eh?' said Holland as he and Salter walked towards the perfectly proportioned maths lab from the car park. 'I wonder if I should approach them myself, once I get my sergeant's exam out of the way.'

'I'd say you lack one of the most fundamental requirements for intelligence work, Tony. The clue is in the title.'

He smiled to acknowledge the jab. 'Ever think about it yourself?'

She shook her head. 'Too many grey areas for me. I like things a bit more black and white. I think that's what appealed to me about maths. Every operation has its own solution and it can never produce a different answer. It's what my prof used to call the beauty of its immutable truth.' She held the door open for him. 'Here we are. What's this one's name again?'

'Ishtara Habloun.'

'I wonder if she will have any higher opinion of our victim's research than Chandra. *Et cetera, sort of thing*,' she quoted. 'Not exactly standard terminology in mathematics. He couldn't have shown more contempt for Lee's work if he'd spat on the ground. Hello, what's going on here?'

The security desk was unmanned, and there were signs that it had been abandoned in a hurry. From up on the second floor, they heard urgent calls and the sound of running footsteps.

'Cover the door,' Holland said, taking the stairs two at a time. He passed a young woman with long dark hair on the first landing. 'Intruder, that way,' she shouted, pointing towards the connecting corridor. 'Sam is after him.'

From below, Salter saw the shadow of a figure in a hoodie sprinting along a corridor on the far side of the offices that ran parallel to the one Holland had set off along. The guard was giving chase. At Salter's shouted alert, Holland turned and sprinted back along the near corridor. Through the offices in between, he could see the figure silhouetted against the plate glass panes of the outside wall. The guard was still in pursuit but he was losing ground.

'Is the door through that connecting corridor to the other building open?' Salter asked the woman who'd descended the staircase and was now standing beside her.

She shook her head. 'It's on digital retina scan. There is an emergency exit at the other end of the hallway, though, past the offices. It's at the foot of the stairwell.'

Salter put in a lung-bursting effort to reach the stairwell on the lower level to cut off the exit, but arrived only in time to hear the door slamming and the blaring of an alarm. She went out into the car park and looked around, but there were no signs of movement. With so many parked cars, the intruder would have had cover all the way to the barrier at the entrance. And the hillside beyond.

She came back inside to find Holland and the guard in the stairwell, both doubled over catching their breath beneath the flashing red light. She shook her head and looked at the guard. 'Any idea who it was?' she said over the noise of the alarm.

'Could have been anybody,' he gasped. 'I can't for the life of me see how he got in.' He shuffled off to file a report with his superiors. He didn't need the officers to tell him there was little more he could do now, beyond shutting off the door alarm and resetting it.

Holland and Salter went back up the stairs to look around. There was no sign of disturbance in any of the offices. They went to the far end of the hallway and Salter tried the door. It opened onto a wide kitchen. She called down to the woman still standing at the foot of the stairs. 'I thought you said this door was locked.'

'From the other side. Both buildings can access the shared kitchen but we can't get into each other's labs. I'll show you.'

She mounted the stairs quickly. Holland's outstretched hand was awaiting her at the top. 'You'd be Ishtara, I presume,' he said with an over-gallant smile. Salter was not surprised. The woman had just the sort of looks and figure that had attracted his interest in the past.

'Any idea what the intruder was after?' Salter asked. 'Lee's work was of interest to the government, I understand. Carbon values?'

Ishtara nodded. 'But it doesn't necessarily mean it was top secret or anything. Confidential at best. For us it's more of a prestige thing. A government-associated project is a great CV-builder for the researcher involved and can lead to bigger things later on. It's typically assigned to the project lead, Amit in this case, but somehow Sampson ended up with it.' She shrugged. 'The carbon aspect was really more his field, I suppose. Let's go through to the kitchen. I'll make us all some tea to calm our nerves.'

The kitchen formed the central section of the glass corridor that connected the two buildings. As with the area they'd just left, its internal proportions conformed perfectly with the golden ratio. Ishtara moved to the counter and sprinkled the contents of a small sachet into three cups before pouring hot water over them. She handed each of them a cup. A heady aroma of cardamom, cloves and ginger swirled up from the watery amber liquid.

'It's my special recipe, all the way from Babylon.'

'Babylon?' said Holland, staring into the cup. 'Is that a real place?'

'Nowadays it's called Al-Ḥillah, but it's where Babylon was. The proud birthplace of mathematics.'

'Not China, then?' he asked. 'Or India?'

'Ah, I see you've already been nobbled by the opposition,' she said, grinning as she took a sip of her tea. 'Place value is undoubtedly important, as are negative numbers, but really neither can compare with Babylon's contributions to the Western world. We introduced the sexagesimal system.'

Holland gave her a blank stare.

'Sixty seconds,' said Ishtara. 'Sixty minutes, 360 degrees. Any of this sounding familiar?'

Salter sensed something in Ishtara's willingness to prolong the social side of things. If it was an attempt to avoid the discussion going elsewhere, she wondered why. She took a sip of the tea. Other flavour notes came through; orange, and perhaps cinnamon. She looked around the kitchen and saw the doors at each end with their digital retina scanners. 'I'm guessing Katie Fairfax's work on air quality would be of interest to all three areas of research your own group is pursuing,' she said. 'And yet her lab is kept separate from the rest of the project.'

'More security measures.' Ishtara raised her teacup and breathed in the aroma. 'Both buildings needed access to this kitchen, obviously, but they didn't want anybody using her lab to enter ours, so they put retina scan locks on both access doors. We don't have access to her lab, and she can't get into ours.'

'Trouble with somebody stealing the milk?' asked Holland, nodding to a large steel fridge in the far corner. It had a metal strap across the front, secured by a lock.

'It's where Katie stores her filter samples until she has a big enough batch to run analysis. She can't afford to have it contaminated, even by accident, so she keeps it locked. We don't have a key to that, either.'

'It sounds like she's isolated from you in more ways than one,' said Salter.

Ishtara shrugged. 'Her work is important to our calculations, but, with the specific types of software programs we are creating, you couldn't really survive in our department without a very solid background in computational mathematics. She simply doesn't have that.' She shook her head. 'I mean, let's face it, collecting and analysing air samples. It's hardly the quest for Fermat's Theorem, is it?'

'I thought that had been solved,' said Salter.

Ishtara's eyes widened in surprise. 'You're a maths wonk?'

'No talent, just an interest. Once.'

Ishtara turned to Holland. 'And how about you, Constable? Do you dabble in mathematics, too?'

'It's the beauty of its immutable truth that attracts me,' he said. 'The way it's so logical and straightforward and makes perfect sense.'

Salter lowered her eyes slightly, as one might at the sight of a runaway train heading for a cliff, but if Ishtara saw the gesture her gentle smile didn't show it. 'Well, the product of a squared integer is the same as the product of the square of the negative of that integer. Two squared is positive four, but then again so is negative two squared. Then there's the whole question of Gödel's second theorem about the incompleteness of mathematics.' She laughed out loud. 'Your eyes are beginning to glaze over. Are you sure you wouldn't rather talk about football?'

Salter regarded the researcher carefully as she turned to give Holland the full benefit of her smile. Although his charm sometimes found favour amongst the most unlikely of targets, once again, Salter couldn't shake the feeling that the woman's playful flirting was an excellent way to divert the detectives from deeper investigations. 'Would you mind going over your own area of study for us?' she asked.

'Sure.' Ishtara shook her head as if to free herself from other distractions, setting her long dark tresses shimmering in a silky wave. Salter couldn't ever remember seeing hair as glossy and healthy-looking. 'I'm using mechanical learning to develop acoustic software that can identify calls of bird species in flight.'

'Mechanical learning,' said Holland. 'That's like AI?'

'It's a sub-branch of it that gives computers the ability to learn tasks or associations without explicitly being programmed for them. It's used to train algorithms to take on various computations. In my case, involving bird call IDs. By overlaying that information onto Amit's migration data, I hope to be able to predict when a particular species is likely to arrive, and even where they're most likely to make landfall. Tracking tags provide spatial patterns of where and when some species of birds migrate,' she continued, 'but even within a species, migratory behaviour may vary across sexes or populations. Once we better understand the migration patterns of a species as a whole, our outfacing project will be able to make recommendations for implementing more species-specific protection measures, like the siting of energy infrastructure such as wind turbines, and mitigating the impacts of light pollution.'

'This other project, that would be the fLIGHT programme,' confirmed Holland, causing Salter to look his way.

'You've heard of it?' Ishtara tilted her head. 'I'm impressed.'

Holland seemed about to say more, but appeared to think better of it. Salter set down her teacup. Only a few small shards of organic matter floated in the remains at the bottom. She noticed Tony was still cradling his own cup. Given his avowed aversion to all things fragrant, she supposed he was awaiting an opportunity to pour the tea away.

'Amit Chandra claims he was at home on the night of the sixteenth,' she said suddenly. 'He says you were, too.'

'Does he? I don't remember telling him that.' Ishtara shrugged again. 'I suppose it's a safe bet, though. We work long hours here and I'm afraid my clubbing days are behind me, for the time being at least. Why are you checking our alibis, anyway? Neither of us would have harmed Sampson. He was our colleague.' Tears started to her eyes for a moment as she stared down into her teacup. 'We cared about him.'

And at that moment, in the sadness that clouded the woman's face, Salter could tell that, for Ishtara Habloun at least, the statement was literally true. The moisture from her withheld tears was still in her eyes as she looked up at Salter. 'I should be getting back, let you get on with the job of finding the person who did this awful thing.'

'We will do everything we can. But we need some help. Especially from somebody who seems to have been as close to him as you were.'

'Once.' She nodded. 'It had been over between us for a while. He'd moved on to Katie Fairfax.'

'So you have nothing to tell us, then?'

For the briefest of moments it seemed like Ishtara's resolve would hold. Finally, it gave way. 'Amit came to me one day and said Sampson had stolen some of his work on predictive algorithms,' she admitted reluctantly. 'He also said he was convinced Sampson had taken some of my own coding for the system architecture. But it didn't make any sense that Sampson would do something like that. He had no use for that kind of material whatsoever. Perhaps it was just some pettiness on Amit's part but, if so, I've no idea why. The two of them never got along, but I can't believe Amit would maliciously accuse him like that. I really can't.'

'But you were never aware of any kind of confrontation between them over these allegations?' asked Salter.

'None, none at all. Look, I'm sure there's nothing to it, just some misunderstanding.' But the shrug was over-elaborate, like someone who might be trying too hard to dismiss something. She paused. 'I really should be going,' she said hurriedly. 'Sam will show you out, but please let me know if I can be of any further help.'

Holland drained his now cold tea in a single gulp and handed Ishtara the cup. 'Lovely, that was,' he said. 'Just like drinking a flower garden. My treat next time, though.'

'We'll see,' said Ishtara. But her parting smile still held her former sadness.

Salter shook her head as the two detectives watched the departing form of Ishtara Habloun. 'I don't know, Tony. I hardly think accusations of intellectual property theft in high-level research like this are the sort of everyday occurrence she seems to be suggesting. With a highly competitive bunch like these mathematicians, stealing someone else's work might well be motive.'

'And that's without the fact that Lee got a juicy government gig that should have gone to the senior researcher, one Amit Chandra.'

So Tony hadn't been entirely distracted by the radiant beauty of Ishtara Habloun then.

'There's one more thing you might not be aware of, too,' he added. 'That escape door, you couldn't see it from the corridor. It's tucked away, completely out of view.'

'And yet our runner headed straight for it,' said Salter thoughtfully. 'Like somebody who knew the layout here.' She nodded. 'I take it back, Tony. You might be Five material yet. If they ever waive that intelligence requirement, that is. Come on, let's see what the others have come up with. I don't know about you, but I think I've had enough of the wonderful world of computational mathematics for one day.'

14

Domenic Jejeune had noticed Tony Holland's Audi as soon as he drew up to the Euclid Lab car park. His intention had been to park there, then walk up to the hilltop and make his way over to the fringe of forest on the far side. Although he had no intention of involving himself in the junior detectives' inquiries, he still felt uneasy about his presence here. He shook his head at the ridiculousness of the situation. As a DCI, he should have been able to go anywhere without invitation, but he knew if word got out that he'd been here, at the Euclid Lab, where all the birding research was going on, Laraby would misinterpret it.

Jejeune parked the Beast on the far side of an old utility shed beside the fenced-in car park. It would be out of sight of the officers if they came out before he returned from his birding. The thought of having to go to such lengths irked him, until he remembered his reason for being here. He had managed to convince himself beyond a reasonable doubt that the soft drumming he had heard the day before was that of a Lesser-spotted Woodpecker, and he had come to find it. He grabbed his bins and shouldered his tripod-mounted scope, and set off up the slope in search of the bird.

Once upon the grassy hilltop, he crossed to the forest and entered at a point close to where he'd heard the drumming. The dense tree cover descended all the way down the far side of the hill. Through the foliage, at the base of the slope he could just see the glinting light of a secluded marsh off in the distance. It was a favourite spot of his and he knew he would be visiting it again soon, but for now he stood and took in the sounds of the forest. Branches creaked in the gathering wind, an occasional call or trill rose from the deeper shadows. From the undergrowth, the grasses whispered in hushed tones.

'There's a peace about being here, isn't there? I do think if more people spent time in places like this, protecting them wouldn't be quite such an uphill struggle.'

He spun round to find a woman standing behind him. In contrast to her cultured voice, her appearance was startling. Though her clothes seemed to be of good quality, they were stained and dirty. Her hair was matted into tangles and she had streaks of dirt on her face and arms. She had the look of someone new to the life of homelessness, battered and worn down by the elements, not yet used to the broken, fragmented rest of rough sleeping.

'Sorry if I startled you,' she said. 'I should have called out when I saw you approaching. You just seemed to be enjoying the view so much I didn't want to disturb you.'

He smiled. 'It's fine. I'm used to having places like this to myself, that's all.'

'There were a couple of Spotted Flycatchers moving through earlier,' she said. 'And what might have been a Hawfinch higher up. I couldn't tell from here.' She opened her hands to show she had no binoculars. 'I doubt that's what you've come here for today, though. Not with that scope.'

'I'm pretty sure I heard a Lesser-spotted Woodpecker drumming up there recently. I thought I'd come and have a try for it.'

The woman nodded her head knowingly. 'Could be. This woodland is a stronghold for them. It's one of the few places I know of that all three species of our woodpecker can be found.'

A call came to them and they stared at each other. 'Curlew?' she asked.

'That's what it was,' said Jejeune. 'But that call couldn't be coming all the way from the marsh, could it? It sounded so clear.'

'I agree. It sounded like it was coming from here in these woods. But then the human ability to identify the direction of sounds is unreliable at best.'

Who was she, wondered Jejeune, this strange woman with such a knowledge of forest birds and calls, and other matters? He took out his phone and opened his bird call ID app. 'Fortunately, the direction a call is coming from makes no difference to this.' He smiled at her disapproving look. 'You're a purist?'

'I'm just not sure I'd place my faith in that if I wanted to put a Lesser-spotted Woodpecker on my list.'

Jejeune shook his head. 'I'd only use it for confirmation, if it's a sketchy look. I'm one of those birders who tends to list a bird only if I actually get eyes on it.'

'Glad to hear it,' she said. 'I worry that technology will take the human element out of birding altogether someday. This whole move towards the use of AI in identifying birds, it seems to undermine the field skills that are still so vital to what a good naturalist does.'

Jejeune tilted his head. 'I think there's always going to be a place for field skills. There's always some nuance, some anomaly that no software is going to be able to pick up. And the data that fuels these birding apps, so much of that comes from citizen science, field observations and recordings. I see it as more of a merger than a competition.'

'I wish I shared your optimism,' she said sadly.

The Curlew call came to them again and Jejeune turned his phone to her. 'At least the AI agrees with us,' he said. 'But I can't believe how much it sounds like it's coming from those trees.' He set up the scope and began scanning the ground around the forest edge. It seemed impossible that he could miss a bird the size of a Curlew, but it was nowhere in sight. He noticed a flurry of movement higher up and focused on a group of large birds squabbling raucously over some berries on a branch.

'No Curlew, but there is a party of Jays there,' he said. 'Care to take a look?' He adjusted the scope height down for the woman and stepped back as she moved in.

He raised his bins as she crouched to watch the Jays through the scope. It was a particularly aggressive dispute, with jousting bills and lancing thrusts, until the victor drove off the others and greedily grabbed the spoils for itself.

'There's no compromise in nature, is there,' she said, still looking through the scope. 'No thought of the greater good, or the species as a whole. Just do what you can to make sure you survive until the next day. I think there's something to that.' She straightened and pointed to Jejeune's hand. 'I wonder if I could ask something of you. That phone,' she said. 'Could you call the police and tell them they need to come out here?'

Jejeune froze. There were a lot of reasons to approach this situation with caution. 'And if they ask why?'

'You can tell them I'm the woman they are looking for in connection with the murder of Sampson Lee. I'm Katie Fairfax.'

*

'If you know the police have been trying to locate you,' said Jejeune as he tucked away his warrant card, 'why haven't you come forward before now?' He hefted the scope onto his shoulder and began to walk out of the woods with Katie Fairfax at his side. As they emerged from the trees, she paused for a moment and looked across at the fluttering yellow police tape round the white metal structure at the far end of the hilltop. Jejeune followed her gaze.

'After Sampson was killed, the bottom just fell out of my world for a while. I got a call from a friend as I was getting ready for work. She said she'd heard about it on the news. I just got in my car and drove around and around until I ran out of fuel. Then I walked. And walked. Until I found myself somewhere I didn't recognise. I've been avoiding the world ever since. But I am ready to come back to it now. I know there are questions that have to be answered.'

'Like where you were the night he was murdered?' said Jejeune.

'I was doing the late run to collect the latest set of filters and install new ones. After that, I came to the lab to store them in the fridge and then went home to bed. I presume I'm a person of interest because the police heard we argued the last time I saw Sampson.'

'What about?'

'I told him he had to release Huebner's name.'

Jejeune spun his head towards Fairfax in shock. 'You knew his name? Before it was announced on the podcast?'

She nodded. 'Sampson told me he had come across it. Only he was pronouncing it Hubbner.'

'It's the spelling of Huebner's legal name, the one used in the legal filings. There's an umlaut on the u.'

'Ah, I see. Well I set him right on the pronunciation anyway.'

'You recognised the name, then?'

'Marius Huebner has been an enemy of land conservation around these parts for a long time. That's why I insisted Sampson had to release his name to that podcaster.'

'But he was having second thoughts? Was he afraid of Huebner?'

'I don't think so. He said he'd simply realised the information could be used for a better purpose. It could correct past wrongs and offer help for the future. A greater good, he called it.'

'What kind of help? Did he mean protecting somebody else? Did he mention any other name?'

Fairfax shook her head. 'He said Huebner's was the only one that comes up.'

'*Comes up* as in continuing references?' asked Jejeune. 'As opposed to *came up* in a single instance?'

She shrugged. 'I'm not sure. *Comes up*, I think. Does it matter?'

Jejeune's expression suggested it might.

'If you are wondering whether he was mistaken, Inspector, I can tell you Sampson was absolutely certain that Marius Huebner was the person at the centre of the blue carbon scandal.' She nodded and her dirty, tangled locks fell forward. 'I understand the idea of the greater good, I really do. But a person has to pay a price for a crime they have committed. They can't be allowed to escape justice in pursuit of something more important, more far-reaching. People need to see that bad deeds are punished. It's what sets the good actions of the rest of us apart. Light is not light without darkness to define it.' She paused to check her outpouring of passion. 'In the end, I must have struck a chord with him, I suppose. He obviously decided to reveal the name to that journalist after all.'

The Curlew call came to them again. Jejeune raised his bins and looked back into the forest. He smiled. A Eurasian Starling was sitting on a low branch in an alder tree and, as Jejeune watched, it gave another perfectly pitched rendition of the shorebird's plaintive cry.

'I found your Curlew,' he said. 'It's a Starling.'

'But it's perfect,' said Fairfax in astonishment. 'It's indistinguishable from a real Curlew's call.'

Jejeune nodded. 'And that's why there will always be a place for field observations. AI systems function on reliable, accurate data. Mimicry, and the injury-feigning tactics of certain species to protect their nests and young, they're undetectable to AI. It's really only humans who can reliably recognise deception.'

'I wonder why it is that I find so little comfort in the idea that dishonesty is one of the last strongholds of human intelligence,' she said with a sad smile.

Jejeune's silence as he hefted his scope to his shoulder to resume their walk to the vehicle suggested he found no more solace in the thought than she did.

15

Marvin Laraby didn't waste much time on niceties when he kicked off the morning briefing. 'I see the DCI is notable by his absence this morning,' he said, surveying the room.

'He's on a course today, I believe,' Maik told him.

'A course, eh?' Laraby nodded at the default response offered by subordinates since time immemorial. 'I wonder if it's one I've played.' The men locked eyes for a moment, equally aware of Jejeune's aversion to golf. The message was clear. In Laraby's world, loyalty came with a price.

'Just a thought, sir,' said Holland, 'but with all that bird-related research, I wonder if it makes sense to let the DCI have a run at this maths crowd.'

Laraby shook his head. 'It wouldn't end well. I've got a lot of respect for the DCI, as you all know, but he does always like to be the cleverest person in the room. He probably couldn't get a position as a tea-stirrer's assistant in that kind of company, and that wouldn't sit very well with him at all. Before we knew it he'd be off chasing wild theories left, right and centre just to show everybody how brilliant he is. Five don't want to hear about some maverick on a crusade of his own. What's going to make them happy is careful, methodical police work.

Like investigating what this intruder was doing at the Euclid Lab, for example. There was a pursuit, I understand,' he said, fixing Holland with a stare. 'Pity it wasn't by somebody young and fit enough to catch the runner before they escaped.'

'To be fair, sir,' said Holland defensively, 'they had about fifty yards on me.'

'Disappeared through an exit door, I'm told. Please tell me you at least got a description.'

'Grey, about seven foot tall, three hinges. Didn't get eyes on the runner, though.'

There was a moment of silence while Laraby decided where the constable's attempt at wit fell. The verdict came down in Holland's favour. 'I see a bright future for this lad,' he said, pointing at the constable as he turned to Maik. If it was a hint that Laraby wanted Holland at King's Landing in the event of a vacancy, Maik's expression suggested that staff retention was suddenly going to become a top priority for him.

'So at least we're making some progress on other fronts,' continued the DCS. 'I'll be happy to be able to report that we have finally found Katie Fairfax. How did Jejeune's interview with her go?'

'Nothing useful,' said Salter. 'She has no idea who would want Lee dead if it wasn't Huebner. Her own alibi seems solid enough. The samples she was collecting are time-stamped when the flaps on the monitoring stations are opened. At the time of Lee's death, they put her fifteen miles away. We had no reason to hold her.'

Laraby received the news in thoughtful silence. 'How about the others up at that lab? There's reason to suspect Amit Chandra's never had the happiest of relationships with the victim. What is it, a bit of jealousy over a government contract and an accusation of IP theft?'

Salter and Holland looked at each other. At this stage there was no point in raising their own suspicions about who Holland had been chasing, but there was no reason not to pile on in other areas. 'It was also Chandra who reported that first intruder,' said Salter. 'He said Lee had propped open a security door right opposite his office to let in some air, which was in breach of the university's policies in the first place. When Chandra spotted the intruder, he was actually coming out of Lee's office, which had been left unlocked. Lee vehemently denied either propping the door open or leaving his office unlocked.'

'Well he would, wouldn't he?' said Laraby. 'Failure to secure sensitive government documents? That's a chargeable offence. Okay, let's give that tree another shake and see what falls out. What about that other security incident up there, the attempted release of Ishtara Habloun's data to that science journal?'

'Nobody saw who deposited the envelope, but the university's internal investigation found that somebody must have put it there the same night as the break-in. Security were actually interviewing Chandra about that incident when Ishtara came in and alerted them to it.'

'What did the woman have to say about it herself?'

There was an embarrassed silence as Holland and Salter exchanged a guilty glance. Laraby looked from one to the other. 'What, neither one of you thought to ask her? Well I can see the standards for investigation at Saltmarsh fall a good way short of ours up here in KL, eh, Danny?'

Salter felt the colour of shame rising to her cheeks. To have this happen on her enquiry, after having being sidelined by Jejeune before? She couldn't be tarnished by this. 'Well, you can thank Constable Holland for that, sir. If he hadn't been putting all his efforts into trying to get her into bed, he might have found the time to ask her about it.'

Holland was too stunned by Salter's comment to respond. He looked helplessly at Maik, but he was in no position to offer anything beyond a questioning stare of his own in Salter's direction. Laraby nodded knowingly. 'Ah, I see. Mind on the job first, Constable, especially when we're talking about a potential key witness. Still, no harm done. There seems to be plenty of reason for another visit out there, so we can ask her then. Can I suggest you write it down though, so you don't forget this time?'

The sardonic grin that had been meant for the Saltmarsh officers was diverted to the door by a soft knocking. An unexpected face appeared. 'First time I've been in a live session.' said Lelia Segal, flashing a tentative smile, 'but I think this news warrants it.'

'Always welcome, Doctor,' said Laraby magnanimously. He spread his hands to show she was free to share her information with the room. 'What have you got for us?'

'A head wound, a second one. When I examined Sampson Lee's skull more closely, I found evidence of another wound, right next to the first, same angle of impact, same block of concrete, only much shallower.'

'So our killer lifted him off the block and smashed him down a second time?'

'I wouldn't say so, no. I think the victim raised his own head slightly after the first blow, but he was too badly wounded and collapsed backwards from the effort, his head striking the concrete for a second time.'

'So Lee was still alive at the monitoring station?'

Segal nodded. 'Only...' She paused for a second, aware that every set of eyes in the room were on her now.

'Go on,' urged Laraby quietly.

'The wounds on the neck from the cord. They were still fresh. I'd say they were inflicted at that scene as well.'

For a moment, there was silence in the room.

'So the cord was replaced in the house after the attack at the monitoring station?' said Laraby. He looked at Maik. 'Could somebody else have been in that house before you got there?'

Maik paused long enough to give the impression that he was considering the idea for the first time. 'It's not impossible,' he said. His impassive features gave no hint of his earlier misgivings, but giving a true answer now relieved none of the unease he felt at previously withholding his suspicions.

Laraby nodded thoughtfully. 'And does this intel give us anything new on TOD, Dr Segal?'

'I'm not going to get much closer than my original window, I'm afraid. We know Lee was still alive at seven p.m. because that's when he emailed the name. Assuming he left immediately afterwards to meet his killer up by the monitoring station – drive there, park, walk up the hill, arriving at the murder scene say, eight o clock at the earliest?'

'With what we know now, it's possible that there was no attack at the house. It could all have been staged afterwards,' said Laraby, 'with the cord taken from the murder scene on the hill and left there.' He shook his head. 'This all seems be pointing towards the involvement of somebody at the Euclid Lab.'

'Not really, sir,' objected Salter. 'I don't see how any of this eliminates Huebner. Surely he's still in the frame?'

The DCS shook his head. 'The more I think about it, the less I like him for Lee's murder.' Laraby made no mention of Jejeune's previous doubts, and barrelled into an explanation before anyone else could point them out. 'By all accounts, Huebner likes the straightforward approach. This business of killing Lee in one place and transporting his body to another, that's not him at all.' He shook his head firmly. 'No, our answer lies up at that lab. I'm convinced of it. For one thing, there may still be more that Katie Fairfax has to offer us. Wherever she was when Lee was killed, it could still have been her that dumped his body in the river. And staged that crime scene at his house, for that matter.' He turned to Maik. 'Danny, can we check to see if she had a key to Lee's place? You said there was no sign of a break-in, so we have to assume whoever went there had access. And Tony, anything yet on that tyre cast?'

Holland shook his head. 'It's not a match for Fairfax's car, but there are a few trucks out in the car park by the lab. I assume one of them is assigned to her for her field work with those monitoring stations.'

'Okay, let's get somebody to take that cast out there and see if it matches any of those trucks. In the meantime, we have enough personnel for a change, so we're going to run simultaneous ops. While Danny's on Katie Fairfax, and Constable Holland is looking at the tyre cast, Lauren, Sergeant Salter, I mean, can see if she can improve on Saltmarsh's previous stellar work up at the Euclid Lab and get to the bottom of this dispute between Lee and Chandra.' He tried to soften his sarcasm with a smile, but Salter's stony stare suggested he had not quite succeeded.

'And Huebner, sir? Do we tell the DCI he's off our radar now?'

'No, we'll leave the inspector to see whether there's any life in that lead. But for the rest of us, our focus is on that lab up at the university. That's where all the evidence is leading us. So we follow it.'

*

The alcove in the hallway had become their default meeting place, and Salter and Maik both headed for it now. 'Am I missing something?' she asked as they arrived. 'Just what is this fixation Laraby seems to have with the Euclid Lab? *That's where all the evidence is leading us.* Really? Only if you discount Huebner as a suspect on the basis of not very much solid police work at all. What happened to looking at the obvious and not trying to be too bloody clever?'

Danny couldn't answer that. He shook his head. '*Ops* and *Intel*. I remember the good old days when we dealt with investigations and evidence,' he said drily.

'And let's not forget his *liaising* with Five,' Salter reminded him. She made a face. 'He'll be asking us to refer to him as Q next.'

'I think he was the gadgets bloke. James Bond's spymaster was M. No idea what it stood for, though.'

'I know "P" stands for prat,' said Salter testily. 'What's going on here, Danny? Is he feeling the heat from Five and now all of a sudden he thinks he has to pull rabbits out of non-existent hats?'

Maik didn't know the answer to that one either. But when a no-nonsense copper like Laraby suddenly started outdoing Domenic Jejeune in his outside-the-box thinking, it might be time to find out.

16

Holland looked up at the unrelenting smoothness of the glass façade of the Euclid Lab. 'A bit boring, isn't it, for all the beauty of its golden ratios. You'd think after spending all day here you might welcome the chance to let your hair down a bit.'

'Please tell me you're not thinking about asking Ishtara out for a night on the town, Tony.'

'You saw us together, discussing that square root business. There was a real meeting of the minds there.'

'I think you might have been one short for that. Besides, you can't go anywhere near her just now,' Salter reminded him. 'She's a key witness in a case you're investigating.'

'Speaking of which, I can't say I appreciated you throwing me under the bus with Laraby.'

'You're getting a bit sensitive in your old age, aren't you?' said Salter defensively. 'And let's face it, with the amount of chit-chat between you, there was plenty of opportunity to ask her about that data that was almost leaked.'

'As SIO, there, it was your responsibility to control the line of questioning. I'm just saying. You made it sound like borderline dereliction of duty.'

'Rubbish. I made it sound like somebody more interested in a date than an arrest, that's all. She's a suspect, Tony, not a prospect, and as such she's off-limits for now.'

It was clear to both of them that the topic needed to be put aside for the time being. But that didn't mean the matter was over. At least as far as Holland was concerned.

'Is she though, really? A suspect.' He shook his head dubiously. 'I'm just not getting that sense from her at all.'

Salter thought about it. Holland was right in that you could sometimes get a feeling about somebody when you questioned them. She hadn't got one from Ishtara Habloun, either. There were definitely layers hidden within her, secrets and evasions, but Salter had never felt that flash, that one intuitive spark, that told her this was their killer. The problem was, they had all been fooled by clever ones before. And Ishtara Habloun was certainly that. As far as Salter was concerned, the jury was still out on her. She could say the same about the man now standing at the end of this corridor awaiting their approach.

Amit Chandra regarded the detectives warily. He was wearing a snug, white golf shirt that emphasised the impressive proportions of his upper body, and they could see the muscles in his arms tensing. He was leaning slightly in the direction of his office, as if he might have taken refuge in it if there had been time.

'He doesn't look all that that pleased to see us, does he?' murmured Holland as they drew near.

'I think it might be you, actually,' said Salter. 'So why don't I go first.' She called out. 'A word, Mr Chandra, if you don't mind.'

'I have something pressing to get to, unfortunately.' He flashed them a nervous smile and turned to go.

'It's about the predictive algorithms you claim Lee stole from you?'

'Is there another word for taking my work without permission?' He sighed, and offered a smile that was meant to show he was being reasonable. It missed by some distance. 'Listen, let's just drop the whole thing, okay? I mean, the guy is dead now. What's the point in pursuing it?'

Salter offered a thin smile. 'The problem is, I just can't see any application in Sampson Lee's field of study for an algorithm of the kind you claim he stole. Identifying conditions and food resources at a site, I mean, it's simply assessment and evaluation of data, isn't it? I don't see a predictive element in it at all.'

Amit looked at the detective with a new respect. But that didn't mean he was ready to open up to her.

'I have to tell you, Ishtara is of a similar opinion about the system architecture you claim he took from her,' said Holland. 'Is she around? Perhaps we could ask her to join us and we can sort all this out now.'

'You need to leave her alone. Your coming here upset her last time. It's not as if she hasn't had enough grief over Sampson Lee.'

'Really, how's that?'

'He just dumped her, out of the blue. After they'd been seeing each other for months. He started seeing Katie Fairfax the same day. That's who Lee was, you see, out for himself, first, last and always. All this making him out to be some kind of good guy, it makes me sick. You need to leave Ishtara out of this. I told you, I can give you a one hundred per cent guarantee she had nothing to do with his death.'

'Really?' said Holland with a smirk. 'You know, I believe that's the first time I've ever got one hundred per cent on anything to do with mathematics.'

'Why don't I find that hard to believe?' said Chandra flatly. He turned to Salter. 'Why are you here, anyway? Am I in trouble for something?'

It struck Salter that this was one of those questions you had answered simply by asking it. 'Is there any reason you should be?'

Chandra's eyes searched up and down the corridor, but it was clear there was no escape route available.

'When we pursued that intruder the other day, he was coming from the direction of Sampson Lee's office,' said Holland. 'Any idea what he might have been looking for?'

'None at all. Sorry.' If he was, neither the man's tone nor his expression reflected it.

'See me, I hear "intruder in a maths lab", I automatically think, "what's he after?"' said Holland easily. 'I mean, let's face it, a few mathematical equations are hardly worth risking jail time for, are they?'

'I take it you've never heard of the Diffie–Hellman key algorithms? They allow for the secure exchange of cryptographic keys over public channels. Every time you use a credit card over the internet or a bank card at a cash machine, you're employing those algorithms. You come up with something like that, it might be worth a bit, don't you think?' Chandra asked coldly.

'You're not doing that work here, though, are you? You're researching bird migrations. So I come back to my earlier question: why would anybody try to steal that?'

Amit stared at Holland but made no comment.

'Not the first time it's happened here, though, is it?' said Salter. 'In fact, it was you that reported the earlier break-in at Sampson Lee's office.'

Chandra shrugged, setting his muscular shoulders rippling. 'I know what I saw. Besides, he even told campus security himself he thought he was being followed. They never saw anyone watching him, but I know they took the report seriously. After all, they've invested enough in security around here.'

'Just why do you tolerate the security measures here, Mr Chandra?' said Holland. 'Be a bit of an ask for me, if I'm being honest, handing in my phone and devices every morning, security checkpoints in and out. Makes me wonder why anybody would put up with it.'

'The facilities here at the university are as good as it gets. These systems they have built allow us to run concurrent iterations of our programs that will ultimately allow the mechanical learning software to train our algorithms. The same combination of mathematical and computing functions would be hard to find elsewhere.'

'So nothing to do with the prestige of being associated with government projects then?'

'What? No. Of course not.'

'See, I'm thinking that, given your low opinion of Sampson Lee in the first place, the fact that he got the nod for that contract must have rankled a bit.'

'What are you talking about?'

'I mean here he is, dodgy character, less qualified than you by some distance, and he's the one who's going to be strutting around with the government project on his CV. But if you start whispers that he's the type of bloke who steals other people's work, maybe the government gets jittery. Maybe they want to take that project away and give it to someone more worthy. Somebody like you, say. I think once Lee had attracted the wrong sort of attention by failing to lock his office when that intruder got in, you just decided to come up with some fantasy about him stealing your work in the hope that it would be enough to tip the scales.'

'This is preposterous.' Chandra looked at Salter for help. 'I'm sorry, what does any of this have to do with Sampson Lee's death? You can't seriously be suggesting I killed him because he had a government contract and I didn't.'

Holland tilted his head. 'Well, the situation is now vacant, as they say.'

'This is madness.' Chandra turned to Salter again. 'Is he for real? Thinking I would kill somebody over this?' She saw the colour rising around his bull-like neck, the muscles flexing in the forearms and biceps. This was a man capable of enough anger to put a cord round a rival's throat and pull hard. And hold on.

'I'm not listening to any more of this,' Chandra said furiously. 'If you aren't going to charge me with anything, I'm leaving.' He reached out and pushed Holland aside as he went past.

'Of the many things you don't want to do at this point, sir,' said Holland, dropping the pronoun heavily, 'putting your hands on me is right at the very top.'

The officers were silent until Chandra had disappeared along the corridor and closed his office door with a loud slam. 'You were right. I don't think he likes me.'

'Not least because you're his rival for someone's affections.'

'Ishtara? She'd never be interested in a plonker like that, would she?'

'Oh, I don't know, Tony,' teased Salter. 'You might have your boyish charm going for you, but I'll bet you couldn't factor out an aliquot sum as quickly as he could.'

'Please tell me they're not together.'

Salter shook her head. 'Only in his mind. I doubt he's ever got as far as even mentioning it to her. But even if he wasn't the reason Lee broke up with her, I'm sure he would have been happy enough to be there to pick up the pieces.'

'So perhaps those allegations about him stealing their work were just a way to discredit Lee in her eyes, then.' Holland shook his head. 'A maths lab, a hotbed of passion. Who'd have thought it?'

'You think because they're mathematicians they're not as much a hostage to their emotions as the rest of us. There is no algorithm for love, Tony. When the heart decides what it wants, no amount of rational calculation is going to change it. Take it from me, Amit has got it bad for Ishtara Habloun. Worse, he's in love with the idea of her. He'd go a long way to protect that.'

Further than floating false accusations about her boyfriend, she meant. The question was, how much further?

17

In her recent quest for greater fulfilment, Lindy had spoken about the necessity of pursuing moments of mindfulness, but Jejeune had no need to go searching for them. He had been drinking in views like this for as long as he could remember. He couldn't imagine any better way to connect with the world than to stand on the edge of an expanse of wetland like this, as the fading light of evening drew it into its embrace. It was a place where a person felt like they were beyond the control of time and circumstance, where what you held on to and what you let go were all within your power. The feeling never failed to bring him a sense of peace.

As he turned to return to the hide behind him a Raven circled in and settled in a nearby treetop. He watched it through his bins as it turned its head this way and that to survey its surroundings, its noble profile clearly recognisable. It was only in association with humans that the bird acquired its malevolent symbolism, Jejeune thought. Here, it was just a majestic creature whose presence had momentarily raised his spirits. With a lean into an air current and a couple of effortless flaps, the Raven was suddenly airborne once again, and he watched as it glided away into the evening's gloaming.

But it wasn't the bird he had come here for. He had just tried, unsuccessfully, for the third time to find the Lesser-spotted Woodpecker, in the woodland that rose up the hillside behind this hide. His brother, Damian, would have undoubtedly found it by now. So would Traz, his good friend and birding expert back in the Americas. Or would they? Sometimes a species simply eluded you. Nemesis birds, they were called, and, no matter how hard you tried, they always seemed to be just out of reach. Perhaps missing this woodpecker was nothing to do with his birding skills after all. Perhaps it was just Marvin Laraby, eroding his self-confidence in more areas than just his policing.

From the corner of his eye, Jejeune saw Kim coming down through the woods towards him. She stood beside him in silence for a long moment, taking in the stillness and the quiet beauty of the marsh. 'How can this place have existed all these years without me knowing about it?' she asked.

'It's pretty secluded,' said Jejeune, 'which is probably why it's not very well known to most people.'

Together they spent another moment gazing over the wetland. Small islands of light danced on the gently undulating surface of the water, while a breeze too subtle to detect moved the tall grasses fringing the marsh. 'The way the light plays on the water,' she said, 'it's like watching pools of copper drifting around. It's so peaceful here I can almost feel my heartbeat slowing already.'

'It's always a good time,' said Jejeune, 'just as the day is winding down like this. There are fewer birds around, but there is something special about seeing them in this setting.'

'I suppose spending time in isolated places like this is all part of the appeal of birdwatching.'

'Birding won't solve all your problems,' he said, 'but it can take you to some pretty incredible places to contemplate them.' But Kim wouldn't seek out a place like this to contemplate her problems. It was the human realm that interested her; their habits and habitats, not quiet, unpopulated spaces like this. In a way, the human psyche was his world, too, he recognised, but it was here that he was most comfortable, out among nature's rhythms, immersing himself in its patterns, its pulses, listening to its heartbeat.

Kim took a moment to watch as he set up his scope and adjusted it to his height before scanning the water. 'Do you bring others here? That nice young lady of yours, perhaps? What's her name, Lindy?'

'To some,' he said ironically. He shook his head. 'No, I usually come alone.' He indicated the hide behind them, nestled into the high vegetation along the edge of the marsh. 'I sometimes spend hours just sitting in there. I'm always amazed where the time has gone.'

'But someone else joined you recently, I think.'

He looked at her, puzzled.

'The telescope was not set to your height,' she said simply.

'Ah. I was trying to find a particular bird for someone. We thought we'd heard a call. It turned out to be a case of mistaken identity.'

Kim nodded like someone who had been reassured about something. She looked all around. Only the silence of the marsh greeted her.

'We shouldn't be disturbed,' said Jejeune. 'Unless Maria decides to pop by.' He gave her a half-smile to show it was a joke.

'You can't really believe she is part of some vast intelligence-gathering network of mine,' said Kim reasonably. 'Maria is simply a hardworking woman who has a smile and a kind word for her customers. Confirming that the nice young DCI who usually pops in for his morning coffee hadn't been there the day before isn't indiscretion. It's conversation.'

'But you knew where to ask. Somebody must have told you that was my regular coffee shop.'

'There aren't that many places in Saltmarsh where you can get a good cup of Colombian coffee.' Kim smiled. 'The good lord may have blessed his children with free will, Inspector, but our choices are often not as random as we might like to think. I don't deny there are titbits I pick up from her every now and again that I might store away for future reference, but your coffee-drinking habits will not be among them.'

'It just seems a touch unethical, building up files on people in that way in case you might need to use something later.'

'Intelligence has only one moral law; it is justified by results.' She smiled. 'Was it Le Carré who said that? Or one of his characters? Probably the latter. It was always the fictional spies who got the best lines. I suppose it means no one can be trusted in this shadowy world of ours. I do hope you don't feel that way about me.' Kim smiled again. 'I take it this request to meet means you might have something of interest?'

'I don't believe anyone at that hearing identified Marius Huebner to Sampson Lee.'

Kim looked interested, but said nothing.

'I believe Lee was shown an unredacted copy of the hearing transcript. That could obviously only have been prepared after the hearing was over.'

'And may I inquire how you came to this conclusion?' Kim asked cautiously.

'I saw the email Lee sent to the podcaster, Johnno McBride. In it, Lee had used the legal spelling of the name:

Hübbner, as it would have been in the transcript. Only somebody who'd seen the name written would know to spell it like that. Plus, Lee told his girlfriend that Huebner's was the only name that comes up, not *came* up. It suggests he was reading it, rather than having been told it in conversation.' Now that he had voiced it out loud, the assertion sounded tenuous. Was he trying too hard? Perhaps this was another symptom of the uncertainty that Laraby had brought to his confidence in his abilities.

But Kim didn't seem to find anything unconvincing about the reasoning. She shook her head in admiration. 'It's fine work, Inspector. And supposing you are right, do you have any idea who might have shown him that document?'

But Jejeune had seen something in Kim's response; a glimmer not of shock, but of satisfaction. 'This is not a surprise to you, is it?'

He received only an enigmatic smile in return.

'I wondered what possible interest GCHQ could have in the death of a low-level program developer for a bird tracking app. A leak from someone present at an in camera hearing, an indiscreet word, a deliberate act even, that would be Five's interest, not yours. But revealing the contents of a classified document that had already been redacted, that points to somebody deeper inside an organisation. And GCHQ is in charge of redacting documents for all intelligence services, isn't it?'

There was a noise of grasses moving in the marsh and Kim turned quickly. 'You're quite sure no one else knows you are here.'

'I told no one,' he said. Her wariness reminded him of a bird at a feeder, skittish, vigilant, never shutting off its watch for danger. Intelligence operatives should have side-facing eyes, he thought, like prey species. But then, of course, they were predators too, voracious in their search for information.

Kim spent a few moments looking out at the water, dark now except for a few patches where the trapped light of the setting sun still reflected, fighting valiantly to hold on to its splendour for a few moments more. 'I take it you haven't shared these latest thoughts with Laraby yet,' she said finally. 'I hear your intrepid DCS is now firmly focused on the maths lab where Lee worked.'

'There's a part of me that says if Laraby is focused on something, it must be wrong.' He gave a gentle smile but shook his head. 'I just don't see it.'

'Really? There is a lot to recommend the Euclid Lab as a focus of investigation, as I understand it. Motives and suspects galore. You still feel Marius Huebner is involved, then?'

'I think he may have been interested in something Lee was working on. Something to do with blue carbon. One of the researchers reported that Lee stole software from Amit Chandra that had no bearing on his own work. I believe Lee may have come up with a way to use that software to identify previously unknown blue carbon areas.'

Even a career listener like Kim couldn't completely suppress an expression of interest. She leaned forward slightly. 'Indeed?'

'I believe Lee was planning to use a predictive algorithm to assess potential blue carbon sites,' said Jejeune. 'It would be a valuable tool in the world's carbon trading schemes.'

'And you think an algorithm like that would be of interest to somebody like Marius Huebner?'

'I do. He doesn't strike me as the kind of man to sit and wait for a list of valuable sites to come his way. He's much more likely to go out and arrange to get it for himself.'

'If true, this is important progress,' said Kim. She took in her surroundings one final time and shook her head. 'It is beautiful here, but it's a bit too quiet for my liking.' She turned and smiled. 'Not to mention it's out of mobile phone range, if I needed to be contacted in a hurry. Perhaps we should find somewhere else for our next meeting.'

'Will there be one?'

'I said you had made progress. I didn't say you had yet provided all the answers we need. So yes, we should meet again. Would you consider yourself a churchgoer, I wonder, Inspector Jejeune?'

'Occasionally. When there's no alternative.'

She smiled. 'St Margaret's in the Field, Tuesday night. The crypt. Seven thirty. Don't be late. We like to start on time.'

18

The figure in the distance would have been instantly recognisable to Lindy even without the presence of the playful dog beside it. She quickened her stride as she approached the pair, holding her hair back as the wind threatened to swirl it in front of her. 'Hey there,' she said. 'Fancy meeting you up here.'

'I thought I'd bring Truth to see his new friends again. Fancy a stroll over in that direction?' Johnno indicated the monitoring station, standing like a sentinel at the far end of the flat expanse of grass. They walked side by side, just far enough apart not to be a couple. Truth ranged all around them, in front, behind, but never broaching the space between them. The breeze flipped Lindy's hair again and she swept it back from her face.

'I'm glad to see you kept your hair long,' said Johnno. 'No need for a radical makeover after we split, then?'

'Oh, it was shorter for a while, but not because of that. I just thought I'd try it. I like it more this way, though. So does Dom.'

She didn't know why it had been necessary to mention him. To remind herself that she was just here with a friend, taking an innocent stroll on a hilltop? To remind Johnno that this was all it was? Whatever the reason, it caused them both to fall silent for a moment.

'It goes without saying it's good to see you again, Lin, as an acquaintance of ours might have put it.' He gave her a cheeky grin, and for a moment she was back in the corridors outside the lecture halls, having just endured another session with the man she called Professor Redundancy. *'I'm sure I don't have to remind you,'* she said in a deep voice, 'but you're going to remind us anyway. *It goes without saying,* so why bloody say it then?' She smiled at the memory of that time in their lives when the future had beguiled them with all its promises.

'Did you ever get round to that novel you were always threatening to write?' she asked him.

He shook his head. 'The last rejection hurt so much I decided to give up the idea altogether.' She looked concerned for a moment, but then a smile broke over his face again. 'It was from ChatGPT. They said even AI writing had some standards.'

Lindy laughed. 'Don't give me that, you were a great writer.'

'I was always a better storyteller. That's why the podcast has been so good for me. Journalism without the grind of writing.'

She nodded in agreement. 'You deserve your success, though.'

'Deserve it? No, I don't think so. Life doesn't treat everybody equally, Lin. It's a sad fact, but it's true. Some people try hard and get nothing for their efforts, while the undeserving get the breaks. I just got lucky with this one. You know how it is, sometimes you turn the corner and there your story is, just waiting for you.'

'Yeah, I always seem to be standing on the wrong corner these days.'

'You've done well enough. A national award, even. Besides, don't look at me as a model of success. I have paid for my career with my personal life. A good story is one thing, but what you've got, with Dom, this relationship. That's something worth having.'

'So there's nobody in your life at the moment, then? I always thought you'd cave in one day, end up marrying some society heiress. What was it you used to call them? The haves and the have-yachts.'

He shook his head. 'There hasn't been anyone since you, Lin, not even casual.'

'Please don't say you're married to your work.'

'Actually, she's more of a mistress than a wife. Albeit a pretty high-maintenance one.'

'Not like me, then.'

'Oh, you were way worse.' He reeled away from her attempted punch and they laughed together. 'In a way I envy you, to achieve the balance you have managed. Career, settled life and partner. It goes without saying that I couldn't be happier for you.'

'Then thank you for not saying it.' They had reached the monitoring station and Truth ran ahead. Though they couldn't see the chicks, the way he was gently nuzzling through the long grass suggested that they were still huddled in there somewhere.

'Is this your dog?' asked the woman working at the station.

'Don't worry about him,' said Johnno, 'he's as gentle as they come.'

'I can see that,' said Katie Fairfax, bending to gently stroke the dog's head.

'Look at those chicks fussing around him,' said Lindy. 'I have to get this for my friend's little boy.' She took out her phone and began filming the tender interactions. Overhead, a Lapwing let out a skittering call and skimmed down towards her, making her duck.

'I doubt she'd actually attack you,' Fairfax told her. 'I'm more worried about them hitting one of those windows down in the valley, to be honest. They get so caught up in their swooping and swerving during their courtship displays.'

Johnno considered the shining sides of the Euclid Lab below them. 'That is a lot of glass,' he conceded.

Katie nodded. 'When you're cooped up in an office all day, I imagine it helps to be able to look out and convince yourself that you have some connection with nature. Which I suppose you do, as long as you don't include hearing it, or tasting it, or feeling it or touching it.'

'Not a fan of the place?' asked Lindy.

'More the architecture. They're working on software to eliminate bird strikes and yet they couldn't find it within themselves to compromise on the size of the window glass. All in the name of the beauty and elegance of proportions.' She pointed to the block at the other end of the connecting corridor. 'That's mine, you see. Masonry and small windows. They're not admitting any numbers, but I'd bet bird strikes on my building are far less than theirs. It just seems a bit hypocritical, that's all.' She caught herself. 'Anyway, that's my rant for the day. I'm sure you've got better things to do with your time than listen to me go on about the evils of the golden ratio. Sorry to have spoiled your nice romantic walk up here.'

Lindy and Johnno smiled without comment. They watched the chicks with the dog for a moment.

'It's hard to believe they're barely a few days old, isn't it?' asked Katie. 'Precocious, they're called, and they earn every bit of that description.'

Johnno turned to Lindy. 'That's what they used to say about you, Lin. A precocious talent.'

'Yeah, where did all that promise go, I wonder.' She smiled at Katie. 'We should be going. It was nice to meet you.'

They continued their stroll, looking back to watch the dog extract himself gently from the attentions of the chicks. He fell into step beside them, trotting along quietly. Lindy turned to Johnno. 'This has been great, but I should be getting back. Dom will be wondering where I've got to.'

'He should have come as well,' said Johnno. 'But I suppose he's occupied with this investigation.'

'That's one word for it,' said Lindy. 'He always gives a case everything he's got, but there's usually a bit less intensity. There's generally just some sense of inevitability, I suppose, that he will get there in the end, so his investigation is not quite so full on. But with this stupid rivalry with Laraby...' She shook her head. 'I don't know, he really seems determined to wrap this one up as quickly as he can. And that means spending every waking hour on it until he does.'

'You think he will?'

Lindy nodded firmly. 'Oh, yes, it's seriously bad news for the killer that he's so committed to this one. He's just so good at what he does. He'll see the things the others miss, put it all together. I wouldn't say I guarantee it, of course, but I would be prepared to say that, if he can't identify the murderer, then I'm not sure anyone else could.'

'It definitely sounds like he will get there eventually.'

'He will.' She nodded sadly. 'But it means I won't be seeing much of him for a while.'

'Perhaps it's time you started your new hiking regimen after all, then,' Johnno suggested.

'Oh, I'm not sure I'm entirely serious about that,' said Lindy dismissively. 'Just a bit of frustration creeping in, I suppose. I mean, me stuck doing what I'm doing and then I see you breaking this big story.'

It was Johnno's turn to be dismissive. 'Ah, I told you, I just got lucky with that one. Your next big story will come to find you eventually. Stay with it, keep chasing. Don't give up.'

'But in the meantime, take up hiking, just in case?' she asked with a sarcastic laugh. 'To cover all those long, lonely times while I'm waiting for Dom to wrap up this case. Oh, the compromises a relationship asks of us.'

'But that's exactly what a relationship is, isn't it?' said Johnno earnestly. 'Compromising, giving up on the things that don't matter to you and finding a way to hold on to those that do? It's inevitable you'll lose some things. But you gain so much more.'

'Do you?' Lindy gave a small, sad smile. 'Yes, I suppose you do.' It felt good to talk about all these things, these feelings she'd been holding inside lately. This was exactly the kind of conversation she wished she could have with Dom. But he was so busy. He didn't have time, for talks, for long walks on hilltops, for anything. She was seized by a sudden moment of guilt. Why had she felt the need to keep it from Dom that she was coming here today? Was it because she had been afraid that he might ask if she was meeting someone? Even if he did, why couldn't she have said? She didn't have even the faintest of ulterior motives, so she would have had nothing to hide. A guilty pleasure, that's all this was, a stolen moment of self-indulgence. Did she have any thoughts of taking it any further? Absolutely none. Then why was she pretending to herself that it might all have been just one great, glorious accident that she happened to meet Johnno on the same hill above the lab at the same time as before, even as she recognised the lie she was burying inside herself? Because that's what deceivers did, that's why.

19

Lelia Segal straightened from her crouch and regarded the figure lying on the hard-packed earth at her feet. 'No broken bones, as far as I can tell,' she said. 'There'll be plenty of soft tissue injuries, though.'

'I can sit up, then?' asked the woman below her.

The ME nodded, dusting off her black, calf-length skirt and brushing a pine needle from her red blouse. 'But I'd get the paramedics to take you off to hospital for an X-ray, just to make sure.'

She looked across at the group of police officers gathered nearby in a clearing carpeted by dusky pine needles. Through a screen of thinly planted trees, they were watching the activities of uniformed officers who were searching the buildings and grounds of the property. Marvin Laraby was standing in the centre of the assembled group, looking across at Talia Rowe with concern.

'I'm so sorry to have troubled everyone with an emergency call,' she told him, 'but for a few moments there, I literally couldn't move.'

'No need to apologise,' he said. 'As far as we can tell, this was an attempt on your life, and we're treating it as such.'

Fairfax looked down again and regarded Talia Rowe frankly. 'I don't usually get to do live ones, but since I was so close when the call came in I thought I'd respond. I know people say this all the time and it sounds ridiculous, but you were lucky.'

Rowe nodded and twisted to stare along the trail behind her, wincing in pain. Were it not for the recently attached flag of police tape, the strand of cheese wire strung across the opening would have been invisible, as it had been when she had ridden this way on horseback a short time earlier.

Laraby stepped aside and summoned Jejeune and the ME to join him a few metres away. 'Thoughts, Inspector?'

Some, his expression said. 'Cheese wire. Crude, but effective.'

'I agree,' said Segal. 'The wire caught her across the top of the chest, but I have to tell you, if that horse she was riding was any smaller this might have been one for me after all. Thankfully her mount is tall, almost seventeen hands, I'd say.'

'Seventeen hands?' Laraby looked impressed. 'An equestrian, Dr Segal?'

'Sagittarius, actually.' She flashed a smile. 'Okay if I get off? I was on my way to a girls' night out.'

Laraby nodded. 'Enjoy yourself. Oh, and, Dr Segal, feel free to drink too much tonight. We dodged one here. Don't be afraid to celebrate it.'

She waved over her shoulder as she left and Laraby turned to Jejeune again. 'Now, I'm going to go out on a limb here, and suggest you might already have somebody in mind for this. You'd better get over and talk to our victim. See if she agrees with you.'

Jejeune crossed to where Talia Rowe was now being helped to her feet by two attendants. She flinched as she straightened into a standing position, but waved away their efforts to help further. Jejeune looked back along the trail behind her. It descended from an open meadow beyond and passed through this small glade of mature pines, pressed tightly to the hard-packed trail on both sides. 'Do you ride around here very often?' he asked.

'Whenever I'm up here,' she said, 'most weekends, anyway.'

'And do you always take this trail?'

'It's the main one back to the barns. The horses hardly need any encouragement from this point. They know the way well enough.'

'Were you galloping, then?'

'Cantering. But it would have been more than enough...' She tailed off as she contemplated the fate she had so narrowly avoided. 'Thank God I was on Dalhousie. He's the biggest horse I have.'

'Of how many?' asked Jejeune, looking around. He could see no signs of the horse. He assumed it had been checked for injuries and led back to the barn.

'Three, but Dalhousie is my favourite. He's a big old brute, and today I love him more than ever for it.'

Jejeune nodded silently. 'Do you have any idea who might have been responsible for this?'

Rowe tried wheeling a shoulder but stopped abruptly as a flash of pain crossed her face. 'I imagine I can guess who you suspect, Inspector.' She shook her head. 'But what possible motive could Marius have for wanting to harm me?'

'Could it be that he suspects it was you who released his name to Sampson Lee?'

'How could I have done that?' Rowe winced again as she lifted her arms to shrug. 'I had no idea he was involved in that scheme. Besides, as his business partner, the revelation would have had the potential to ruin me.'

'Would he have any other motive?'

'None at all. Okay, it's true that, now his name has been released, banks are calling in their loans and shutting off his lines of credit. He can't get access to money anywhere. Personally, I suppose, he is effectively bankrupt.'

'Would that be a reason to harm you?'

'Well, I mean the terms of our partnership stipulate that if one of the partners is unable to fulfil the duties due to death, illness or other incapacity, administration of all company assets reverts to the remaining partner. In other words, if I die, Marius gets control of everything.' She shook her head vehemently again, causing another wince of pain. 'Look, Marius is capable of incredible rage at times and I admit I am truly terrified by his outbursts sometimes. But I can't believe even he would consider doing something like this.'

Only she could, thought Jejeune. And despite the blue-eyed innocence of her stare, she wanted him to believe it, too. Especially after she'd so conveniently laid out all the details for him.

'I wonder, do his financial troubles impact the donations the partnership makes to the fLIGHT programme?' asked Jejeune.

Rowe pulled a face. 'No. They're paid out of a separate trust the company holds. He set it up himself. Or had it set up, I should say.' She hesitated for a moment. 'I was too busy,' she added weakly.

'It's a sizeable amount. Had he ever shown any previous interest in the company?'

'None whatsoever. It came completely out of the blue. I asked him what brought it on and he just shrugged and said it was a worthy cause.'

'Any other worthy environmental causes out there ever catch his eye?'

'I doubt you'd be asking if there was the slightest doubt about that answer, Inspector.'

Danny Maik strolled over to join them. 'The ambulance is ready to leave, Ms Rowe. Last chance to get a ride to the hospital.'

'I'll be fine, thank you, Sergeant. Just a few aches and pains. If anything changes, I'll make my own way to hospital. Thank them for their care, would you? They've been so kind.'

Jejeune saw a warmth in her smile towards Maik that he had not been treated to himself in the entire time he'd been speaking to the woman. There had been a guardedness to her that he had seemed unable to breach. 'I'll go, Sergeant,' he said. 'You can take this from here. We were just discussing Marius Huebner.'

Maik looked around the clearing and the surrounding land. 'Has he ever been here?'

'It's my retreat,' Rowe said emphatically. 'As far as I knew, he wasn't even aware of it.'

'Why the secrecy?'

'Privacy. I can work on things here without any disturbance. As you know, Marius doesn't involve himself in electronic communications at all, but that doesn't mean he doesn't like to see paper reports. I prepare spreadsheets here and take them into the office. He scrutinises them carefully, and if he ever comes across anything that doesn't makes sense, he asks me.'

'As somebody involved in the financial side of things, you have a maths background, I assume?'

'I have a background in finance. Most people assume it's the same thing but, as any financier or bank manager will tell you, it most assuredly is not.'

Maik nodded. 'Do you use predictive algorithms in your line of work?'

'Almost certainly, I should think. I would imagine every piece of financial planning software I use has them built in. But I don't develop any myself, if that's what you're asking. Why?'

'Somebody seems keen to focus our inquiries in that direction, that all.'

'Then it would appear that I'm not your girl, Sergeant. Sorry to disappoint.'

'According to my colleagues, Marius Huebner says you can give him an alibi for the time of Sampson Lee's death. That would be the evening of the sixteenth.'

'I'm not sure I can.' She flinched slightly as she tried her shoulder's range of motion again. 'I'm all but certain I left the office early that day. As far as I know, Marius would have been alone there after about four thirty. I didn't see or hear from him again at all until the next morning.'

Maik nodded with satisfaction. 'Okay, I think that'll be all we need for now.'

'Sergeant,' said Rowe. 'If this really was an attempt on my life, do you think it's possible the person could try again? Only, I feel a bit vulnerable out here by myself.'

'We could find you a hotel,' suggested Maik, 'if it would make you feel safer.'

'Actually, I'd prefer to stay here, but perhaps... a police officer outside? Just for a couple of days? So I can work from the safety of my own home.'

'I think you might want to just lie low for a few days and get some rest, instead of worrying about work,' advised Maik.

Rowe shook her head. 'That's impossible. If I am going to demonstrate to our clients that it's business as usual at HR despite Marius's legal problems, I need to act quickly, before gossip and suspicion harden into mistrust. I need to show them that the business operations of the partnership and the private conduct of one of the partners are not one and the same thing.'

'So you intend to just carry on as if nothing has happened here?' asked Maik incredulously.

'I admit I am a bit shaken, but I'm sure I'd recover faster here than some hotel room. And there's no reason I can't do some work here while I do. I already have everything I need with me. I know a police presence may seem like a silly request, but it wouldn't be for long.' She gave him another warm smile. 'Just until I feel a bit less unnerved by everything.'

In and of itself, thought Maik, it wasn't a silly request at all. In fact, it was perfectly normal under the circumstances. But it was perhaps unusual that it was being made by a person who was as calm and rational in the face of a violent attack as anybody he had ever seen.

20

'Morning, Inspector,' said Laraby brightly as Jejeune entered the incident room at King's Landing. 'I forgot to ask you yesterday, how was your course? Learn lots, did you? What was it, brushing up on your maths?'

'DNA. Specifically airborne DNA particles. It's called environmental DNA, eDNA for short.'

Laraby nodded tersely. 'Yes, thank you, Inspector. You're not the only one who's up on the latest developments. Right. So, what do we make of the attempt on Talia Rowe's life? Do we like Huebner for it?'

Holland shrugged. 'Let's just say, if she crossed him in some way, it'd be no surprise if he tried to offer her a trip to the glue factory.'

'Tony!' said Salter in disgust.

'What, I'm just saying…'

Yes, you are, she thought. But you wouldn't just be saying it if Danny was still your sergeant. Maik's expectation that everyone extended the victims of a crime the same kind of reverence he did was one of the first things a junior officer learned. Often at intimidatingly close quarters. It was a lesson some of the newer recruits here at King's Landing would be receiving now. She wondered how they were adjusting to each other, Danny and his new colleagues. He said everything was going smoothly over here, but she would not have expected him to burden her with the truth if things were otherwise. The few officers she knew personally at this station were decent enough people – diligent, honest, professional – but if they balked at the way Laraby wanted something done, Danny would be the one they would be looking at to smooth things over. How long would it be before Danny became both bridge and barrier between them and Laraby, as he had so often between Jejeune and Shepherd?

At the front of the room, Laraby was shaking his head slowly. 'Some people just can't seem to stay off our radar, can they? Here we are just about ready to dismiss Huebner for Lee's death and up he crops again, front and centre, as the prime suspect in an attempt on his partner's life.'

'I'm not sure about that,' said Jejeune cautiously.

Laraby might have been trying to suppress his sigh, but he made sure enough of it was audible to make his point. 'I'm sure we'd all like to think we're being treated to everything you know, Inspector,' he said.

Jejeune inclined his head in a gesture Maik recognised. Everything he knew? Unlikely. And everything he thought or suspected, even less so. It was always going to be easier, given the nature of his relationship with Laraby, for Jejeune to hold on to his theories until they had been confirmed or otherwise, rather than release some half-formed thought only to have to walk it back later, with Laraby all the while suspecting him of either duplicity or incompetence. It saddened Maik that progress here in the station was being hampered by such considerations, but they were the uncomfortable reality in this case.

'Something about the assault feels off,' said Jejeune. 'As far as motive goes, with Huebner's own personal assets frozen, maybe trying to take over the partnership is plausible, but the method doesn't make sense.' He turned to Holland. 'How many times has Huebner cropped up on the radar of Serious Crimes?'

'At least half a dozen.'

'And how many charges has he faced to date?'

'That would be a nice round number. Zero.'

'Does that sound like someone prone to clumsy, offhand attempts like this? Huebner is careful, calculating. Plus the whole scene felt...'

'Staged?' asked Laraby sarcastically. 'Understandable, I suppose, you miss obvious signs that somebody has planted evidence at Lee's cottage and suddenly you start to see false leads everywhere.'

'I do get the impression Huebner is the kind of bloke who would want you to know he was coming, though,' said Holland. 'He'd feed off your fear.'

'He strikes me as the type who'd enjoy taunting us, as well, if he did it,' said Salter, 'but there's been nothing from him at all.'

'We checked on social media?' asked Maik.

'True to his word, he has no online presence at all. Talk about the ghost in the machine. To run a business empire and still manage that is no easy trick to pull off. There's not even any evidence that he has an email account of his own.'

'Or a smartphone, as he reminded us,' said Holland.

'But if not Huebner, then who?' said Laraby, becoming visibly frustrated. He drew a steadying breath. 'Okay, let's park it for now. I'm willing to take the DCI's views on board, but we will continue to treat this as a legitimate attempt on Talia Rowe's life until we know otherwise. We'll put all the proper protections in place as requested. And let's get somebody good on it. We want to reassure her we're taking this seriously.'

'PC Goodwin comes to mind,' said Maik. 'She's about as steady as they come.'

Laraby nodded. 'Good choice. Shelley Goodwin is exactly the kind of reassuring presence Rowe will want out there. Set it up, Danny, and then let's get you out to have a word with Huebner, just in case.'

'I was the one who spoke to him previously,' Jejeune reminded him.

Laraby nodded. 'I doubt your softly-softly approach put the fear of God into him, though.' He turned to Maik. 'You need to let him know where we stand on people putting themselves about in our bailiwick, Danny. You can tell him, when I find out who it was that assaulted that woman, I shall be looking to put my size twelve on his Adam's apple and press down hard.' He gave a cold smile. 'Metaphorically speaking, of course.'

'If you'd like, I can be the Saltmarsh officer present,' offered Salter.

Laraby held up a hand without looking at Maik. 'Appreciated, but Danny will handle that on his own. So,' he declared, drawing a line under the discussion, if that was what it had been, 'where are we on the Lee murder? Just for the novelty of it, I'm wondering if we might actually get somebody in here and ask them some questions.' He looked around the room. 'I don't know how things are done out there in Saltmarsh these days, but here in King's Landing we do occasionally like to get a suspect in, if only to see what they look like.' He glanced towards Holland. 'Katie Fairfax was on our radar, as I recall. Any more on that?'

Holland shook his head. 'No joy in matching that tyre cast to her truck yet. I keep going back up there but, every time I do, she's out collecting her air filters.'

'That's convenient, isn't it? I want you to stay on her, Tony. I don't care if you have to track her down at one of her monitoring stations. I want that tyre cast matched as soon as you can.' He turned to Jejeune. 'So I'm hearing there's some real promise being offered by these airborne DNA samples, Inspector.'

'Air filters do collect DNA samples, but you can only use them for identification as far as species level. You could never use eDNA collected this way to identify an individual human being, for example.'

Laraby digested the information for a moment. 'That's not what I'm hearing. There have been a number of advances lately.'

Salter and Holland exchanged a quick glance. Together, they watched Jejeune's reaction. It was clear that, wherever Laraby was getting this information, it wasn't from anything the DCI had read in his research. 'The science is pretty clear,' said Jejeune carefully. 'A professor named Libby Leclair in Toronto is the leading authority on this, and, according to her, there really doesn't seem to be any grey area. Identifying an individual from eDNA can't be done.'

'Well, we'll have to agree to differ on that for now,' said Laraby blithely.

The officers sat in stunned silence. Unless he had something he wasn't sharing with them, Laraby's conviction seemed to be completely unsupported by any facts. In turn, Salter, Holland and Maik all looked towards Jejeune. But he was staring resolutely ahead, resisting all attempts at eye contact.

Laraby seemed to sense the silent resistance in the room. 'Okay, let's broaden the scope. Is there anybody else out there who's set our antennae quivering? This boy, Chandra, for example. These predictive algorithms Lee stole from him. There's a lucrative market out there for that kind of software if you can find the right buyer. Plenty of motive there, I'd have thought.'

'I have my doubts Lee took that work, sir,' said Salter. 'I had a look at this blue carbon project he was working on, and predictive algorithms seem to have no application in that kind of research at all.'

Jejeune looked up in surprise. 'Are you sure about that, Sergeant?'

Salter nodded. 'Yes, sir. It's basically just assessment and evaluation of data. It involves complex calculations, but there's no application for predictive algorithms anywhere that I could see.'

Jejeune shook his head sharply. 'That can't be right. There must be something. We should have some third-party experts look at the research. Ask them point-blank whether a predictive algorithm would apply.'

Salter shrugged. 'Up to you, sir, but I'm pretty sure they will tell you the same thing I am. You don't have to be a mathematician. All you need to do is look at the program parameters. It's common sense.'

'I'm sure it is,' said Jejeune, finally reining in his agitation in favour of courtesy, 'but let's check with them anyway.'

Laraby had been following the exchange with interest. 'It's sounds like whatever theory you had in mind might be a bit of a non-starter, Inspector. That's okay, happens to the best of us. As I said, I encourage all of you to come up with lines of inquiry. Just make sure everybody's in on them. Of course, if this one's not going to pan out, we can just move on.' He flashed an enigmatic expression in Salter's direction. Perhaps it was redolent of their earlier connection, thought the watching Danny Maik, perhaps it was merely satisfaction at seeing Jejeune put firmly in his place. Either way, it was a long way from disapproval.

'Chandra does seem very anxious to give the girl an alibi, you know,' said Salter.

'Do we like her in any of this?'

'This fLIGHT project of hers,' said Maik. 'For somebody with no previous interest in bird studies at all, it seems a strange investment for Huebner to make. And with his current money troubles, I'm surprised he hasn't withdrawn the funds that have been set aside for it.'

'As far as I understand, it's an indentured trust,' said Laraby. 'That means highly protected funds and terms that it's all but impossible to challenge. That money couldn't be further out of Huebner's personal grasp if it was on the moon. Still, perhaps it's worth a chat about the programme with Habloun. Sergeant Salter, I'll leave that in your capable hands. Danny, you can bring it up with Huebner as well when you're there.' He turned to the room one final time. 'For the rest of you, remember, our primary line of inquiry is still the Euclid Lab. I'm convinced the answers are up there, so let's find them.'

'Predictive algorithms? Laraby?' Salter shook her head. She and Maik were in the same alcove outside the incident room as before, but Salter wasn't keeping her voice down this time. 'What's going on here, Danny? Until a few days ago I would have bet Laraby thought an algorithm was a new kind of music. And where did this sudden expertise in indentured trusts come from? Let alone eDNA.'

Maik nodded. 'I wonder if it might not just be easier for him to invite Five in to do a guest speaker spot instead of having to relay all this information himself.'

'You think he's being fed all this stuff by them? Why? Have you talked to the DCI about this?'

'No need,' said Danny. 'I think he was there a long time ago.'

'So what are you going to do?'

'I know how these people work. They don't operate out of a sense of altruism. If Laraby is being given information, it's only to take the investigation where they want it to go. I need to find out who at the service has most to gain by controlling the direction of this inquiry.'

'How do you propose to do that? I'm fairly sure information like that is going to be protected.'

He shrugged. 'I have a few back-channels I can try.'

'I don't know, Danny,' Salter said warily. 'This feels dangerous, drawing attention to yourself like this. Wouldn't it be better to let the DCI handle this? He might have more currency with the government agencies, given his past heroics.'

Maik shook his head. 'Political affiliations have shifted a lot since then. Most of his promoters and protectors are long gone. And not all of his recent convictions have gone down well with people in high places. They won't trust him any more. I'll just put out a few feelers, see where they lead.'

'Well just be careful. The last thing you want to do is get on the wrong side of these people. They'd be bad enemies to make.'

It was good advice, thought Maik as he watched Salter make her way along the corridor. But he had a feeling that, as far as the department was concerned, it might already be too late for that.

21

Jejeune sensed a watcher as he closed the door of the Range Rover and began to make his way across the church car park. But it was not among the couples or small groups slowly making their way towards the open door at the side of the church. Nor in the small, neatly kept cemetery, separated from the car park by a low wrought-iron fence. The surveillance was coming from above. He looked up into the branches of an ancient oak tree. On one bough that stretched out over the tarmac he saw the silent, still form of a Tawny Owl. He had no doubt that the bird was now aware of his gaze but it remained motionless, aloof almost, as if convinced its position up here rendered it safe from any harm this human could bring.

Jejeune stood for a moment, staring at the bird. Owls were perhaps Lindy's all-time favourite members of the avian world. He smiled as he recalled the time he'd told her the collective noun for owls was a parliament. She'd commented that she had only ever seen owls sitting around looking half asleep and doing absolutely nothing. 'So perhaps you birders do sometimes get it right, then,' she had said mischievously.

But that was back in those carefree days when she wasn't questioning the world and her place in it. Lately, things had changed. For example, what would this watching owl, in all its mythical wisdom, make of Lindy's sudden announcement just before he'd left tonight that she had bumped into Johnno up on the hilltop the previous day? 'He was out walking Truth,' she had told him breezily. 'He said to say hi. Johnno, that is. The dog never mentioned you. He was too busy fussing around those chicks again. Honestly, you should have seen them together, pressing in all around as he nosed them one by one. It was adorable. I even took some video.' But she hadn't shown it to him. She'd become distracted and moved on to another topic, as the Lindy of those carefree days of her recent past was wont to do.

He left the owl to its vigil and joined the crowd filing in down a set of narrow stairs to the brick-lined crypt. He settled onto a folding metal chair and watched as two women, Kim and another willowy woman of a similar age, mounted a small stage.

The song they struck up filled the room with its ethereal sound. Kim manipulated a theremin, cradling her hands around the twin antennae, coaxing volume with one and beguiling tones from the other. Overlaid with lilting flute notes from her partner, it created a musical experience unlike anything Jejeune had ever heard. He sat absorbed, as did the rest of the audience, allowing the composition to swirl around them and fill the small, low-ceilinged room with its haunting, mystical beauty. It seemed to transport them to another place, where light and emotions and ephemeral winds danced in the air.

Jejeune watched Kim closely, observing how she induced the sounds from the theremin without touching the instrument, inviting them to contribute their beauty, their joy, as if by mere force of will. The duo moved through a number of pieces, some recognisable as show tunes or old standards, others, he was sure, original compositions, perhaps even written for this evening. At the end of the recital, after the applause had died down, the crowd stood and began to disperse. Low murmurs of approval mingled with the clattering and scraping of the metal chairs being folded and stacked against the back wall of the crypt. Jejeune sat patiently until Kim beckoned him towards the low stage.

'I can only assume that was your first theremin recital,' she said with a smile. 'What did you think?'

'It was astonishing,' said Jejeune sincerely. 'In a good way.' He was not given to fulsome praise but could make his approval clear when something warranted it. 'It was such an inspired pairing of instruments, with the flute.'

'*Capturing at turns the poignancy of loss and the joy of discovery*, as one of our critics said.' Kim nodded. 'It was something the flautist, Nadia, and I had been discussing for a while, blending the sounds of possibly the world's oldest instrument with the newest. If you'll excuse me, I just have to say goodbye to Nadia, but I do hope you'll stay. I believe we need to catch up.'

He nodded and watched as she moved off to talk to the flautist. He noted the interaction between them, the casual hand on the woman's forearm, the smile, the slight tilt of the head to acknowledge a point, but all the while alert for developments elsewhere in the room. Kim returned carrying a chrome case, which she set down on the ground and opened up. It was lined with blue velvet memory foam that had been pressed into various shapes. She turned to begin packing away the theremin, carefully disconnecting the two antennae from the oscillator box and pressing them into their moulded foam slots in the lid. Then she carefully laid the central unit into the space between.

Jejeune cast a glance around the room as she worked. Most of the crowd had dispersed by now, but one small knot of concertgoers was still huddled in a corner, engrossed in conversation. When she had finished packing the instrument away and closed the case, Kim straightened and let her eyes rest on the group for a moment until they finally moved off. She looked at him now the two of them were free to speak of other matters, but still Jejeune hesitated. Kim stood by patiently, like someone who had spent a lifetime waiting for informants to wrestle with their demons before deciding to bare their souls.

'The theory I had, about the algorithm for blue carbon.' Jejeune shook his head. 'I'm afraid it doesn't hold up. It seems predictive algorithms such as the one Chandra accused Lee of stealing have no function in the blue carbon research he was doing.'

Kim was silent for a moment as she digested the information. 'And do we believe them, the people who told you this?' There are those at the lab who have their own involvements with Lee, do they not? The girl, Ishtara, for example. A woman scorned, I think...' Her look towards Jejeune was not that of someone seeking to confirm information but of someone who was already absolutely sure of it.

'I think it's generally felt she'd lack the physical strength to strangle Lee in such a brutal way.'

Kim shook her head slowly. 'Once the ligature is in place and begins cutting into the neck, it's all but impossible for a victim to remove it. After that, it's simply a matter of resolve. Does the assailant have the commitment, the will, to keep pulling and see it through?'

In the echoing emptiness of the now deserted crypt, Jejeune reflected for a moment on a life that so frequently brought him to discussions of disturbing topics like this in such genteel settings. 'I don't know,' he said. 'I simply can't see the motives for either Chandra or Habloun killing someone by strangulation from behind. Theft of your intellectual property, or a romantic betrayal, these are deeply personal things. Anybody seeking to avenge them would surely want to look their victim in the eyes, to let them know who was doing this to them, what they were being punished for.'

Kim looked at him for a moment and smiled softly. 'We should go,' she said.

Outside, a warm starless night had settled over the car park. Jejeune looked up, but the Tawny Owl had abandoned its roost and only the bare oak limb now hung above them. As far as he could tell, he and Kim were the only two living creatures left, standing here in darkness on the edge of the cemetery.

Kim paused for a moment, listening. 'You didn't feel moved to mention this meeting to anybody, did you?'

He shook his head. 'I didn't tell anyone.'

'Not even Lindy? What would she make of your secret liaisons with an older woman, I wonder?'

Jejeune smiled. 'In the nicest possible way, I doubt she has the subtlety for clandestine observation. She's more likely to march up to you and ask you point-blank what's going on. She doesn't really have a lot of time for secrecy.'

'Are you sure, Domenic? We all keep secrets, even from those we love. Perhaps especially from them, to try to protect them.'

Jejeune looked at her for a long moment. Was it possible that that she was already aware of Lindy's meeting with Johnno? 'Not Lindy,' he said. 'Even when she's unhappy, she's willing to talk about things. Eventually.'

Kim shook her head slowly. 'This encounter with the podcaster must have upset her, I imagine,' she said. 'Becoming reacquainted with someone from our earlier days can be unsettling; seeing where we are now, how far we have drifted on life's tides from the dreams we once held.'

Jejeune nodded thoughtfully. 'I've told her the work she does is important. Journalism is vital.'

'But not print journalism, perhaps. It's an electronic world now. Digital media has taken over. When was the last time you saw someone under thirty reading a magazine? When was the last time you read one?'

In truth, Jejeune couldn't remember the last time he had read anything for pleasure. He truly could not. And that, he realised, might too be a symptom of whatever Lindy was feeling these days; the all-encompassing nature of his work, of this case.

Kim looked around, scrutinising the dark corners of the car park. She noticed Jejeune watching her.

'Forgive me. The price of liberty is eternal paranoia.'

'Le Carré again?'

'Probably, or Len Deighton. There were others of course, but those were the two who came closest to getting it right. They understood, you see, in that era, before this digital onslaught of satellite tracking and monitoring devices, that spying was about the human elements: trust, fear, insecurity. In one sense I suppose that has never changed.' She nodded resolutely. 'It would have been Deighton. His spies were people first, human beings with human motivations and human weaknesses.'

She paused for a moment, as if deciding whether to share her thought. 'You do need to consider the possibility that not everything at the Euclid Lab is as it seems. If not for calculating blue carbon values, is there perhaps another reason Lee could have wanted that algorithm?'

'Because he was working on something else, you mean?' Jejeune shook his head in rejection. 'The way the resources are allocated, it would have been immediately apparent to the others if computation time was being used by Lee for something beyond the scope of his project.'

Kim sighed. 'Then as far as our interest in the investigation goes, it seems we are at an impasse. And with it comes the end of our association, sadly. You have a killer to catch, and, once you find the person, you will presumably have a motive. In the meantime, GCHQ will be conducting an internal inquiry to discover who showed the document to Lee. I have enjoyed our time together, Inspector. You really do have an agile mind. If you'd ever be interested in a position with the service, I'd be happy to recommend you.'

He smiled his regrets. 'I don't think I'd enjoy the compromises I'd have to make.'

'I fear you will need to make them anyway, Inspector. Before this case is over, I'm afraid it will demand them of you. However, I wish you success.'

She hefted the chrome case and began walking across the car park, taking a set of car keys from her pocket as she did so. Jejeune didn't know where she had parked, but his Range Rover was the only car in the lot. She stopped for a moment and turned to him. 'If anything extraordinary does come up in your inquiries,' she called, 'you know how to reach me.'

He nodded. At the coffee shop. Through Maria.

22

Marius Huebner was standing at a tall upright filing cabinet when Danny Maik entered his office. The top drawer was open and various papers and files were strewn haphazardly around on the floor. It looked like somebody had been searching for something. And they had been in a hurry.

'What's this then?' asked Huebner, turning at Maik's appearance. 'Somebody else coming in to lay down the law? Hope you've got more about you than that last pair.' He shook his head. 'Killing somebody to silence them, after they've already let the cat out of the bag? I ask you, have you ever heard of anything so ridiculous?'

'What's going on here?' asked Maik, ignoring the question. 'Have you had a break-in?'

'Of a kind, I suppose. I think something's gone missing.'

'Do you want to file a police report?'

Huebner met the sardonic comment with a hard stare. 'No thanks. I'm used to handling these kinds of things on my own. I find the personal approach goes a long way.'

'I can see why HR does so well, with you handling its negotiations,' said Maik drily.

'There's no need for the heavy stuff if you know how to read people properly.' Huebner tapped his temple with a thick, gnarled finger. 'Up here, that's how you best people. Get inside their head and start putting yourself about a bit.'

'In that regard,' said Maik easily, 'I'd like to talk to you about an attack on Talia Rowe yesterday.'

'Oh yes?' Huebner slammed the file drawer shut, ready now to give his full attention to the other man. 'What happened to her, then?'

'Somebody strung a strand of cheese wire across a trail when she was out riding on her property.' Maik paused, in case Huebner might want to ask about the outcome. He didn't. 'Fortunately she wasn't badly hurt, but a few inches higher and it could have been nasty. Fatal, most likely.'

There was a long beat of silence as Huebner took in the information. It didn't escape Maik's notice that he hadn't asked where Talia Rowe's property was, or even express any surprise that she had one. 'Were you up in the woods by her place yesterday?' he asked.

Huebner shook his head. 'Not much of a fan of the outdoors.'

'Wrong answer,' said Maik.

'What?'

'That's the answer to the question, "are you much of a fan of the outdoors?" This process will go a lot faster if you answer the questions I ask instead of making up ones of your own.'

Huebner nodded a grudging approval. 'They really have sent their brightest and their best this time, I see.' He gave another thoughtful pause. 'Now the thing is, Sergeant, I could do as you suggest and answer all your questions, but let's face it, I'm the only bugger who knows whether those answers are going to be true or not, aren't I? So how about this as a plan instead. You poke about up there, ask around, see if anybody saw anything, have a good old search of the property, and, if you come up with one single shred of evidence that I was anywhere in the vicinity, you come and see me and we'll chat some more. How does that sound?' He opted for a more genial tone. 'This is that DCI, isn't it, the Canadian bloke? He's had me in his sights ever since that boy's death. Like a dog with a bone, that one, they say, when he latches on to you. Well you can tell him from me, I never laid a hand on Sampson Lee. Besides, I have an alibi for that time. I was here. With Talia.'

'She says otherwise. She says she went home early that afternoon. She said you were still here, all alone, when she left.'

Huebner nodded with what might have been understanding, light shining off the pink dome of his pate. 'So that's what she's saying, is it?' he said finally.

'So,' Maik said, 'you can see how not wanting to help me out in the attack on her is hardly doing your case any good. You know, we don't have a lot going for us when we're running a police investigation these days. We can't put ourselves about a bit, get up close and personal with people. We have to rely on them telling us the truth if we're ever going to get anywhere with a case. And getting a verifiable alibi is one of those things we place a lot of stock in when evaluating a suspect's guilt.'

'Then verify it. Ask her again. Tell her I said I'm sure she'll want to recall how she was here all evening. With me. Perhaps she just got her dates wrong. Maybe she's not as good with numbers as she claims.' The man looked past the sergeant into the corridor, where he seemed to notice a small aquarium on a stand for the first time. 'Here's another bunch faffing around in the dark,' he said. He moved past Maik, approached the tank and reached below to switch on a light. A swarm of small, brightly coloured fish swam to the surface immediately.

'What are those, guppies?' asked Maik.

Huebner nodded. 'What were you expecting, piranhas?' He searched around the tank and found a small tube of fish flakes on the shelf below the aquarium, and sprinkled them liberally into the water. The fish began feeding frenetically right away. 'Look at 'em, poor little things. Probably not had anything to eat for days. Talia normally looks after them, see.' He looked along to the far end of the hallway, where an office sat in darkness with its door closed. If this was Huebner's way of pointing out that Talia Rowe had been absent for a while, he'd apparently picked up a nice line in subtlety since his earlier interview with Jejeune and Holland.

Huebner spent a moment watching the guppies as they darted about the tank. A thought seemed to come to him suddenly. 'She's told you she's afraid of me, am I right? Talia.'

'Does she have any reason to be?'

Huebner shrugged. 'Throwing me under the bus like that about my alibi, a way to make enemies, that is.' The coldness of his delivery was a stark reminder of the latent power the large man possessed.

'The police department won't stand for threats against a potential witness in a case, whether it's intended as intimidation or something more permanent,' said Maik matter-of-factly. He raised his eyebrows slightly to await Huebner's response. If the other man intended to escalate the hostility, this would be where it would happen. But he seemed disinterested in continuing the conversation.

'Okay, so now you've told me about the attack on her. Is that it, Sergeant?'

'Not quite,' said Maik genially. 'Can I ask you why you were so interested in making contributions to Ishtara Habloun's fLIGHT programme?'

'They do good work. I have an interest in helping out all of God's creatures. Birds' – he indicated the aquarium – 'little fishes.' He looked at Maik. 'I'll bet she's even floated the idea of a restraining order against me, hasn't she?'

Danny wasn't sure whether he'd been completely successful in disguising his surprise. Police protection would be a handy substitute for an order without necessarily raising any flags. 'Is there any reason why she'd feel she needs one?'

Huebner shook his head contemptuously. 'None at all. But it would suit her needs to have one. At least for the time being.'

Maik tilted his head questioningly. 'Would you care to elaborate?'

'Not at the moment, no. But I will tell you this for nowt. There's more to that woman than meets the eye. There will come a time when I'll be happy enough to talk to you about Talia Rowe, Sergeant. And when that day comes, you'll want to hear what I have to say, count on it.'

'I'm around, if you need to reach me,' said Maik.

Huebner nodded slowly. 'You seem like a decent enough bloke, quick on your feet, good at your job. But you won't get to the bottom of this, not with all those operating procedures you're on about that police officers have to observe these days. What this case needs is somebody who can get in and poke about a bit without having to worry about probable cause or the rights of some delicate little wallflower who's going to wilt if they're asked a few questions without a lawyer being present.'

'I am officially advising you not to consider going that route yourself, Mr Huebner.' Maik waited a moment to make sure the comment had landed. 'I'll see myself out.' He took one last long look at Huebner's office. 'As long as you're sure you don't want to report that missing property.'

'Thanks all the same,' said Huebner, turning back to the filing cabinet. 'But that won't be necessary. I think I've just realised where it is.'

23

Lauren Salter was uncharacteristically quiet on the drive out to the Euclid Lab. So much so that Tony Holland, sitting beside her in the driver's seat of the Audi, even had to supply his own put-down.

'I'm not imagining it, am I? There was some kind of magnetism between me and Ishtara the last time we were out here?' He looked over at her. 'What, not even a snide comment about opposites attracting? It's not like you to miss a soft lob like that, Sarge. Everything all right?'

'Yeah. It's going to help today if we can just keep our mind on the job for once.'

Holland couldn't shake the feeling that Salter wished he hadn't volunteered to make the trip out here with her. He supposed he could understand her tetchy mood. Every time she offered to follow something up in this case, either Laraby or Jejeune seemed to want her somewhere else. But it was not his fault she was being sidelined like this, and, after he had been frustrated once more in his attempts to track down Katie Fairfax to check the tyre cast, the chance to see Ishtara Habloun again seemed worth a few moments of moodiness from his sergeant. Still, their exchange settled into a sullen silence that neither of them broke until they were through the lab's security check and had mounted the stairs to the second floor.

Amit Chandra and Ishtara Habloun were standing side by side at the top the stairs waiting for them, their shoulders all but touching. They looked like they might be preparing to offer a joint defence against something.

'Detectives. The lure of mathematics just too strong to keep you away? What is it today, a discussion on the Zermelo-Fraenkel set theory?' To Salter, Ishtara's smile looked strained, but Holland was prepared to meet it at face value anyway.

'You were right,' he said. 'The West does have a lot to thank Babylon for. I looked it up. Your lot even invented zero, didn't you? Back in 3 BCE.'

'We tend to think mathematicians discover concepts rather than inventing anything,' Chandra told him shortly. 'Zero was always around. The Mayans got there independently a hundred years later.'

'Really?' said Holland, still firmly focused on the woman. 'What are the odds of that?'

'Not as high as you might think,' said Ishtara. 'As Amit says, maths concepts already exist, we just have to reason them out of their hiding places. Okay, they may take some refining, but really we just have to reach into the intellectual cosmos and extract the pieces we need. There's every possibility that people working on opposite sides of the world could come up with the concept of zero at the same time. The workings of a mathematician's mind are a strange and wonderful thing, Constable Holland.'

'I imagine the constable finds the workings of any mind strange and wonderful,' said Chandra drily. 'Can we help you with something? We're in the middle of recalibrating the system software. It's a long and tedious process and we'd like to get back to it, if it's all the same to you.'

'Can't AI do it for you?'

Holland had intended the remark to be sarcastic, but Chandra took it seriously. 'It does perform some of the functions, but each adjustment requires manual input from the operators, so no, it can't do it all on its own. We have to be here.'

'How about that,' said Holland. 'Man and machine working together in perfect harmony.' He turned to Salter. 'Whatever next, humans getting along?'

She ignored the remark. 'I'm wondering if you can tell us anything about the blue carbon studies Sampson Lee was involved in, Ms Habloun.'

Ishtara looked across at her associate uncertainly, 'I'm sure Amit could help you there.'

'We'd like your take,' said Salter shortly.

'Okay. Sampson's work involved documenting the resources that awaited the migrating birds arriving at certain sites. We're talking about the species mix of the local ecosystems, the nesting habitat, the terrain. It would allow landowners to redesign disruptive construction projects or farm operations, or delay them until the breeding season had passed. They might also be able to manipulate water levels to accommodate waders.'

'You know a lot about that project, don't you, for a place that operates in such a silo mentality. How is that? Pillow talk?'

'Now just a minute,' said Chandra, stepping forward, 'that's uncalled for.'

Ishtara held up a hand. 'It's fine, Amit. No, Sergeant, not pillow talk, just a professional interest.'

'Would you know enough about the work to pass information on to somebody else, I wonder? This fLIGHT project you're running. It's an expensive undertaking. That monthly contribution from Marius Huebner is a godsend, I would imagine. Only he doesn't seem like the type to do something for nothing. Much more of a quid pro quo businessman, by all accounts. Quo, in this case, being information on Sampson Lee's blue carbon project, the specific sites he was working on. Is that what Huebner was buying with his monthly payments to fLIGHT?'

Holland's face darkened. He realised why Salter had kept her intended approach away from him. She hadn't wanted him, through some serious, guarded opening, to tip the woman off that a bombshell like this was coming. In fact, she had used his breezy chit-chat to set Ishtara up. Salter wanted the element of surprise to rock her back on her heels like this. But understanding his partner's motives for blindsiding him didn't make Holland appreciate them any better.

Chandra rushed in to defend Ishtara again. 'You're saying Lee found out about the arrangement and threatened to expose it, and either Huebner or Ishtara, or perhaps both, killed him to silence him? That's insane. Ishtara would never, ever be involved in anything like that.'

'I've never met Marius Huebner, or even been in contact with anyone from HR Holdings,' said Ishtara. 'The donation came as just as much of a shock to me as anyone. I wasn't going to turn it down, obviously' she added, 'but I would never hurt Sampson. I loved him.'

'Even after he so unceremoniously dumped you for Katie Fairfax?' asked Salter coldly. 'That must have hurt. After all, you had been seeing each other for months.'

Ishtara nodded. 'At first, yes, of course I was devastated. I never saw it coming. I never even picked up on any connection between them at all.'

'I imagine it created quite a bit of friction around here.'

'Things were awkward for a while, but it didn't last long. I mean, we're all adults. I even think with a little more time Sampson and I could still have worked things out and remained friends.' She lowered her head. 'But now we'll never have that chance.'

She began to weep into her hands. Amit reached out to comfort her, but she turned away from him and disappeared along the corridor.

'You shouldn't have done that,' he told the detectives angrily. 'Bringing up that business with Lee again. I told you she had nothing to do with his death.'

Salter ignored the comment. 'What do you know about the role of predictive analytics in her fLIGHT project?'

'Enough to know they are central to it. The acoustic data is fed into a machine learning algorithm known as a convolutional neural network. The data is then processed using statistical operations tuned to detect and respond to certain patterns. The algorithm calculates which class of sound has been activated most strongly and predicts the most likely species.'

'And in your own work?' pressed Salter. If Laraby was interested in the role these equations might be playing in all this, trying to establish a connection between them and a viable motive seemed like a good place to start.

'Migration is dynamic, and the birds fly through climates and landscapes that are constantly in flux. We need to know all we can about where and when they are migrating.'

'But don't tracking tags on birds already give you that information?' asked Salter.

'Seventeen million birds migrate across the UK each year. Tracking only gives us a snapshot of a small number of those. And that data tells us where birds have been, but not necessarily where they're going. Our ability to protect migratory birds is only as good as the science that tells us their routes and destinations. For that, we need precise imagery of the landscapes and oceans they are going to traverse. But the satellite images we get are fragmentary. The space station doesn't follow a linear orbit around the Earth, its path undulates, more like a sine wave. It takes forty orbits to get the same image of the same landscape from the same angle. Piecing those fragmented images together into a single coherent picture is where the use of predictive algorithms comes in.'

'So this predictive algorithm,' said Holland, desperately trying to keep up, 'it's intended to work on future waves of migrant birds, then?'

Chandra did nothing to hide his contempt. 'Of course it's for the future. Do you know anybody who makes predictions about the past?'

The comment would not have sat well with Holland on his best day. But, already angered by Salter's ambush on Ishtara and, by extension, on himself, too, his tolerance had reached its limit. 'Speaking of the past,' he said in a restrained tone that Salter recognised as a sign of trouble brewing, 'I've been looking at reports of earlier incidents here at the lab, and you know what isn't in there? Any mention of those thefts of your intellectual property. I mean your colleague Ishtara said you suspected Lee of stealing system architecture she had designed as well. Two counts of intellectual property theft. It would be a serious charge, if it was ever brought. But the university has no record of you lodging any report about this, let alone making a formal complaint.'

'Yeah, I just decided, why bother. It all came to nothing anyway. Like I said before, best to just let it go.'

'I wonder if the reason you didn't report the thefts is because, if anybody looked into them, it would become quite clear that Sampson Lee never stole anything. Not predictive algorithms from you, nor system architecture from Ishtara. I'm beginning to wonder if anything you've told us from the beginning of this case is true, Mr Chandra. And that includes you having an alibi for the night of Sampson Lee's murder. Frankly I've had it up to here with your lies. Unless you want me to up your status to prime suspect right now, along with all the indignities and inconveniences that go with it, this might be a very good time to start telling us the truth.'

Chandra took a step back from the latent hostility in Holland's delivery. He looked across at Salter, but it was clear she had no intention of reining her constable in. He lowered his head. 'Okay, okay. It's true that there's no application for predictive analytics in blue carbon research, or for the architecture he took from Ishtara. But Lee was working on something else. I came back here one night and found him running iterations, multiples of them, through the system.'

'What was it he was working on?

'I couldn't say, but it was a big program. He didn't know I'd seen him, but when I came in the next day I checked the logs of what had been run. It was so big he needed to manipulate the system settings to accommodate it. Messing around with the underlying parameters like that could have compromised all the work we had done here for the entire day, possibly longer.'

'Did you confront him about it later?'

He shook his head. 'But I told Ishtara. If he had been caught working on his own project, the university might have suspended the entire programme to investigate. He was putting the whole project at risk. So we decided not to report it.'

'How do you know the work he was doing wasn't already approved by the university? Perhaps they'd just left you out of the loop.'

'As project lead, I have oversight of all new programmes. I also checked all newly approved projects for other departments. There was nothing. He was definitely doing this work for himself.'

'Why didn't you tell us this in the beginning?' Holland nodded as understanding began to settle. 'I'll tell you why. Because when I was chasing you the other day, you were coming from his office, where you'd gone to get that program now that he's dead.'

Chandra was silent for a long moment. 'He steals my work to build some private program of his own,' he said finally, 'and he thinks I'm going to stand around and let that happen?' He shook his head vehemently. 'I did go there looking for whatever he was working on, but I didn't find it.'

'Well there is no way he could get it out of here, is there? Not with all this extra security. Was he looking to sabotage some of the work being done here, do you think?'

'I have no idea what he planned to do, but there doesn't seem to be any trace of the program on the servers now.' He looked at Salter again. 'Look, I know it was stupid not to report it, but we were only trying to protect the overall project here.' He paused. 'I assume I can get back to work, now that I've told you everything,' he said. 'And I trust you won't be coming round here to bother Ishtara and me any more.'

Holland wasn't so sure about that. As far as he was concerned, Chandra had only added to the web of secrets and deceptions going on at this place, but for now, he would let the man hold on to his belief that he was no longer under suspicion.

As soon as Chandra had disappeared from view, Salter gave Holland a nod of approval at an impressive performance.

'How's that for keeping my mind on the job?' he asked. But his customary laddish grin was nowhere to be found as he turned and headed back towards the car.

24

A lone figure approached Lindy as she was waiting on the hilltop. She looked behind Johnno for a moment, but it was clear he was on his own.

'Where's Truth?' she asked.

'Vet's. Just a routine check-up.'

She nodded. 'Ah yes, one of the hidden responsibilities of dog ownership.'

'And a costly one, too,' said Johnno as the two of them began to stroll slowly along the same path as before. 'You were always the one saying we should get a dog, weren't you? You never got one yourself after you left?'

'Dom said he can never be sure he'll be around to walk it, which I think is code for he wouldn't want to take it birding with him. I can't really commit to being around all the time, either, so it wouldn't be fair to it. Pity though, I did want one. I always fancied a Samoyed; a little white ball of fluff. Which of course grows into a much bigger white ball of fluff leaving dog hair everywhere.'

'So there's to be no pitter-patter of tiny feet around Lin's place anytime soon then?'

Lindy gave a wan smile. 'If Dom doesn't have time to walk a dog, I hardly think now's the time for us to be thinking about starting a family,' she said.

Johnno nodded. 'And I don't see you staying at home to raise a kid anyway. One of those great women behind every great man.'

'I'd be perfectly okay being the merely competent woman, as long as it wasn't in anybody else's shadow. But I can't even seem to manage that these days.'

'Everything in your life seems to revolve around Dom,' said Johnno, stopping for a moment. 'I think I've figured out why that is. Duck farmers in China make sure they are the first thing young ducklings see when they emerge into the world. After that, the birds will follow them anywhere, utterly devoted to them, every step of the way. Dom was the first thing you saw when you came out into the world after your relationship with me.'

'So what, now you're saying I'm just mindlessly waddling along in his wake. Woah, way to go with the imagery there, Bucko. I'm beginning to understand why ChatGPT rejected your writing.'

'Relax, Lin, it was a joke. Where's that famous sense of humour of yours? Not one more compromise you made for the sake of your relationship, I hope. Look, I'm just saying maybe you lost some of your independence when you hooked up with him. Not in a bad way, I'm sure it's what you wanted, what you intended. But the trouble is, once you give something like that away it's hard to get it back. A very wise woman once told me our gains are only temporary. It's only our losses that are truly permanent.'

Lindy recognised her own ham-fisted stabs at philosophy as well as anyone. 'I should be grateful for all the wonderful things I have in my life, I know that. But I just can't seem to find my joy these days. I feel like none of this, where I am, what I have, what we have, is enough any more. I know that's on me, and it makes me a horrible person, but I can't help it.'

Ahead of them, they saw Katie Fairfax dressed in a PPE suit, carefully extracting a tray of filters from the monitoring station. She waved to them but Lindy subtly leaned into a change of direction that veered them away from her. 'Maybe it's just that Dom is so wrapped up in this case all the time. It's as if he feels he can't fail, as if anything but his absolute complete and undivided attention will result in Laraby besting him. And he won't have that. Oh, no, not Dom.' Lindy bit her lip to fight back a sob and shook her head. 'This time nothing else seems to matter to him, and I mean nothing. He doesn't have time for the personal things, like moving a relationship forward, or considering where we go with next steps, that kind of stuff.' She managed to find a brave smile, the wind tousling her hair as she turned to Johnno. 'It's so good to have you to talk to. I don't think anybody really knows me as well as you do.' The smile saddened. 'We never did quite get there, you and me, did we? But the almosts we had were pretty good.'

He nodded. 'The Corner Café, the Leonard Cohen, the Passionfruit Rum.'

'God, yes, the Passionfruit Rum. I haven't had that stuff since, I don't think.'

Johnno returned her smile. 'We might have shared a few dreams over a few drinks, back in the day, but it was never going to work out between us. Still, "No Regrets", eh?'

She nodded. 'The greatest break-up song of all time. At least, according to you. I remember you even had tears in your eyes when you played it that last time.'

'Ah, it's just that amazing guitar solo at the end. Gets me every time.'

In her mind, Lindy recalled the moment, and her parting words as she was leaving. *If there is anything you need to say to me, now would be the time to say it, Johnno.* But he hadn't. The molasses baritone of the song's vocalist rose in her memory. 'It was true, wasn't it? The words to that song. You didn't want me back?'

'*We'd only cry again. Say goodbye again,*' he quoted with a lopsided grin. 'I wanted you to be happy, Lin. And that wasn't with me. I'm more convinced of that now than ever, seeing you with Dom. But you have to tell him what it's doing to you two, this case. I know he's under pressure to solve it, but he can't abandon you in his pursuit of it. He needs to find time for you as well.'

'I know.' She began to tear up again. 'But I can't make him see that.'

'You must.' He paused for a moment. 'Listen, you and Dom should come over. I'll cook something. Linguine alle vongole, maybe.'

'Your famous clam sauce? I'd forgotten what a foodie you were. Talk to Dom about the food groups and he thinks you mean hot and cold.'

'He's a good man, Lin. And you two are great together. Or could be. I'm sure he would acknowledge that all the pieces are there. He just needs some encouragement to recognise what the next step should be. Perhaps you need to take charge, force the issue, give him an ultimatum. You shouldn't have to wait for ever. You're too good for that.'

'But what if it backfires? If he shies away and I lose him?'

'Then you were always going to.'

She shook her head and looked around the hilltop at the couples, strolling hand in hand, happy to be with each other, talking, smiling, together. 'Now is not the right time,' she said.

'No time ever is going to be right for a conversation like that. So you just have to decide – how long are you going to put it off? There's a great big world waiting out there for you, if he decides he doesn't want to be a part of your future.'

She looked at him uncertainly. 'I hope he does.'

'I'm sure of it. I've seen the way he looks at you. He loves you. But you have to ask yourself if that's enough. This is not the Lin I know. Afraid of what's waiting out there? *We are our past, but we are not yet our future.* Wasn't it you that said that to me, as well? There is still time to change where you are heading. You always were honest with yourself. I hope that's not one more compromise you've had to make for the sake of your relationship.'

Lindy was still coming to terms with how she might handle the comment when her phone buzzed. 'Ms Hey? Lindy? DCS Laraby here. I'm Domenic's… I'm overseeing a case he's working on. I've been trying to reach him but his phone is off.'

Lindy pulled a face at Johnno as she listened to Laraby. There seemed to be a strange urgency to his tone, but she reassured him with a breezy laugh. 'Yes, he does that sometimes. When he's going somewhere the reception is particularly spotty,' she added hastily. 'I'm sure he'll check in soon.'

'Any idea how I can reach him? It's a matter of some importance.'

'I'm sorry, I don't know where he is. It's migration season. Frankly he could be anywhere.' She bit back her regret at having given him some ammunition about Dom's birding, but his concern seemed elsewhere.

'His vehicle will have a tracking device on it. Can you contact his insurance company, the twenty-four-hour emergency assistance department, and ask them to activate it?'

'Can't you do that?' asked Lindy, aware that her tone to Domenic's boss was sharper than it might have been.

'We'd need a court order. It would be much faster if you requested it.'

'Do you really think that's necessary? Honestly, DCS Laraby, he does this all the time, I'm sure it's nothing to worry about.'

'Ms Hey, can you please do as you have been asked.' There was no mistaking the tension in the man's voice now. Lindy gripped her phone more tightly, and Johnno crowded in to hear. 'Is anything wrong?'

'No, not really wrong as such. Just a routine check on an officer we have out in the field.' Laraby's attempt to dial back on the urgency was fooling no one. 'It needs to be completed immediately, that's all,' he added lamely.

Fear began to grip Lindy's chest. Since when was a routine check-in a matter of such importance? And enough of a problem that a commanding officer would try to misrepresent the situation. 'What's going on, please?'

'We need the location of his vehicle. As soon as possible. Tell the insurance company you're acting on a request from the police. I'll hold.'

Lindy left the call on hold and scrolled through her address book for the number of the insurance company. Her own tone and the mention of police involvement got her to an administrator quickly, and it was only a matter of a few minutes before she reconnected with Laraby.

'Dom's car is parked at the Fleming campus of North Norfolk University,' she reported anxiously. 'It's been there for the past twenty minutes. In the same spot. The diagnostics report suggests that it's been running all that time. So why isn't he answering his phone? Has something happened to him?

'I'm dispatching officers to the location now. I'll keep you informed.'

Lindy saw Johnno gesturing and understood immediately. 'We're closer. I'm closer,' she said. 'I'm just on the far side of the hilltop. 'I can get there faster than a police response unit.'

There was a momentary silence from Laraby's end. 'Okay, see if you can locate the vehicle, but do not approach it. Is that clear?'

'Clear,' she said, nodding to Johnno.

'When the officers arrive on scene, show them where the car is and then follow their instructions. Again, I repeat, do not approach that vehicle until we get there.'

But by now, Lindy's phone was in her pocket and she and Johnno were sprinting side by side down the long hillside to where they had parked their cars. Laraby's warning had been repeated to dead air.

25

They took Johnno's jeep. After speeding away from the parking spot at the base of the hill he drove rapidly, hauling the jeep round the bends so sharply, Lindy was having to hold on to the roll-bar to avoid swaying out through the open doorway. With her other hand she clutched her phone equally tightly, pressing it to her ear. She was waiting for the insurance company to confirm if they could pinpoint the location of the Range Rover with any greater accuracy.

'On the far side, they're saying,' she told Johnno. 'Somewhere over by the Euclid Lab. That's as specific as they can get.'

Johnno took a corner fast enough to have the tyres squealing in protest, rocking the chassis and yanking into an oversteer as he straightened, sending Lindy swaying outward in her seat again.

'What the hell is he doing there?' she asked angrily. 'On his own. Surely everyone will have packed up for the day by now.' She banged the jeep's metal dashboard with her hand. 'This is him trying too hard, trying to beat Laraby, damn him.'

'He'll be okay, Lin,' said Johnno, reaching for a tone that wouldn't agitate her still further. 'We're almost there. We'll find him. And then you can give him a piece of your mind and everybody will feel better.'

The university complex came into view as they crested the last rise in the road. It looked like a small city. A few lights burned in buildings, but large parts of the campus were silent and empty now that people had gone home for the day. Behind the buildings, the twilight was fading fast and a greying sky was turning darker. As Johnno pulled onto the grounds, he slowed down. Ahead of him, a maze of roads, lanes and bike paths snaked off in every direction He stopped at an intersection and looked across at Lindy.

'The lab,' she said impatiently, 'the lab. You can see it from the rise. It must be somewhere over in that direction.' She pointed. 'That side, there, down by those buildings. Try there.'

Johnno turned in the direction she had indicated and began driving along a road lined on both sides with ranges of buildings. 'Slower, slower,' said Lindy. 'He could be parked anywhere around here.'

Johnno slowed to idling speed, creeping along at a pace that allowed them to check every gap between buildings, every loading dock, every alleyway. The last of the daylight was beginning to dwindle now, filling the recesses with dark pockets of shadow that forced them to peer deeper into every space as they passed. The jeep was barely moving at walking pace as they crept along the empty roads, past the deserted shells of the darkened buildings.

'It's not here,' said Lindy, craning forward to scan a loading bay intently. A sudden surge of panic seized her. 'Oh, God, what if they got it wrong?'

'It has to be here, Lin,' Johnno reassured her. 'The insurance companies locate vehicles every day using that technology. They're not going to be wrong.'

'But what if they are?' she persisted. 'What if all that artificial intelligence is wrong for once? Dom could be miles away, in trouble, waiting for help, and we're driving around in circles out here.'

'He's here, Lin,' Johnno told her firmly. 'We'll find him. There's a big car park over there. Maybe we missed the blindingly obvious.'

But as they rounded the corner, they could see even from this distance that the sulphur-lit expanse of fenced-in tarmac was empty. Johnno fell silent. Only the sound of the Jeep's off-road tyres on the road surface filled the air around them now.

'There,' Lindy shouted. 'I'm sure I saw a glint of something. Back up, back up. On the far side of that little hut, tucked in beside it. Is that a reflector? It is. It's him, Johnno. It's Dom.'

Johnno sped up, and turned in to park on the side of a narrow lane that passed in front of a small utility shed. He could see the outline of the Range Rover clearly, but it was backed up towards the door at an odd angle. Even from here, he could hear the sound of the engine running.

'Let's go,' said Lindy, straining against the seat belt latch. 'I have to see if he's all right.'

'Laraby said no, Lin. He said to wait and call in. The police should be here any moment. Call Laraby now and say we've found the vehicle.'

But Lindy wasn't waiting. She cast off the seat belt and jumped out. Johnno followed her, catching up just as she got to the vehicle. 'He's not in there,' she said staring around frantically. 'Where is he?'

But Johnno had already seen enough to guess. The Range Rover was backed tightly against the single door of the hut with its exhaust angled exactly at a small envelope-shaped slot, pumping its fumes directly into the building. 'We need to get this thing away from the doors,' he said. He ran round the driver's door and tried it. 'Locked. We can't even shut it off.' He scrambled onto the bonnet of the vehicle and then up onto the roof. A single, small window loomed above him. It was fastened shut from the inside and covered from the outside by a heavy wire mesh. But even stretching up on his toes from the roof of the Range Rover, the window was still above Johnno's head height. He took out his phone and reached up to his fullest extent to angle the phone downwards through the window. He snapped off a series of shots and pulled back his phone. He scrolled through the photos, still standing on the roof of the Range Rover. 'Call the cops now, Lin,' he said as calmly as he could manage. 'Tell them Domenic is trapped inside the hut with exhaust fumes being pumped in. He's unconscious on the floor.'

But Lindy didn't call. She tore at the driver's door handle and beat on the window with her fist. Johnno jumped down from the car and came round beside her, looking around frantically. There were no sounds of sirens in the distance, no neon-blue flashes of any help on the horizon any time soon. Lindy turned to him, her eyes filled with tears of panic. 'We have to get him out of there, Johnno. He's going to die.'

'There is one thing I can try,' he said. He crossed to his jeep, fishing a coin from his pocket as he went. He bent down in front of the vehicle and used the coin to unscrew the number plate, then ran back to Lindy with it in his hand. 'If I can slide this down alongside the window, I might be able to jam it against the locking bar in the door. It might not be long enough but it's worth a try.'

He peeled back the rubber seal at the base of the driver's-door window and began to slide the flat metal plate down gently. But the rubber flipped back, pressing firmly against the plate, preventing further progress. He tried again, and a third time, but got the same result. 'I can't do it. I need to hold the rubber back and slide the plate down at the same time. You do it, Lin. Come inside me here. Hold the plate by the edge and, as I reach round you to yank back that seal, slide the plate all the way down and jam hard.'

Lindy wriggled under Johnno's arm into the tight space between him and the door. She could feel his body pressing hard against her as he reached round on both sides to grab the rubber seal with his fingertips. Holding on to the edge of the plate, Lindy slid it down into the gap. But even at its fullest extent it found no resistance. She backed up her grip until she was only holding the metal edge with her fingertips. She jammed the plate down again but still didn't strike anything. 'It's not working,' she said. 'The plate's not long enough.'

'Closer to the front, then. It's a shorter distance to the locking bar.' They shuffled along, side-stepping in unison. Lindy could feel Johnno's breath on her neck as he pressed in behind her. She felt droplets of sweat on her shoulder as he strained to haul back the rubber seal. She slid the plate in gently and jammed down hard. Once, twice. Clunk. She uttered a tiny spontaneous sigh of joy, and spun to face him. His arms were still either side of her. 'We did it,' she said, her eyes shining. 'It's open.' Her body was arched backwards against the door, Johnno's pressed against her, both breathing hard from their exertions. Johnno peeled an arm away and yanked open the car door. He slid in, jammed the car into gear, and accelerated away a few metres before turning the key off and hauling on the handbrake. By the time he got back to the hut, Lindy was already inside. She was kneeling beside Domenic, cradling his head on her lap. He was still unconscious.

'He's still breathing. We have to get him out of here into some fresh air.'

Johnno came round and helped her lift Domenic from the ground. But he was completely unresponsive, lolling forward in their grasp. Together they dragged him from the hut and laid him on a small patch of grass outside. The sound of distant sirens came to them now on the still night air. 'We should get him up, walking,' said Lindy, looking down at him. She knelt beside him and stroked his face. 'Dom, can you hear me? It's over. You're safe now. Wake up, Dom, help is coming. They will be here any second. You're going to be fine.'

Johnno stood a few paces off, looking over Lindy's shoulder at the man lying on his back on the grass in front of her. He'd only ever seen recoveries like this in the movies, but in the successful ones the victim had been responsive by now; choking and gagging and staggering around maybe, but able to get up, or at least move. He couldn't ever remember seeing a movie where someone came out of the situation looking like this and it ended well. *Fine?* He hoped this wasn't more of Lindy's misplaced optimism. But the police were pulling up at the scene now, and an ambulance with them. They would all have their answer soon enough.

26

'How are you feeling?'

Marvin Laraby's face might not have been the first thing Domenic Jejeune expected to see when he opened his eyes in his hospital bed, but the DCS's look of concern was genuine enough.

'I've felt better,' said Jejeune. He had a severe headache and his mouth felt dry and fuzzy.

'That'll be the ketamine.' Laraby shook his head. 'Nasty stuff. The doc says you'll probably be feeling the effects for a while yet. Your neck will hurt, too, I imagine, at the injection site.'

Jejeune's hand involuntarily went up to the side of his neck where a plaster was in place.

'No evidence the exhaust fumes had much of an effect, thankfully,' continued Laraby. 'Goes without saying you'll be off until you've received full medical clearance to return to work. Not that there's any rush. I can't have you working this one anyway, for obvious reasons.' The delivery was an uneven balance of concern and officiousness, but Jejeune gave Laraby the benefit of the doubt. The other figure standing behind him had come into focus now, and this, perhaps, was someone he might have expected to see at his hospital bedside.

'Lindy is outside,' said Danny Maik. 'We've promised not to keep her waiting long, but we wanted to ask you a few questions first, if you're up to it.'

Jejeune nodded weakly. They wanted his impressions, his own memories of what had occurred, as accurately as he could recall them, before Lindy came in and told him where he'd been found, when, in what condition, creating a scenario into which his recollections might neatly begin to mould.

'What happened to me?'

'You were found unconscious in a storage shed at the uni. Your Range Rover had been backed up to the doors and the exhaust was being pumped inside. Even if you had come to from the drug, there would have been no way for you to escape.'

Jejeune nodded. 'The storage shed. There was a noise inside.' He paused. 'The door was slightly ajar. I eased it open further.'

'Did you call out?'

He shrugged. 'I can't remember. Probably. I do remember going inside. It was dark. No light.'

'Any sounds, scents?'

He shook his head, stopping quickly as a dull pain began throbbing at his temples. 'Whoever it was must've been beside the door. I don't remember the needle, just staggering around for a moment. I could see the open door but I couldn't get to it.'

Laraby pursed his lips. 'Did you find out anything before you were attacked?'

Jejeune made as if to shake his head again, but remembered the throbbing it had caused just in time. 'I'd only just arrived.' A moment of revelation seemed to come to him. 'I was going to check the truck. I was there to see Katie Fairfax.' He looked at Laraby questioningly. 'To arrest her?'

The DCS ignored the question. 'Was her truck there?'

Jejeune nodded. It didn't cause the same kind of pain in his temples. *Affirmative, good*, he registered. 'In the car park. It was the only one there.'

Laraby looked at Maik significantly. 'It was gone by the time we found you,' said the sergeant. 'The lot was empty. So you didn't see anybody else around, notice anything off when you approached the shed?' His tone was almost apologetic. Even in his groggy state, Jejeune understood. With Laraby standing beside him, Maik had no choice but to ask, but it was a given that, if his former DCI had seen anything out of the ordinary, he would have thought to mention it by now.

'I'd only just arrived. I didn't have much chance to look around.'

'And somebody went to great lengths to make sure it stayed that way,' said Laraby bitterly. He steeled himself for sincerity. 'We'll get them for this, Inspector, Domenic. They think they can do one of our own, they've got another think coming. I won't let this go, it gets top priority. Only...'

Jejeune waited.

'I don't want to declare it an attempt on the life of a serving member just yet, if you're all right with that. As soon as I do, we'll have half the police officers in the county down here, crawling around all over the place, getting in the way. Give me a couple of days, let's see if we can get to the bottom of this ourselves. Whoever it was clearly didn't want you poking around there at the uni. Whatever they were trying to stop you uncovering, it was worth doing this to you.' He paused. 'We'll give this everything we've got, Domenic. I promise you. If we get nowhere in forty-eight hours, I give you my word, I'll declare it an attempt on life and let the major crimes unit take it from there.'

Jejeune offered another pain-free nod. 'The Beast. That's what they used to block the doors? I parked beside the hut. They must have moved it...'

'The only prints we found were yours, Lindy's and McBride's,' Laraby told him.

'Johnno was there?'

Laraby and his sergeant looked at each other. 'He's the one who rescued you,' said Maik. 'Him and Lindy.'

'Quick thinking,' said Laraby. 'Good job, too.' He looked back towards the door. 'I should get going. Let your girl come in here. But remember, if there's anything you need, you let me know. I mean it, Domenic. Anything. Understood?' The moment of sincerity sat between the two men uncomfortably until Maik stepped in to relieve it. 'I could bring in some of my Motown tunes, if you like. Help you pass the time.'

'Are you joking?' asked Laraby, seizing on the escape route. 'Set his recovery back weeks, that would. Besides, where's he going to find a Victrola in here?'

Maik gave a dutiful smile. His DCS had striven so hard for the human touch, Danny was prepared to give him the win on this one. He joined Jejeune in watching as Laraby bustled hurriedly from the room before turning to the DCI. 'How's the pain?'

'Better, all of a sudden.' Jejeune managed a smile.

Maik matched it. 'I don't think they cover compassion on the superintendent's courses. The concern was genuine, though. He was beside himself when he knew you'd gone missing out there. Almost frantic until they found you. Any further recollections, with the passage of time?' Since Laraby had departed, Maik meant.

'Nothing. The cast for the tyre matched Katie Fairfax's truck. He'd suggested I talk to her about it and bring her in if I didn't like her answers.'

'He sent you? No wonder he's remorseful. A bit below the pay grade for a DCI, I'd have thought.'

'He said you were busy and Salter and Holland were off on a call.'

Maik fell into a thoughtful silence for a moment. 'I should get Lindy,' he said finally. He didn't need to repeat Laraby's offer of help. Jejeune knew he could ask Danny for anything. They both knew he wouldn't.

He crossed to the door and held it open as Lindy burst past him with a grateful smile. Johnno followed at a more sedate pace, nodding at Maik as the sergeant left. By the time Johnno turned, Lindy already had Domenic in a tight embrace.

'I was so scared, Dom,' she said, releasing him from the hug finally. 'When you wouldn't wake up…'

'It was the drug, not the fumes,' he said, brushing a tear from her cheek with his thumb. 'I'm fine now.'

She shook her head. 'No, no, you're not. You will be, but the doctor says you need rest. No rushing back to work. Promise?'

She pulled away slightly so she could look into his eyes. She was going to wait for an answer. He treated her to one of his newly mastered nods and turned to Johnno. 'I understand it was you who rescued me?'

'We'd just bumped into each other,' said Lindy hurriedly. 'Johnno offered to drive while I was on the phone to that bloody insurance company, trying to get a location on your car.'

Johnno smiled benignly in support of Lindy's account. 'Hey, at least you've got birds to watch,' he said brightly, pointing at a feeder outside the window.

Jejeune looked outside, but didn't offer the smile Lindy expected. 'It needs to be closer to the window,' he said.

'Surely you can see it from here,' said Lindy. 'It's only about four metres away. Even I can tell what birds are on there. That one's a Chaffinch and that colourful one is a Goldfinch, isn't it?'

'I can see them okay,' said Jejeune, hefting himself up in the bed slightly. 'But at that distance, they can generate a decent velocity before they get to the window. If a predator comes by and they scatter from the feeder in panic, one of them could hit the glass hard. I might ask them to move it closer, so the birds can't get up enough speed in case they do fly into the window.'

'Seems like a simple enough solution,' said Johnno. He watched as a squirrel approached across the lawn and eyed the baffle on the feeder's post. 'Any chance you have another one up your sleeve to keep squirrels away from the feeder?'

'Sadly not.' Jejeune smiled, entering into the lightness that seemed to suit them all. 'The solution to some problems lie beyond the realms of human intelligence.' He became serious for a moment. 'Though I hear I'm indebted to you for your own ingenuity.'

'He was great, Dom. Honestly,' said Lindy. 'He knew just what to do with that number plate.'

At Jejeune's puzzled look, Johnno went into a brief explanation of the rescue. He left out the part about Lindy's help at close quarters. 'You meet a lot of interesting characters when you do a podcast like mine. Not all of them earn their living on the right side of the law. It's amazing the things you can pick up.'

'Well, for once I am extremely grateful to the criminal element,' said Jejeune. 'And to you.'

A sudden thud at the window startled them all. They looked to see the shadow of a large bird flying off swiftly and a small shape lying on the window ledge. It was the Goldfinch.

'Sparrowhawk,' said Jejeune flatly. 'Is the finch dead?'

As Lindy watched, it rose to its feet and sat motionless on the ledge. It seemed unharmed by the collision, but it was a few moments before it flew off.

'I'll ask the nurse to talk to the maintenance crew about moving the feeder. Even if this one recovered, the next one may not.'

'I'll do it,' said Lindy. 'You concentrate on your own recovery.'

They turned at a knock on the door. A young nurse entered, pushing a tray loaded with medical devices. 'Vitals,' she announced officiously. 'All visitors outside, please.'

Another time, Lindy might have taken the trouble to explain why that wasn't going to happen, but today she simply looked at Jejeune sternly. 'If she asks how you feel, tell her the truth,' she said. 'There's no extra points for bravery.' They all smiled, since that what they were required to do, and then Lindy became serious. 'I'll be right outside, Dom. Don't worry. I'm not going anywhere.'

It was a strange parting line but, as the nurse prepared the tray to check Domenic's vital signs, he reflected that it wasn't the only statement from this morning's visits that had given him cause to wonder.

27

From the way Laraby strode into the room and stood before them, legs splayed, as he glowered around the room, the message was clear. This was not a day for the usual light banter. They were here on serious business today.

'How's the inspector?' he asked the room in general.

Maik took on the question, as everyone expected he would. 'He has his medical assessment later on today. All being well, if he's cleared he should be able to report for duty tomorrow.'

Laraby gave a short nod, not giving anything away. 'And what better way to greet him, then, than by handing him the person who tried to do him? I want a result on this, and I want it fast. We go after this lot like a pack of junkyard dogs. We tear into their lives and we go through the scraps. This is one of our own we're talking about and I won't stand for it.'

Holland felt he was on safe enough ground to address Laraby's point for the whole room. 'The problem is, sir, we simply don't have enough on any of our suspects to warrant bringing them in. Not for any of the cases. They might have sketchy relationships with a victim, or some dodgy motives, but it's like trying to nail down soap. Nobody we've had on our radar clearly has motive, means and opportunity; for Lee, for Rowe, or for the DCI.'

Despite his obvious agitation, Laraby accepted the point at face value. 'Can we at least start to prioritise them, then? Huebner; he's no friend of the DCI. How's it look with him?'

'He has no alibi for the time of Lee's death, which is to say he claims he and Talia were meeting, but she doesn't back that up. As for the DCI, he can't even be bothered to offer up an alibi. He just says he has one but isn't interested in sharing it yet.'

Barely suppressed to begin with, Laraby's exasperation boiled over. 'What the bloody hell is he playing at?' he shouted. 'Get over there Danny, and impress on Mr Huebner that, unless he decides to cooperate with an inquiry into an attack on a senior officer of the local police force, I intend to come after him with everything I've got.'

Danny might put it another way, but, judging by his own reaction to Holland's news about Huebner's alibi, the suspect would still be left in no doubt as to how the station felt about the attack on Jejeune.

'Any other angles looking good?' asked Laraby abruptly. 'Huebner is obviously connected to Lee, but I can't see his connection to that Euclid Lab.'

'Talia Rowe is the connection,' said Salter. 'Through his investment in this fLIGHT programme. Huebner asked her to look into it, to talk to Ishtara Habloun about it. But she says she's never heard of Rowe. Worth another chat? With either one? Both?'

'Good, yes. Let's get somebody on that.' He looked around the room expectantly. Was it Maik's imagination or did Laraby seem to be waiting for one of them to suggest a specific suspect he already had in mind? If so, Maik had an idea who it might be.

'The reason the DCI was there, sir,' he began cautiously, 'at the lab. It was to check on the tyre cast, I understand?'

'I already did that,' said Holland, puzzled. 'It was a match. To Katie Fairfax's truck.'

'The DCI was there to bring Fairfax in,' admitted Laraby. 'Her truck was there when he arrived, but by the time we got there, after he'd been attacked, it was nowhere in sight. Neither was she. Listen,' he said defensively. 'The DCI had already had previous contact with her. I had no reason to suspect anything would go south.'

'Nobody could have foreseen that, sir,' said Holland.

Laraby's expression suggested he hadn't been mollified by Holland's obsequious assurance. The absolution he required was from Jejeune himself. And he wasn't here to give it. He was still lying in a hospital bed. 'I went back and had a look at the DCI's notes from his initial encounter with Katie Fairfax,' said Laraby carefully. 'She said the reason for their argument that afternoon was that Lee had told her he knew the name of the person involved in defrauding the government over the blue carbon scheme, but he had decided not to release it to the journalist.'

'He claimed he was going to hold out because he thought the information could be put to better use elsewhere, didn't he?' said Holland.

'The greater good?' said Maik. 'Or maybe it was that Huebner put the frighteners on him.'

'Either way, we know Lee did eventually decide to pass on that name. But what if Fairfax thought he really did lose heart? She lures him to the monitoring station and strangles him. It's an attack from behind. He's not going to have the chance to tell her he changed his mind and did send the name after all. Now she's got a body on her hands, so she drives it to the river, and stops off at the house afterwards to stage it as the murder scene to throw us off?'

Silence greeted Laraby's scenario. Somebody needed to point out the obvious. 'She has an alibi, sir,' said Salter evenly. 'For the time of the murder.'

'Does she?' asked Laraby. 'Somebody was fifteen miles away collecting those samples at the time, but we have no way of knowing who that was.' He raised his fingers and counted off his points. 'An argument with the victim that she admits to. The victim's blood at her work site. A key to Lee's house, where there was no sign of forced entry. And now, a plausible motive.'

'Not to mention the tyre cast match,' added Holland.

'And then there's that,' agreed Laraby firmly. 'Bring her in, constable. It's time to ask Ms Katie Fairfax a few pointed questions.'

There was no need for Salter and Maik to retreat to the alcove after the briefing. The pall of Laraby's remorse that had hung over the meeting meant that nobody wanted to stay around for long afterwards. Besides the two sergeants, only Tony Holland remained in the room. He raised his eyebrows as soon as the last of the King's Landing crew had departed. 'Blimey, Laraby's feeling it.'

'He should,' said Salter, 'seeing as he was the one who sent him out there. A DCI, on a simple bring-in? What was he thinking?'

'That it should have been easy enough,' said Maik. 'I wouldn't have disagreed with him on that.'

'Me neither,' said Holland. 'He had reasonable grounds to bring Fairfax in. He followed all operational protocols. Fairfax had no prior history of violence or resisting arrest. No weapons or drug charges. It happens. It's always a risk you take when you send somebody out, but I can't see why he's beating himself up unduly for this. Okay, the DCI caught a bad one. But he's all right, thankfully.'

'And I suppose it was Laraby's own actions that ultimately set the rescue in motion,' said Salter grudgingly. 'So he could at least give himself a bit of credit for that.'

'What's this now?' asked Holland, who was clearly hearing the news for the first time. 'It was the DCS who sent out the alarm? What was all that about?'

Maik turned to him. 'When you did your stint at the Met, was it standard practice for commanding officers to do routine checks on officers in the field?'

'No,' said Holland, drawing the word out. 'They tend to treat people like adults down there. The inference being you'll call in all on your own if you find yourself in a dangerous situation, or are about to enter into one. Why? Is that what happened here?'

'When he couldn't raise the DCI by phone, he got in touch with Lindy to see if she knew where he could be reached.'

Holland stared at Maik. 'How long had Jejeune been out of contact?'

Maik tilted his head. 'A couple of hours, max.'

'I have longer lunches than that,' said Holland. 'Talk about keeping tabs on the DCI's every move. That's borderline workplace harassment, that is.'

'This personal feud they've got going, it's getting out of hand if Laraby is taking things that far,' said Salter. 'Still, I can't see the DCI bringing a formal complaint. It was only Laraby's ridiculous checking up on him that ended up saving his life, after all.'

Holland stood up to leave and shook his head. 'The worst of intentions; the best of outcomes.' He gave an ironic chuckle. 'Funny how life works sometimes, isn't it?'

Maik's expression suggested he wasn't seeing the humour in it at all. In fact, he seemed to be finding something faintly disturbing about the whole thing. And there was something else concerning him, too; the way Holland had studiously avoided making eye contact with Lauren the entire time they had been talking. Every comment, every reply, every gesture; they had all been directed solely at Danny. Surely this couldn't just be the residue of her hanging him out to dry at that earlier briefing? But whatever was going on between them, it would have to wait because, now Holland had left the room, the way was clear for Danny to cover some other ground with Lauren. 'This business of Laraby checking up on the DCI. It doesn't sit well, does it?'

She shook her head slowly. 'Not after such a short time, and with no indications of a problem.' She paused. 'At least, none that we were privy to. You think somebody tipped him off that Jejeune was in trouble? Who? His MI5 contact?'

Maik's expression told Salter she was on the right track, at least as far as his own suspicions went.

'But how would they have known?' she asked. 'The only way they could have is if they were following Jejeune themselves. And why would they do that? If they wanted to know where he was, they could have just asked Laraby. After all, he sent him there.'

'No,' said Danny quietly, 'that's not the only way. They would know where the DCI was if they were the one who had told Laraby where to send him.'

Salter gave a sharp intake of breath. 'Which he does. And then he suddenly has second thoughts, a bad feeling about it.

So he calls Jejeune and, when he can't reach him, he starts to panic.'

'And when he finds out he's been attacked, he realises he's the one who put him in harm's way. By sending him out to where somebody else told him to.'

Salter nodded. Hence all the hand-wringing and remorse. And the determination to find out who did this. 'So his contact at Five wanted Jejeune poking around the Euclid Lab to shake something loose,' she said. 'And they were willing to put him in harm's way to do it. This is a ruthless person Laraby's dealing with, Danny. Ruthless and dangerous. We need to find out who it is. Did you ever hear anything back from your contacts?'

He shook his head. 'Even without the Official Secrets Act, this lot look after each other. Nobody is admitting to knowing anything about any MI5 liaison with Laraby.'

'Then perhaps we need to ask the liaisee. I might be able to get Laraby to talk to me. Just between friends.' She tipped her head and smiled. 'You know, for old times' sake.'

'I can't ask you to do that, Lauren.'

'Then don't. To be clear, Sergeant Maik, you are not involved in my decision to act, and have no influence upon it whatsoever. Anything I do will be of my own volition. Now, let's get down the pub and you can buy me a Chardonnay and a ploughman's while you try to talk me out of it. And fail miserably.'

28

Holland gave an exasperated sigh as the Audi approached the police station and he caught sight of the crowd of reporters gathered at the front entrance. The team were on shaky enough ground, bringing Katie Fairfax in like this on such circumstantial evidence. The fact that Laraby had quietly let the media know that they now had a person of interest helping with their inquiries wasn't going to improve matters. He understood that the DCS had been under a lot of pressure from the brass to do something to counteract the press's constant barrage of negative publicity; pointing out their lack of progress and failure to even bring in a single person for a formal interview. But subjecting the woman to a sideshow like this wasn't going to do much for her inclination to cooperate with the inquiry.

Holland pulled up into a side street and opened the passenger door for Fairfax. 'Sorry about this,' he told her as she stared back towards the reporters. 'Word must have got out,' he said halfheartedly. 'We can take the side entrance here, save going past them.' He led her down a narrow passage and into the station, where they followed a maze of corridors to the interview room. His instructions had been clear. *Wait for Laraby*. The DCS was going to be doing this one himself.

Another mistake, in Holland's less than humble opinion, after allowing himself to be stampeded into bringing someone in before they had enough on her. It was a further sign of the twin pressures Laraby was feeling from brass oversight and his own remorse over the attack on Jejeune.

Laraby entered the room with Lauren Salter in tow. Holland expected to be dismissed now Laraby had a female officer as his second, but he was offered a seat in the corner of the room. Numbers for intimidation, he thought. He doubted it would have much effect on the young woman sitting with her back to him. From his brief conversations with Katie Fairfax on the way, Holland got the impression she was already bristling with indignation at being summoned here. He had a sinking feeling that Laraby's confrontational approach was going to encourage some testy push back from her.

'What am I doing here?' she asked Laraby as soon as he had finished the preamble for the recording devices. 'Sampson Lee was my partner. I've lost somebody I loved and now, on the basis of absolutely no evidence whatsoever, you think I had something to do with his death?' Her voice was a model of controlled disbelief.

'Not think, Ms Fairfax, know,' said Laraby crisply. 'What can you tell me about ketamine?'

'Only that it's a Class B disassociative anaesthetic and analgesic.'

'But you don't use it in your work?'

She looked at him in astonishment. 'In the collection and analysis of environmental DNA samples? No, Superintendent, I don't.' She smirked and shook her head. Holland could perhaps have signalled to her that this might not be the way to go with Laraby, but Fairfax didn't look in his direction.

'Impressive knowledge, then, for somebody who's not using the stuff. For any legal purposes, anyway.'

'Not really. Just part of a post-secondary-level education in biochemistry.'

Laraby pulled a face. 'This partner of yours, Sampson Lee, he was a clever bloke, too, wasn't he? A mathematician, a software program developer. And you're not either of those, I understand.'

'I've just told you my field is environmental DNA. What's your point?'

'That your former boyfriend's field requires a more, shall we say, elite level of intelligence. I'm sure that made you feel a bit inadequate at times, like you were out of your depth around him. Wouldn't sit well with somebody like you.'

'You can't be serious?' Her tone suggested she had been prepared to be amused with such an outlandish idea, but had now decided to be offended by it. 'I'm exploring groundbreaking DNA research. It's on the cutting edge of its field, with the potential to change the way we approach major conservation initiatives around the world. You really think I'm going to suffer from a crisis of confidence because somebody else can do a few sums better than me?'

'Not just one somebody, though, is it? It's a bunch of them up there, a cliquey little group that would have no time for anybody who was not quite up to their intellectual standard. Breed a lot of resentment, a snub like that.'

'You're suggesting I killed Sampson because I felt left out of a maths club?' Most people could probably manufacture a convincing display of surprise. But it was doubtful many could have found the perfect pitch of outrage and disbelief Fairfax managed. She looked across at Salter as if to suggest reining her superior in might be a very good idea. 'You know I'm half tempted to stay here and find out what other idiotic theories you've managed to come up with. But on the whole, I think my time can be better spent elsewhere.' She stood up. 'Unless you intend to charge me with something, I believe I'm free to go.'

'Sit down, Ms Fairfax,' Laraby told her firmly. 'There's something else you need to explain to us. It's a piece of evidence. You know, that thing you've been suggesting we don't have. But first, let's get to your alibi for the night Sampson Lee was murdered. Out collecting samples, wasn't it? Or did you have somebody do it for you? We found a key in Sampson Lee's desk. It fits the lock on the flap of the monitoring station where the filter trays are stored.'

'What? I never gave Sampson that key. I have no idea how he got it.'

Laraby ignored the denial. 'If you're in the habit of passing out keys to all and sundry, anybody could have collected those filters for you, replaced them with the new ones, and reset the programming.'

'Not quite anybody,' said Fairfax. 'I doubt you could, for example. Would you even know where to start?'

Laraby regarded her with undisguised hostility. 'Big thing, for you, isn't it, trying to show how clever you are.'

'If by clever you mean well educated, I'd say that's demonstrably true. I have eight years post-secondary education. How about you?'

'And because you're clever, you think we won't be able to get you for this crime, is that it?'

'You won't be able to *get* me for Sampson's murder because I didn't do it. And quite frankly, I'm tired of being considered a suspect just because his blood was found at the station.'

'Not just blood, Ms Fairfax, hair and tissue. And yet you didn't notice a thing. Right there, at your work site, where you argued with him to convince him to release a name he had come across to a podcaster. To be clear, he never identified this person to you, did he, by any chance?'

'I...'

Had Jejeune not reported it? She couldn't understand why, but she realised that it would only provide more fuel for Laraby' suspicions if she admitted she had known Marius Huebner's name before Sampson was killed.

'Would you not expect it to say so in the inspector's report if I had told him that?' she replied haughtily.

'I've got a team of people here who are looking at evidence against you as we speak. They're all clever, too, and between us we're going to prove you killed Sampson Lee, regardless of how much of a genius you think you are.'

'Well, you know what Jonathan Swift said about genius. *You shall know it by this sign – all the dunces shall be in confederacy against him.*'

Salter smiled, despite being lumped in with the confederacy, but the comment quickened Laraby to anger.

'A senior officer was attacked near the lab two days ago. In the storage hut by the car park. He was coming to see you to confront you about a piece of evidence. Was it you that attacked him, Ms Fairfax?'

'No, it was not. Is the officer all right?'

Laraby ignored the question as he pressed on with his interrogation. 'Your truck was there when he arrived, but it had gone by the time the rescue team showed up. Were you lying in wait to assault a police officer who was coming to question you, possibly bring you in?'

'I drove off to go on my rounds, I presume. I had no idea he was even there. And as for lying in wait, how on earth would I even know he was coming?'

Laraby shook his head. 'An answer for everything, eh, Ms Fairfax? Well, try your luck with this one. We found a tyre print on the riverbank where Sampson Lee's body was dumped, and, because it had rained earlier, we know it was made around the exact time of Sampson Lee's death. The thing is, the print is a match to your truck. The truck you've already admitted to being out in that evening.'

'I brought it back after my shift. A couple of people saw me on my way in. I parked it in the car park, the controlled access car park, and drove my own car home.'

Laraby nodded. 'And came back later, when everybody else had gone home for the night. And then you drove the truck containing Sampson Lee's body down to the riverbank. Unless, of course, you can come up with another plausible explanation as to how a track from a tyre of your truck, to which you had the keys and which was parked in a locked car park to which you have the access card, could be found at the site.'

'How about I try my luck with this one?' said Fairfax angrily. 'Whoever killed Sampson transported his body to the river in another vehicle. Then, after the parking lot is all locked up tight for the night with my truck inside it, that person comes back, jacks up the truck, removes the tyre, wheels it around the barrier, puts it in their own vehicle, leaves the imprint and then comes back the same way and replaces the tyre on my truck. Is that plausible enough for you?'

Laraby was visibly taken aback. 'And why would somebody go to all that trouble?' he asked as he tried to find a way to recover.

'To have you lot chasing their tails all over the place. Like you are now.' Fairfax stood up again. 'I take it this time I am free to go.'

The anger seething in Laraby's silence after the woman departed was palpable. That such a straightforward explanation had never occurred to any of them added another layer of humiliation to the proceedings. It was a moment before the DCS could trust himself to speak. 'Bloody university types. They can't resist lording it over you with their learning, can they? Quoting Jonathan Swift, for God's sake.'

'And English is not even her speciality,' said Holland.

Salter flashed a look to suggest his contribution was not helping.

'The jack compartment in the truck bed isn't locked,' said Holland, hurrying towards safer ground. 'It's definitely possible that somebody could have accessed it, jacked up the truck and removed the tyre, just as she said. If they replaced it the same night, nobody would be any the wiser.'

'Check it out, constable, the tyre, the wheel, the jack. We might get lucky with a fingerprint.'

Salter shook her head. 'Unlikely, sir. Those minute particles off the monitoring station post, they have been identified as leather. It looks like the killer wore gloves.'

Laraby inclined his head. 'Even if they get any matches off the tyre to that leather, that might get us somewhere.'

It might, thought Salter. But not to Katie Fairfax. That chance had gone. She was their best suspect, the only one linked to any crime by physical evidence, and that had all just disappeared in a puff of smoke, in no small part because of Laraby's ham-fisted approach to the interview. She looked across at him now: angry, frustrated, still wounded by his guilt over Jejeune. Once the results of today's interview became known, they wouldn't do him much good with either his superiors or the press. As much as it pained Salter to say it, such a reckless approach to the investigation hardly deserved any better. Of more interest to her just now, though, was the effect that today's interview might have on Laraby himself. With any luck, it just might have made him a bit more vulnerable.

29

To anybody who knew the inspector as well as Danny Maik, it was no surprise that he had insisted on making the trip out to HR Holdings, even if it was only with 'observer' status, for Maik's interview with Marius Huebner.

The DCI's return to work had been as low-key as he would have wanted, but there had been some interesting information awaiting him. Laraby may have gone out of his way to keep the attack on Jejeune off the police grapevine for now, but word had got out, locally at least. The IT team had a lot of respect for the DCI's meticulous approach to any evidence they brought him, and they had been working, unbidden, around the clock to find the investigating officers something new to go on. Maik could imagine their pleasure when they had finally managed to turn up something useful on Marius Huebner. Or, at least, related to him.

Huebner didn't bother coming out to greet them after they knocked on the front door of the building. 'You know where I am,' he called. 'Come on through.'

They made their way to his office, as neat and tidy now as if it had never seen the kind of disarray Maik had encountered the last time he was here. 'Looks like you found whatever it was you were looking for, then,' he said.

Huebner shook his head. 'No, but, as I told you, I know where it is. It's just a folder containing some financial documents.'

'Wouldn't there be electronic records of them anyway?' asked Jejeune.

Huebner looked at him frankly. 'I like everything on paper. I'm a bit old school that way.' He considered Jejeune again for a moment. 'It was you who ran into a bit of bother the other day, wasn't it? How you doing now? All better, are you?'

'We're wondering where you were during the time of that attack,' said Maik evenly. 'I hear you claim to have an alibi but you don't feel like sharing it.'

'You hear right. But why are you looking at me in the first place?' He jerked a thumb in Jejeune's direction. 'Why would I want to kill this bloke?'

'It's Inspector Jejeune,' Maik said with barely suppressed anger. 'Detective Chief Inspector, as a matter of fact. We're thinking it might be connected to the fact that Sampson Lee came to see you, shortly before his death.'

Maik waited but Huebner apparently didn't feel like contributing anything yet. 'We got the tracking records for Lee's phone,' he continued, 'and they place him here, the day before he was murdered. What did he come to see you about?'

'Well, it seems to me all you have is evidence that his phone was here,' said Huebner thoughtfully. 'But even leaving that aside for the moment, he might well have come by, but I wasn't here. That's the trouble with all this technology, isn't it? It only gives you half the picture.'

'Even coming here was a dangerous thing to do, given your avowed interest in teaching him a lesson.'

'Not mine, Sergeant. AI, remember?'

'Can I ask why you decided to invest in Ishtara Habloun's fLIGHT programme?' asked Jejeune as if the other conversation had not existed.

'I told your sergeant,' said Huebner, casting a glance Maik's way, 'they do good work. Did you know millions of birds are killed every year from colliding with buildings? Think of it, all those little birdies dying just because people can't be bothered to switch off a few lights when they leave work at night. It's tragic, is what it is.'

'Actually, fewer than half of bird collision deaths are light-related, probably closer to a quarter in fact. The vast majority die in strikes with windows that have no clearly visible markers. They usually happen in the bottom five or six storeys of buildings as well, the equivalent height of the canopy of tree cover. If they're flying higher than that, they're likely going to go over the building anyway. The time of day is a factor, too. The early hours of the morning seem to be the worst, rather than the dead of night, as you might imagine.' He paused to check the effects of the information on Huebner. He received only a blank expression in return. 'It's the sort of research I might have done into the subject if I was thinking of making a significant investment,' he said.

'Ah, well, there you are, see. You take a more intellectual approach. Me, I'm more instinctual. I like to go with my gut.'

'And did your gut tell you anything about a profit margin?' asked Maik. 'Only as far as I can see, there isn't one.'

'Oh, I wouldn't be so sure about that, Sergeant. There can be big money to be made in apps these days. Ever hear of this one called Merlin?' He nodded at Jejeune. 'He will have. It went from one million subscribers to five million virtually overnight.'

Maik turned to Jejeune. 'Those birding apps are free though, aren't they?'

'Maybe so,' said Huebner, 'but advertisers would be willing to pay a lot of money to get that many eyeballs on a sponsored link, if they ever decided to go that way.'

'You seem to know a lot about it. For a technophobe,' said Maik flatly.

'Money is a great motivator to expand your horizons, Sergeant. You want to get a Yorkshireman's attention, speaking to him through his wallet is usually a good way to go about it.'

'Speaking of that, we're hearing things might be a little challenging for you these days, in terms of your personal finances.'

Huebner nodded slowly as he digested the sergeant's comment. 'Ah, that's where she's going, is it?' he said finally. 'The thing my partner may have failed to mention is that, as part of the plea deal I made, any future changes to the company structure would need to be approved by an oversight committee appointed by the government. If she was to die, especially under suspicious circumstances, the finances would be tied up so long I'd be lucky if they were released in time for my grandchildren to use as their retirement fund.'

There was enough sincerity in the response for the detectives to consider it seriously. 'Can I ask how you even learned about the fLIGHT research programme in the first place?' said Jejeune eventually.

'I asked Talia to look into it.'

'Which she told us she didn't do,' said Maik sharply. 'So how did you get to know all the ins and outs of it, you not being an internet kind of person and all?'

Huebner shifted his feet around to stand more squarely to Maik. 'Is there any point to all this, or is this just more flailing around because you've got nothing? Just like last time, and all the previous times you've come here throwing your weight around. It's bordering on harassment.'

'Do you want to call a lawyer?' asked Maik pleasantly. 'They might advise you to share your alibi with us and be done with it.'

Huebner shook his head. 'Waste of time. You wouldn't believe it anyway. And it wouldn't be corroborated.'

'Let us worry about that. Just point us in the right direction'

'Thanks all the same, but I think I'll save it in case I ever need it. Of course, unless you've got anything more on me, that won't happen. There won't be a single shred of evidence connecting me to this attack on you, Inspector.'

'Are you in touch with anybody from your childhood, Mr Huebner?'

It would have been hard to say who looked the most surprised at the question, but Maik at least had more practice in recovering from such non sequiturs. Huebner simply stared at Jejeune for a moment. 'I didn't really have many friends when I was growing up. A bit of a loner, I suppose. But feel free to have a look into my background if you like. After all, you haven't really got anything else going for you at the moment, have you? Must be a daunting task, trying to solve a case with so many challenges at every turn. Take this cheese wire business for example. You try and trace the source of that piece up at Talia's, you could spend the rest of your career on it. Somebody could even have ordered it online, had it delivered to a rented mailbox in somebody else's name and nobody would be any the wiser, would they? So I'm told, anyway. As I said, I'm a bit of a Luddite when it comes to all these ecommerce transactions, so perhaps I'm mistaken.' He offered them a cold smile.

'Well, I must be getting on. Those little fish out there aren't going to feed themselves. So unless there's anything else, gentlemen...'

'You know,' said Maik, returning the smile in kind. 'If I find out somebody has been less than honest with me, I just keep coming back until they decide to tell the truth.' He paused. 'That could mean we'd be seeing a lot of each other in the near future.'

'Oh, I don't think you'll be coming back,' Huebner told him frankly. 'Either of you. I told you, there are security implications over whoever leaked my name. The service aren't going to be content to let matters rest in the hands of a local police force, however competent they may be.' He flashed the men a mirthless grin.

'That's the second time you've suggested that,' said Jejeune. 'Is there any particular reason you think the authorities would be willing to close down an ongoing police investigation?'

Huebner shrugged. 'All I'm saying is they won't be too happy if you continue poking around where you shouldn't. And they might choose to do something about it.'

'Is that a threat, Mr Huebner?' asked Maik formally.

'Only to a policing career, I would have thought. But of course, if that's all a man has, that might be enough, mightn't it? Have a nice day, gentlemen. Goodbye.'

30

Lindy and Jejeune stopped on top of the rise to take in the scenery. The crisp, clean forms of the Euclid Lab glittered against the greenery that cascaded down the hillside from their vantage point and carpeted the valley below. On the far side of the buildings, more green-clad hills rose to the horizon.

'I don't know,' said Lindy, shaking her head. 'I understand the concept of the golden ratio, the beauty in its proportions and all that, but it does look like a bit of an eyesore when surrounded by all this natural vegetation. Don't you think so, Dom?'

Something had changed between them. They used to walk in easy silence, but now she seemed to feel the need to fill the voids with conversation. It was almost as if she was searching for some shared connection that had been lost, some reassurance that everything was still the same. 'So are we going to talk about it?' she asked suddenly.

'About what?'

'Johnno said you called to go over the events of that night.'

'Yes. I did.'

'But, curiously, he said you seemed to be asking him to recall the details in a backwards order.'

Jejeune said nothing. He continued staring out over the valley, in the direction of the Euclid Lab with its precise, perfectly defined lines.

'I remember you once told me that someone who is lying can't seamlessly reconstruct events in reverse order,' said Lindy. 'Not without a lot of practice, at least. It was all perfectly innocent, Dom, us being together. If you wanted to know why we were, why I came in his car to rescue you, all you had to do was ask me.'

'He said you just bumped into each other. That there was nothing to it.'

'There wasn't. It was all perfectly innocent.'

She'd said it twice now, the way people did when they meant something sincerely. Or wished they did.

'Dom, look at me. Do you trust me or not?'

'Do I have any reason not to?'

She shook her head and gave a bitter laugh. 'The preferred answer there, Inspector Jejeune, might have been *Yes, Lindy. I trust you completely*. Oh Dom, even somebody as utterly thick as you are must know how I feel about you.'

He thought he did, once. But lately, with this shadow of discontent that had been lying between them, perhaps he wasn't so sure any more. 'You just seem to have been so unhappy lately. I know I haven't been around much. It's this investigation, there are just so many things going on with it, inside and outside the case. But it will be over soon, I think.'

'Do you?'

'I'm getting closer to understanding what happened. And once it's done, we'll go away, Lindy. I promise. Somewhere nice, for a long break. And no birding.'

But even his wan smile that had dried tears and forced grudging smiles in the past failed to land with Lindy today.

'We'll see,' she said in a voice heavy with resignation. She sighed. 'You know that thing where people say, *It's not you, it's me*, but really they mean it is you, after all. Please believe me when I tell you it's not you, Dom. I should be happy. I know that. I have a great partner, a lovely home, everything. But I can't find any contentment in that any more. And I'm not sure what I do about that.' She wanted to reassure him, but at the same time to tell him what was truly in her heart. And the two messages were irreconcilable. 'I'm not ungrateful, Dom,' she said finally. 'Really I'm not. I'm just... I don't know, restless, I suppose.'

Restless as in no longer ready to let their relationship drift along aimlessly, she meant. But that wasn't a conversation he could have at this time. Not with everything else that was going on. And yet he knew that if he shut her down now, she would never speak to him about it again. And that would change things between them for ever. Salvation came in the form of the woman dressed in a PPE outfit standing at the top of the rise, bent over her monitoring station.

'I should talk to Katie Fairfax,' said Jejeune. 'I need to apologise for what happened at the station.'

'She looks busy,' said Lindy. 'Maybe we should talk more about us.' There seemed to be a kind of panic in her eyes, as if she was afraid, perhaps, of losing the moment.

'Five minutes, that's all,' said Jejeune and began walking towards Fairfax. Lindy followed reluctantly, but quickened her pace as they approached, so she arrived a step ahead of him.

'Long time, no see,' she said, flashing her eyes wide.

Fairfax looked behind her, puzzled. 'No dog again?'

It was Jejeune's turn for a quizzical expression. 'Again?'

'Like last time.' Fairfax looked at Lindy and saw a kind of alarm in her eyes.

'I thought you said Truth was here?' said Jejeune, turning to Lindy. 'You said you'd taken footage of him with those chicks.'

Finally, Katie recognised in Lindy's eyes the universal appeal from one woman to another for protection from a man. 'Of course he was here,' she said. 'Cute dog,' she added weakly.

'I just wanted to tell you we're not all in a confederacy against you. Or any other geniuses,' said Jejeune, hoping the light touch would find a more receptive audience in Fairfax than it had with Lindy.

She nodded. 'Ever hear of the Dunning–Kruger effect? People with limited competence in a particular domain tend to overestimate their abilities. I'd say your DCS might be a candidate. Anyway, thank you for not mentioning the fact that Sampson had identified Marius Huebner to me. It would have made the situation so much worse if he'd been aware of that.'

Jejeune smiled nonchalantly, but Lindy stood beside him in stunned silence. Withholding evidence like this from Laraby must surely be compromising their investigation. Was Dom's desire to defeat Laraby so strong it was even beginning to cloud his judgement?

A Lapwing fluttered to the ground near them and began dragging its wing. 'Ah, you're not fooling me this time,' said Lindy. 'I know your game, trying to distract us from your babies.' She looked around but could see no sign of the chicks. 'I wonder where they are.'

Jejeune watched the bird for a moment. 'It takes a lot of effort for her to put on a display like that,' he said. 'The chicks can't be far away, if she's willing to continue performing it like this.'

'I feel so sorry for her,' said Fairfax, shaking her head. 'Going to all that trouble to put on a performance everybody already knows is a sham.' She turned her attention back to the monitoring station. 'Could I ask you to step back while I replace these filters. I'd like to minimise the risk of contamination as much as possible.'

Lindy and Jejeune shuffled back and watched as she donned latex gloves to remove a container the size and shape of an ice-cube tray and set it carefully beside the monitor. Methodically, she withdrew a series of golf-ball-sized filters and set them in the tray before sliding it into an insulated bag and zipping it shut. Then she reversed the process, using new filers from a second tray in another bag to replace those she had removed. Finally, she recalibrated the gauges and reset the dials. Only when she had completed the process did she peel off her gloves and look up at them again.

'Welcome to my alibi,' she said. 'This is what I was doing the night Sampson died, the procedure Laraby tried to imply any idiot could do.' She shook her head. 'You know that DCS of yours is never going find the killer if he's so hell-bent on proving it was me. And just because he couldn't pin it on me this time doesn't mean he's lost interest. We both know I'm always going to be top of his suspect list unless I take action to clear myself.'

'I'd strongly advise you against investigating anything on your own,' said Jejeune.

'Oh, I'm not going to do anything dangerous. But I do think there may be a way these eDNA samples might shed more light on what happened up here that night.' She looked at Jejeune. 'Can I ask you a hypothetical question?'

It was Jejeune's experience that when people asked hypothetical questions they weren't usually looking for hypothetical answers, but it was clear Fairfax was going to ask anyway. 'At the moment, the field of eDNA falls into a really vague, undefined area of law. Would it have any validity, legally, if I tried to use evidence from these samples to clear myself of suspicion in this case?'

Jejeune shook his head. 'It's impossible to say until it has been tested in court.'

'I suppose what I'm getting at is, if these data are not going to be admissible in the first place, I don't need to hand them over. If it's not evidence, then I can't be charged with withholding it, can I? I mean, not even that Neanderthal Laraby can have it both ways.'

'Are you saying these filters might hold evidence that could clear you?'

'It's nothing more than an idea I have, at the moment. But I intend to run further analysis on the filters from around the time Sampson was killed to see if they can tell me anything.'

Jejeune thought back to his exchange with Laraby on the subject earlier. 'To be clear, there is no credible research anywhere out there to suggest a human being can be identified from the eDNA samples collected by these filters, is there? The researcher in Canada...'

'Dr Leclair.' Fairfax nodded her head firmly. 'She's been unequivocal from the beginning in stating that you're never going to be able to identify an individual from the DNA collected this way. An airborne DNA sample collected through our filters might only yield a hundred base pairs. The entire human genome has about three billion. That's an unbridgeable gap. To have any chance of identifying an individual, you would need vast multiples of the amounts of DNA we collect, in longer, intact strands. Using this method, at best you'd be able to ID it as coming from the human species.'

'But you still intend to analyse the samples further?'

Fairfax seemed to realise that to say anything more might invite questions she was unwilling to answer at this time. 'Don't worry. If I do come up with anything I think could be useful to your investigation, I'll be in touch.'

'That would be the way to do it,' said Jejeune. He handed her his card and turned to Lindy. 'We should be going.'

'You go on,' she told him. 'I'll catch up.'

She watched Jejeune walk away before turning to Fairfax. 'Thanks,' she said. 'For not saying anything. It's all innocent, but, I don't know, somehow it just wouldn't seem that way.' Why did she feel this need to explain to a stranger? If her last stroll up here with Johnno was as innocent as she claimed, why was it necessary to justify it?

But if Fairfax sensed Lindy's internal conflict, she seemed unbothered by it. She shrugged. 'It happens.' She looked across at Jejeune, standing now at a distance with his back to them. 'He seems like one of the good ones, but really, these days, it's just so hard to tell, isn't it?'

'I'm so sorry for your loss,' said Lindy. 'It's been overlooked a little bit in all this. I thought it wouldn't hurt to let you know someone has noticed.'

Fairfax nodded her thanks, unable to find words. Her eyes misted over. 'The last time I saw him,' she said quietly, 'it was here.' For a fleeting moment, the time revisited her; the sharp lines of the Euclid Lab carving through the valley, the Nightjars flying over the hill, their churring calls as soft as the approaching twilight. 'We argued. We fought. And I never saw him again.' She shook her head. 'We never would have lasted. The relationship was already coming apart at the seams. The kind of work we do, it demands everything of you. But still, I miss him. And I regret the way things ended.'

From a small tussock of grass beside them, the female Lapwing uttered a faint peep, and together they watched as the bird shuffled into a resting position, fluffing its feathers around it and tucking its head under its wing. 'Looks like she's all done with her performances for another day,' said Katie.

But Lindy didn't smile. She could understand why the bird had settled in to rest. The business of deceit could be so exhausting.

31

It was perfect. Not a formal setting, with Laraby still at the front of the Incident Room having just dismissed the assembled troops, or seated behind the desk in his office, looking up at Salter's hesitant knock before summoning her in, but this, a casual encounter in the hallway, with the DCS studiously perusing the drinks on offer from the vending machine and her the only other person in sight. Until Tony bloody Holland swung round the corner and spoiled everything.

'All good?' he said, misinterpreting her look of frustration as contempt.

'Yeah, fine.'

Laraby looked up at their exchange. 'Everything all right between you two?' he asked. The uncomfortable beat of silence told him he wasn't going to get an answer, and he turned his attention to the machine. He settled on a bottle of water, hitting the selection buttons in a way that suggested he might resent the amount the machine was charging for it.

'Tech have something,' said Holland. 'They have uncovered evidence from Lee's laptop that a file was deleted shortly before he sent the podcaster that email.'

The unopened bottle dangled from Laraby's hand, forgotten. 'Do they have any idea what it was?'

'The file folder is empty now but it looks like a document was transferred from a hard drive. Only, they have no way of knowing what was on it.'

'Surely Tech can recover deleted files, can't they, Constable?'

'Yes sir, they can. But when they retrieved this one, it was blank.'

'Blank?'

'It was a Word doc but it had no words on it. The text had been erased before the file was saved. The tech bloke said the delete button is not the most devastating weapon on a computer keyboard. It's the backspace key. Once the text itself has been erased and the file is saved, there's no way to recover it, unless there are earlier versions saved to the cloud.' He paused. 'There weren't.'

'So they have no idea what that file was, then?'

'They don't, but I do. If Lee was working on something extracurricular, as Chandra claims, that could well have been it.'

'And you think he managed to get it out on a hard drive despite all that security?' asked Salter.

'There was no hard drive on Lee's body, nor at the house or his place of work,' said Laraby. 'So let's see if we can find it. I want a sweep of all of Lee's known locations, including a fingertip search of the area around the monitoring station.'

'We'll need clearance for that,' Holland told them. 'There's a nest of young birds right at the base of it. Environmental ops will have to sanction it.'

'Shouldn't be a problem, though,' said Salter. 'They're only Lapwings. I don't think they're especially rare or protected or anything like that.'

'Thank God for that,' said Laraby, remembering his water finally and unscrewing the lid to take a drink. 'Want something?' he asked them both. 'The coffee's a lot better here than at Saltmarsh, I'm happy to say. You can't underestimate the value of morale in a department.'

The comment fell flat. The blank expressions on the officers' faces suggested that there might be a bit more to teamwork than a good cup of coffee. 'Anything more on that business with the tyre?' the DCS asked into the awkward silence that had descended over the group. 'Any prints on the wheel or the jack?'

Holland shook his head. 'Nothing. I wouldn't mind making a collar in that one soon, though. I could use the time off.'

Laraby looked perplexed. 'Time off?'

Holland nodded. 'It's all there in the Employee Handbook, sir. According to the Health and Wellness section, I'm entitled to a minimum of ninety days medical leave after a car-jack arrest.' He raised his hands. 'Thank you, ladies and gentlemen. I'll get that application into Enviro for the fingertip search.'

Laraby turned to Salter as Holland turned the corner, and shook his head. 'I can't help it. I like the lad.'

Salter's expression suggested he should perhaps try harder. Holland's jokey interruption hadn't made what she needed to do now any easier.

'So how's everything with you, Sergeant?' asked Laraby.

'Yeah, fine, yeah.' Her willingness to linger in his presence might have suggested he could revert to calling her Lauren, but he had clearly decided to pass on the opportunity for now. She was relieved not to have to correct any misconceptions before she got to what she needed to.

'And Max, still football mad, is he?'

'Norwich City crazy. Worse than ever,' she said.

He nodded. 'Danny'll steer him straight. He's a good man. He's right for you. I'm glad for the both of you.'

'How about you?'

'It's all about work for me now,' said Laraby, taking another sip of his water. 'You don't rise up to this level without putting in the hours. It's a choice you make, isn't it? There wasn't anybody after I left Saltmarsh. I just kept it that way.'

Meaning she'd been the last romantic interest in his life. This wasn't going to get any easier. She decided to act before it got worse. 'Sir, there's something we need to talk about.'

'Concerning the case?'

Her silence answered him. He looked up and down the empty corridor. 'About us?'

She shook her head. 'The check-up call on DCI Jejeune. Some of us thought it was a bit early. He'd only been out there a couple of hours.'

'Turns out it was just as well I made it, though, wouldn't you say?'

She didn't return his smile. 'It's just... well, it suggests you knew something was wrong. Or at least suspected it.'

It was Laraby's turn for silence. He took a long drink from his water bottle.

'Nobody thinks you're to blame for what happened, obviously, but he was there at your direction. Only, if you did think he was going to be in danger, it sort of begs the question as to why you'd have sent him out there in the first place.' She paused again, but it was clear Laraby wasn't going to meet her halfway.

'Is there a point coming any time soon, Sergeant Salter?' he asked formally.

'Sir, your source, at MI5. How sure are you about them?'

Laraby stared at her.

'It seems to us they must have been the one to tip you off that Jejeune was in trouble. Only, how did they know? Did they follow him? Did you tell them where he was going? Did they suggest it, even?'

'Even if they did, they weren't the ones responsible for the attack on DCI Jejeune,' he said firmly. 'It was somebody who didn't want him sniffing around that Euclid Lab.'

'Sir, those Lapwing birds up near the monitoring station, they have this trick of feigning an injury to lead people away from their nest. All I'm saying is, the direction they want to take you, it's not the one you should be going.'

'And just who is this *us*, Lauren? Exactly how many at the station think I'm being led down the garden path here?'

'Nobody has said anything about you being manipulated or misled by your source, sir. I give you my word.'

'No, but they're thinking it, right? Why would MI5 deal with a muppet like me, instead of the service's golden boy?'

'DCI Jejeune knows nothing about this line of inquiry.'

'What line of inquiry is that, then?'

Salter sighed resignedly. 'Danny went through some old contacts at Thames House. Nobody was willing to give up the name of your contact. They denied knowing anything about an officer being assigned to act as liaison for the police.'

Laraby gave a short, contemptuous laugh. 'You'd hardly expect them to say otherwise, would you?'

'Danny knows a bit about them. They suggest you collaborate, so you give them everything you've got. Only anything they give back will already have the important stuff redacted before you ever get to see it. Any information you receive will be designed to take you where they want you to go, regardless if it's the right direction or not.'

'He knows all about them, does he, Danny?'

'He said your contact probably wouldn't even tell you their name. It's not you, sir, it's the way they operate.'

'Yeah, well, he's not always right. For one thing, I've got these.' He pointed to the DCS pips on his collar. 'And the respect that comes with them.' He shook his head. 'I can't give you that name, Sergeant Salter. Sorry.'

'We just want to be sure your source is acting in the investigation's best interests, sir. That person put the DCI in harm's way, whether it was intentional or not. Whatever personal issues you might have with Jejeune, we do have a duty of care to him, the same as if he was a private citizen. More, even. He's one of us. If there are people out there looking to do him harm, we need to know who we're dealing with.' She paused and shrugged. 'But if you can't find out the name, you can't.'

'I don't need to find out,' said Laraby his voice rising angrily. He lowered it again and looked up and down the empty corridor. 'I didn't say they hadn't shared their name with me. I said I couldn't reveal it. I am bound by the Official Secrets Act.'

'Ah, well, I suppose that's it then. Even if you wanted to help protect the DCI from another attack, you can't.'

'I told you, I know who I'm dealing with. And I am completely confident that they are acting in good faith. This conversation is over.'

He finished his drink and looked around for somewhere to put the empty bottle. It was a moment before he looked back to her.

'The thing is, sir, even though those Lapwings up on the hill are trying to lead you away, you can be sure of one thing. They aren't taking you into any danger. We just wanted to be able to say the same about your contact. I understand, though. It's out of your hands. You're powerless to do anything.'

Laraby scrutinised her intently, and for a moment she wondered if she'd pushed it too far. For all his faults, the DCS was no fool, and he had spent a career dealing with people who were being less than honest with him. He seemed to weigh his options for a moment.

'Do me a favour, Sergeant. On your way past my office, pop in and check that I closed the lid on my laptop. I have a nasty habit of leaving it open sometimes. Who knows what somebody might see. No need to report back to me. If the laptop is closed when I get back to the office, I'll know everything is safe and sound.'

He crushed the water bottle in his powerful hands and threw it in the recycling can as he headed off down the corridor, in the opposite direction to his office.

Maik picked up the phone on the first ring.

'You're buying dinner,' Salter told him, 'and you're not getting away with fish and chips from that place on the seafront at Wells, either.'

'I take it you got the name of Laraby's source.'

Lauren liked a bit of a production before a big announcement, so he was expecting a dramatic pause. He wasn't disappointed.

'Karla Imogen Montgomery,' she announced finally.

'Can't say I'd like to write that name out on a charge sheet too many times,' said Danny.

'That's probably why she tends to go by her initials. K.I.M. Kim.'

32

Johnno emerged from the kitchen in his London flat carrying two mugs of tea.

'Builder's?' Jejeune tried to keep his voice as neutral as possible. Enthusiasm was out of the question. He took the proffered mug, looking on it as the price of visiting the man who believed he had saved his life. The two men crossed to the window as before to take in the views over the city. Jejeune chose to study the garland of painted flowers round the window instead.

'This painting...'

Johnno nodded. 'Lin. And the one round the doorway there. As soon as she moved in she wanted to spruce the place up a bit. She said it looked like the waiting room of a bus depot.' He grinned. 'She probably wasn't wrong.'

Jejeune stared at the flower paintings thoughtfully. Lindy had proposed doing something similar in their first place, he remembered. Catching sight of his expression, she'd said it didn't matter, and had abandoned the idea. How many other compromises had she made, he wondered, how many other plans had she shelved to fit her life into theirs? Into his?

'So nothing special on the agenda today then, Domenic?' Johnno made a point of looking at Jejeune to gauge his answer.

'Not really. I just wanted to thank you properly. In person. Now that I've recovered.'

'It was nothing. Only glad I could be there to help.' Johnno took a sip of tea. As impossible as it seemed to Jejeune, he actually appeared to enjoy it. 'No thoughts on who it could have been who attacked you?'

Perhaps he had some, said Jejeune's silence, but he wasn't sharing them.

'Definitely connected to the case you're working on, though, you think? The Lee murder?'

Jejeune took a moment to look out over the glittering urban landscape. Stories galore waited out there; for a podcaster, or a journalist feeling a bit restless and dissatisfied with her life. One more thing Lindy had given up to be with him out in the rural wilderness of north Norfolk. 'The email you received from Lee, were you expecting it?'

Johnno shook his head uncertainly. 'When we'd spoken in the past, I was pretty sure he was going to go ahead and release the name, but he had shown some doubts towards the end.' He shrugged. 'I'd been clear in my previous podcast that there was always the possibility I wouldn't be able to reveal the name in the end, so when he hadn't come through when the time came to record my new one, I decided to dedicate the whole thing to how tricky it was to deal with unreliable and reluctant sources. And then, about an hour before it was due to go out, in comes the email. I had to spend the next hour frantically re-recording the entire thing. I barely got it done in time to stream it.'

'What happened to the old podcast? Did you erase it?'

'No, I have a copy of it around here somewhere. I can't see why you'd need it, but it's yours if you want it.'

Jejeune shook his head. 'That won't be necessary.' The tech department had already verified that Johnno's podcast had gone out from this IP address; the same one Lee's email had come in to. 'I was just wondering if that previous podcast also discussed the dangers of revealing something somebody wants to remain hidden.'

'Not in so many words, but a future one might. I'd probably advise my listeners to consider the implications before releasing that kind of information, sure.'

'Did you? Consider them?'

'Of course. My own brand is fearless, not foolish. I mean, Marius Heubner is a dangerous man. People who cross him tend to run into some serious bad luck somewhere down the road.'

'So you knew him?'

'I've never met him in person. I wouldn't want to get that close.' He nodded. 'But, yeah, I recognised the name.'

Jejeune asked to see the email again. 'Unless you've already deleted it.'

Johnno raised his eyebrows. 'I don't think your DCS would be too happy about that, do you?' He reached for his tablet and called up the email. Jejeune nodded as he read. 'It has an umlaut. It's the legal spelling, as it would have been on the official transcript from the hearing. Had you ever seen that spelling before?'

Johnno thought for a moment. 'You know, I can't recall ever having seen the name written at all, but, as I say, I'd heard it. Is it important?'

'If Lee wanted you to reveal it, you'd think he might have gone with the normal spelling, just to be sure you got the pronunciation right. Not everybody would know how to pronounce a "u" with an umlaut. He didn't.'

Johnno tilted his head. 'Fair point, I suppose, but with or without an umlaut I was going to know who he was talking about. I mean, let's face it – *Marius Hübbner, Marius Huebner, north Norfolk land developer.* It wasn't going to be a coincidence, was it?' He looked impressed. 'Umlauts? Pronunciations – jeez, Domenic, that's top-drawer stuff. Lin was right, you really are pulling out all the stops on this one.' He levelled his tone to sincerity. 'She's sure you'll solve it, you know. She says you'll stay with it, no matter what it takes, until you have. But just make sure you know the cost of doing so, that's all. I know about Laraby, a little. Lin has explained. That kind of pressure, the feeling you have to prove yourself, believe me, I get it. But just be careful not to sideline Lin in the process. The rest of the group, Maik, Salter, that constable, they seem competent enough. Surely you can leave some of the heavy lifting to them. Your relationship is something great. Don't sacrifice it just to prove something to Laraby. You find the right one, you need to hold on tight.' He paused and offered a smile to relieve the intensity. 'Listen to me, sounding like I know what I'm talking about. Okay, here endeth the relationship lesson for the day. How's that tea? You need a top-up?'

The trilling of Jejeune's phone saved him from having to cast around for an excuse.

'Hey you. What's new?' Lindy's voice was filled with the kind of light enthusiasm he hadn't heard for days.

'Not much. How about you?'

'Me? I've just had a big story come my way, that's what.' It wasn't possible to tell if Johnno could hear Lindy's voice from where he was standing but, if Jejeune was going to continue the call, there seemed to be no way he could avoid telling the other man who it was. 'Lindy,' he mouthed.

Johnno nodded in understanding and moved over to take in the view from the window again.

'Well, that's great news,' said the detective, watching him go. 'Can you tell me what it is?'

'Only that Katie Fairfax is wondering whether you had any more idea as to whether the police might accept the filters from the day of the murder as evidence.'

'Has she figured out a way they can tell her something? You need to advise her she's required to take them to the police if she has, Lindy.'

'She says no. But she's on to something, Dom. I could hear it in her voice. And she wants me to have the story when she gets it.'

He flashed a look over to Johnno. There seemed to be little point in trying to keep anything from him now. He would have already been able to piece together the gist of the conversation from Jejeune's own contributions. 'Lindy, this is not the story for you. Tell Katie Fairfax she needs to get the police involved. Even informally. I'll chat to her myself, if she wants.'

'Oh no,' said Lindy playfully. 'You're not taking this one away from me, Mister. If anything comes of this, she will contact the police, I'll make sure of it. But for now, the background, her thinking, how she plans to go about collecting and using the filters, that's all mine. I just wanted to share my good news with you. Where are you, anyway?'

I'm standing in the living room of the flat you used to share with your ex-lover, looking at flowers you painted on the wall. Johnno had his eyes averted, but Jejeune had the impression that somehow he knew what she had just asked. He ignored the question. 'Lindy, I don't want you to pursue this. It's too dangerous. Somebody has already been murdered. Let this one go.'

'I can't do that, Dom. I need it.'

'I know it means a lot to you, but there will be other stories coming, good stories. Big stories.'

'No, Dom, there won't. Not like this. This one has the potential to be huge. I can't let it pass me by.' She sighed sadly. 'I called you because I wanted you to be happy for me, maybe offer to take me out to that Italian place to celebrate my good fortune. But it seems like that was too much to ask. I have to go.'

'Lindy, wait...' But he spoke into the dead air of a terminated call.

'She's onto a story?' asked Johnno. He shrugged. 'Sorry, I couldn't help but overhear. Good for her. I told her something would pop up sooner or later. It always does.'

'I wish it hadn't been this one. She could be putting herself in danger if she follows it.'

'We both know she's never going to let something like that stop her.'

Jejeune looked around the flat, and out the window beyond, at all the things Lindy had given up, unbidden, to be a part of his life. Did he have the right to ask her to give this up, too, even for her own safety?

Johnno answered the question for him. 'You need to let her pursue this one, Dom. Watch her, by all means, keep her safe. But let her do it. Maybe that will be enough to settle her, to quell all this restlessness in her. I hope it will. For both your sakes.'

Was that reason enough, wondered Jejeune, to allow her to put herself in so much danger? No, it wasn't. He would do anything to protect her, and if that meant stopping her from following this story then he would do that, too. He took one last brave swig of the tea, then handed Johnno the mug. 'In case we don't meet again,' he said, 'what you did, that night at the lab. I won't forget it. Thank you again.'

Johnno smiled, but this time he didn't dismiss it as nothing. Both men knew that it was far more than that.

33

According to Danny Maik, Detective Chief Inspector Domenic Jejeune was back. Perhaps not fighting fit and firing on all cylinders yet, but sharp enough to match wits with Marius Huebner and come out unscathed. Holland was looking forward to what he might make of Amit Chandra, somebody who also fancied himself as a bit of an intellectual heavyweight. He was going to have a front-row seat for this bout. He wished he had brought popcorn.

'I'm telling you, sir,' he said as the two men approached the glass cube that was the Euclid Lab, 'they're not what you'd expect, this maths crowd. Not a pocket protector between them. Just a whole lot of jealousies and betrayals and deep-seated passions. It's a bit disappointing in a way; all that intelligence and learning and they are really no different to the rest of us. Cleverer, perhaps, but still just as flawed. Makes you wonder about human nature as a whole, doesn't it?'

It was a curious remark, and Jejeune looked at him.

'Sir, all this time we're spending up at KL. I think the DCS is beginning to take a bit of a shine to me. If I asked for a transfer, it's not impossible he'd agree.'

Jejeune stopped short. 'Is there a reason you'd want to?

'It's just taking a bit of getting used to, working under Sergeant Salter.'

Jejeune waited.

'She blindsided me recently. Over Ishtara. Okay, she may have needed to get somewhere with her, and she knew how I felt about her, but it's not the way Danny would have gone about it if he was still my sergeant. It's not the first time either. She hung me out to dry over something else recently, too.'

Jejeune shrugged. 'Have you talked to her about it?'

Holland nodded. 'A bit, yeah. And then I walk in on her and Laraby in a corridor, and I get treated to a look that says she can't wait to get shot of me.' He shrugged. 'You know what, forget I said anything. I'm just a bit restless, I suppose, with all this moving and changing happening and me stuck not going anywhere. New sergeant, new rules, I guess. It was just the appeal of reconnecting with Sergeant Maik. But you can never go back, can you, sir? Things are never going to be the same.'

'No, Constable,' said Jejeune. 'They're not.' He just hoped other people he knew had the wisdom to see that, too. 'So what can you tell me about the people we're about to interview?'

'Well, Chandra might think this story about Lee's secret programme has got him off the hook, but as far as I'm concerned he still has plenty of reason to kill Lee.' He smiled. 'For a clever bloke, if he did it, offering up yet another motive like that would suggest he certainly isn't the smartest of villains.'

'And Ishtara Habloun?'

'She had reason to be aggrieved with Lee,' said Holland, 'and no alibi. And she did lie to us, by omission at least. But' – he shook his head – 'the ones who've done something wrong, they know why you're coming for them. She might be hiding something, but she had no idea she was being looked at for murder.'

'So she's either innocent, or very good at pretending to be?' asked Jejeune. 'There's a romantic link between them, I understand.'

'Chandra seems infatuated with Ishtara, but I don't think the feeling is mutual. Definitely a one-way connection, I'd say.'

Jejeune nodded. Sometimes, his small smile seemed to say, one way is all it takes. 'This might not look like it's going to be too productive at first, Constable, but stay with me and let's see where things go.'

And instead of blindsiding somebody, thought Holland, that was exactly how you did it.

They entered the bright, white lobby to find Ishtara Habloun and Amit Chandra waiting for them. The man's scowl was uninviting, but Jejeune could see how Holland might have trouble remaining objective in the face of a beguiling smile like the one Ishtara was offering them.

'I wonder if we could have this meeting up in the connecting kitchen area,' said Jejeune cordially. 'I'd like to see the layout, if you don't mind.'

'Sure,' said Ishtara. 'I can make us all some tea.'

'Oh, I don't think there's any need to go to all that trouble,' said Holland quickly.

'It's not builder's, is it?' asked Jejeune, picking up on Holland's reluctance.

'Builders? I don't know what that is,' said Ishtara, looking puzzled. 'It's Babylonian. I'm sure you'll like it. Amit, in particular, really enjoys it.'

The four of them trooped up the stairs into the kitchen area. Jejeune inspected the digital retina-scanning devices on both adjoining doors and nodded approvingly.

'As secure as it gets, Inspector,' said Chandra. 'Neither we nor Katie can gain entry to the other's lab space. Just as the uni wants it now.'

Jejeune approached the fridge with the metal strap fastened across it. 'Katie Fairfax's air filter samples are stored in here, presumably,' he said. He opened a small cabinet next to the fridge. 'And the empty trays and new filters are kept in here.' He nodded again, like someone trying to commit it all to memory. Holland watched silently as Jejeune made his way round the room. His DCI was right about the visit not seeming too productive. Yet.

Jejeune turned to take in the view through the large, plate glass window. 'Excellent views of the hilltop from here.'

'Yeah,' said Ishtara as she busied herself with the tea-making. 'A bit too good. A raised corridor like this, suspended between two buildings, with a plate glass window this size, it could be an absolute kill zone for flying birds. When I pointed it out, the uni offered to go with film or silhouettes on the windows, but they are woefully ineffective.'

The DCI nodded. 'Best practice in Canada seems to be what you have here, a matrix of dots spaced at two-inch intervals.'

'We are having a lot of success with it. Our bird strike rates are way down. And now that we've trialled it here, I'm hopeful they will approve it for the rest of the building. I've told them if they want to keep their BREEAM certification, it's the only way. A building is not truly sustainable until it is as bird friendly as it can possibly be. After that, who knows – maybe the university as a whole can get on board.'

'And the uni will stand for that, will they?' asked Holland, subtly declining Ishtara's offer of tea with a hand gesture. 'All that added expense?'

'It's been calculated that over thirty million birds a year are killed by colliding with buildings in the UK alone,' said Ishtara. 'If we can prevent even some small percentage of those deaths it's still a huge number of birds saved. All through a few tiny dots that nobody even really notices after a couple of days.'

Jejeune looked out through the large window again. 'You have a perfect view of the monitoring station from this vantage point.' He turned to Chandra. 'Is this where you saw the argument between Katie and Sampson Lee?'

The man nodded. 'But I don't think we can tell you any more about that than we've already told the constable here and the other officer.' He looked at Ishtara. 'Or anything else to do with the case, really.'

'Then perhaps I can tell you what I think,' said Jejeune pleasantly. He turned back to Ishtara. 'That any envelope with sensitive data inside would have been put into the mail tray by you. To heap more suspicion on Sampson Lee.'

She stepped back a pace. 'What?'

'Deliberately attempting to implicate someone else in wrongdoing is a crime, Ms Habloun. You can be charged for it.'

'No, no. None of this is true. I didn't do it.'

Holland stood by silently. He was surprised, but the DCI's warning was still in the back of his mind.

'Ishtara is innocent,' said Chandra. 'You've got this all wrong. She didn't do this. I can one hundred per cent guarantee it.'

'See, that's the second time you've given us an assurance like that, Amit,' said Holland. 'But as I see it, there's only two ways you can be that sure. One is if you put that envelope in the courier box yourself, which we know isn't the case since you were being interviewed by the campus security at the time. And the other would be if you were with Ishtara at that time, which we can eliminate for the same reason.'

'No, Constable,' said Jejeune quietly, 'there is a third way to be sure. And that's if it didn't happen at all. There was no envelope, was there? And the break-in didn't occur, either, did it?'

Holland nodded slowly in understanding. 'No wonder Lee denied leaving those doors unlocked.' He shook his head. So they had all got it completely wrong then, himself included. The part they had rejected at first, that Lee had stolen material from the other researchers, had been true all along. It was the reports of the break-in and the attempted leak of Ishtara's work, which they had accepted without question, that turned out to be the lies. But, as with his earlier warning, Jejeune knew the right way to go about things. Holland doubted the earlier errors in judgement would ever be referred to again.

'You asked Ishtara to lie about the envelope to help ensure the new security measures would be put in place,' said Jejeune, staying with the friendly, conversational tone he had used throughout. 'You wanted the security to be so tight Lee couldn't get that program out.'

'I didn't force Ishtara to lie,' said Chandra. 'She agreed to say it.' He looked appealingly at Jejeune. 'Sampson was risking everything we're doing here. If the university had found out someone was working on a private venture, consuming their resources, their technology, and using stolen intellectual property to do it, they would have shut down the entire project.'

'What Sampson was doing threatened all the promise our work holds for the future,' said Ishtara. 'These programs represent the final phase of a multi-generational approach to environmental research, you see. The first phase, back in the early days, was accumulating the information, the knowledge of migration patterns, of bird behaviour. It told us what we still needed to know, what we had to measure. In the next phase, we developed the technology to gather that data and analyse what it was telling us. What we are doing here now, developing the mechanical learning and predictive algorithms, will allow us to know how and where to apply the knowledge we have. It's the kind of information we need to effect real change, to intervene while there is still time to make a difference. It was all this that Sampson was putting at risk through his actions.'

'You know what I notice most when I receive those images from the satellites, Inspector,' said Chandra. 'It's the dark, curved spaces at the top of them. They remind me that the photograph is of a planet, our home, all alone out there in space. But not just our home; that of all the other species, too. I couldn't stand around and watch their continued existence being put at more risk over one man's selfishness. We just thought if we made it impossible for Lee to get his program out of the facility he would simply abandon working on it and focus on the blue carbon study again.'

'But he didn't, did he? And he did manage to get that program out of here somehow. There was evidence on his computer that a Word file had been downloaded from a hard drive.'

The researchers looked at each other in shock. 'How is that possible? The security here is airtight now.'

'Could he have committed it to memory?' asked Holland. 'I mean, you lot don't have to check your brains in at the door, do you?'

Amit looked incredulous. 'Are you serious? Whatever it was, it would have been far too complex to commit to memory. Lee didn't have the mental capacity required for that. It's not like he was some kind of Clifford Cocks, for God's sake.'

'Who's Clifford Cocks?' asked Holland.

'A former GCHQ employee,' said Chandra. 'He was actually the first to develop the Diffie–Hellman algorithm I was telling you about.'

'Only he did it a long time before them,' continued Ishtara. 'When he first joined GCHQ he was told they were trying to develop a system for the secure exchange of cryptographic keys. A team had been working on the problem for years without success. Cocks went home that night and thought about it, and he came in the next day with a solution.'

'But very few people have that kind of mental processing capability,' said Chandra, 'and Lee certainly wasn't one of them. If he got that program out of here, it wasn't by memorising it.'

Ishtara turned to Jejeune. 'You said he had it on a Word file,' she said. 'That doesn't sound right. A program involving predictive algorithms of the kind he stole from Amit would take up dozens of pages, possibly hundreds. It's not how I'd choose to save a sophisticated software program.'

Jejeune looked at Chandra. 'You're certain you have no idea what it was he was working on.'

'None at all.' He turned to Ishtara. 'Neither of us. But it almost certainly wouldn't have involved a Word doc. It's hard to see an application for predictive analytics in a language-based program. Especially a program of that size.'

'Yes,' agreed Jejeune thoughtfully. 'It is, isn't it?' He drained his tea and offered Ishtara the cup. 'Thank you for your time. We'll show ourselves out.'

'Inspector,' called Chandra as the detectives turned to leave. 'Lee's program, whatever it is. If it got out into a commercial market and it became known that it was developed here illegally, it would still threaten the future of our research.'

'It hasn't surfaced yet,' said Jejeune. And to Holland, the DCI's tone suggested that it wasn't likely to.

34

Danny Maik was sitting in his Mini just down the road from a nondescript townhouse when his phone rang. Reluctantly, he turned down the volume of the song he was listening to, consigning Brenda Holloway to whisper 'Every Little Bit Hurts' to herself while he chatted to Lauren Salter.

'Anything happening?'

'Not yet,' said Maik.

'Do you feel like you're on a proper spy mission?' asked Salter with a laugh.

'If you mean one that's boring, uncomfortable and probably unproductive, then I suppose so.'

'So it wouldn't be for you then, a life in the service?'

'I'd have a hard time coming to terms with the choices they'd ask me to make.' Danny had been around long enough to recognise that compromises were inevitable, but that didn't mean he was going to scale back on his own efforts to bring the guilty parties to justice. He was happy enough leaving decisions about what happened to them afterwards to people higher up the chain of command.

'Well, boring or not, just be careful out there. Remember what I said.'

Right after she had revealed the woman's name to him in that previous call, she meant. According to her file, their target tended to go off script at times. But in her last couple of cases, that approach hadn't worked so well. She had not been given a sanctioned op since. Danny had received the information in silence. And there was one more thing, as Salter had put it in a cautionary tone at the end of the call. 'Danny, those last two failed ops. They both involved loss of life.'

The front door of the house opened and a woman came out and climbed into a small grey Kia. 'Okay, activity,' said Maik, stirring forward in his seat.

'Now remember, you're just going to follow her and see where she goes. With any luck she'll be meeting somebody. But no heroics. Promise me, Danny. She'll be good at what she does if she works for MI5. And if it was her who set up Jejeune, she is dangerous.'

Maik nodded to himself. If the information in that file was right, she was more than just dangerous. She was under pressure, and, like any person with nothing left to lose, that made her unpredictable. Ruthlessness, volatility and desperation. It wasn't a great combination in any suspect, let alone a highly trained intelligence operative. The woman eased her car into traffic and Maik moved the Mini out a few cars later.

'Heading west on Bagley Street,' he reported. He thought about turning up his music again. Brenda Holloway would have resolved her romantic dilemma by now, but there were a number of other excellent tracks on the mix. But a cautious pursuit of a suspect meant keeping a clear line of communication open. And Salter's tone now reminded him of the situation they had put themselves in.

'We are right about this, aren't we, Danny? We're not getting ourselves into something all based on some horrible misunderstanding?'

'The DCI is convinced somebody chose that particular river deliberately as a place to leave the body,' said Maik, waiting for a break in the traffic to slide into the next lane, where he could remain in Kim's blind spot for a while. 'I think it was suspended in the centre like that to slow up the investigation, by starting a turf war between Jejeune and Laraby over boundary jurisdiction. It bought the killer time to clear up the mess after things went south with the botched murder up at the monitoring station.'

'But that doesn't prove she was involved. Anyone could have put that body in there.'

'Could they? When did you find out Laraby was coming in to replace Shepherd?'

'Me? When Shepherd told me she was leaving on holiday.'

'Whoever wanted to exploit the rift between them already knew Laraby was coming in as temporary DCS. Somebody would need access to a high level of police information for that. It's her,' he said firmly. 'She's involved in this somehow.'

The car ahead indicated and drew to a stop at the kerb outside a coffee shop. Maik drifted past in the Mini, paying no attention whatsoever to the woman craning forward in her driver's seat to look along the street.

'She's pulled over,' he told Salter. 'I think she's waiting to pick someone up.' He guided the Mini to the kerb on the far side of the road a good way up and watched the grey car in his rear-view mirror.

In the silence of the waiting, faint strains of the Spinners came to him. 'It's a Shame'. He turned it up to listen but his eyes never left the mirror.

'Anything?' Salter's voice was taut with tension, a staccato counterpoint to G.C. Cameron's silky vocals.

'Nothing yet. Maybe her contact isn't going to show.'

'I don't like this, Danny,' Salter told him. 'I'm starting to get a bad feeling about it. We should abort this now. We've got her name. We can ask the ACC to take it up directly with Five. We don't even have to get Laraby involved.'

'We don't have enough to justify anybody taking action. At best, all we've got is suspicions. Well-founded ones, agreed. But we need more. And as soon as we raise the flag, she'll be gone. We'll never see hide nor hair of this woman again.'

The silence suggested Salter understood his point. In Danny's world, you committed a crime, you paid for it. There was no bigger picture to consider, no greater good. And if the crime you committed involved putting DCI Jejeune in danger, or worse, if you represented a threat to him yourself, then the sooner you were taken out of action the better. Maik saw the woman lean over to unlock the passenger door and offer a short wave to someone.

'Her contact is coming,' said Maik. 'They must be in that shop.'

'Can you see them?'

But for a moment all that came to Salter were the dulcet tones of the Spinners. Danny Maik could find nothing to say. Because the person who had just come out of the coffee shop, descended the steps and got into the passenger seat of Kim's car was Domenic Jejeune.

'What?' Salter all but screamed the question. 'Was he being coerced? Did she force him into the car?'

By now the Kia was five vehicles ahead of Maik and he was trying to nudge the Mini back into the flow of traffic.

He didn't want to attract attention to himself, but he wasn't going to wait much longer for an opening. He spotted a gap and accelerated, lurching the small car into it. 'No evidence of it,' he told Salter now that he had settled into the traffic. He was trying to remember if he'd noticed the DCI's expression. Had he seen a smile of recognition? He couldn't be sure. But no signs of surprise, or shock, that was for sure. Those had belonged to Danny.

'We need to make sure he's okay,' said Maik. 'Send him a text, something normal. A bird. Announce a rare bird sighting, see if he'll respond.'

'What kind of bird?'

'Any. I don't know, google one. If he's able to use his phone, then it's unlikely she's holding him against his will.'

Danny saw the Kia's left indicator blinking up ahead and his stomach churned. He'd been hoping the car would stay in town, where the steady ebb and flow of the street traffic would have offered him some cover. But they were heading out to the country. Following along the high-hedged lanes and tight turns would be much more difficult, and all but impossible to do while staying out of sight. It was only a matter of time before an experienced operative like Kim spotted him. And then, a pursuit of a very different kind might begin.

He made the turn on the same light as the Kia, but now there was only one car between them. By the time they left the last of the houses along the roadside, that car had gone, too. Only countryside flanked them on both sides now. In the background, Martha Reeves and the Vandellas had taken over the soundtrack with 'Nowhere to Run'. The two cars proceeded along the lane, Maik holding back as far as possible. 'Make that call now, Lauren,' he told her urgently. 'I need to know if I have to go and get him out of that car. Once I start to close in, she'll be on to me and I might not get a second chance.'

'I'm trying.' There was panic in Salter's voice. 'I can't find a bird. They all sound the same to me; rare, extirpated, vulnerable, what the bloody hell's the difference?'

'It doesn't matter,' said Maik, his voice rising as he fed off her panic. 'Any bird, just get a call in to him.'

But it was too late. The Kia took a late turn at a speed that couldn't have been anything other than an evasive action. Maik dropped the Mini a gear and took off in pursuit. But as he emerged round the turn, the other car was nowhere in sight. He'd been driving these roads for as long as he could remember and knew this stretch well enough. Nobody could have disappeared round the next bend that quickly. He brought the Mini down another gear and began trundling along slowly, checking between the flickering gaps in the hedgerows that lined the lane on both sides. Kim must have slipped in behind them somewhere and now be driving parallel to the lane along the fields on the other side of the hedge. It was the only explanation for her having been able to disappear so quickly. He three-pointed the Mini round in the lane and headed back, scrutinising the hedges carefully for a gap wide enough for a small car to squeeze between. There: an overgrown track that farm equipment had once used to access the field, long since narrowed by the encroachment of the hedgerow on each side. He eased the Mini onto the track and through the gap, and slowed still more as the tyres hit the bumpy dirt surface of the furrowed field. A hundred metres ahead of him, the Kia was inching along cautiously, hugging the edge of the hedgerow. Maik feathered the Mini's speed up slightly, hoping Kim's attention would be focused on peering through the screen of bushes, looking for signs of his car on the road. But she spotted him in the mirror and took off at speed, throwing up clouds of dust from the hard-packed earth. Maik accelerated in pursuit, but she reached another gap in the hedgerow first and sped through it, back out onto the road. Maik came through as fast as he could but braked hard as the Mini's tyres hit the road surface. He looked around. He was at the corner of a crossroads; narrow lanes curved away in four different directions, each lined by high, dense hedgerows. There was no sign of the Kia along any of them. He sat listening to the sound of the Mini's engine, the faint strains of Martha and the Vandellas floating ethereally beneath it. *Nowhere to run, baby. Nowhere to hide.* Finally, he called Salter.

'I lost them.'

'Oh, Danny,' she said.

But there was no time for sympathy or reassurances. 'Did you get that message to him?'

'I did. I told him something called a Serin had been seen. No response yet.'

'Text him again,' said Danny. 'And get an alert out. Grey Kia.' He gave her the number plate. 'Two passengers. Last seen, intersection of Gardner Road and Freemantle Lane.'

'Direction?'

There was a beat of silence after Salter's question. 'No idea.' The resignation in Danny's voice was palpable. 'She could have taken him anywhere.'

35

Kim watched through net curtains as Maik's Mini drove along the street. It had been fifteen minutes since they had pulled into the driveway of the small cottage, one of a few lining the quiet lane less than two miles from the crossroads. It was the second time the Mini had passed the house. It hadn't slowed down either time.

'He certainly is persistent, our follower,' said Kim, turning away from the window to address Jejeune. 'Normally, that's a quality I admire. Do we know of anybody like that in our shared worlds, I wonder?'

'Lindy can be a bit tenacious at times,' he said, trying to buy some more time to let his racing mind settle. Kim had made them both a cup of tolerably good coffee and he took a drink of his now.

'Yes, but she doesn't drive a Mini, does she? She's gone electric these days. And besides, why on earth would she be following you? She trusts you, doesn't she? I'm sure she has no reason not to.'

He had been alarmed at first. Kim's evasive manoeuvre into the field from the lane had come without warning, although perhaps not quite, given her first question as he got into the passenger seat after exiting the coffee shop: 'Did you mention our meeting to anyone?' But it wasn't until they were on the far side of the trees, tracking parallel to the lane, that she announced that a car had been following them since they left the coffee shop. 'Beige Mini, bulky-looking driver. Ring any bells?'

Jejeune had denied it did, and had maintained his silence as she had played her game of hide and seek with the Mini along the lanes and hedgerows of the Saltmarsh countryside. Only once had her attention been drawn his way, when a text pinged on his phone.

'A bird sighting,' he said, looking at the screen. 'An alert. For a Serin.'

Kim had nodded. 'Ah, yes, the notorious birding network. Speaking professionally, I have to tell you, we hold it in great esteem.' She had asked if he would be going to go to see the bird, but he rejected the idea.

'Probably a misidentification,' he said as nonchalantly as he could manage. 'It happens.'

They had not spoken again until they were in the house. As soon as she pulled into the driveway, Kim had clicked a remote. A long section of fencing across the far end of the driveway had rattled noisily sideways along a track, giving access to the rear garden. 'So much more convenient for back door deliveries,' she had told him with a smile.

As soon as the car was through, the fencing rattled back to its former position. From the road, all that was visible beside the cottage now was an empty driveway with a fence at the end of it. Anybody looking for an elusive Kia would concentrate on those houses with a garage next to them, or those flanked by narrow alleys and passageways. The last place you'd pay any attention to was a small cottage with an empty space beside it. The simplest deceptions are always the most effective, thought Jejeune.

Kim sipped her coffee thoughtfully. 'So it seems our faith in you has been justified, after all. You have made something of a breakthrough, your message said.'

'Not in who killed Lee,' said Jejeune, 'but perhaps why.'

His phone pinged again. The same bird alert. 'They do seem very keen for you to go and see this bird, Inspector. Are you sure you don't want me to drive you somewhere? We could talk on the way.'

'It's sounding less and less likely to be an accurate sighting. If there was anything to it, a number of the other birders in the area would already be messaging about it.'

'Are you saying you don't trust your source?' A faint smile touched the corners of Kim's mouth.

'Let's say I'd rather await further verification before I race off anywhere.'

She nodded. 'Danny Maik,' she said suddenly. 'Your sergeant. He drives a Mini, doesn't he?'

'He's not my sergeant any more.'

'Oh, but he is, Inspector Jejeune. In every way that matters, he is. I hear he's been looking into me, asking for my file and such. What's his interest in me?'

'That is something you'd have to discuss with him.'

'How much do you trust him?'

'Completely.'

'Then you should ask him what it is he thinks he knows. And perhaps you can satisfy him that it is not my intention to impede your investigations in any way.'

Jejeune looked around the tiny living room they were in. It was sparsely decorated, but with enough attention to period and pieces that you might believe you were in the home of a retired widow, if you hadn't been ushered in through the back door in an arrangement that was clearly designed to keep new arrivals out of sight of the prying eyes of neighbours. A safe house, he thought, here on the outskirts of Saltmarsh. How many times had he driven down this street without knowing, because there was no reason for him to have known? How many more places like this existed around here that he was unaware of, how many more operatives drinking coffee in street-front cafés. And watching? What was this strange, unsettling world he had found himself drawn into?

Kim joined him in gazing around. 'Odd, isn't it, how normal it all looks, how benign. And yet, to think of the things that may have been discussed within these very walls. I imagine you'd be surprised to know how many momentous decisions affecting the lives of so many people are made by a few individuals in innocuous little rooms like this one.' She paused for a moment. 'Now, you were saying about progress?'

'I think Lee was killed over a program he developed, but not a blue carbon one. He used predictive algorithm formulas he stole from Amit Chandra and he built it using architecture from Ishtara Habloun, putting it together and test-running it on his own time, late at night.'

Kim nodded. 'The latest intelligence suggests predictive algorithms are going to be the new frontier in espionage. What do you know about them?'

'Not enough to confidently see how they could fit into this case at first. But this particular algorithm is designed to analyse gaps in data and calculate plausible solutions.' He paused. 'A blank Word doc file was found on Lee's laptop. I think it once contained a redacted copy of the transcript from the Huebner hearings. And I think Sampson Lee found a way to reverse the redactions, using a program he had designed exclusively for that purpose.'

Kim smiled softly. 'Did you know in the good old days even copying and pasting was sometimes enough to undo redactions. Sadly, things have moved on considerably since then. New levels of redaction are highly encrypted. In theory, from predicting missing information in a dataset to analysing gaps in redacted text is not that much of a stretch. In practice, of course, you'd have to run millions of iterations of letter combinations to fill in the missing words. The university certainly has the facilities to do it, but it would require a considerable feat of programming.'

'One that would be of great interest to the intelligence community.'

Kim nodded. 'The secrets an algorithm like that could expose would be of interest to a lot of people. Consider who and what could be at risk. Confidential informants, those in witness protection. Not to mention the national security implications. Documents detailing military operations are often so heavily redacted they are unintelligible to the casual reader after release. An algorithm that can decode redacted documents could cause immeasurable harm to a great many people. We would indeed be very interested in it.'

'When we met at the hide, and I told you Lee had seen the document, it wasn't a surprise to you.'

He received only the same enigmatic smile as before.

'You knew he was working on this, didn't you?'

'A law unto themselves, these algorithm developers. It does pay to stay abreast of how they are keeping themselves busy.'

'If that Word file on Lee's computer contained the unredacted document, it means that he had already managed to get the program out of the lab. And now it's gone. Did you take it, when you went into the office after he was murdered? Before closing the door on your way out?'

'I left everything as I found it. Including the door. I'd hoped there might be a copy of the program on the laptop, but there wasn't.'

'So someone else got there before you? The person who closed that door?'

'Possibly. Or perhaps Lee had the hard drive with him when he was killed at the monitoring station. Either way, the fact that it hasn't surfaced yet suggests whoever has it knows the value of what they have, and intends to make use of it. But I sense you're not telling me everything, Inspector, even now. Do you know where that program is? I would remind you that it's in the highest interests of national security that you hand it over if you do.'

'I don't have the program and I don't know where it is.'

Kim stared at him for a moment, assessing the truth of his words, and of the unspoken ones that lay behind them. 'Very well,' she said finally. 'Come, I'll give you a ride to the marsh, or wherever this bird is. Unless, of course, there is anything more you wanted to tell me.'

Anything more? Not that he wanted to tell her. So he would hold off saying that Sampson Lee had continued to work on the program *after* the security measures had been put in place at the university. Or that it made no sense to continue working on a project he wasn't going to be able to get out of there. So then he wouldn't need to say, either, that it all pointed to the idea that Lee must have already had a plan in place to get it out. And that it almost certainly had to have involved Katie Fairfax.

'A lift back to the coffee shop will be fine. I'm certain by now it's a false alarm. I think it's fair to say if it was a verified sighting, there would be a lot of other alerts pinging on my phone by now.'

'How disappointing.' She smiled teasingly. 'You really should get yourself some better sources.'

36

Lindy found a broader smile than Domenic had seen for days when she caught sight of the Mini in the car park of the Board Room.

'Danny,' she exclaimed delightedly. She got out of the car along with Jejeune and approached the sergeant's Mini, where vocals as smooth as melting chocolate could be heard over a lush soundtrack. Maik had started again on yesterday's mix, having been unable to give it the necessary attention at the time. By now it had progressed to the Originals' 'Baby I'm for Real'.

'Mind if I have a listen?' she asked, leaning in. She rocked her head easily for a few moments to the mellow beat. 'Brilliant,' she said, straightening. 'It's the only chance I get to hear Motown these days, meeting you in car parks.'

'Do you miss it?' he asked.

'Yes, Danny,' she said sadly. 'I really do.' And for a moment, they both knew she wasn't talking about the music. 'I have something to send you. I took some video of a dog playing with some little chicks. I think Max would love it.'

Maik doubted it would be of interest to a boy of Max's age. He had long outgrown his interest in the cute, fluffy things in life. But Lindy hadn't been around Max in a while, and Danny knew children tended to be frozen in the minds of people at the age they'd last seen them. He thanked her anyway, and the men waited together until she'd driven away before they went inside the pub.

The Board Room promised comfort, privacy and good quality beer. To Danny's mind, there were few better places anywhere for a celebration. Of sorts. As soon as they were seated at a table, he raised his glass. 'To your safe return, sir,' he said. 'You had us a bit concerned there for a while.'

'I could tell,' said Jejeune, raising his own glass. 'But why you were following me in the first place?'

'Not you, her. She is DCS Laraby's MI5 contact, after all, as you must have already worked out for yourself. I presume that's why you were meeting her.'

Jejeune took a sip of his beer and looked around the room for a moment to disguise his shock. But even here, amid the warm ambience of the wood-panelled walls and the welcoming security of this familiar setting, he couldn't bring himself to tell Danny the whole truth. Not yet anyway. 'How did you work it out?' he asked before Maik could ask him the same question.

Danny shrugged. 'We got her file. Heavily redacted, as you might expect, but there was enough in there to confirm that she'd acted as liaison on various other cases over the years as well.'

'Laraby shared her file with you?'

'Let's say no. But it is definitely her he's been in contact with. However you found out yourself, you were right. Old contacts still in high places, I presume?'

Both men turned at a sudden eruption of noise from a nearby table. The board game gods had thwarted another strategy and the players' mixed emotions had spilled out into the otherwise sedate atmosphere. With sheepish smiles and apologetic waves, the tranquil mood of the room was soon re-established. Jejeune sat back and sipped his beer again. His former sergeant deserved the truth after the lengths he and Salter had gone to in order to watch over him, and the unease at deceiving him sat like bile in the back of his throat. 'I haven't been made aware of anything to suggest she might constitute any sort of a threat,' he said finally. 'What was it that had you concerned, specifically?'

'We think it may have been her who had Laraby send you out to the lab that night. It could have been a deliberate attempt to put you in danger.'

'If I ever was.'

'Yes, I did wonder about that,' said Maik, nodding thoughtfully. 'It occurs to me that diesel fumes might not be the way to go if you were really intent on killing somebody. I can't ever remember a report of anybody dying that way.'

'There would be a few cases over the years, I'd imagine,' said Jejeune, more relaxed now that he had successfully navigated their conversation away from how he had uncovered Kim's identity. 'But the incidence of death from diesel fumes would be pretty small,' he agreed.

'You'd think anybody going to all that trouble might check what kind of fuel they'd be using. Unless there was a reason they went about it that way.'

Jejeune gave a soft smile. 'If you have any thoughts on that, Sergeant, I'd be interested to hear them.'

Maik tilted his head. 'An attack on a senior officer like that, it has certainly made sure that the entire focus of the inquiry is now on the Euclid Lab. In fact, if I needed a police department looking in one particular direction, but I didn't want an officer's death on my conscience, that might be exactly the way I'd go about it.'

'You think somebody wants to deliberately point us there?'

'Or away from somewhere else.'

Jejeune looked interested. 'So where do we end up, then, if we follow a path away from the Euclid Lab?'

Maik shrugged. There were more than enough suspects who might fit the bill. He had laid out an avenue of investigation. He would leave it to Jejeune to see where it led. Exactly the way they used to do it. He picked up his beer and held it aloft, allowing the light from the window to filter through it, setting the amber liquid aglow and laying patterns on the tabletop. 'Fractals,' he said. 'Endlessly repeating shapes. One of the areas of mathematics where people find beauty.'

'There are others?' asked Jejeune with a crooked smile.

'*Mathematics, rightly viewed, possesses not only truth, but supreme beauty*,' he quoted, nodding authoritatively. 'Bertrand Russell said that, so I'm told. I've been hearing a lot about mathematics since Lauren started going up to that Euclid Lab. I never realised how important it was to her.' He shrugged. 'You think you know somebody, but there're always hidden aspects to them, aren't there?'

Jejeune nodded thoughtfully. 'There are.' He was moving in so many worlds he was unfamiliar with: algorithms, intelligence services, unravelling personal relationships. He felt adrift, unanchored from his comfortable life of work, and home, and certainty. Birding, too, had always been a safe haven for him. But he doubted it was going to lead him to his answers in this case. He would need to step out into these other worlds for that. One bird, though, had unexpectedly appeared on his horizon recently.

'I meant to ask. A Serin, Sergeant?'

'That was Lauren. I told her to choose a rare bird and she just picked that one.'

'Well, you can tell her I'm impressed.'

'Though not enough to end your meeting with Kim to go chasing it,' said Danny, raising his eyebrows.

'If it had been a genuine sighting, my phone would have been lighting up like the Yarmouth seafront at Christmas.' He smiled. 'You really did think Kim represented that much of a threat?'

Maik took another long drink of his beer. 'I think her involvement in all this might run a bit deeper than feeding lines to Laraby and taking you on tours of the countryside,' he said. 'According to her service file, she has a background in all this program development, predictive analytics, algorithms and the like.'

Jejeune left his own beer untouched as he stared directly at his former partner in surprise. 'Now that, Sergeant, is something she failed to bring up in our little chat.'

'The thing is, that same file suggests she's had a couple of setbacks recently. She's looking at early retirement unless the tide turns for her very soon. She has no family; the service has been her whole life. They kick her out, she's going to be left with nothing. She's an old spy fighting for her life. You may feel she's harmless enough, sir, but I think she's about as dangerous as it gets.'

Jejeune digested the news in silence until Maik casually raised his glass again. 'I was wondering,' he said, 'how's Lindy's knowledge of diesel engines?'

'I think we might have the edge on her there, Sergeant. And on Johnno, too.'

Maik nodded. 'Are you going to mention it to them?'

Jejeune shrugged. 'He believes I'm alive because of his actions. They both do. There's no reason to tell them otherwise.'

Out of habit, Maik had set his phone to vibrate when they had entered the pub, but even that noise was enough to provide an unwelcome distraction to the patrons on the next table. Maik snatched it up and heard Lauren Salter's urgent question, asked in lieu of a greeting: 'Where are you?'

'With the DCI. He was just commending you on your knowledge of local bird rarities.'

'You need to get over to Katie Fairfax's lab now.'

'What's going on?' he asked. But he was half-standing already. Jejeune followed suit.

'I'm sending a link to Laraby's press conference. He's just announced a new lead. He claims we can identify the human DNA collected by the filters at the monitoring stations.'

'Bloody hell,' said Maik, unconcerned about disturbing anybody now.

'Exactly,' said Salter. 'With the killer still out there, he's just put a target on Katie Fairfax's back.'

Whoever else had an interest in coming here had arrived first. Even as they approached the complex, Maik and Jejeune could see that the rear door of the eDNA Lab was open. Jejeune urged a little more speed from the Beast and pulled up beside the utility shed. The space he had parked in before was taken up by Katie Fairfax's blue Honda.

'Let me out here,' said Maik. 'I'll check the shed and meet you over at the lab.'

Jejeune pulled the Range Rover onto a grassy verge beside a small patch of landscaped shrubs along the car park fence and hurried over to the lab door, where Maik was waiting for him.

'Nothing in or around the shed, but tyre marks on the gravel here look like somebody left in a hurry.' Jejeune nodded and looked behind him at the blue Honda. It hadn't been Katie Fairfax. If she was still here, and that other car had already left, it didn't bode well for what they might find inside.

Maik pointed to the splintered wood of the jamb where the door had been crowbarred open. 'Somebody came prepared,' he said. He eased the door open and they went inside. A series of small offices opened off the corridor on each side. The door of every one was open, but there was no sound coming from any of them. The two detectives entered and began moving slowly along the central corridor, easing back the office doors fully and peering in as they went. Nothing. They met at the foot of the narrow staircase that went up to the second floor. Maik led the way. A single door faced them at the top of the stairs. Unlike the others, this one was closed. Maik rocked a three-count, then snatched open the door, bursting in so quickly only someone with a weapon already aimed at the doorway could have reacted. But there was no gunshot, no knife blade, no swinging blunt instrument. There was no movement at all. The room was empty.

Maik stood aside to let Jejeune enter. It was a small study, with an overlarge desk surface dominating most of the space. A half-full coffee cup sat beside a space big enough for a laptop. 'No computer, but no charger and no bag either,' said Jejeune. 'It looks like she may have managed to get out before whoever it was arrived.'

On the far wall was the adjoining door to the shared kitchen. Though it was fitted on the other side with digital retina-scanning software, on this side it had only a simple hand lock. It wasn't engaged; the door was ajar. Jejeune eased it fully open and peered into the kitchen. 'It looks like they got what they came for.' He indicated the fridge in the corner behind the door. The metal locking strap once folded across it now hung forlornly from its hinge. A short crowbar lay on the floor beside it. Jejeune opened the fridge and saw a series of containers like ice-cube trays arranged in neat rows: Katie Fairfax's filters. There was a gap where one of the trays had been removed.

'If I were a betting man, I'd wager that's the set of filters from the day of Sampson Lee's murder,' said Maik. 'I'd bet that crowbar has no prints on it, either.'

Jejeune nodded. They'd get tech in to catalogue and identify everything, and forensics would dust for prints, but he had no doubt his former partner was right on both counts. 'Call it in, Sergeant,' he said.

37

Holland's Audi arrived first. Salter pulled up separately in the following vehicle. If either Jejeune or Maik had any thoughts about the fact that the two officers hadn't ridden together, they kept them to themselves.

'The DCS will be along shortly,' Holland told them. 'But it's not going to be pretty when he does get here. First things first, though, is Katie Fairfax okay?'

'She's missing,' said Maik, 'but there are no signs of a struggle or any injuries. All indications are she left of her own accord. In a hurry, mind. But whoever came after her looks to have got the eDNA samples.'

Holland took a step to the side as Salter arrived. She asked the same question, but he left it up to Maik to fill her in.

'What happened?' asked Jejeune. 'Where is Laraby?'

'He's been ordered to make another press announcement. He's taking care of that now.'

'Hasn't he done enough damage with his first one?' asked Maik drily.

'This one is to recant the previous information about eDNA, and to clarify in no uncertain terms that we have no leads from it that may result in imminent arrests. He'll be along as soon as he's done.'

Jejeune watched as the forensics team pulled up and deployed into the building to begin their sweep for trace evidence. He could hardly imagine the humiliation the DCS would be feeling as he stood before the cameras to admit he had announced dangerously incorrect information. 'How can he have got this so wrong?' he asked.

'Apparently, he was shown a confidential government report that said it was possible to identify human DNA from samples collected using air filters,' said Holland. 'It meant only that the DNA can be identified as coming from a human, as you said, but the way it was written didn't make that sufficiently clear. He took it to mean it could identify an individual's DNA. As soon as the press got hold of his announcement, the ACC's phone started lighting up and the brass were on him like a shot.'

'He didn't think to get the information verified by an expert in the field?'

'The document was classified. Besides, he was already convinced Katie Fairfax had been lying to him,' said Salter, 'or at the very least withholding information. With the pressure he's been receiving from upstairs to get a result, the press all over him about the lack of progress, and…' They waited. '… and the fact that he still holds himself responsible for putting you at risk, sir, it was inevitable that, if he got anything he felt even remotely resembled progress, he was going to announce it. The idea that we would soon be able to identify the killer using their DNA would have been like an answer to all his prayers.'

And now it had turned into a nightmare. A grey Lexus ES slewed to a stop behind the forensics car and Laraby got out. His face was still dark with anger. 'No sign of the girl?' he asked without preamble.

'No, sir,' Holland said. 'But there's no reason to think she's been harmed. It looks like whoever came here took the samples they were after and left. So we can assume she is alive and in hiding for now.' The glowering silence that met the remark seemed to demand another contribution from Holland. 'Sir, I can't see why they would need to harm her now. Even if they thought she might be able to prove something with those samples, she doesn't have them any more. Whatever information they contained has gone.'

'The person who killed Sampson Lee is no fan of loose ends, Constable,' said Maik. The implication was clear. Laraby had claimed they had enough evidence from the samples to make an identification. Only Katie Fairfax could have provided the police with that information. Whoever had come here wanted those samples, but they weren't about to leave Fairfax around to testify as to what they might contain. No hastily issued press statement to the contrary was going to change the killer's mind about the threat she posed.

'Right,' said Laraby. 'We can leave forensics here to look around and see what they can find, but the priority is the safety of this girl. She's frightened, she's panicking, she's vulnerable. Get every uniform we have on it, her place, known hangouts, friends she might be staying with. Nobody stops for breath until we find her and bring her in safely.'

'She could be anywhere, sir,' said Salter reasonably. 'It seems to me best chance we've got of keeping her safe is to get to Lee's killer before he can get to her. We might be better served concentrating our efforts on that.'

Laraby fought back the anger at her response to acknowledge the wisdom of it. 'Spies, special briefings, privileged information, I'm sick of it, all of it,' he said. 'We go again. From the beginning. And we run the investigation properly this time. With no outside influences. We look at everybody: Huebner, Rowe, Habloun, Chandra, the lot.'

He turned and began marching towards the Lexus. Halfway there, he spun round to face them. 'Has anybody even bothered to check up by the monitoring station yet?' he snarled impatiently. 'Start up there.'

They watched him reverse out of the driveway and slam the still-rocking car into gear. Perhaps Maik could have pointed out the unlikelihood that Katie Fairfax would have fled her offices in a panic before a killer arrived, and then blithely gone about her duties up at the monitoring station regardless, but, given the DCS's present mood, even Danny decided that discretion had its merits.

Jejeune took his bins from the Range Rover and scanned the hilltop. 'I don't see any movement up there,' he told Maik, 'but I do know one place she might have gone. It's on the far side of the ridge, past the forest. We could get everybody to move their vehicles and then we could drive around. Or we could take a walk up over there. It's a bit of a hike but…'

But it might offer a chance for a quiet chat just between the two of them. Maik got the message. He turned to Salter. 'It might be a late one for me. I know we had agreed to go out for a bite to eat together,' he said, 'but after you've wrapped up here, perhaps Constable Holland could put his hand in his pocket and treat you for once. I'm sure the two of you could find something to talk about.'

Holland twisted his neck. Had the problems between him and Salter been so obvious, he wondered, or did Danny Maik just know them so well? 'Sure, I could stand her a curry at that place on the high street.' He turned to Salter. 'Unless you've got something else you'd rather do?'

She gave a small smile. 'And miss the chance to see your face when the bill comes? Not likely. But let's have a good look around here first, in case Katie Fairfax left something behind that these amateurs missed,' she said, nodding in the direction of the two senior detectives.

Jejeune turned to Maik as the men began striding up the steep path towards the monitoring station. 'Problem solved?' he asked.

'I'd like to think so. It's hard on everybody, an adjustment like this.' Maik shrugged his large shoulders. 'It'll just take some time before everybody finds out where the land lies after all the upheavals.' And perhaps where their loyalties lie, thought Jejeune.

There was no one near the monitoring station when they reached the summit, and no evidence that anyone had been around earlier. They carried on to the woods on the far side and entered a cathedral-like silence, darker and cooler by degrees than the open grass only a few metres away. Their feet padded quietly on a carpet of moist, dead leaves as they moved.

'Seems to me, the DCS left a couple of names off that list,' said Maik as they walked. 'Katie Fairfax herself, for one.'

Jejeune nodded. 'I agree. Just because she has gone into hiding doesn't mean she wasn't involved in the earlier crime in some way.'

'Crime? It occurs to me as well, sir, that, if we can now discount the attempt on you as a distraction, we're still at two.'

Jejeune was silent for a moment. 'Are we, Sergeant?'

'You never were convinced by the attempt on Talia Rowe's life, were you?' asked Maik. 'What is it that bothers you?'

Jejeune shook his head. 'A feeling. Plus there's a motive we don't have yet. I'm certainly not buying Huebner's desperation to inherit the business.'

Maik pointed through a labyrinth of tree trunks that descended the steep incline on the far side of the hill. 'Through this way is it, that place you were going to check out?'

'There's a hide at the bottom of the hill,' said Jejeune. 'It's a long shot, but Fairfax does know this area well. I'm pretty sure she'd be aware of it.' He stooped to pick up a small feather. It was black with white markings, and stiff to the touch.

'Can you tell what species it is?' asked Maik.

'It's a tail feather from a Lesser-spotted Woodpecker,' he said. 'See how firm it is?' He ran his thumb along its length to demonstrate its resistance. 'The bird braces it against the tree trunk for better leverage when it's drumming its bill against the trunk.' He gave an ironic grin and looked up into the treetops. 'I've been trying to see this bird all week. This is as close as I've come.' Here they were, the thought, in the middle of searching for a young woman at the centre of a murder investigation, and they were discussing birds. Why did this feel so easy, so natural, when everything else about the investigation seemed so forced and fraught with conflict? Danny was right, acknowledged Jejeune. It was going to take some time for everybody to come to terms with the new circumstances they now found themselves in. Himself included.

They descended the slope carefully, bracing and balancing against the slippery footing. From the outside, the hide had an air of abandonment about it. But instincts couldn't always be relied upon and they approached the structure with caution anyway, coming in stealthily from either side and rounding the corners tentatively until they could peer in through the slats. Empty.

On the far side of the narrow clearing, the marsh itself was as silent and still as the hide. The light glinted on the water like the fractals from Maik's beer glass in the Board Room earlier that day. 'You said a couple,' Jejeune reminded him as the two men stood side by side looking out over the wetland. 'A couple of names Laraby had left off the list. You meant Kim, didn't you?'

'*Special briefings, privileged information,*' said Maik. 'It's pretty clear where Laraby got that false information about the eDNA.'

'And here we are again, spinning this way and that, spending more time on damage control than moving forward. But what motive would she have for stealing the eDNA samples?'

Maik shook his head. 'I don't know how she would be involved, or why,' he said. 'But I do know this – a career spy like her would have traded in her morality a long time ago. And the ones promoted from the field are the most dangerous of all. They're not squeamish about doing what's necessary. They don't particularly care if they collect a few casualties along the way.'

38

Johnno was playing his bins over the Euclid Lab buildings when Lindy arrived. The rushing of the wind around his ears had disguised her approach and he started slightly when she touched his elbow. The dog, though, had watched her all the way.

'The birds are over in the other direction,' she told him, indicating the forest behind them.

'Area 51,' said Johnno, lowering the bins and smiling at her. 'Looks innocent enough, doesn't it. Nice neat proportions, a few maths wonks toiling about. And yet so much going on in there behind the scenes, apparently. Intrigue, jealousy, murder. Appearances. You never can tell, can you?'

Lindy reached down and patted Truth behind the ears. He looked up and licked her hand. 'Has he seen his little friends today?'

'We haven't been over that way. We just got here. We had an urgent message from somebody to meet us here. Breathless, some might have called it. Usually a good sign, coming from a pretty woman.'

Lindy smiled. 'Thanks for coming, Johnno.'

'Always,' he said. 'Come on, let's walk. You always did find it easier to talk about stuff when you weren't looking at me face to face.'

They strolled together along the hilltop, the glass walls of the lab reflecting the sunlight in the valley below. The mercurial wind swirled around them, and Lindy drew her light jacket tightly around her as they walked. 'I'm on a story,' she said, bowing her head slightly into the breeze. 'A big one. They want to meet. Tomorrow.'

Johnno nodded approvingly. A lot of people contacted journalists about stories they felt they should share. Many of them had second thoughts, so meeting as soon as possible was always preferable. 'The less time they have to stew over it, the better.' He looked at her sideways. 'Unless you already know your source is fully committed to this.'

'Nice try. A good journalist never reveals their sources,' said Lindy. 'And neither should mediocre ones. Especially to unscrupulous podcasters who would likely swoop in and steal their story out from under them.'

He put up his hands. 'Never happen. This one's all yours and I'm happy for you.'

But Lindy didn't return his smile. She let her eyes trail Truth as the dog made his way up to the monitoring post. Unattended, the structure looked like a forlorn white monument to mark the place where a man had died. The dog sniffed around the base for a few moments and then moved on. 'I don't know if I should go through with it,' she said. 'Dom thinks it could be dangerous.'

'Have you told him about this meeting?'

She shook her head. 'The thing is, he could be right. The source was the victim of a crime yesterday, a break-in. They are hiding out at the moment, afraid to go home. They think they might be able to supply some evidence about an open case but they don't want the police involved yet. I don't know what to do.'

Johnno stopped and looked at her. 'To be clear, they called you after the break-in and told you they still want to meet?'

Lindy nodded.

Johnno thought for a moment. 'Lin, I would never, ever counsel you to keep secrets from Domenic but, if you want some advice from an old hand, don't say anything until you have had the meeting. This source is obviously very keen for you to have this story, but if the police get wind of it now they'll step in and take it from you.'

She sighed. 'I know you're right but I'm just so tired of all the evasions, the deceptions, the... this...' she said, holding her hands out to indicate the hilltop they were standing on.

'This is nothing, Lin. This is just two old friends meeting to take a walk with a dog.'

He was right. So why did it feel like so much more? 'I just wanted to talk to you about it because Dom was so unsupportive when I called him about the first contact.'

They watched the dog for a moment, tracking back and forth, nose to the ground on the trail of something. 'I know,' said Johnno. 'I was there.'

She spun suddenly, shocked. 'You were together?'

'He came to the flat. He wanted to thank me again, you know, for the other night.'

Or was there another reason, she wondered. Was he there looking for clues, for lies by omission, for deceptions? 'So you already know about my lead then?'

'I overheard. Parts. But I could have worked it out anyway. There's only one big story in town, Lin. And certainly only one that's dangerous enough for your boyfriend to be this worried about you. Is Katie Fairfax really on to something?'

'She thinks she is. Or might be. She needs more results before she can be sure.'

'Dom might be right, you know. Somebody has already died over this business. And now there's this break-in. Perhaps you should listen to him and drop this story.'

'I can't.' She looked out over the valley, her eyes glistening. From the wind? From something else? 'Those people down there in that lab, they're making a difference. The fLIGHT programme, the predictive analytics. Everybody's doing such vital work, really important stuff that will make the world, or at least some tiny part of it, a better place. Even you are. But you can't say that about the work I'm doing, can you? Trivial pieces that nobody wants to read. And now I have this one. I just don't know what I should do.'

'Walk away, if you're unsure. We used to say the story was the only thing that mattered. But we were kids then, we didn't know any better. We didn't have other priorities, other lives, futures worth protecting.'

But what future did she face if she didn't do this? Daily battles with her editor for the right to cover stories that didn't matter to anybody. A life as a partner to somebody brilliant, whose career was still on the upswing? Johnno was right. She hadn't worked this hard, come this far, to be one of history's great women behind a great man.

'No,' she said firmly. 'I'm going through with it. I'm going to have that meeting.'

Johnno nodded. 'If she's in hiding, she'll want it to be somewhere quiet. Just be careful. I can be your backup if you want, waiting nearby, in case anything goes wrong.'

Lindy shook her head. 'It's fine. We've arranged to meet at my house. I just had to make sure it was a time Dom was not going to be around.' More deceptions, her expression said. More lies by omission.

They watched silently as Truth tracked around the hilltop, sniffing, exploring. There was no sign of the chicks today, and no sign of any adult birds either. Perhaps they had sensed the sadness of the place and abandoned it for somewhere happier.

'I'm leaving.' Johnno spoke without looking in Lindy's direction. 'Heading back to London. For good this time. I've helped the investigation as much as I can up here. They say any follow-ups can be done by Zoom, so I'm free to go whenever I like.'

Was it Lindy's imagination, or did he sound relieved?

He nodded. 'You're right. We shouldn't be doing this. No matter that it's innocent. I shouldn't be up here, walking around with you, talking about your relationship with Dom. You two are good together and I'm happy for you. Truly I am. But I have moved on, to other things, another life. You have too. It's with Dom. I just hope you can both see that.'

Lindy tilted her head, allowing her hair to swirl around unchecked. 'We should get together one last time before you go. The three of us. I think Dom would like that.' She turned to him. 'He is truly grateful, you know, for what you did.'

'I know. But we've already said our goodbyes. I'll head out tomorrow. I have a few things I found when I was back in London – photos, a couple of mementos. I think you'd like them. I meant to give them to Dom to bring back up here for you but I forgot, so I brought them up myself. Maybe I could drop them by before I go.'

Lindy hesitated. 'Sure,' she said after a moment, 'that would be nice.'

'I'll pick up a bottle of the good stuff on the way. Really bring back the old days.' He held up a hand. 'Don't worry, my intentions are purely honourable.'

'That'd be a first,' said Lindy, searching for a smile. It was her second choice for a comeback line. The first had been *How disappointing*. But up here on this hill, all of a sudden she didn't trust herself to be able to find the correct tone to deliver that one. It was just a few old photographs and memories, she thought. She could have said no. Why had she agreed?

'If you'd rather not, I can always post them,' he said, sensing something in her brave, uncertain smile.

'No, it sounds like fun. We really should say goodbye properly. Let's do it.'

'Great,' he said. He whistled to Truth and the dog came trotting over slowly. 'It shouldn't take too long. What time do you want me to come over?'

'Say, three?'

He nodded. 'Sure. And I'll make sure I'm gone long before your source is due to arrive. Promise.'

She watched him walk away, the dog by his side. *No Regrets*. Did she mean it? Or was she still hanging on to some last thread of hope for something else? Some answers gave you the truth, and some gave you lies. But what answers did you get when you were too afraid to ask the question at all?

39

A warm evening breeze brought ethereal strains of music from the church crypt; as before, the blended harmonies of theremin and flute seem to float on the air, plaintive and yearning, like thoughts of loved ones. Jejeune leaned on the low fence and looked out over the graveyard while he waited. Behind him, the church's eighteenth-century façade was bathed in shadow, although the sky was barely beginning its slide towards sunset. The few muted streaks of purple looked like waves on the distant horizon.

He looked up as a chorus of high, single-note calls laid a canticle over the music. A bind of Common Sandpipers flew over, heading out towards the coast to roost for the evening. Their route would take them over the rise and across the valley where the glass cube of the Euclid Lab lay, but, as long as they maintained their altitude, the birds would be high enough to avoid any casualties. Tonight, at least. He watched their flight across the sky until they disappeared. Like the now silent music from the crypt, they had barely seemed to belong to this world, but they had touched his heart as they passed anyway.

'Waiting and thinking,' said a voice beside him. 'A spy's life. And what are your thoughts today, I wonder? About the dear departed?' Kim indicated the row of gravestones in front of them. 'About how many of these people had died of unnatural causes, taken too young, by disease or accidents or darker acts?'

'More about the intersecting of lives, about coincidence, or otherwise.'

'Heady stuff for a quiet evening in a churchyard,' said Kim. 'Maria mentioned you may have other thoughts, too. Come, let us sit a while.' She indicated a bench just on the other side of the fence, set there to offer visitors to the graveyard a place for quiet reflection.

'My sergeant thinks it was you who staged the attack on me at the Euclid Lab.'

'Ah, so that's why our Mini-driving friend was following us.' She offered a thin smile. 'He thought you were in danger. And did he have any thoughts as to why I might have taken such a drastic course of action?'

'He thinks it was to focus the attention of the investigation up there as a way of misdirecting us from where we should be looking.'

'At the intelligence services, you mean?' She gave a genuine chuckle. Jejeune got the impression it didn't see the light of day very often. 'I can assure you, Inspector, if the service was involved in this neither the Saltmarsh constabulary nor King's Landing would be anywhere near it by now.'

He nodded. 'That's what I thought. I believe you staged that attack to make sure I was focused in the right direction.'

'Subterfuge upon subterfuge, which lie is the truth? Again, you seem to find yourself in our world tonight.' She looked out over the gravestones for a moment before continuing. 'You seemed determined the answer was not at the lab, while I remained convinced that it was. You are undoubtedly our best hope of finding that program, so I needed you to be looking in the right direction.'

'Your involvement in all this, it wasn't a chance development, was it? Just another assignment. Not with your background. You have a high degree of expertise in algorithm development.'

'Do I indeed? And where does that knowledge lead you, do you think?'

'To the fact that Sampson Lee was recruited by you to develop that program. Perhaps you even guided his efforts.'

Kim stared out over the graveyard at the horizon. The purple-pink waves in the sky were rolling closer, gathering in the light as they approached. It was going to be a beautiful sunset.

'Despite the lamentable fact that we are no longer a part of the EU, we still have an obligation to share certain things with our intelligence partners. Officially developed anti-redaction software would be one of them. A program developed outside official government channels, however, would be subject to no such obligation.'

'So the government doesn't know about it?'

'It's not sanctioned by them. It's not quite the same thing, but it does offer our lords and masters a desirable distance; indeed, our ladies and mistresses, too.'

And who better to run it, thought Jejeune, than someone on her last chance, needing success, desperate for it, even. What lengths might somebody like that go to in order to secure their legacy, he wondered.

'Of course, such an arrangement couldn't be funded by the government, so we turned to the one place that has the resources and software necessary to develop such a project.'

'A university.'

'But particularly, the program development arm of a School of Applied Mathematics and Computer Sciences that deals with predictive analytics.'

Jejune looked back at the church. The waning light behind it seemed to be projecting it forward into the floodlights almost, the shadows deepening into the rough-hewn stones. It gave the façade a new and slightly more sinister aspect.

'Why did you give Laraby that eDNA report? You must have known he would misinterpret it and rush to announce a breakthrough in the case.'

'His preoccupation with Katie Fairfax was becoming obstructive. Despite my insistence on concentrating on the Euclid Lab, he kept focusing on her, the only one up there not involved in algorithm development. The man's incompetence is truly staggering. Is it a requirement for advancement in the police service now, I wonder? Still, I suspect he will be more ready to follow your lead now he has been suitably chastened for his faux pas.' She shook her head slightly. 'He has only himself to blame, really. One would think he'd learned his lesson about the dangers of an association with the intelligence network after the attack on you, but privileged information is a powerful drug; that little rush of being on the inside, knowing what others don't. And as with any addiction, those who crave it are vulnerable. He requested a government report on eDNA research, and I supplied it; current and confidential. It's touching how much faith people have in the written word, isn't it? And of course one does tend to cherish the information one has had to work hardest for. Secrets most of all.'

'But still, you put Fairfax's life in danger by allowing Laraby to make that announcement.'

'Only until you have apprehended the killer,' said Kim dismissively. 'Until then, I trust she will have the good sense to stay under the radar. I take it you are getting closer to finding out who murdered Sampson Lee?'

Closer, thought Jejeune, but not there yet. 'Why him?' he asked. 'Amit is clearly the more talented programmer. Why settle for somebody who needed to steal predictive algorithms and system architecture, rather than a person capable of developing them?'

'Lee had traits that were of use to us. Not least the drive and ambition not to let moral qualms stand in his way. Chandra seems to possess a more black and white view of the world, of right and wrong in particular. Perhaps such a binary mindset is the measure of a true mathematician.' She smiled to show it might have been a joke. 'It's doubtful he could have been persuaded to see the bigger picture.'

'Beyond right and wrong, you mean.'

'A bench overlooking a graveyard is no place to be judgemental, Inspector. I told you this case would demand compromises from you. Can you imagine what this and all my other cases have asked of me? I have done what I have done, given what has been asked of me, so people like you can hold on to your own morality. But sooner or later, compromise comes to us all.'

'Including Lee. Because he was someone you could turn into a true believer.'

'Once a person is in our fold, it becomes easier to help them see things our way.'

'Or so you thought.'

Kim turned to look at him, puzzled.

'He was still unpredictable, wasn't he? No matter how well you programmed him, there was always that one random aspect, the human factor. The element that made you wonder if he wouldn't keep the program for himself once he had developed it. After all, it's not just the single function of decoding redacted documents, is it? You spoke of the harms, but the design features behind the program must have other applications that would be of great benefit to the wider world.'

Kim sat still, looking silently at the darkening sky, like someone trying to judge exactly when the encroaching night would envelop them.

'Clifford Cocks came up in conversation at the Euclid Lab,' said Jejeune. 'They are clearly in awe of his talents and achievements.'

'It would be surprising if it was otherwise,' said Kim, 'given the nature of the work they are pursing up there. He was a pioneer in the development of encrypted algorithms.'

'He was with GCHQ too, wasn't he? Lee would have known that Cocks developed the encryption key long before Diffie and Hellman. But GCHQ suppressed it.'

'Not at all. They merely chose to explore its possibilities for their own purposes.'

Jejeune tilted his head to indicate that the distinction was immaterial. 'It shows that the agency is not averse to withholding something that might have benefits for the world in general in favour of what it alone decides is the bigger picture. Perhaps Lee believed it could happen in this case, too. Maybe he had a change of heart about handing the program over to you. Perhaps his decision to release Huebner's name and expose the scandal is an indication that he wasn't buying your argument of the greater good after all.'

Only the sound of the night wind in the branches of the nearby oak disturbed the long silence on the bench below it. 'He did not have any second thoughts,' said Kim finally.

'Not even about leaving Ishtara?'

Kim turned to him. 'I'm not sure I know what you mean.'

'You were not going to let Lee continue on a path to develop a program without already having some way to get it out of the lab. It was your idea to have him form a relationship with Katie Fairfax, wasn't it?'

Kim smiled enigmatically. 'Sex was probably the first weapon ever used in espionage. I'm sure it's still as popular as ever. But really, who can tell where our hearts will lead us? Once they decide on a course, you, me, Lindy, we are all helpless to resist.'

The reference to Lindy was intended to distract him, wound him, even. He had long ago realised that Kim knew exactly what weapons to use to deflect unwanted inquiries. She looked at him directly. 'I need you to recover that program, Inspector, and deliver it to me.'

He looked at Kim, her features receding into shadow in the fading light. 'And if I can't?'

'Then I may be forced to make a deal with the person who has it. Because I can assure you, they will come to me at some point. Perhaps they will only want money. That will be easy; expensive but quickly dealt with. But what if the algorithm has fallen into the hands of an idealist, someone more attuned to your own way of thinking? That will be a much trickier negotiation.'

'And you'll deal with this person even though they are almost certainly the murderer of Sampson Lee?'

'I won't have any choice. The greater good, Inspector Jejeune, will have made that decision for me.' She looked at him earnestly 'Find it for me. Find that program. And allow me the chance to hold on to any last remnants of my own morality that remain. I'll await your call.'

40

Danny Maik and DCS Laraby were standing in the lobby of the King's Landing police station, awaiting the arrival of Marius Huebner for his formal interview. Maik would have preferred to have been in the interview room already. He liked to be well prepared when suspects arrived. Holland was supposed to be the one waiting here to escort Huebner down to the room. But he was nowhere in sight.

'Nothing on Katie Fairfax yet?' asked Laraby.

The sergeant could see the fear in the other man's eyes, feel him waiting to flinch away from any news. 'No, sir. No sightings, no reports. We've checked all her known haunts, relationships, acquaintances. Nothing about her phone, either. It seems likely she's dumped it to avoid being traced.' To Laraby's credit, ever since Katie Fairfax had gone missing the DCS had seemed more concerned with her fate than his own. Though the shame of his humiliating climb-down in front of the press would still be burning within him, he hadn't allowed it to affect his focus on the investigation.

'She can't stay in hiding for ever,' said Laraby. 'The minute she surfaces, I want to know about it.'

Holland approached them at speed, but made no apology for being late. He dived straight in with his news. 'Sir, the security guard at the Euclid Lab just called. Apparently, after the attack on the inspector, the university issued a work order to have a CCTV camera installed on the shed. He's not checked yet, but it may have been up and running when the lab was broken into. We may have footage of who took those samples.'

'Get over there now, Constable. I'll take this interview.'

Maik and Laraby looked at each other. It had been a long time coming, but it seemed they had finally caught a break in the case. It was with something approaching geniality that Laraby greeted Huebner's appearance on the steps of the station. 'Mr Huebner, thank you for coming in.'

Marius Huebner entered the small lobby, filling it with his presence. 'What's this?' he asked, looking around at the two officers. 'The welcoming committee?' Behind him stood another large individual. He had cold eyes and a colder expression, and his battle-scarred face told you he had been earning his living the hard way for a long time.

'Who's this, then?' asked Maik. 'Your new BFF?'

'This is my driver. I don't trust myself behind the wheel these days. Find myself susceptible to a bit of road rage.' He gave a flat smile. 'Could be to do with all this police harassment I'm getting.'

'I'm here to inform you that your status on this case is officially that of a suspect,' said Laraby formally. 'Now that can go either way, depending on the outcome of today's interview, Mr Huebner, so let's get started, shall we?'

Huebner flipped an arm back over his shoulder. 'Give me your phone and wait in the car,' he said to his companion.

He closed his hands around the phone and gave it to Danny Maik.

'What do I want this for?'

'You'll need it for what I'm going to tell you. Through here, is it?' Huebner pointed along the corridor that led to the interview rooms and set off, leaving Maik and Laraby to catch up.

None of the men was in much of a mood to waste time once the formal interview information had been duly logged on the recording, 'Mr Huebner,' said Laraby, 'you are here because you have no alibi for the time of Sampson Lee's murder.'

'I do.'

'It remains unsupported,' said Maik flatly. 'You are also suspected of involvement in an attack on Talia Rowe. Again, we were not able to verify your alibi through independent sources.' In light of his recent chats with Jejeune, Maik was ready to give Huebner, and everybody else, a pass on the attack on the DCI, but Laraby had not been privy to those conversations.

'You're also unwilling to reveal the alibi you claim to have for the attempt on the life of DCI Jejeune,' said the DCS. 'Three for three, Marius. I might be looking to get out from under some of that suspicion if it was me.'

'I went to see Talia. That's where I was during the time the DCI was attacked.'

Laraby sat forward. 'So if I'm getting this right, your alibi is that you were visiting the person who has failed to support your previous alibi?'

'It was at her request. Talia asked me to come by.'

'I was with Ms Rowe when she requested police protection, Mr Huebner,' Maik told him. 'She seemed quite keen on keeping you away. And yet you're now saying she agreed to meet with you. Invited you over to her place, in fact.'

'I told you that you wouldn't believe me. She slipped out the back, so that sharp-eyed female copper you've got on the front door wouldn't see her. We met in the laneway that runs behind her property.'

'And she'll confirm this, this time?'

'She won't need to. Miladdo outside drove me up there.' He nodded towards Laraby. 'You like checking phone locations and all that business, check his. It'll show you.'

'As you pointed out previously, Mr Huebner,' said Laraby, realising the need now for formality as the revelations became more serious, 'it'll show his phone was there. It won't be able to verify whether you spoke to Talia or not.'

'What did she want to talk to you about?' asked Maik.

'She wanted to discuss finances.'

'Must have been a short conversation,' said Laraby. 'I'm hearing you don't have any these days.'

'Ah, you shouldn't believe everything you hear, DCS. You know that. When we knew I was going to face a hearing, I was confident I could strike a plea deal. But I didn't expect they'd let me walk away scot-free. I knew they would impound any funds they could get their hands on. So I squirrelled away as much of it as I could before I went into the hearing. It's amazing some of the ways you can keep your money out of the government's hands if you know they're coming for you. All perfectly legal, too. Well, mostly, anyway.'

Maik's expression suggested it wasn't something he'd be looking to be amazed by any time soon. 'Do you even have the financial nous to do that?'

'No, but I knew somebody who did.'

'Talia made those arrangements?'

'That would be a question for her.'

'And would your contributions to the fLIGHT programme be a part of this new financial structure she set up?'

'No, that was all done through a separate trust.'

'Which Talia set up as well?'

Huebner shook his head. 'No. I got outside help on that one. She had no interest in getting involved.'

Maik drew a breath. 'So I suppose the big question that remains is why did you go to all that trouble to invest in a programme that deals with migratory birds?'

Huebner sat so still for a moment that the detectives wondered if he was having some kind of medical episode. But there comes a point in every contest when the will of one of the combatants gives out. It may not be physical fatigue, or mental. They may not even be in a losing position. The resolve to continue competing simply evaporates and the person gives in.

'I invested in the programme because Sampson Lee told me to,' said Huebner. 'When he came to see me.'

'So you did see him that day?'

'It took him a while to get to the point, mind you. He was a bit twitchy. I thought it might be because he was afraid of me, but he kept looking around, like he was trying to make sure nobody had followed him. I didn't see anybody out there myself, but we went indoors anyway. He settled down a bit then. Got a bit brassy, in fact. He said he knew it was me who had set up the blue carbon scheme, that there was no point in me trying to deny it. He'd seen my name in the official transcript of the hearings. He pointed out that if he released it, both my personal life and my business would be in ruins.'

'And I assume he wasn't just giving you this information so you could start getting your affairs in order,' said Maik.

'He said he thought I should have gone to prison for a long time, that he was disgusted that I was going to walk away free after compromising all that blue carbon work he'd done.

And then he said he had decided he wouldn't release my name anyway.'

Maik allowed his eyebrows to lift slightly, as if he might be having trouble coming to terms with this news. In the other chair, Laraby made a less subtle contribution, blowing air out through his lips. 'And did he say why?'

'He told me my days of making profits off environmental projects were over. I was going to start supporting one now. Generously. There was a research project called fLIGHT, which was looking into ways of preventing building strikes by migratory birds. I would be making monthly contributions to this project from now on, through a trust he'd set up.'

'And how did you respond to his blackmail? I mean, I can't imagine the prospect of making generous contributions to anything for the foreseeable future filling somebody like you with any great joy, let alone a project to save birds. Those monthly payments could end up costing you a lot of money in the long run.'

'I tend to deal with the situation at hand rather than worry about problems further down the line, Sergeant. I wasn't interested in how much this might cost me in the future. He said he wasn't going to release my name to the public. That was enough for me. I knew that I could have lost everything if he revealed my name. Loans would get called in, lenders would freeze up on me. I'd never survive.'

'So what did you do?'

'What any man would who'd been given a reprieve. For the sake of appearances, I asked Talia to look into fLIGHT, in case anybody ever asked why I was investing in it. But she could have told me it was a retirement scheme for suicide bombers and I'd still have forked out the money. I deposited enough to cover three years' worth of monthly payments into the fund, as directed. Then I tore around like mad making sure all the earlier arrangements I'd made were still in place. I was worried if Lee had somehow been able to get my name, other people might, too. And they might not be as willing to settle for a contribution. All it would take was some fanatic with more interest in morality than money and I was done for.'

'But those payments are still going on,' Maik pointed out. 'The last one cleared yesterday. Why didn't you stop them after your name was released?'

'I tried to. I looked into it as soon as the podcast announced my name. That's what I was doing the night he was murdered, consulting a financial specialist. But it turned out Sampson Lee was the sole administrator of the trust. Unless he alone changed the terms, as long as the funds are available that programme will get its monthly payments. Of course, his death changes all that. Once the probate court looks into it, they're going to realise the original deposit came from an offshore HR Holdings account. They were partnership funds, but one of the partner's names doesn't appear on any of the documents. If Talia brought a challenge, it would probably stand up and the trust would have to return the funds.'

'You strike me as a person who wouldn't want to dance to somebody's tune without knowing why,' said Laraby. 'Even if you had no choice in the matter, you would still have asked Lee what was so special about that particular programme.'

'He said it was to apologise to the girl, Ishtara. For the way he had treated her. That this was his way of making it up to her. He said he wished he didn't have to break up with her that way. She deserved better.'

'Then why did he?'

'He didn't say, but it was pretty obvious that he regretted it.'

'Just to be clear, Lee didn't ask you to make any contributions to the eDNA work of Katie Fairfax, who was his actual girlfriend at the time? Or to Amit Chandra's migratory study programme, the one he had originally stolen the algorithm from in the first place?'

Huebner shook his head. 'There was no mention of giving any money to either of them. Hardly surprising, though. The only one he truly seemed to have any feelings for was Ishtara. We can justify doing almost anything in the name of making a profit, or idealism. But do the dirty on someone in the name of love, it's hard to forgive ourselves for that one, isn't it? Or so I'm told. To be honest, matters of the heart are just as much a mystery to me as the world of technology.'

But Marius Huebner smiled at the men in a way that suggested perhaps he knew a thing or two about both. 'That's your lot,' he announced flatly. 'All I know. All I can help you with. So if we're all done here, I'll take my leave of you gentlemen.'

After he stood and left the room, Laraby and Maik looked at each other. Marius Huebner had casually given them a compelling motive for someone wanting Sampson Lee dead. But it was clear that somebody else had an equally vested interest in ensuring he stayed alive. It would take some time to untangle all these intertwined motives, but one thing was clear. Together with the footage Holland was on his way to retrieve, they were suddenly a lot closer to solving Sampson Lee's murder than they had been before.

41

Lindy felt foolish as she looked in the mirror. She had gone to a lot of trouble with her appearance again today, far more than anyone would just for an old friend coming by to drop off some stuff and say goodbye. And if it was that obvious to her, surely her frustratingly astute ex was going to pick up the signal immediately. But what signal was it? Even she didn't know. She sighed with frustration and thought about ditching the make-up, changing into something more casual. But it was too late now. Johnno's jeep was pulling up in the driveway. He came in carrying a large cardboard box filled with papers and books and old photographs. Truth trotted in obediently through the open door behind him, carrying a rawhide bone in his mouth.

'Relax,' Johnno said, 'I know it looks like a lot, but there's a couple of old T-shirts and posters in there, too.' He set the box on the living-room floor, then eased out his back as he stood. He had made an effort, too, with tight grey jeans and a turquoise shirt she had bought him. He would pretend not to remember if she mentioned it, but she knew him well enough to know otherwise.

The dog settled in on the rug in front of the fireplace and began gnawing on the bone. 'He'll be set for a couple of hours with that,' said Johnno, smiling. 'But don't worry, we'll be gone long before he's done. I know you have your meeting, presuming it's still on?'

Lindy tilted her head. 'I haven't heard otherwise.' A source getting cold feet was an occupational hazard, but her tone left no doubt she had far more riding on this one than usual.

'Got any glasses?' Johnno fished in the box on the ground and produced a bottle of Passionfruit Rum. 'It's a bit early, I know, but it seemed appropriate for our last date.' He smiled to show he was joking.

Lindy hesitated for a second and then disappeared into the kitchen, returning a moment later. 'The best I can do for now,' she said, handing him a pair of wine glasses. He poured for them both and they settled into chairs, close, but not too close, to sip their drinks. 'Bloody hell,' said Lindy, making a face, 'I don't remember this stuff being so strong.'

'You're just out of practice,' said Johnno, 'you used to knock it back by the bucketload. Okay, I suppose we'd better get started if I'm going to be out of here on time.' He reached into the box again. 'First item: one CD, Hall and Oates, vintage era. Containing the song you mistakenly claimed was the greatest breakup song of all time.'

'"She's Gone",' said Lindy. She stood up, crossed to the DVD player beneath the TV set, slipped the disc in and shuffled to the track. They listened for a moment in silence, until Lindy shook her head. 'This one, "No Regrets",' she said, cradling her glass to her chest, 'why were our parents' generation so good at breakup songs, do you think?'

Johnno took the question seriously, thinking about it for a moment while the slow four-bar beat played on in the background. 'I suppose it's because they knew enough to accept when something was over. They came to terms with the finality of it, and prepared to move on without each other, instead of trying to have the best of both worlds like we do now; done but not quite, in case, you know, maybe there's something still there, some thread to hang on to, some hope.' He shook his head. 'That's no way to be living your life.'

Something died inside Lindy. She took a big gulp of the rum and poured herself another glass. The CD moved on to the next track, but neither of them were really listening to it any more. They began sifting through other things in the box, moving closer to each other as they laughed, sighed, and shook their heads in wonder at a past life caught in memories.

Lindy was aware of a faint cold sensation on her cheek. She opened her eyes to find Truth nuzzling his nose against her. She sat up suddenly and looked around. She was on the floor of her living room, propped against the sofa. Johnno was lying beside her, his turquoise shirt opened a couple of buttons down from the neck. Her hand was inside, resting against his chest. She withdrew it quickly, sat up straight and nudged him awake.

'Johnno, get up,' she said urgently. 'You need to leave.'

'What? Oh, right, your meeting. What time is it anyway? Oh, my head,' he said, sitting up. 'You're right about that stuff. We must be getting old.' He looked at the photos strewn around beside them, and one of the empty wine glasses lying on its side. 'How long have we been asleep?'

Lindy reached for her phone but it wasn't in her pocket. She looked towards the dog, who had retreated to the rug. Only a few small remnants of the rawhide bone were still evident. 'Judging by what you said, it must have been an hour or more.' She looked at the clock in the kitchen. 'It's four thirty. Come on, get up.'

'I need to get the jeep out of your driveway before your source gets here,' he said as he buttoned his shirt. 'If Fairfax thinks you've got company, she might get spooked and not come in.'

'You can't drive after all that booze.'

'I'll stash it in the first available parking place and Uber it from there. Promise,' he said. 'How about you? Want me to put on a pot of coffee for you before I leave?'

'No rush on that, apparently,' she said sadly. Johnno looked up to see her reading her phone. She stared at the screen and sank back on the couch in silence.

'Fairfax's going to be a no-show?' asked Johnno. When she looked up, he could see the devastation of crushed hopes in her eyes.

'The DNA testing proved to be a bust, after all. *So sorry,*' she read, '*but I don't see any point in meeting now. Goodbye. K.*'

'Maybe she'll have a rethink and get back to you,' offered Johnno. But the suggestion lacked the conviction to be anything other than consolation. 'I'm so sorry, Lin. I know this one meant a lot to you.'

She cradled the phone in her lap, staring down at it as if she might be able to change the message by sheer force of will. 'There will be other stories,' he said. 'I know there will.'

'Not like this one. This was it, Johnno. I truly believe that, my last shot at something good, and big, and important.' She shook her head again.

He picked up the two glasses and the empty bottle and held them as he looked at her.

'I should get going,' he said. 'Unless you want me to stick around for a while.'

She shook her head. 'No. You bugger off back to swinging London, and I'll stay here with my crappy life. That sounds about right.'

'It will turn for you, Lin. It will.'

She found a smile for him from somewhere. After all, it wasn't his fault. He didn't need to be here. He could have already left, instead of staying here trying to console her. This wasn't his job. But the person that role fell to wasn't here. He was off solving crimes, protecting citizens, making the world a better place. And leaving her at home to fend for herself in her moment of disappointment. 'Okay, pity party over,' she said. 'Truth looks like he needs a drink after all that chewing.'

They went into the kitchen and Lindy took a bowl from the cupboard. She filled it with water and set it down for the dog. Truth went to it immediately and started drinking gratefully.

'I know how he feels,' said Lindy, watching him, 'my mouth feels as dry as a biscuit.'

'Mine, too.' Johnno poured a glass of water and handed it to her and then drew another for himself. He leaned back against the counter, holding the glass at belt level like a gunslinger. How many times had she seen that pose? she wondered. So much of their time together came flooding back to her every time they met: small habits, expressions, turns of phrase. How many other memories did she have buried inside, how many other emotions lying dormant, just waiting to be rekindled by some fleeting smile or a gesture?

'You're right,' she said, 'you should be going.'

He looked at her and understood. 'Look, Lin, if you want to say I was never here, it'd be okay with me. I don't want to cause any trouble between you two. And really, it's not like anything happened.'

Perhaps not, she thought, at least not in the way he meant. 'I'll tell him you dropped by,' she said. 'Though maybe I'll spare him the details about how we got drunk and literally slept together on the living room floor.' She smiled and threw a dish towel at him. 'Help me to dry those glasses and then you can get going.'

'Yeah, London's not happening now, obviously. After I've moved the car, Truth and I can just have a quiet night back at the B&B. I'll come back for it tomorrow and head off then.' The dog looked up at the sound of his name. 'Whaddya say, pal, Chinese takeaway and a movie tonight? No booze, though. I think I've had enough for one day.'

He stood beside Lindy at the sink as she washed the glasses. He dried them and set them on a shelf, then wiped down the empty Passionfruit Rum bottle and placed it in the bottle bin. He hefted the cardboard box from the living room and set it in the cupboard in the spare bedroom.

It had been some time since they spoke and the silence was beginning to feel deliberate.

'So this is it, then,' said Johnno. He held out his hands and she put hers into them. But he didn't draw her close. There was going to be no goodbye kiss, no final embrace. 'Remember to have that talk with Domenic, Lin. Yes, he's got the case to solve, but he can't sacrifice his relationship with you to do it. Tell him you need a few days away, a weekend even, just the two of you. It's a good relationship you have, a great one. Don't allow him to let his work be the end of all that. Listen to somebody who knows, somebody who decided on a career at the expense of everything else. It's not worth it.' He looked at her earnestly. 'You know, I never intended to do any damage,' he said. 'I stayed around because I thought I might be able to help with the case, offer some background, but I see now that I should never have come up here.'

'No, Johnno, I'm glad you did. It's been good to see you. Really good. But you're right. It's time to move on.' She offered a brave smile. '"No Regrets", right?'

He nodded and opened the door to allow Truth to walk out ahead of him. 'Exactly. No regrets.'

42

'Given that the DCS has just upgraded Ishtara Habloun's status to "Suspect" in the attack on Talia Rowe,' said Salter as they approached the Euclid Lab, 'it's probably time to abandon your hopes of a happy ever after with her, Tony. I suppose you'll just have to find somebody else with that golden ratio of beauty.'

Whatever had lain between Salter and Holland the last time they had been here had been lifted away, and the lightness between them felt like fresh, clean air. Holland shook his head as he held the lobby door open for her. 'It'll be a hard job talking to women about their proportions,' he said. 'But I'm willing to take it on.'

They smiled at each other. It was just like old times. Except that it wasn't old times. It was all strange and new, and even their banter seemed to have a Maik-sized hole in it at times.

'It's still a bit weird, isn't it, Danny being gone? I mean we're working with him now, but once this is done, so is all that. It'll just be you and me and the DCI; that's the Saltmarsh crew now.'

It was undeniably true that real change was coming. But for now they were still all a single team, trying to get one step closer to solving the murder of Sampson Lee and the attempted murder of Talia Rowe. And now, they felt, they might finally have a foothold.

They waited in the bright, perfectly proportioned marble lobby as the security guard summoned Ishtara down from her office.

Her radiant smile faded as soon as she realised Tony wasn't going to return it. She'd never really expected Salter to. 'Detectives, so what is it this time? More algorithms, predictive analytics? Honestly, I never thought I'd say this but I'm getting a bit bored of talking about them.'

'How about a change of subject, then, Ms Habloun?' said Salter pleasantly. 'Like your exact whereabouts the evening the attempt was made on Talia Rowe's life?'

Was she that good? wondered Holland. He would have put a lot on Ishtara's shocked reaction being genuine, but things were shifting around so much in this case he was beginning to wonder if he could trust his own judgement any more. Certainly, the surprise in Ishtara's voice when she spoke didn't settle things one way or the other. It could have been genuine. Or not.

'You suspect me of having something to do with the attack on her? Where would you even get an idea like that?'

'Those whereabouts,' said Salter patiently.

Ishtara shrugged and flapped a hand in the air. 'I don't know. Home, I assume. I am never anywhere else these days, other than here. What possible motive could I have for wanting to harm that woman? I've never even met her.'

'Yeah, that's part of the problem, Ishtara,' said Holland. 'You should have, you see. Huebner asked her to come out here and have a look at the fLIGHT programme with a view to investing in it. But Talia Rowe was so dead set against the idea, she refused point-blank to have anything to do with it.'

'And I doubt she was any more fond of the idea when Huebner went ahead and invested partnership funds in fLIGHT anyway,' said Salter. 'Quite a lot of them, as it happens.'

'I told you, I have no idea why he did that. I never asked for that funding. It just arrived.'

The officers had no way of knowing how long Amit Chandra had been behind them, but it was long enough to form an opinion on the proceedings. 'This is idiotic,' he said, coming round them to stand at Ishtara's side. 'Ishtara would never do anything like that. She's completely innocent of the attack on that woman.'

'And here we go again,' said Holland. 'Another hundred per cent guarantee, is it, Mr Chandra?' He inclined his head. 'Sorry, but we might need a bit more than a character reference from Ishtara's number one fan. Because of the structure of trust the funds are held in, with Sampson Lee dead there is only one person who could put an end to the payments: Talia Rowe, through a legal challenge.'

'One that our legal experts suggest would stand a good chance of success,' said Salter. 'I'm guessing yours told you the same. I'm quite sure you would have checked out the status of the fund. Especially after you received notice from Rowe's lawyers the day after Sampson Lee died that she intended to instigate proceedings to freeze the payments.'

'You're suggesting Ishtara tried to kill Rowe to protect the fLIGHT funding?' said Chandra. 'She would never do that. Ishtara is not a killer. She doesn't have it in her.'

'Again, touching,' said Holland, 'but not quite the definitive proof of innocence that we're after. I'm betting when he told you he was setting up the fund, Sampson Lee never mentioned the possibility that in the event of his death Talia Rowe might be able to step in and turn the tap off. He probably wasn't even aware of it himself.'

'He arranged that funding? Sampson did? Oh God, what an incredible thing to do.' Ishtara hugged herself tightly, fighting back her emotions, and Chandra reached to support her. Holland and Salter exchanged a glance. This was no performance. Ishtara Habloun genuinely had no idea it was her ex-boyfriend who had set the fund up for her.

'Sampson Lee made arrangements with Marius Huebner for those payments to be made to the fLIGHT programme, Ms Habloun,' Salter told her. 'Now I accept that you may not have known that, but, once they started rolling in, I imagine the prospect of losing that money would have been very upsetting. You might even have been angry enough to try and prevent it. The fact that you have a strong motive and no alibi for the evening in question means that we are now treating you as the prime suspect in the attempted murder of Talia Rowe.'

'No, she has an alibi,' said Chandra. 'She told you. She was at home.'

'There's no one to corroborate that.'

'I can,' he said. 'I saw her.'

The four figures stood motionless in the lobby. A silence as cold and unblemished as the white marble tiles settled over them for a moment.

'You were there?' asked Salter finally. 'At her home?' She turned to Ishtara. 'Why didn't you tell us this?'

Ishtara looked at her wide-eyed, then turned her glance on Amit and then Holland, before returning it to Salter. 'I didn't know. I didn't know he'd come by.'

'To be clear, sir,' said Holland carefully, aware that the proceedings from this point on were likely to be subject to some fairly close scrutiny once they got back to the station, 'you saw Ishtara, but you didn't go in the house?'

'I was driving. Past. I do sometimes. Drive. It's something I do.'

'And what do you do on these drives. Do you go anywhere special?'

'No I just find somewhere and park.'

'And then what? You listen to music? Have a smoke?'

'I just sit. In my car.'

The halting, fragmented delivery didn't sound like lies or evasion, but it carried the air of something else. And Salter knew what it was. But Tony Holland hadn't picked up on it yet. 'So on the very evening she needed an alibi, you just happened to be driving past Ishtara's house and you looked over and you saw her?' he asked. 'That's very convenient, isn't it, Amit? And she had no idea you'd driven past?'

He looked at Ishtara and she shook her head, refusing to take her stare off Chandra. Holland still hadn't got there, and Salter doubted now that he would. He was ready to dismiss Chandra's statement as a pack of lies. But she knew it wasn't. Because she recognised that other element lying behind his words. It was guilt. 'Had you driven past there before, Mr Chandra?' she asked quietly.

'I checked in on her once or twice.' He turned to Ishtara. 'I was worried about you. The way Sampson left you, the state you were in afterwards. You should never have been with him. I could see that he would only hurt you. You should have left him.' He shrugged sadly. 'But the heart wants what the heart wants.'

'And what does your heart want, Mr Chandra? To protect Ishtara, to watch over her? To make sure no harm comes to her. So you drive there every night after work, and you park outside her house and you watch her?'

'She was wearing her green smock,' he said. 'She had washed her hair and she was sitting on the sofa with her feet tucked up under her. She was watching TV and eating a biriyani.'

Holland saw the look of horror beginning to spread across Ishtara's face and turned sharply on Chandra. 'What else did you see?'

'Nothing. I would never... You can only see the living room and kitchen from the street. You can't see into the bedroom. Nor the bathroom.'

Salter looked at Ishtara and she nodded confirmation, hugging her thin arms round her tiny waist, trying to shrink herself away from this terrible truth.

'I watch you every night, Ishtara,' said Chandra, his eyes pleading for understanding. 'From my car. Sometimes I see your shadow on the wall and then, every once in a while, you'll stand or walk close to the window and I will get to see you. It's enough for me, just knowing you are in there. Safe. I just stay there until I see your living-room light turn off when you go to bed and then I drive home.'

Ishtara's voice was small when the words came, as if she was dragging them from somewhere inside her. 'This is not right, Amit, It's not normal. It can't even be legal, can it?'

'It can't be considered a crime if it threatened no harm to you and caused you no emotional or psychological distress,' Salter told her.

'But that's only because I didn't know about it. If I had known, of course it would have.'

'I understand that, but the fact is it didn't.' Salter turned to Chandra. 'But it must stop now, Mr Chandra. Do you understand? Any further actions like that now Ishtara is aware would constitute a crime.'

'I would never hurt her.'

'It would cause her distress. She would feel unsafe.' She turned to Ishtara. 'Have Mr Chandra's actions or conduct here at work ever made you feel uneasy?'

Ishtara shook her head. 'No, not ever. Until now.'

'So this would be the perfect time to stop. You need to get counselling, Mr Chandra. And you both need to reassess your work relationship now.'

'Just one more question, Amit,' said Holland. 'Were you also outside Ishtara's house the night Sampson Lee was murdered?'

Chandra hung his head. 'I've been there every night since he broke up with her. She didn't kill Lee. And neither did I.'

Salter looked at the crestfallen young woman. 'I believe Sampson Lee did love you, Ishtara. The fund he set up was to apologise for the way he treated you. I don't know why he did that, but I don't think he would have gone to that much trouble if he had stopped caring for you.'

Ishtara began crying softly, but this time Chandra made no move to comfort her. He retreated to his office, leaving her to shed her tears alone. But whether they were for a betrayal by a man she had loved, or by a friend she had trusted, the officers couldn't have said. Broken hearts, even those of mathematicians, hold no answers.

43

Lindy was sitting outside when Jejeune pulled the Beast up in the driveway. She was in one of her favourite spots, perched on a rock overlooking the inlet where the water levels rose and fell with the tidal flow. It was a beautiful evening, soft and calm, with the gentlest of breezes still holding on to the last of the day's warmth. And yet, even approaching from behind, Jejeune could tell she was unhappy.

She half-turned to look over her shoulder at his arrival. He noticed she was wearing sunglasses. 'Oh, hey,' she said. But she turned back immediately to look out over the water again.

'All good?' asked Jejeune, coming to sit beside her on the rock. He knew it wasn't, but asking if anything was wrong would undoubtedly lead to a denial. Like most people, Lindy expressed her feelings best when she wasn't being asked for them.

'Just lamenting the loss of a big story,' she said. 'And looking out over that big wide world out there, wondering if another one will ever come my way.'

'It will, Lindy. I know it was hard for you not to pursue that story with Katie Fairfax. You must know I would never have asked you to give it up if I didn't think it was important.' He shook his head. 'There's a lot going on in this case and most of it is below the surface. Dangerous undercurrents,' he went on. 'It was safer that you left it alone.'

Her shock at realising he didn't know the truth stunned her into silence for a moment. He wasn't aware of the meeting she'd set up. She had only confided that information to one person. And it wasn't the man who was sitting beside her now.

Jejeune took something from his pocket and began twirling it absently between his fingers as he joined her in staring at the water.

She raised the sunglasses to her forehead. 'Is that a feather?' she asked.

He looked down, as if seeing it for the first time. 'A tail feather, from a Lesser-spotted Woodpecker.' He offered it to her with a smile. 'A gift, for you. By way of an apology. I'm sorry I haven't been around much.' He shook his head. 'It's this case. Everyone is guilty of something, everyone is lying, but I'm not sure any of them committed the crime I'm investigating. It's so strange. I've never had a case quite like it.'

'And working with Laraby can't be helping,' she said, staring at the feather.

'He's preoccupied with finding Katie Fairfax at the moment. At least that's keeping him off my back.'

At the mention of the woman's name, the urge to reveal her truth rose in Lindy. She wanted to tell Dom everything, about Johnno being here, about the cancelled meeting, about the true reason for her disappointment. But she looked down at the feather between her fingers again, his apology. And she couldn't. Instead, she would deflect.

'So who's your killer then, Mr Detective?' she asked, reaching deep for a brightness she didn't feel.

'Somebody clever,' he said thoughtfully. 'And perhaps lucky, too. Somebody who either deliberately left us clues leading in the wrong direction or just had things fall that way.'

Lindy nodded. Intelligence and luck. It was a bad combination in a killer. 'If you think you're being led in the wrong direction, you could do worse than study those dodgy birds on the hill,' she said.

'The Lapwings?'

'They might be dishonest but they are not going to be devious. If you traced a straight line back along the path they're leading you, I'll bet you'd find their nest, in exactly the opposite direction.' She looked at him and raised her eyebrows. 'Could be that's the way you're going to find your killer, too.'

'It's a thought,' he said. He looked at her and smiled. 'There are a lot of reasons I like you,' he said, 'and your own devious mind is not the least of them.' He kissed her on the cheek and stood up. 'Do you want a drink?'

'No thanks, I've got a bit of a head.' She flipped her sunglasses down again. 'I'll get you one though if you like.' She started to rise.

'You're fine, you stay here, watch the sunset.'

A mild panic rose in Lindy as she saw him walking back towards the kitchen. Had they cleaned everything up? Yes, glasses washed, bottle in the bin. Why hadn't she told him about Johnno's visit? Why was there this circle of deception swirling around everything she did, everything she thought? There was nothing to hide. A visit between two old friends, reminiscing about past times. That was all. Except it wasn't.

Jejeune took a half-empty bottle of wine from the fridge. He might have gone for a single malt himself, but Lindy had a habit of changing her mind about not drinking if he sat down beside her with a glass of something, and, if she was going to reach over for a sip, he wanted it to be something she liked. He opened the cupboard to reach for a wine glass, but they weren't in the usual spot. They were on the shelf above, the one she sometimes chided him for using because she had to stretch up on her toes to reach. He took down one of the glasses, spotless and gleaming. He opened the bottle bin and saw the empty Passionfruit Rum bottle lying there, its surface as clean and unblemished as the glass. He reached down and touched it, allowing his fingertips to rest on it for a moment. The bottle had been washed and dried off. Why would somebody do that? There was only one reason. To remove evidence. Of something.

'Got it?' asked Lindy with a smile as he returned.

'I did.' He resumed his seat beside her and offered her the glass, but she declined. 'How's your head?'

'Ah, I got into some old liquor I found,' she said. 'Drowning my sorrows. Always a bad idea.'

'It must have been so hard to give up that story,' he said. 'I'm sorry I couldn't have been around.'

'Oh, Dom,' she said, 'I really thought it was my chance at something big again. And now it's gone.'

'Katie Fairfax couldn't use eDNA to ID anybody, Lindy. It's simply not possible. You heard her. This Dr Leclair back in Toronto knows more about the subject than anyone and she's adamant. It can't be done. Whatever it was that she was going to offer you, it wasn't the killer's ID.'

Lindy was keen to let the subject slide as quickly as possible. 'Well' – she shrugged – 'whatever it was, the story's gone now. Time to move on.'

'There will be other stories, I know there will.'

The echo of Johnno's exact words cut her like a blade and she fought to hide her pain. Jejeune watched her carefully. Something was troubling her, but she was doing everything in her power to disguise it from him. She seemed to be veering between the precipice of despair and artificial high spirits these days. Somewhere in the middle ground was the real Lindy, but he couldn't reach her. 'Can I ask you something?' he said. 'Have you had the feeling recently that you were being watched?'

Lindy started, unable to hide her shock. 'Watched? Where? By you?'

'Me?' Jejeune's shock matched Lindy's. 'No, by someone you didn't recognise. There is an interest in the case from the intelligence services. They like to cover all their bases. I just wondered if you were aware of anybody following you lately.'

She shook her head. 'No, nobody.' She still seemed alarmed by the idea. 'Would they report back to you?'

'I'm not part of their investigation. They would keep it internal.'

His reassurances seemed to have calmed her and he could see the relief flooding back into her now. 'You should be part of their intelligence team. They'd be lucky to have you. You are a good person, Dom. A really good person.'

It was a strange thing to say and Jejeune stared at her for a moment. 'Once this case is over, I'll take some time off,' he said. 'We can go away somewhere.'

It was a promise he always made when a case was consuming him. And he always meant it. They would go away. Afterwards. Until another case came up. And then it would be after that one. Always afterwards. Was that where she would always come for him, she wondered. Afterwards? She ran her thumb along the feather in her hand. 'Lesser-spotted?' she asked. 'That would be because of these two dots here? Hey, maybe they're Morse code. Perhaps this is the clue you've been waiting for. Your killer's initials.'

Jejeune smiled and shook his head. 'Two dots is "I". We do have a suspect with that initial, but I doubt it's her that killed Sampson Lee. She loved him.'

'Are you sure? Dots don't lie, you know,' said Lindy, trying for a playful tone that seemed just beyond her. 'Oh, speaking of which, the hospital called. They said instead of moving all the feeders, they were going to be installing film with little dots on it on the windows.' She looked puzzled. 'Would that really work to help prevent bird collisions?'

Dots. On feathers, on windows. Perhaps they were pointing him to the truth after all. He stood up suddenly and handed her the half-empty wine glass. 'I have to go. I'm sorry, Lindy. I'll make this up to you. I promise.'

She called to him as he turned to go. 'I was wrong, Dom. About you being a good fit for intelligence work. You wouldn't be able to live with it, a morality that says nothing is good or bad, just whatever advances their cause. You know the difference between right and wrong. I just wanted to say that, that's all.'

For the second time, a comment of hers left him uncertain, not about what she had said, but why. But he couldn't stay to find out. He had a lead to follow, one that explained a lot and began to make sense of everything. If it worked out.

He left Lindy sitting on her rock overlooking the inlet, alone with her sadness. And her guilt.

44

PC Shelley Goodwin had become one of Maik's favourites in the short time he had been here at King's Landing. She knew her job, and did it well, following orders without fuss or the constant need to follow up that Danny found increasingly frustrating these days. The constable ushered Talia Rowe into the interview room, offering Maik a significant glance as she departed. Having picked up on the other woman's potential as a problem witness only enhanced the young PC's standing in the sergeant's eyes.

'Thank you for coming in, Ms Rowe,' said Maik as she sat down across the table from him. 'Constable Goodwin got you here safely, then?'

'She's a very capable young woman,' said Rowe. 'I feel quite safe with her outside my door.'

Maik nodded. 'Oh, she'd certainly keep away anyone you didn't want there. Like somebody you felt might pose a threat to you, for example.'

Rowe turned her ice-blue eyes on Maik. She didn't blink. 'Why am I here, Sergeant?'

'Constable Goodwin didn't tell you?' Maik feigned surprise. 'We're going over everyone's alibis and whereabouts for the time of Sampson Lee's death.'

'Didn't we cover all this in our earlier interviews?'

'We're going back to the beginning,' Maik explained amiably. 'Just checking everything again from the start.'

'Not the most reassuring sign of progress in an investigation, I'm sure you'll agree.' She gave a flat grin. 'So, how can I help you?'

'We'd like to establish your whereabouts during a couple of incidents, including the attack on Inspector Jejeune.'

'I had nothing to do with that,' Rowe said indignantly. 'Why on earth would I want to attack the inspector?'

Maik leaned forward slightly. 'I think it's fair to tell you that both the inspector and myself are convinced you were not involved in that attack. But it would still be helpful for us to know where you were at the time.'

'Helpful to whom?' asked Rowe.

Maik had a lot of time for people who didn't try to pretend they were something they weren't. It would have been a hard sell, anyway, for Talia Rowe to try to convince people she was stupid.

'Marius Huebner claims he was with you at the time of the attack,' he said evenly. 'Phone tracking puts him there.'

'He doesn't have a smartphone,' she said defiantly.

Maik inclined his head. 'No, but his driver does. And it puts him in the laneway behind your house at the property for over an hour during that period.' He gave her all the time she needed, but it became clear Rowe was not going to respond. 'A man you had specifically expressed concerns about came to see you, and you didn't see fit to let any of us know about it? Not even that nice Constable Goodwin stationed out in front of your house. My DCS is wondering why that might be.'

'But not you, Sergeant? Is that because you already know?'

'Once again, it seems Huebner is relying on you to be his alibi. And since you declined the last time of asking, I'm wondering why he would do that again.'

'He was with me this time. I am prepared to confirm that.' She'd learned to use her frank stare to good effect in dealings with men. The trouble was, that wide-eyed look would have been an equally effective asset whether she was trying to convince you of the truth or a lie.

'And the last time?'

'Marius asked me to say I was with him at the time Sampson Lee was murdered. But I wasn't.'

Maik nodded slowly. 'And that's where we run into a problem, Ms Rowe. After we spoke to Huebner, we just assumed you would corroborate his alibi. However, what with all that commotion surrounding the attack on you' – he raised his eyebrows – 'I don't mind admitting, that off-hand denial you gave us sent us haring off after Huebner without a second thought.' He waited, but Rowe seemed to have a very clear idea of when speaking would be to her advantage and when silence would be the better route. The decision seemed to suit Maik anyway.

'When we did come to have that second thought, however, it was that, if Marius Huebner wasn't with you at the time, then we had no alibi for you either.'

'No one ever asked me for one,' said Rowe. 'I simply assumed everyone considered it so preposterous that I could have been involved in Sampson Lee's death, they never bothered.'

Maik offered an apologetic smile. 'That's not quite the way it works. And for the record, not everyone thought it was preposterous. For a start, DCI Jejeune seems to think you had a couple of very strong motives for killing Mr Lee.'

Rowe went for a derisive laugh, but it missed by a long way. Her deft use of silence seemed to be deserting her. 'It's ridiculous. Why would I want to hurt Sampson Lee? I never even met him.'

'No, but you were asked to look into a program he had discussed with Marius Huebner. He wanted you to cast a glance over the fLIGHT operation as a precursor to donating considerable sums to it. But you didn't investigate it at all.'

'It was obvious Marius was going to throw those funds at it anyway. It would have been a waste of my time.'

'Time that could be better used creating and posting those AI-generated threats; you know, the ones that make it seem like Marius Huebner is threatening Sampson Lee's life.'

'Now wait a minute,' said Rowe. A lot of the surface shine had disappeared now, and the streetfighter beneath was beginning to emerge. She nodded emphatically. 'Yes, I did post those videos. But it was nothing more than sentiments he had expressed in private.'

'So why did you do it?'

She was silent for a moment. 'Sergeant,' she said finally, 'your investigations involve finding the murderer of Sampson Lee and the person who attacked DCI Jejeune. None of my activities are in any way connected to those matters.'

'And if I was to ask what those activities were?'

'I have no wish to lie to the police, but it wouldn't be a lie until you asked a question and I gave you an answer I knew to be untrue.' She looked at him and treated him to the unblinking blue-eyed stare once more. 'I would ask you not to put me in that position. I give you my word that my activities can be of no help whatsoever in solving your cases.'

'You know what I think, Ms Rowe? I think the long game would be to set up Marius Huebner from the beginning.'

'And my motive?' She wasn't going to give an inch. She would make him work for every piece of progress as he moved forward. That was okay. Maik was as patient as he was relentless.

'Huebner had got himself into a situation where he was going to be siphoning off a sizeable chunk of the company's assets to put into a trust fund Sampson Lee had set up. As the partnership's chief financial officer, that wouldn't have sat very well with you at all. But if Huebner wasn't in the picture any more, say in prison for threatening Sampson Lee, well, you'd be in a position to do something about it, wouldn't you?'

'The terms of the trust were iron-clad.'

'As long as Lee was alive, yes. But before Lee died, you already knew what would need to happen in order for you to change those terms. According to the trust's administrators, that's where you were the evening Sampson Lee was killed. You couldn't give Huebner an alibi because you were exploring a way to recover the donations he was making. So let's look at the situation, shall we? You post threats by Huebner against Lee. Then you arrange to have Lee killed and Huebner gets arrested for it. With Lee gone, you are free to challenge the terms of the trust and get the partnership's funds back. And with Huebner banged up, you can take your time shifting the rest of the partnership's money around in hiding places an army of tax accountants would have trouble finding, let alone poor old tech-challenged Marius Huebner.'

'Come on, Sergeant,' said Rowe, all pretence of hauteur gone now. 'Do you really think I'm capable of coming up with a scheme like that?'

'Oh, yes, Ms Rowe, I do. And so do one or two other people here at the station. Capable of that, and of some fancy improvisation when things went wrong. When we didn't arrest Huebner for the murder, you had to think fast. That day the DCI and Constable Holland first saw you at the offices, you were moving out some boxes of documents. The constable even remembers giving you a hand to load one of them into the boot of your car. When I went to see Marius Huebner a bit later, he was looking for those files. And I think he had just realised where they were.'

'If he thought I'd taken those documents, do you not think he would make it his business to get them back?'

'I'm sure he would. And the best way to combat that threat would be to have some police protection in place. Only, the police coffers are hardly a bottomless pit these days, Ms Rowe. In the absence of a clear threat, there would be no justification for assigning a police officer to look after you. But a serious attempt on life, involving cheese wire strung across a riding trail, say, well, there's not a police service in the country that's going to deny a protective detail after that, is there? And under the cover of that protection, you had all the time you needed to complete the transfer of those partnership holdings to offshore accounts in all those exotic, faraway places.'

'As I said before, I had nothing to do with the death of Sampson Lee, or the attack on DCI Jejeune.'

Maik looked into those wide blue eyes. He had no algorithm to guide him, no software scan to run, or pulse monitor to read, nothing to measure eye-flickering or breathing patterns. It was just one human being looking into the eyes of another and trying to find the truth.

'The reason you invited Huebner over for a chat, was that to tell him you had now completed the transfer of all those funds?'

'Did he say it was?'

She knew he had not. Huebner would not have told the police anything.

'You knew you were safe enough around him now. With you in complete control of the company finances, all tightly protected with end-to-end-encrypted keys and such, he would never dare touch you.'

'I didn't detect a question in any of that, Sergeant.'

Maik shook his head. 'No, but I think I'm right in saying you won't be needing the services of Constable Goodwin outside your front door any more, will you?'

'Actually, since you mention it, I am feeling a lot more secure now. I will of course notify the police if that situation changes. Now, am I free?'

To go? Yes, thought Maik. But of suspicion? No, not by a long way.

45

Standing at the front of the Incident Room, Marvin Laraby looked like a shadow of his former self. The self-assurance that used to pulsate from him like a force was gone. Any energy and dynamism he showed now was coming from a place of desperation. He looked across at Lelia Segal, who was standing at the side of the room.

'Something particular bringing you here today, Dr Segal?' he asked.

'I was told I might be needed to clarify something a bit later on,' she said. If she had failed to add what, or by whom, it was by design.

Laraby was content to let it go unexplained for now. 'First things first,' he said. 'Still no news about Katie Fairfax?'

Salter shook her head. 'But no Jane Does matching her description either. As far as we know, she's still safe.'

Laraby greeted the positive news with a nod, as if to suggest the other kind might be on the horizon. 'Care to share your update on the camera, Constable?' he asked, turning his gaze to Holland.

'Camera?' asked Salter. 'What camera?'

'The one that was installed at the lab after the attack on the DCI. It was on the shed. It would have recorded the intruder who took the filters during the break-in.' Nobody in the room missed the conditional tense. 'Somebody stole the drive.'

'I don't get it,' said Salter. 'Why go to all that trouble, why not just smash the camera before they went in?'

'Because they didn't know it was there,' said Maik. The inference was clear. Somebody else beside the intruder now had the drive. And since the assumption was that the intruder and Sampson Lee's killer were one and the same, it meant this same somebody else now knew who the killer was.

'So what can we take from our interviews with our suspects?' asked Laraby. 'Marius Huebner was kind enough to drop a couple of new motives into our lap. Have we checked those out?'

Salter nodded. 'Ishtara didn't know those funds for the fLIGHT programme were set up by Lee, but it's pretty clear she would have gone a long way to protect them. She appears to have an alibi for the time of the attack on Rowe, though. And as for Lee's murder, she definitely had motive at the time but, again, she does appear to have an alibi.'

The DCS nodded thoughtfully. 'Given to her by Amit Chandra, meaning he has one, too. If we believe he was actually there.'

'Same story with Talia Rowe,' said Maik. 'In terms of motive, she didn't do a lot to clear herself of suspicion when I spoke to her, but her alibi for the time of Lee's death seems to hold. As does Huebner's, now we know he was with his financial adviser.'

'So what we have is plenty of motive for killing Sampson Lee, but no opportunity,' summarised Laraby. 'Every suspect we have has a rock-solid alibi between seven and eight thirty p.m. on the night of the murder.'

Jejeune turned to Lelia Segal. 'Can you confirm the entire time-of-death window?'

She shrugged. 'Certainly quite a few hours before the body was discovered at six a.m. But because of the body's prolonged immersion in the water, forensics can't help much more than that. However, other factors help us narrow down the window considerably, and I'm comfortable enough with what they tell us. We know Lee was still alive at seven p.m., because he sent the podcaster the email with Huebner's name at that time. Some time after that he went to the hill, which is definitely where he was killed. I did the drive and the hike myself. It took me about an hour, give or take, so I would suggest the earliest he could have died would be around eight.'

'I think it may have been earlier,' said Jejeune.

All eyes turned to him. Danny Maik had known it would be coming soon. He had sensed that the DCI was getting closer; the quiet thoughtfulness as he evaluated the evidence, his absences during the interviews. But even he was surprised to hear that Jejeune was proposing a different time of death.

'I believe the program Sampson Lee was working on was designed to recreate content that had been redacted from documents. I think he completed that work and produced an effective functioning model that he used on the Huebner hearing transcripts.'

'How would he manage that?' asked Holland. 'He couldn't get the transcript into the lab, and he couldn't get the program out.'

'Katie Fairfax took care of that for him.'

'She was his accomplice?'

'Not wittingly. Lee couldn't get a hard drive into or out of the lab, as you say, because of the security, but he could go into the shared kitchen where Fairfax kept her tray of filters.

Anything she carried in or out in those trays wasn't subject to search. Why should it be? There was a digital retina scan on the kitchen door blocking her access to the Euclid Lab, and one preventing any of the others from entering hers.'

'So using a key he's had copied, Lee slips a mini hard drive into one of the filter trays up at the monitoring station one day,' said Holland. 'Fairfax unknowingly takes it into the kitchen, unloads her filters into her fridge and stacks the tray in the storage closet.'

Salter nodded. 'Then Lee retrieves it, and now he has a portable hard drive inside the complex on which to load his program. Once he's done that, he just reverses the process to get the hard drive out.'

'So his relationship with Katie Fairfax, that was all just a front to allow him to do that?'

'From his point of view, I think so,' Jejeune told Laraby. 'She certainly cared for him, but even she said she didn't think he was interested in her.'

'His affections were still with Ishtara,' said Salter. 'He didn't leave her because he stopped caring about her. It was because he needed to use Katie Fairfax to get his program out of the lab. Which is why he felt the need to atone for his betrayal by setting up the payments from Huebner.'

Jejeune nodded. 'Once he had the program out, I believe he used it on a copy of the redacted hearing transcript he had downloaded onto his own laptop at home.'

Laraby nodded. 'Which explains how he got Huebner's name in the first place. But how does that affect the timeline? We know that email was sent at seven. Tech have verified that.'

'Yes, but I don't think Lee sent it. I believe he was already dead by then.'

There was a moment of stunned silence as the room took in the implications of the DCI's statement. Laraby looked at him. They would need more than just some more casual musings from Jejeune. But he knew that.

'Marius Huebner's legal name is spelled using an umlaut, those two little dots above the letter "u".'

Laraby nodded. 'The official unredacted transcript would have been careful to ensure the legal spelling was used throughout the proceedings.'

'But a predictive algorithm used to recreate missing characters wouldn't factor in umlauts. I spoke to three experts in predictive analytics yesterday. I asked them if, theoretically, they were going to design a program to do this, how they would go about it. They all said they would base it on probability of text spacing, context, syntax, font size, even. The capital m is the widest letter in the alphabet, the lower-case i is the narrowest. There are a number of other considerations the program would have to factor in. It would have to filter and rank improbables while still considering words and meanings one might never have anticipated. But they were all in agreement that you couldn't reliably factor in diacritical marks like umlauts. The recreated document Sampson Lee saw would not have featured them in the spelling of Huebner's name.'

'But the email did,' said Maik.

'Marius Huebner told us he added the "e" when he was younger to stop kids from saying his name wrong,' said Holland. 'Surely whoever sent that email to Johnno McBride would want to make sure he'd know how to pronounce the name properly. So why didn't they use that spelling?' He nodded in answer to his own question. 'Because they wanted us to believe Lee had unredacted the transcript with his program and got the name from it. And on there, it was spelled with the umlaut instead of the "e".'

But Jejeune was shaking his head. 'Not unredacted, constable. The missing parts of the transcript were recreated. By a mechanical program that couldn't account for umlauts. That's the difference.'

Mechanical learning software could train the predictive algorithms. They could create the data, run the iterations, and refine and rerun and come up with the probabilities and possible solutions. But none of that could ever make a leap like this, between tiny white spots on a bird's tail feather and window glass, and a small diacritical mark above a letter. No mechanical program could do that. Only a human mind could. And only a special few of them, at that, thought Maik wryly.

'I follow your logic, sir,' said Salter, 'but if it wasn't Lee who sent that name to McBride, who was it? Who actually benefits from revealing it? It's not clear how Chandra or Ishtara would have even known about Huebner's involvement. Talia Rowe certainly saw an opportunity to get control of the company once the name was revealed, but she surely wouldn't have made the decision to release it herself. Having Huebner's name out there was hardly good for the company's brand. And he's not going to release it himself, is he?'

'So nobody benefitted from releasing Huebner's name, then? Is that what you're saying?' asked Laraby. 'Here's the thing.' He leaned forward as if taking the entire room into his confidence. 'I don't care. Our victim was last seen alive around five p.m. and we now know he was almost certainly dead by seven. One of these people killed Sampson Lee, and that means one of them is going to have no alibi for the period between five and seven p.m. on the night of the murder. So let's get out there and find out which one.' He looked around the room, allowing his eyes to drift Jejeune's way for once. 'This is good work, everyone. We're closing in. Now let's finish it off.'

But they weren't looking at Laraby's beaming face any more. The appearance of the duty sergeant in the doorway always drew interest, and his demeanour now suggested they might all want to be paying particularly close attention. As soon as Laraby followed their gazes in the direction of the duty sergeant, he knew.

'A body's been discovered, sir. In the woods up on the hilltop.' No one needed the sergeant to provide any further details. They could have supplied them themselves. *Female, mid-twenties, tentatively identified as Katie Fairfax.*

46

Perhaps Domenic Jejeune had been holding on to hope. On his drive over, listening to the radio dispatcher declare a tier one incident, there had been no mention of the victim's identity. The staccato crackle of messages back from the first responders to the hilltop beside the Euclid Lab had confirmed a body but no more. But as he emerged from his vehicle, he saw the sadness on the faces of the people in white coveralls clustered together in a small clearing a few metres back into the forest. It was all the confirmation he needed.

Lelia Segal had ridden with Holland and was already here, staring down at something on the ground in the midst of the gathering. As Jejeune reached the edge of the forest, she broke away from the group and approached him, peeling gloves from her hands. She nodded. 'It's Katie Fairfax. Strangulation. Ligature.' The ME's flat tone was fighting for detachment, but the sorrow and anger were seeping through anyway.

'Time of death?'

'It was raining until lunchtime yesterday. The ground beneath the body is wet, but the corpse itself is dry.' She shrugged. 'Late afternoon, based on the degree of rigor?'

Jejeune looked around the hilltop where he and Lindy had strolled only a few days earlier, encountering Katie Fairfax along the way. 'This is a popular spot. And yet the body's only just been discovered?'

'It was a bit deeper into the woods. A dog walker found it. An attempt had been made to hide it, but it was a rush job. Another fifty yards in and there's a ravine with a lot of fallen logs. If the body had been left there, it's likely it wouldn't have been found for a while.'

A killer in a hurry? He stood for a moment, deep in thought. A skittering high-pitched call pealed through the air, startling him. He looked up instinctively and, when he returned his eyes to the scene, they found Laraby's.

'Lapwings,' he said. 'They nest up here. All the activity is disturbing them.'

'Then I'd say they'll have to just get over it, wouldn't you, Inspector? We're going to be here a while with this one. Confirmed ID?'

Jejeune nodded. He stood aside and together they looked across at the body of Katie Fairfax. She was lying face down in a shallow depression. Leafy branches had been tossed over the body but, even from here, anything more than a cursory glance revealed the outline of a human being. How long would it have taken to drag the body those extra fifty yards? The killer would have been in the cover of the woods already, away from any witnesses on the hill. Why were they in such a rush to leave the scene?

'No doubt you have a theory.' Laraby's tone was defensive, but the connection between Katie Fairfax's death and Laraby's earlier press announcement was so obvious it didn't need making. And the obvious sometimes had a way of leading you away from the truth. There was always the possibility, thought Jejeune, that Katie Fairfax's murder had another cause.

Together they stepped through the forest litter and approached the body. Jejeune crouched down beside it. He remembered adjusting his scope lower for the woman. She looked even smaller now, almost petite. But death had robbed her of more than her stature. It had stolen Katie Fairfax's secrets too, like the one that Lee had confided Heubner's name to her before he had been killed. Jejeune regarded the body carefully. Below her ear, he saw the end of an angry red line that curled round her throat. It would run to the far side of her neck, he knew. It looked narrower than the one he had seen on Sampson Lee, closer to cheese wire than a computer cord. But it was still strangulation with a ligature, a surprise attack from behind. He stood and turned to Laraby.

'So she comes out of hiding and the person who's been after her just happens to be waiting here?' said the DCS. 'We never were fans of that kind of coincidence down at the Met, were we, Inspector?' He looked at Fairfax's body for a moment. 'We need get this one fast,' he declared firmly. 'Whatever the motivation behind Lee's death, the killing itself was messy, amateurish. This one; it's cold, ruthless, calculated. This girl was followed here. She was stalked, hunted down. It shows our killer is getting comfortable with this kind of work. And that means anybody else who gets in their way is likely to end up meeting the same fate.'

In front of them, the white-suited figures moved around the periphery of the scene, taking their searches further into the woods. Sunlight filtered through the upper canopy of the forest, but down here, for a moment, it was just the three of them in the cool dark shadows; a young girl, a DCS who carried the guilt for having set the killer on her trail, and Domenic Jejeune, who didn't have answers yet, but was closing in fast.

Laraby turned and looked back to where the monitoring station could be seen in the distance, and beyond that the sharp, uncompromising lines of the Euclid Lab. 'What was she doing here in the first place?' he asked. 'I'm trying to keep a low profile. Am I going to be hanging around near my place of work? A site that's already been the scene of one murder?'

Jejeune shrugged. 'Perhaps she had arranged to meet someone.'

Maik came over to join them. Behind him, Jejeune could see the small group the sergeant had just left: Salter, Holland, Lelia Segal and a couple of uniformed officers. They were all staring intently in this direction.

'We've found her phone, sir. If you'd like to come and take a look.'

Jejeune was puzzled. Why could Maik not have just brought it over with him?

'Anything on it, Sergeant?' asked Laraby.

'Yes sir.' Jejeune couldn't remember ever seeing Maik hesitate for so long. For a moment, it seemed uncertain whether he would continue at all.

'Well?' said Laraby impatiently.

'Her last text, sir. It was to Lindy.'

They were standing off beside the vehicles, at a distance from the others.

'A woman who we are actively searching for contacted your girlfriend and you didn't think this warranted a mention?'

'Her call to Lindy about the story was before she went missing.'

'But not this last text, Inspector,' said Laraby. 'That one wasn't before she went missing. Katie Fairfax contacted Lindy within what Dr Segal suggests were her last few hours. That text was her last known contact with anyone, as far as we can tell. So what do you know about this meeting they were supposed to be having, the one Fairfax postponed at the last minute?'

'Nothing.'

'She didn't mention it to you?'

'No, of course not. I would never have let her go through with it. I had advised her not to follow the story up. I didn't think she had.'

Laraby nodded thoughtfully. 'We need to talk to her, as soon as possible. You can ask her to come here if you like. She can stay over here, away from the scene.'

Jejeune nodded. Bringing Lindy here would work. It would be more formal than going to the house to interview her, but would save her the indignity of a trip to the station, when she might start to get defensive about protecting her sources. He moved away to text her, and looked up at Laraby. 'It might be best if I handle the interview.'

Laraby nodded. 'But I want it done right. Sergeant Maik will be with you. We need answers to our questions. All of them. Katie Fairfax postponed that meeting for a reason. Perhaps she was already on her way to meet her killer.'

The watching group, sensing that the confidential conversation was over, began to approach. Jejeune's phone pinged and he looked at the screen. 'She's on her way,' he told them.

Laraby looked around at the group. 'Right, so, before she arrives, let's get some things straight, Inspector. Are you aware of any other meetings she had with the victim since she disappeared?'

'No, but Lindy's a reporter. She's entitled to keep her meetings confidential.'

He saw Maik turn his head slightly. Even to Jejeune, the response sounded weak and defensive.

'And you were not with Lindy when she received this text at…?' Laraby pointed at Holland.

'Four-ten p.m. on Tuesday.'

Jejeune shook his head. 'No. She was at home.'

'Alone?'

Jejeune shifted slightly. It was the discomfort of all those he had interrogated over the years, those who knew something but didn't want to reveal it. He thought about the glasses on the high shelf, the washed-down bottle of Passionfruit Rum. 'I don't know,' he said.

He expected Laraby to press further, but the DCS seemed content to let things rest for the moment. 'I'll expect your report directly, Sergeant,' Laraby told him. He strode off to join the group searching deeper in the woods.

'We can wait for her over there, if you like.' Maik indicated a patch of ground a short distance away, where a couple of the police vehicles were still skewed haphazardly from when they had pulled up in a hurry. The nasal call of a Marsh Harrier floated down from the pale blue sky and they stopped walking and watched as the bird drifted in over the treetops. For a long time the two men stood in silence, side by side on the windy hilltop, each lost in his own thoughts.

The electric car crept up noiselessly and pulled to a halt near the other vehicles. Even through the windshield, Jejeune could see Lindy had been crying. He went round to the door and opened it.

'Oh, Dom,' Lindy sobbed. 'This is so terrible. That poor woman, that poor, poor woman. This is all my fault. She came to me, and now she's dead because of it.'

'No Lindy, you're not to blame for this.' Jejeune was crouched down awkwardly beside the open door. 'Katie Fairfax knew she was putting herself in danger by coming out of hiding. And yet she still chose to do it. It was her decision.' He wished she would get out so he could draw her into him, hug her, comfort her. But she remained sitting in the car seat, sobbing fitfully, angrily dashing away the tears as they rolled down her cheeks.

'But it was me she trusted to tell her story,' she said between sobs. 'It was my job to protect her. And I didn't.'

Jejeune looked at Maik helplessly. He seemed unable to penetrate the barricades of her regret. Perhaps Danny might do better. 'Can I ask you a couple of questions about your involvement with Katie Fairfax, Lindy,' asked Maik calmly from behind Jejeune. The DCI stepped aside so Maik could approach her more closely. 'You can stay in the car if it's more comfortable for you. I'll come and sit in the passenger seat.' He moved round and got in, closing the door behind him. 'Were you in constant contact with Katie Fairfax, Lindy?' With another person, Maik might have called her 'the victim', thought Jejeune.

Lindy shook her head, but she left her eyes on her hands, still clasped tightly in her lap. 'One phone call before she went missing and then an exchange of texts afterward to set up a meeting.'

'And she said she would be bringing eDNA evidence to show you? Evidence that later proved to be a bust?'

Lindy nodded and through the open driver's door Jejeune saw a teardrop fall onto her hands. If anyone other than Maik was conducting this interview, he would have reached in to take the hands in his own.

'It's why she cancelled the meeting,' she continued. 'But it was strange. From her earlier message I got the impression that she already had the data. I mean how else would she know what it was telling her? But I must have sounded doubtful, like I didn't believe her. Obviously she felt she needed something more to convince me. Right?' She looked at him questioningly. 'Oh Danny, she died because of me, didn't she?'

'That's not true, Lindy,' said Maik.

'Yes, yes, it is. I'm the reason she was here.' She began to cry again. 'She was coming up here to get more data because I wouldn't believe her. It's all my fault.'

Maik looked across to invite his DCI's consolations, but Jejeune seemed unable to offer anything.

'She is the one who cancelled the meeting, Lindy,' Danny told her gently. 'There is nothing you could have done to prevent this.'

Lindy nodded, as if somewhere inside herself she knew she needed to accept that. But she kept her shoulders hunched, her hands clasped together in her lap, protecting her guilt anyway.

'Did she say what she was looking for in the samples?' asked Jejeune.

'She said it was to do with the amount of Lapwing DNA in the readings. It had changed. And she had found something else, a second sample that explained something odd that she'd seen. Together, she thought it suggested who had been there that night.'

'She told you that?'

'I said I was going to need to see the data. I asked her to bring it to our meeting. But she must have thought it wasn't enough and she came here to get more. Otherwise, what was she doing up here?' She lowered her head again, shaking it slightly. 'If only I had been able to respond to her text straight away.'

'You didn't hear it come in?' asked Maik.

Lindy shook her head. 'No, I...' She looked at Jejeune. 'I was listening to some music.'

On a vintage CD I found in the DVD drive, thought Jejeune. A CD I don't recognise.

Lindy managed a brave smile for Maik. 'You know me, Danny. I like to crank it up a bit. Can I go home now, please?'

'Yes, that will be all we need.' He turned to Jejeune. 'I can bring the Range Rover back, if you wanted to drive Lindy home, sir.'

'That's okay,' she said. 'You're needed here, Dom. I'll be fine, honestly. I'll see you later.'

As the car pulled away, the Marsh Harrier called again. It had been joined by its partner and they were engaging in their sky dance of courtship. Jejeune spent a long time looking up to watch them. It was clear he had no intention of meeting his sergeant's questioning glance, so Danny walked away to his own car in silence.

47

Marvin Laraby looked like a man who had spent the night replacing sleep with recriminations. Those gathered in the Incident Room for the morning briefing knew the silent accusations of those sleepless hours would have impressed on him the full extent of his responsibility in Katie Fairfax's death. He alone had raised the possibility that she held the answer to the murderer's identification. And that pronouncement must surely have been the catalyst for the murderer to strike again. The team's response to his error in judgement, and its results, had been awaiting him when he entered. The silence and uncomfortable shifting in the chairs; they were their own accusations. 'The ACC has just been on the phone, sir,' said the desk sergeant, appearing in the doorway. 'The press office are complaining about you being unavailable for an update. They're looking to schedule a briefing.'

'There will be no further comments to the press for the time being,' said Laraby testily.

'There's a concern about the level of public interest, I believe,' said the sergeant tentatively. He seemed to be aware that he was on shaky ground. 'The ACC said he wants to discuss it with you personally.'

Laraby swept his arm up in front of him and consulted a large watch. 'Come back in ten minutes and look for me, Sergeant. You won't be able to find me, and then you can truthfully go back to the ACC and say you don't know where I am.'

'Erm, it's just, I mean, it is the ACC, sir,' said the sergeant dubiously.

'You have your orders, Sergeant.'

Laraby watched the officer disappear and turned to face the others in the room, to make sure his message had got through to them as well. Nothing was going to be allowed to get in the way of the job they had to do.

'I've excused DCI Jejeune from this briefing so we can speak freely if need be,' he said crisply. He turned to Danny. 'Dr Segal is confident in placing time of death some time during the afternoon of Tuesday.' He turned to Maik. 'I'm assuming Lindy has an alibi for that time?'

Salter stirred. 'Sir, I don't think...'

But Maik held up a hand. 'She spent the afternoon at the house. I'm confident her phone would put her there at the time the text was sent.'

Laraby nodded. His point had been to demonstrate that nobody was going to get a free pass on this case now, no matter how they were connected, or to whom. 'To be clear,' he said, 'Katie Fairfax did tell Lindy at first she thought her data could lead to identifying the killer? An actual ID?'

Danny Maik nodded.

'So since we now know that there is absolutely no way she would have been able to extract identifiable individual DNA from those filters, what was this evidence she was originally planning on bringing to Lindy, then?'

'She said it was to do with the DNA of Lapwings, the varying amounts of it.'

Laraby seemed aware that he was in no position any more to be dismissive or cynical about leads. But his vulnerability didn't sit well with him, and he made little effort to disguise a sour expression. 'Well, whatever it was, even though she didn't think the evidence panned out in the end, it was enough to get her killed. And, with Lindy eliminated, we're back to the same set of suspects as before.' He raised his hand and counted off the fingers. 'Marius Huebner, Talia Rowe, Amit Chandra and Ishtara Habloun.' He shook his head firmly. 'Let's get them in. All four at the same time. Danny, Lauren, Tony, let's have one of you on each of them, simultaneously. The DCI can take Huebner. We start with alibis for the time of Katie Fairfax's death. Then we move on to Sampson Lee's. As we know, his time of death has been revised backwards, so we're now looking for somebody who can't provide a valid alibi for the earlier time of Lee's death, or for Fairfax's.'

'We can't go back at them a third time, sir,' said Salter reasonably. 'They're going to claim it's harassment.'

'And they'll be right,' said Laraby, becoming more animated. 'We're not going to stop until we've harassed the truth right out of one of them.'

Holland shook his head dubiously. 'If they've got any sense, they won't show up without legal counsel. '

'Fine by me. Because when we find the one with no alibi for either murder, I want them to have the best legal representation they can get sitting right beside them to explain their options, which will be cooperate now, or go down for the count.'

The tang of remorse and self-recrimination that had pervaded the briefing left little appetite for any after-meeting banter. Once Laraby had departed, the assembled officers picked up their belongings and proceeded from the room in silence.

Laraby was sitting behind his desk, head bowed over paperwork, when Holland entered his office. He leaned back in his chair. 'Well, do we have our killer?'

'Sir, you'll want to see this.'

'Spare me the drama, Constable. Just tell me what you've found out.'

'No, sir. I think you really need to see this.'

Laraby rose wearily from his desk and followed Holland along the corridor. They entered the well-appointed observation suite, where Jejeune, Salter and Maik awaited them. A bank of four individual monitors sat with their screens in pause mode. Grainy images of separate rooms showed each of the officers seated at a table, across from the four suspects and their legal representatives. Holland hit the play tab on the first screen and paused it after the first sentence, then moved on to each of the screens in turn, doing the same.

'I received a WhatsApp message,' Rowe told Holland.

'A voicemail,' said Huebner to Jejeune.

'A text,' Chandra informed Salter.

'An email,' Ishtara said to Maik. 'From an unidentified sender. It contained coordinates, and said I should be there at four.'

'Four o'clock,' said Huebner.

'Exactly,' reported Chandra.

'On the dot,' confirmed Rowe. 'The location turned out to be the hill behind the Euclid Lab, the north-west corner.'

'South-west corner,' said Ishtara.

'South-east,' declared Huebner.

'North-east corner,' reported Chandra. 'It said I would learn something to prove Ishtara's involvement.'

'To incriminate Huebner,' said Rowe.

'To show Amit was guilty,' said Ishtara.

'To implicate Talia,' said Huebner.

Laraby stared at the screens for a moment in silence and then turned to the detectives. Holland nodded back towards the screen and played the next sections of the recordings in the same order.

'I waited maybe thirty minutes,' reported Rowe.

'Twenty-five.'

'About half an hour.'

'Almost an hour,' said Chandra. 'But it was clear no evidence was coming, so I went back to work.'

'Back home.'

'To the office.'

'To the lab.'

Silence hung in the room for a long moment. 'Phone data verifies they were all where they say they were, except for Huebner. But his driver confirms it's where he dropped him off. And waited for him.'

'So one of our suspects lures the other three to the site to ensure none of them would have an alibi. They were all alone, out of sight of the others?'

'From where they had been told to stand, none of them could have seen the others. And any one of them could have left their phone in place and climbed to the hilltop where Katie Fairfax was killed,' said Maik. 'They would have remained out of view of the other three the whole way up.'

Laraby nodded thoughtfully. 'So nobody could be sure of where anybody else was, and at the same time, they were invisible to the others, too.'

'This is like that Schrödinger's cat thing isn't it?' said Holland.

It wasn't, but Salter let it go. She had other mathematical aspects to introduce. 'There's more,' she told them. She took a marker and stood beside the whiteboard. 'If you plot the exact coordinates of where each person was sent, you get this.' She indicated four black dots on the board that she'd previously marked. 'But if you connect these points, the shape becomes clear.' She used a long ruler to precisely draw a line between each dot, before standing back.

'An elongated diamond shape,' said Laraby.

'Also known as a rhombus,' said Salter.

He stared at the shape for a long moment in silence. 'Based on these locations, the point at the centre of this shape, that's...'

'Yes, sir,' said Salter. 'The exact central point of this rhombus is the monitoring station where Sampson Lee was murdered. There's something else, too. The angles of the longest points at the top and bottom of the shape are exactly 36 degrees. And if you draw one more line through the centre of the shape to connect the two dots at the sides, you have two isosceles triangles, each with the perfect golden ratio.'

Laraby looked at the monitors for a moment. 'Identical alibis? Giant geometric shapes being drawn all over the landscape? Somebody's playing games with us. Somebody who thinks they're clever.' He looked across at Jejeune. 'You're quiet, Inspector. Nothing to add?'

'The timing,' he said thoughtfully, looking at the whiteboard. 'Whoever invited the others wanted them there during the time-of-death window so they'd have no alibi. It suggests they had already decided on the exact time they intended to kill Katie Fairfax. But the killer must have known the others would start to suspect it was all a hoax when the promised evidence hadn't materialised by four thirty or so.'

'And then they'd start to wander off,' said Maik, picking up on the point. 'That text to Lindy came in at ten past four, meaning Fairfax was still alive then. If the killer wanted the others present at the crime scene during the time of death, that only leaves a window of twenty-odd minutes. It's pretty tight to climb the hill, track down Katie Fairfax, kill her and hide the body and then get back down the hill to retrieve their phone and leave.'

'For somebody who had planned everything else so meticulously,' said Salter, 'it makes no sense that they would cut things so fine.'

But perhaps it did, thought Jejeune, once you knew who benefitted from the release of Marius Huebner's name. He did now. And he knew, too, who had stolen the CCTV hard drive from the shed beside the Euclid Lab. The last of the other pieces had begun to fall into place, as well. And they were all leading him in the same direction.

48

Kim looked around the coffee shop as Jejeune took his place across from her at the corner table. 'Maria tells me they'll be closing down shortly. Renovations.' She sighed. 'I can't see why. I think this place is perfect as it is. Still, nothing ever stays the same, does it, Domenic?'

Certainly not the nature of relationships, he thought. In the space of a few short days, this woman had been a confidante, a mentor, an asset, and an ally to Jejeune. Now she was a suspect in at least one crime, almost certainly more.

'I take it you're not here to arrest me,' she said matter-of-factly. 'We both know you have no evidence whatsoever to connect me to that young girl's death.'

She flickered a smile over at Maria, who returned it. Was she on watch, Jejeune wondered. Had she been asked to be on the alert for any signs that some brutish young man might try to force her good friend into going with him against her will? She needn't have worried. Jejeune had known Kim wouldn't be leaving as his prisoner today as soon as she had suggested this location for the meeting. Given Laraby's current problems with the media, having one of his senior officers conduct a high-profile arrest of a resisting intelligence officer in a high street coffee shop was the last thing he needed making the evening news.

'You don't leave anything to chance, do you?' he asked. 'I'll bet if I went to talk to the security team at the university, I'd find out the idea to install a camera on the shed after my attack didn't come to them in a blinding flash of inspiration. I imagine somebody in some vague position of influence suggested it to them.'

Kim said nothing.

Jejeune looked through the large plate glass window of the Daily Grind. The human traffic was ambling along the street at a steady pace. In some jurisdictions in Canada, a renovation for a street-front establishment like this might well require the installation of bird-friendly glass. He wondered what the passers-by would make of a grid of two-by-two dots embedded in the window. He imagined that in no time at all they would become so accustomed to the sight, the dots would fail to even register with them. It would be the same with the customers inside the shop. But some would notice, and the person sitting across the table from him was one of them. The small details were important to Kim.

'I couldn't see what you gained by giving Laraby that false information to announce. It seemed like a lot of trouble to go to just to embarrass him into focusing on the right avenue of investigation. And then I heard about the missing CCTV hard drive. You knew Laraby's press conference would panic the killer into trying to retrieve those samples. And you would have footage of them doing it.'

'And why would I want that, I wonder?'

'To trade it, for the redaction reversal program. Somewhere along the way you lost faith in me that I would turn it over to you, and you decided you'd need to deal with the killer instead.'

'I'm sorry to say faith in human beings is one of the first casualties of intelligence work. But you're wrong. I never doubted your intentions, Inspector. Rather, I always knew you would hand the program over to the authorities once you'd recovered it. But it is necessary that it comes to us, instead. For the greater good, you see.'

'Two people have already died. There is no good in that, greater or otherwise.'

'Those people will not be forgotten. We will find a way to make sure their families are compensated. They will be supported in their grief.'

'But they will be denied the justice they deserve. Whoever killed those people needs to be held accountable. Someone has to pay.'

'Perhaps I have already paid that debt for them, Domenic. Look what this has cost me, this case, this life. I have given up so much of myself, I can no longer even recognise who I once was.'

'Then end that cycle. Do the only moral thing left, hand over that footage and let the killer be brought to justice.'

'I'm afraid an appeal to my better angels will be a lost cause. Over the years they have been sacrificed at too many altars.' Kim sipped her coffee and offered a small smile. 'You've done well, Domenic. I doubt many others could have even got this far. But you can stand down now. You must allow things to take their natural course.'

Outside, people walked past. People who believed in a system of justice, whose faith in that system meant trusting that guilty people were punished for their crimes. And no one was sacrificed to some higher cause. He shook his head. 'I can't do that.'

'Perhaps it's too late. If it's true, as you say, that I once had the footage, then perhaps I have already made that deal and I now have the program.'

Jejeune shook his head. 'Whoever has that program knows its value. They have killed for it. Twice. They aren't going to let that go without some sort of guarantee against prosecution. And they don't have that yet. As long there's the slightest chance that they could still be charged with the murders of Sampson Lee and Katie Fairfax, they won't hand it over. To you, or anyone else.'

'But there isn't, surely? That chance? There is no evidence to prove who killed Sampson Lee. And that elaborate charade up on the hill beside the Euclid Lab has eliminated any possibility of discovering which one of your suspects could have killed Katie Fairfax. Designating them cold cases must be just a formality now.'

'The cases won't be closed. Because I think I can prove who killed both Sampson Lee and Katie Fairfax.'

Kim looked shocked for a moment. She sipped her coffee delicately while she regained her poise. Jejeune looked around him at the people in the coffee shop. All going about their daily business, unaware of what was being discussed at this table. The whole world could be found in this room, Kim had told him: the trusting, the cynical, the innocent, the guilty.

'The irony is that you and Laraby were right, you see. Katie Fairfax did believe she had found a way to use eDNA data to identify Sampson Lee's killer.'

Kim stared at him over the rim of the coffee cup. 'Did she happen to say how she intended to do this?'

'She said the Lapwing DNA would lead her there.'

'Yes, those little Lapwings,' said Kim with a small smile. 'You know, I suppose I have always identified with them in a way. They indulge in their deceitful behaviour, and that's what most people know them for. It's even their collective noun, isn't it, a deceit of Lapwings? But consider what is really going on. To protect their nests or their young, those birds must draw the danger towards themselves. Their strategy is really based on a system of self-sacrifice. If there is such a thing as a noble form of deceit, then theirs must surely be it.' She shook her head. 'But why would Katie Fairfax make such a ridiculous claim?'

'Is it ridiculous? Somebody else believed it was possible. They killed her because of it. Of course, they sent a text to Lindy saying the eDNA results wouldn't help. But Katie Fairfax was already dead by then. I think she did find a way to use those samples to identify who killed Sampson Lee. I've sent the filters to Canada, where I'm having them examined by the leading expert in the field.'

'Ah, the redoubtable Dr Leclair.' Kim shook her head. 'Why are you doing this, Domenic? You must know, as I do, that, whatever information those samples may contain, it won't be the killer's DNA, and surely nothing short of that would lead to a conviction. So is this all just to prove something to Laraby, to show that against all odds, with no possibility of success, you are still willing to pursue a lost cause? It defies logic.' She gave another soft smile. 'But then, that is what sets us apart from our AI counterparts after all, isn't it, these ridiculous, irrational, unjustifiable choices we make.'

Something in his silence made her look up. She saw his eyes, the resoluteness, the unwavering intensity, and she realised finally what was driving him, why he would never give up on this no matter what appeals she made to reason. 'You already know who the killer is, don't you?'

He nodded slowly.

'Then can't that be enough? Cases are all about understanding, for you. I can see this. It's not about the clues and the evidence, or what can be proven or prosecuted. It's about uncovering the truth about what went on, and why. And you have all that now, every secret, every motivation. Be content with that. It will end your career, you know, bringing this case. The CPS won't pursue it. To do so would require friends in high places. Laraby has none, these days. Nor, I'm sad to say, do you. To insist this case is brought and have it fail, you will have sacrificed, and lost, everything. It's a high price to pay for defending your principles. I urge you to think about the bigger picture, Domenic. I know you are no fan of compromise, but sometimes it's not just the sensible path. It's the only path.'

Jejeune drained his coffee and slid the cup away. 'This was never a government project, was it?' he said suddenly. 'Unsanctioned or otherwise. The government have no idea that a redaction reversing program has been developed. This is your operation.'

'The last hurrah for a fading spy at the end of her career?' she asked ironically. 'Perhaps it is. But the goal is still the same. The greater good. Always the greater good.' She sounded almost bitter.

'And that's why you can't afford to let a case against the killer go to trial. Because it will all come out into the public arena and you will have lost the chance to use that program for whatever purposes you have in mind.'

'There is more to this than you can possibly understand. I must have that program. And that can only happen if I can offer to exchange it for the evidence that would allow you to bring a case against the killer: the CCTV footage. But it requires you to end your investigations into the cases.'

Jejeune looked around the room. He thought about what Kim had said about monumental decisions being made in small, anonymous spaces like this. And now he had made his. He had done all he could to convince Kim to give him the footage. He knew that, now, things would swing into high gear. There would be a request to Laraby from the CPS to either provide evidence that might lead to a conviction or drop the cases. Meanwhile, Kim would be contacting the killer to try to secure the program before its existence became public knowledge. Both things would take time, but not much. He probably only had twenty-four hours to make his move. It would all depend on what those results from Canada told him. If they arrived in time.

Kim looked at him sadly. 'I can see now that you cannot be persuaded from your chosen course. Perhaps that's no surprise. But should things not unfold the way you desire from this point on, I do want you to remember, Domenic, that I did try to get you to drop these cases of your own volition.' She stood up and looked around sadly. 'I suppose we're both going to need to find a new place for our coffee,' she said, 'I doubt we will be seeing each other again. And that will be such a pity.' She extended a hand and Jejeune rose to shake it. 'Goodbye, Inspector Jejeune.'

49

Danny Maik was sitting in the car park near the Euclid Lab when Jejeune pulled up in the Range Rover. Even before he turned off the engine the DCI could hear the strains of a Motown song coming to him.

'The more things change, eh, Sergeant? Is that Smokey Robinson?'

'It is,' said Maik with mild surprise. '"The Tracks of My Tears".'

'I think I might finally be starting to get the hang of this Motown,' said Jejeune with a smile.

'Imagine that, after all this time.'

The two men got out and made their way to a path leading up to the summit of the hill. They began their ascent, content to let the morning sounds of the north Norfolk countryside fill the silence between them. Blackbirds called from the low scrub along the forest edge to their left, and above them a Skylark was exclaiming its joy at the new day. Maik knew there would be a purpose to the meeting, and the location, but he would be patient. In the old days it always took Jejeune some time to get started. But he always managed to reach his destination in the end.

'The results came back from Canada,' said Jejeune eventually as they walked. 'They told me what I needed to know.'

Maik nodded. 'Are we there, then?'

'There. And nowhere. I'm confident Dr Leclair's testimony would stand up in a court if she was called upon. A lot of the science around this eDNA is new, but what she can tell from the samples cannot be disputed.'

'And it points us to a killer?'

'It points me to one.' He stopped and shook his head. 'I'm just not sure it would be enough for others.' For a moment he scanned the treetops of the forest. Maik realised he wasn't carrying his binoculars. He couldn't remember a time when he'd seen the DCI out on a walk like this without them.

Maik wouldn't ask his former boss to run the evidence by him. He suspected he had brought him here to do just that, but he would choose his own time. He did wonder, though, why they couldn't have done this over a pint in the Board Room if Jejeune wasn't planning to fit in any birding. 'Anything particular we're looking for up here, sir?' asked Maik as they resumed walking up the hill.

'Bodies,' said Jejeune. 'A few of them, in fact.'

It wasn't his style of humour, but Maik looked over to check for a smile anyway. There wasn't one.

'When I came home in the evening after Katie Fairfax had texted her, Lindy said she'd been drinking,' said Jejeune suddenly, keeping his stare resolutely on the path in front of him.

Maik was reeling as much from the abruptness of the topic's introduction as the content of it. 'All afternoon?'

Jejeune nodded. 'To the point of getting drunk.' He fell silent as they crested the rise and emerged onto the flat hilltop. If the DCI was hoping to find bodies up here, thought Maik, he would be disappointed. He could see only living people on the expanse of grassland; a couple of dedicated joggers battling their way around the perimeter, couples strolling hand in hand, a man throwing a Frisbee for a leaping golden retriever. Bathed in the soft sunshine of morning, with the light breeze carrying the calls of songbirds to them, it seemed hard to believe that this hilltop, and the woods nearby, had been the scenes of two murders. They made their way slowly towards the white monitoring station at the far end of the flat expanse.

Jejeune paused and looked up into the trees, standing for a moment in utter stillness, just watching. Patience, thought Maik, that was what set birdwatchers apart. The willingness to stand motionless, like this, for long moments, waiting for a flicker of movement, when most of us would settle for a quick glance before giving up and continuing on our way. It was the same kind of patience that would allow Jejeune to wait for his evidence to come from Canada when he already knew who the killer was.

'Are you hoping to see that bird, sir?' Maik asked. 'The one whose tail feather you found.'

'Hoping, but not expecting, Sergeant,' he said. 'I think this one will get away. Sometimes, no matter how hard we try, life has other outcomes in mind for us.'

Maik nodded slowly. 'I was wondering, if you still had that feather, if I could have it for Max? He has a school project on local wildlife. I think a tail feather from a woodpecker, so stiff like that, used as a lever, it would be an interesting thing for him to take in.'

'I gave it to Lindy as a gift. I can ask her for it, if she still has it. Would you need me to label it with the species, or do you remember it?'

'Lesser-spotted Woodpecker,' said Maik. 'As opposed to the larger one with the greater spots. I'm guessing that would be the Great-spotted Woodpecker,' he said with a soft grin. 'I think I might finally be starting to get the hang of this birding.'

'Imagine that, after all this time. I found glasses,' said Jejeune with the same abruptness as before. 'Two of them, washed and dried, up on a shelf Lindy can barely reach. There was an empty bottle, too, Passionfruit Rum, in the bottle bin.' He gave a pained smile. 'I would have bet she didn't even know what that was for'.

'You think there was someone there with Lindy that afternoon?' Maik recoiled from his own question. But he knew his DCI wasn't telling him this to share his personal anguish. He *suspected* there was someone there. But only suspected. Because he hadn't been able to bring himself to ask Lindy directly. Why was that? Because he feared the answer? Or because he wasn't sure he would be able to believe her when she gave it? A wave of despair rose within him at the situation his former DCI found himself in.

They strolled on in silence until they reached the monitoring station. Jejeune began looking around the concrete base, expanding his search in ever-increasing circles. He stopped, eyes to the ground, and Maik joined him. The tiny corpses of the four Lapwing chicks lay huddled together, their striped downy plumage camouflaging them even in death.

'Your bodies,' said Maik.

Jejeune nodded sadly. He bent to touch them gently with fingertips.

'If you want a necropsy done on them,' said the sergeant, 'it strikes me that Lelia Segal might be up for that sort of thing.'

'I think they've found a good one there, Sergeant. She's going to prove a valuable asset in the future. But I already know what killed these chicks.' He pointed to the concrete plinth at the base of the monitoring station. 'Let's take a seat. There are a couple of things we need to discuss.'

They sat side by side, looking out over the valley and the glass cube of the Euclid Lab. Behind them, on the opposite corner of the plinth, Sampson Lee, his skull already crushed, had raised his head one final time in an effort to save his life. He had failed, but the message he had left had brought Jejeune to this point.

'We always assumed the killing here was a matter of opportunity. That the original intention was to kill Lee at the house, but something went wrong and the killer ended up following him here. But it wasn't. The killer always knew Lee would need to be killed here.'

Maik looked at his DCI. 'To prevent him from handing over the hard drive?'

Jejeune smiled. Their skills melded so well together. For the first time since Maik had left Saltmarsh, the fact that they would no longer be working with each other seemed to really strike home with the DCI.

'Lee had made arrangements to hand it over to Kim. It was why he told Katie Fairfax he'd had a change of heart and wasn't going to release the name to Johnno. The killer was already up here, watching when Fairfax arrived carrying the tray of filters containing the hidden hard drive. As soon as she locked them in the storage box and left, the watcher knew Lee would come up and unlock it to retrieve the hard drive. Once it was in Kim's hands, it would be too late. So they had to act fast, before the handover took place. They could have jimmied the flap open, but nobody knew about the existence of the hard drive, and they wanted it to stay that way. Why would anybody want to break open a flap to steal a few air filters? So they waited until Lee had unlocked the flap with a key he had copied without Katie Fairfax's knowledge. And then they struck.'

'But it was supposed to be a clean kill, I'm guessing, using the computer cord so the body could be taken back to the house and the scene staged to make it look like Lee had been murdered there.'

Jejeune nodded. 'After sending Huebner's name. But the fall against the plinth ended all that. There was no way to get the body in the house with such horrific blood loss and try to make a convincing case that Lee had died there. So the body was taken to the river.'

'And the killer took a branch from one of those trees over there with them to make sure the body stayed suspended between jurisdictions long enough to allow them to stage everything, including that tyre print from Katie Fairfax's truck.' Maik might have pointed out to another detective that this was getting them no closer to any answers. But Domenic Jejeune constructed his scaffold carefully. You could keep up if you followed closely, but there was always a reason he put the pieces in the order he did. Danny stayed silent.

'I know who killed Sampson Lee, Sergeant. But I'm not sure I can share that information with you.'

'I don't work for you, now, sir. I'm entitled to know.'

Jejeune nodded. 'You are. But once I identify the killer, a lot of things are going to happen at once. There are those with influence who believe it is in the greater interest to let this all go, so Laraby is going to be pressured into convincing me to drop the case.' He paused. 'I'm not going to do that.'

'No, sir.'

'And I am aware of evidence that exists which would cause Laraby too many difficult questions if he insisted on dropping the cases. So, reluctantly, he's going to step aside and let me continue. The same will happen with the chief constable's office. Once the case is eventually presented to the CPS, they are going to be under a lot of pressure from certain sectors not to prosecute. But with the evidence I could present, the only way they could justify declining to bring a case against a double murderer is by trying to discredit my investigation. That would involve calling you in, to testify that I failed to follow procedure somewhere.'

'I was there every step of the way,' said Maik. 'You didn't put a foot wrong on this one, sir.'

Because no one could prove you had suspicions about a staged scene at a cottage if you hadn't shared them aloud. And Katie Fairfax had taken to her grave the secret that Lee had revealed Huebner's name to her. Jejeune paused. 'They are going to come down hard on anybody who won't help them make their case.'

'I'm a big boy. I can take care of myself.'

'I know that, but if I take this forward and it ultimately gets shut down anyway, I might not survive the fallout. If you were to back me on this, they would have no choice but to let you go, too. There is no need for both of us to put our careers on the line.'

Maik was silent for a long time. Up on the hilltop, a pair of Lapwings took to the air, swooping and twisting on the blustery winds, their high-pitched calls carrying over the noise of the wind. He wondered if they were the parents of the chicks whose frail, tiny bodies were lying dead in the grass a few feet away. 'I've never really had this gift of seeing the bigger picture,' he said. 'To my mind, whoever killed Lee and Katie Fairfax deserves to be behind bars. And I for one would welcome the chance to help put them there.'

Jejeune nodded. Had there ever been any doubt about where his ex-sergeant would stand? Slowly and methodically, he walked Maik through his findings; the sequence of events, the details, and the microscopic, fragmentary evidence that linked them all. Maik listened without comment or question.

When Jejeune had finished, Maik looked behind him at the stand of alder trees on the forest edge. 'So suspending Lee's body from that branch in the river was just to create a jurisdictional dispute. It wasn't about exploiting the personal rift between you and Laraby at all.'

Jejeune shook his head. 'There was no way the killer could have known about Laraby and me. That was just coincidence.'

Imagine that. After all this time, said Maik's smile. 'Those alder trees, they would all have individual DNA, wouldn't they? No matter how well you cleaned out your vehicle, you'd leave some tiny fragment in there, enough for a match with that branch they transported from here to the river.'

'Yes, you would. But you'd need to make the case with your best evidence before you ever got a search warrant for the vehicle.'

Maik nodded. Evidence whose existence *you are aware of*, he recalled. But you don't yet have. You want the person who does have it to hand it over voluntarily, but you aren't sure they will. And that has stopped you from asking for it. What would happen if they refused? Would you be willing to demand it, under threat of prosecution? And be prepared to face the consequences? Again, the thought of the dilemma facing his former DCI brought Maik almost crushing sadness.

The men stood up together and Maik took one last look at the tiny bodies of the Lapwing chicks. 'These birds, sir, in the end, I suppose what killed them was a case of misplaced trust.'

Jejeune nodded. 'A simple mistake. But the consequences proved fatal.' He extended a hand. 'If this does turn out to be the last case we work on together, I want you to know I couldn't have wished for a better colleague, Danny.'

Maik grasped his former DCI's hand and shook it firmly. He smiled. 'It's not always been straightforward, sir, but it has been an honour and a privilege to serve with you.'

Jejeune nodded and drew in a breath. He looked out once more over the edge of the hilltop, where the sun slanted along the valley, glittering off the glass walls of the Euclid Lab. 'Ready, Sergeant?' he asked. 'I think we've covered all we needed to up here. Time to finish things off.'

50

Domenic Jejeune had chosen a table beside the fireplace in the Board Room. It was a favourite of the police officers who met in here, set back and secluded, a long way from casual eavesdroppers. There was no fire burning in the hearth tonight. Instead the pub's windows were open slightly to let in the evening's fresh spring air. But it was the privacy that was Domenic's main concern.

He stood up as his guest arrived. 'Thank you for coming so quickly.'

'You made it sound like I didn't have a choice.'

At this stage, perhaps you did, thought Jejeune. But soon that would change. Once he had started speaking his listener would be compelled to stay until the end.

'Would you like a drink?'

'No, thanks. If this is as important as you claim, I think we should just get on with it.'

Jejeune inclined his head. 'Fair enough. I want to start, though, by telling you I don't blame you for what happened that afternoon at the house.'

There was a long pulse of silence, as if a decision to deny the premise was being considered. If it was, in the end it was rejected. 'Nothing happened. A few drinks, some tunes, a couple of old friends reminiscing about past times, that's all.'

He shook his head. 'Oh no, I think a lot more that that happened. But I don't hold you responsible. For any of it. The fault is all mine. I got so wrapped up with this case, I wasn't there when my partner needed me. I could see she was in trouble but I couldn't make time for her. I was away, and that left a gap, a space that could easily be filled by someone else, someone from earlier in her life, someone who could be there for her when I wasn't.'

He waited to see where the silence would lead them. It ended up not being where he had hoped. 'Well, I'm sure this is not why you asked me here, so if it's all the same to you, maybe we could get to the point.' The smile was perfunctory, the tone defiant.

'I know,' said Jejeune, sitting forward in his chair. 'What happened. How. Why. All of it.' The two pairs of eyes locked and continued staring at each other until one set blinked. It wasn't Jejeune's. He would wait now for the response to guide him. Denial, and he'd press hard. Evasion, perhaps less so. But all he got was another flat stare, more interested now, but no friendlier. 'This should be worth hearing. Go ahead, I'm all ears.'

'It begins with a man who wanted a name, for his podcast. Somebody had contacted him and told him he knew the identity of a person involved in a scheme to profit from government purchases of blue carbon sites. It was a big story, the kind that a career journalist dreams about. And this man thought he had it. He even announced in his earlier podcast that he was going to be able to reveal the name in his next one. But then his source had a change of heart.'

There was an uncomfortable shifting in the seat across from Jejeune, but no other response. He pressed on.

'The source said he had decided he wasn't going to reveal the name after all, that more good could be done by withholding it and making better use of the information. Only, the podcaster had put his reputation on the line with that earlier announcement. Listenership was likely to be at an all-time high for his next show, so he was hardly in a position to allow somebody's second thoughts get in the way of all that, was he?'

Jejeune stopped to see if his listener had any reaction. His look was met only by another silent, unblinking stare.

'I imagine at this point our podcaster began to wonder what had caused such a sudden change of heart. And so he began following his source, Sampson Lee. Tracking him from a distance would be my guess, observing him through high-powered binoculars, possibly even 12 x 50s.' Jejeune tried his luck with a small smile, but there were no takers on the far side of the table. 'And while he was following Lee, the man observed a couple of very interesting things. The first was a meeting between Lee and a person named Marius Huebner; a man with a history of sketchy land deals and a reputation for ruthlessness and greed. Surely, this had to be the mystery figure, the man whose name Lee was originally going to reveal. So the podcaster had his scoop, after all. Now all he needed was for Lee to confirm it, on the record, in time to reveal it in his next podcast.'

'Can I ask, just as a matter of interest, why you're telling me all this?' The tone was intended to be light, playful almost. But the strain of reaching for it came through instead, and the uncomfortable shifting in the chair opposite became more pronounced as a result.

'I want to show you that I really do have the whole picture. So there's no point in protesting, or denying, or attempting to find alternative explanations. Believe me, I've looked for them. I've considered every possibility. This is the truth of what happened.'

'The truth?' exclaimed Lindy. 'Is that what you call this?' She sounded angry and bitter. But not dismissive. No, the other undertone in Lindy's remark was fear.

'I believe when Johnno asked Lee to confirm the name, he not only refused, but even said he'd deny it if he went ahead with the announcement. But we both know how Johnno would handle a situation like that. He'd release the podcast anyway, and deal with the fallout from the denial later.'

Jejeune tried to reach her with a small smile again, seeking agreement even on this small point of Johnno's personality. But Lindy couldn't allow the defenses she was erecting to be breached. As before, Jejeune was left to proceed only into her silence. 'The second thing Johnno found out when he was following Lee proved to be an even bigger story than Huebner. Because the way Sampson Lee had discovered Huebner's name in the first place was by developing a program to recreate redacted documents.'

Lindy sat forward abruptly. All the lightness had gone from her now. There was no dismissive irreverence or affected insouciance. Only a laser beam of focus met him across the table, a cold hard gaze. She could sense where he was going now, and she was challenging him to continue. If he dared. Jejeune's throat felt dry. He wished he'd thought to get a couple of drinks, glasses of water at least. But he knew if he interrupted his narrative now, he'd never get Lindy to resume this journey with him. So he pressed on.

'All of sudden, it all made sense. The reason Lee wasn't willing to confirm Huebner's name, the reason for his change of heart in the first place, in fact. It was because he'd already made a deal to hand this program over to someone else. But Johnno wasn't prepared to let that happen. Imagine it, a program that could reveal all kinds of secrets: military, political, legal. If anybody was going to have a goldmine like that, it would be him. So now, Johnno needed a solution that could not only prevent Lee from denying he had given him Huebner's name, but would also ensure that he secured that program for himself.'

He paused again. On the other side of the table, Lindy's facial features were slipping into a mask of horror and disbelief.

'And that solution was to murder Sampson Lee.'

Jejeune wasn't sure what reaction he had expected. He just knew this wasn't it; a stunned, controlled silence, as Lindy marshalled a response. 'You're wrong,' she said finally. 'When Lee was killed, Johnno was miles away, re-recording his podcast to reveal Huebner's name. It had arrived only minutes before. There's that email. That proves it.' She sounded desperate, but her hollow words lacked conviction.

Jejeune shook his head. 'No Lindy, he wasn't. By the time he sent the email to himself from Lee's computer, he already knew Huebner's identity. He re-recorded that new podcast long before, and played it from his London flat while he was up here killing Sampson Lee.'

She shook her head. 'No, you don't know this, you have no proof, no evidence. It's all just wild supposition, one of your typical off-the-wall theories. Only in this case they're targeting someone for a particular reason. And we both know what that reason is don't we, Dom? Well, I don't want to hear any more.'

Lindy made as if to stand up. The scraping of her chair as it was drawn back seemed overloud against the quiet background hum of the room. But no one looked over. It was still just the two of them, either side of a small, round table, staring at each other.

'Want to? Probably not, but I think you need to listen anyway, Lindy. Because the person who killed Sampson Lee also committed the second murder. The one of Katie Fairfax. Johnno McBride killed them both.'

She sat down again heavily. 'No, that's crazy,' she protested, shaking her head. 'You have this wrong, Dom. It wasn't Johnno. He was with me that afternoon.'

'No, Lindy. He put something in your drink. And then, when you were passed out, he got her new number from your contacts and sent Katie Fairfax a text from a burner phone, under your name, saying it wasn't safe to meet at the house and you'd meet her up in the woods instead. Then he slipped away to kill Katie, deleted his text from her phone and sent you one from it saying the DNA evidence was a bust. He returned to the house before you came round.'

'No, that's not true. It's not.' She was shaking her head again. 'What you think you know and what really happened are two different things, Domenic. I know Johnno. I know he couldn't be capable of these things. I don't believe it.'

'Yes,' he said as gently as he could, 'you do. Perhaps not at first. I could hear the uncertainty in your voice. But it's gone now, because you know, don't you, Lindy?'

'Who the hell do you think you are?' she asked angrily. 'I'm not one of your bloody suspects to be put under the microscope and have my responses analysed. I won't stand for it.'

Jejeune forged on relentlessly. He was heading towards an uncertain outcome, but he had nowhere else to go. 'You know it's true because it's the answer to the question you've been asking yourself since Katie first contacted you. Why you? If she wanted to expose a story nationwide and didn't trust the police, who is the obvious person to go to? Johnno already has a background in the story. He has credibility and an established reputation. He has a national podcast audience that dwarfs your circulation. It's immediate and impactful and could have got the news out there in minutes. So why not go to him with it? There's only one reason you'd choose to bypass an outlet like that and go to a journalist for a small-circulation local magazine. Because the story was about him. Johnno recognised it as soon as he found out Katie had called you, that day I was with him at the flat. He knew then that Katie had found a way of identifying him. And he knew he had to kill her.'

Lindy's features twisted with shock and pain. 'No, Dom, no. He was with me. He was...' Jejeune could see her mind tearing at her memories, searching for something to prove that he had made a mistake. But if she knew anything about his wild, off-the-wall theories, it was that, when he had reached the point where he was willing to voice them out loud like this, it was because they were right. Always. She slumped back into her chair as if she could no longer support herself.

He wanted to reach out and hold her, to tell her everything would be okay. But he was no longer sure that it would. Something had happened that afternoon at the house. He didn't know what, but there was a distance between them since that hadn't been there before. On the hill, at the scene of Katie Fairfax's murder, it had been Danny she had turned to for solace, as if perhaps she felt she couldn't find it from her partner any more. What had happened to them? All he knew was that he could no longer be sure of her, of her feelings, of her intentions. Or even of her cooperation.

'Johnno killed Katie Fairfax, Lindy, but, unless his alibi falls apart, I can't get him for her murder.'

'You want me to say he wasn't there that afternoon?'

'I want you to tell the truth, Lindy. Only that.'

The truth, he thought. The only thing that's left to us after all the lies and evasions and deceptions have been stripped away. Her testimony. And her evidence. Lindy held the keys to both murders. But he was sure now that he couldn't ask her for them. And he didn't know where that left them. This, this was where the truth had brought them both.

Lindy stood up. 'If that's all, then, I'll be on my way.' She walked away without saying goodbye.

51

It was late when Jejeune left the station. The investigation file for the murder of Sampson Lee was on his desk, and beside it lay the one for Katie Fairfax's murder. By the time he had finished explaining them to Laraby in the morning, it was inevitable that they would go forward as a single, linked case file. He had not spoken to Lindy since she left the pub the night before. He had come back to the station afterwards to begin putting the files together before grabbing a few hours' sleep on a couch in his office. He had called her repeatedly throughout the day today, but she hadn't picked up. He tried again now, but declined to leave a message. What they needed to discuss had to be said in person.

He had no wish to go home. It was a soft, warm evening and it beckoned him outdoors. He made his way to the Euclid Lab, dark and quiet now the occupants had gone home for the night. He parked the Beast beside the shed, unable to suppress a shimmer of unease as he got out. But no one was lurking in the shadows when he looked around, and he left the vehicle to begin his long stroll up the hill and over to the hide on the far side. The sunset would be lying on the quiet water of the marsh by the time he arrived. It would be a time of few birds, only evening specialists like Woodcocks and Water Rails, perhaps. But it was not the birds he was coming for tonight. He needed a place to think, to recoil from the blows the world had delivered lately. And to reflect on his future.

The window slat facing the forest was open when he arrived at the hide, but he could see no signs of activity. He opened the door and a small voice came from the darkness of the far corner. 'Hello, Domenic,' said Kim. 'I thought you might come here tonight.'

While he was still recovering from his surprise, she pointed to a scope already set up and focused up into the forest canopy. 'I'm not much of a birder, but I believe there may have been a Lesser-spotted Woodpecker up in the treetops.'

Jejeune crossed to the scope and bent to press his eye into the eyepiece. He adjusted the focus slightly to compensate for the failing light and swivelled the scope back and forth. He saw no signs of movement. 'If it was, it's not there now,' he said, easing back from the eyepiece and straightening up.

'No?' Kim shrugged. 'Well, sometimes our quarry eludes us no matter how relentlessly we pursue them, don't they? They just always seem to be one step ahead. I understand Johnno McBride has been detained in London,' she said without missing a beat. 'Pending your further instructions. Is he saying anything, I wonder?'

Jejeune shook his head. 'He seems to be expecting someone to come to his rescue, as if they might be able to wave a magic wand and make the case against him disappear.'

'Oh, there is no need to rely on magic wands,' said Kim. 'There are easier ways of making cases disappear.' There was a coldness to her smile that Jejeune had not seen before. In fact there was an air of ruthless detachment about her, like a person utterly fixed on an outcome, without time for niceties.

Maik's words from an earlier time came back to him. *The ones promoted from the field are the most dangerous of all.*

'I'm told he's not been confronted with any evidence yet. I do hope you're not resting your hopes on a confession. I have to say, Johnno McBride doesn't seem the type to throw his fate on the mercy of the court.'

'I can produce evidence that places him at the scene of Sampson Lee's murder. It will be enough for a warrant for his laptop.'

'His laptop?'

'We will run an AI acoustic listening program to analyse the recording of his podcast. Technology might not make errors, but its one great flaw is that it is operated by humans. And they are a long way from perfect. We will find proof, some buzz or chime or background noise on there, to pinpoint exactly when that podcast revealing Marius Huebner's name was actually recorded. And when we do, Johnno McBride will face charges for the murders of Sampson Lee and Katie Fairfax.'

'I take it he didn't have a hard drive with him when he was picked up,' said Kim.

'You won't be getting your program, I'm afraid. Johnno McBride will be using it to make other deals to get himself out of prison. The government are going to be very interested to know a program like that exists. They will wait for his court case to reach its inevitable conclusion, and then they will offer to commute his sentence in return for him handing it over.' Jejeune paused. 'It's a deal he will be happy to make.'

Kim shook her head. 'I am here, as I'm sure you've already realised, to ensure none of that happens.' She gave a deep sigh. 'I did want this to be your choice, Domenic, but I suppose I always knew it was one you would never make. So, now I must take that choice away from you. Just the one phone, is it? I wonder if you would be kind enough to turn it off and put it on the seat beside you while we talk?'

'There's no service out here.'

'No, but it will still have one of those nasty recording devices on it.' As before, her smile held more threat than warmth. Jejeune took out the phone and laid it on the seat beside him. She nodded with satisfaction. 'So let's review where we are, shall we? The evidence you need to connect McBride to Lee's murder lies with Lindy, doesn't it? I have to tell you, she doesn't seem inclined to offer any help.'

Jejeune stared at her, shock etched on his features. 'You went to see her?'

'Not as Kim the intelligence operative, of course. But someone purporting to be Johnno McBride's Airbnb host did visit her today. Apparently, he'd left a few things behind during his hasty departure, and, as luck would have it, Lindy's address was among them. The host went round in the hopes that she might have a forwarding address. Oh don't worry, Domenic, Lindy has no idea who she was talking to. She does believe he's guilty, by the way. I could see it in her eyes. She's having a hard time convincing herself that it could be true, but somewhere deep down she knows it is.'

She looked at him and something in Jejeune's face told her: his insecurity, his uncertainty, his pain. 'You're not at all sure that she will turn that evidence over to you, are you? So now you must ask yourself if you are prepared to force her to, through legal channels.' Kim shook her head. 'I doubt any relationship could survive that, let alone one as troubled as yours seems to be. Would you be willing to sacrifice your future with Lindy to pursue your justice, I wonder?' She considered his face carefully in the fading half-light of the hide. 'Do you know, Domenic, I'm not really sure I can tell.'

'Johnno McBride is guilty of the murder of two people. He has to answer for that. I will bring the case forward.' He looked her in the eyes. 'There's no way you can prevent that now.'

'Perhaps I already have.' She sighed and looked out through the slat. 'Eternal vigilance can be so exhausting, can't it? Threats can come from anywhere. Who would think of checking for a nerve toxin on the eyepiece of a scope in a bird hide, for example?'

Jejeune's first reaction was to smile, but the look on Kim's face made it fade immediately. He looked over at the scope. The black eyepiece cup glistened with a shiny substance. As the realisation set in, his mind began racing and he was forced to support himself with one hand on the wall of the hide. His thoughts seemed to be spinning out of control. Was it true? Could it be? Did he feel any symptoms, a faint racing of the pulse, a spiking temperature? His brain began frantically analysing the previous few minutes. Had there been something in the coldness of Kim's demeanour, he thought now, that had told him all along that she knew how this would end, despite his resistance?

'You should sit down, Domenic,' said Kim calmly. 'You need to keep your blood pressure and respiratory rate under control as much as possible for the next few minutes.'

Jejeune felt his way to the bench and collapsed onto it.

52

'Someone will come looking for me,' said Jejeune. He was still slumped over, but the panic had subsided for the moment. His heart was racing, but he had not detected the onset of any other symptoms yet.

'But will they find you? Lindy will not be too worried if she can't reach you. Not exactly unknown, is it, a call to Domenic Jejeune's phone going to voicemail? Nobody is going to start a search for a long while. And even after they did, you parked at the lab, I take it? Once they found the vehicle, how long would it be before somebody thought to look all the way over here?'

Danny would, he thought. Danny would know where to look. If he could just hold on. How long did he have? Long enough for someone to miss him and raise the alarm? Long enough for his trusted friend to come and save him, one more time? He saw Kim's calm, untroubled expression and he knew his answer. No. Not long enough. No one would be able to get here in time to save him.

He looked up at her. 'Killing a serving police officer? Are the stakes really that high, for one simple redaction algorithm?'

She tilted her head. 'For some. Perhaps there are those who have committed transgressions worthy of redaction who now find themselves in positions of power. They would be extremely vulnerable to having their earlier actions revealed. Our past sins don't disappear as we get older, Domenic, they merely go into hibernation. Even if the statute of limitations on a crime runs out, the statute of public judgement never does.'

Jejeune's skin was moist with sweat. He checked his pulse, but he was too distracted to count properly. 'The files are on my desk. Others will follow up.'

'Will they? You are notoriously secretive about your investigations. I hardly think you'll have shared your conclusions with anyone yet. Not the whole picture, anyway. But you live a charmed life, Domenic. Fate has granted you the one thing that may yet save your life.'

His heart quickened at the words, but it seemed impossible that Kim would put herself in the position to gain everything she wanted and then give him a reprieve.

'Ketamine, cheese wire, nerve toxins on surfaces an unwary birder will neglect to check; do you know why such crude methods have endured in this technologically dominated age we find ourselves in? Because they are effective. Yet none of those things are necessary when you possess the most powerful weapon of all: your opponent's heart.' She gave a soft smile, the warmest he had seen from her. 'It is the one true incalculable left to us, isn't it, our humanity? The one variable that defies any analysis, that can never be factored into any algorithm, that sets us apart from the machines. After all, what hopes does a simple computer program have of understanding human hearts when even we who possess them find their workings so impenetrable? So yes, believe me when I say the threat of death from a nerve toxin still hovers over you, Domenic. But your heart may be your saviour yet.'

He stared at Kim uncomprehendingly. Since his entry into this hide, he had been surprised, alarmed and, now, terrified. But none of those emotions could survive his hope.

'You knew about my expertise in algorithms,' she continued. 'That could only have come from my service file. It's a classified document. The ultimate irony is of course that the information should have been redacted before the file was released to the police. It was missed by somebody. A simple mistake' – she spread her small hands – 'and look where it has left us. Failing to protect a classified document would be a career ender for Laraby. Of course, he may do the noble thing and assume responsibility himself, shielding his troops in a selfless act of leadership. Do we think he will do that, Domenic? Or do we think, instead, that he might be prepared to give up Lauren Salter to save his own career?'

Kim waited, but Jejeune offered no answer. She nodded. 'So Salter will be prosecuted under the Official Secrets Act, charged with accessing classified information without clearance. And then sharing that information with other unauthorised persons.'

'I will say I asked her to do it.'

'And if not you, Danny Maik?' She smiled coldly. 'We can ask anything of people, Domenic. But unless you have some evidence that she was acting under orders, I'm afraid your gallant gesture will count for nothing. You need to understand, prosecution under the OSA is not discretionary. If GCHQ request it, a case will be brought. And as for merit, well, a world of irrelevance can be hidden beneath a cloak of a "Classified" designation. It won't be necessary to prove the information's value, merely that it should have been protected from unauthorised distribution.'

'And your role in all this, an unsanctioned operation to develop a redaction-reversing program? How will GCHQ feel about that?'

'I have survived quite a lot in my career,' said Kim. 'I shall survive this, too. But Lauren Salter will not. She is guilty of those crimes, Domenic, and she will go to prison for them. But what of the aftermath? The spiderweb of tragedy, I call it, spreading out across the lives of all those interconnected people like so many cracks in a mirror. How will poor Max cope with losing his mother? How will Danny adapt to the role of single parent? And then, of course, there is Lindy. What would she think when she knows you had the power to prevent all this suffering, all this pain, and you chose not to, that you allowed it to happen because of some inviolable personal morality? Because you can prevent all this, you see. You can close your investigation into the deaths of Sampson Lee and Katie Fairfax, citing lack of sufficient evidence to bring charges. After all, it's not untrue.'

'And if I do.'

'Then you will not die today. And any charges against Lauren Salter, or Laraby, go away. Permanently.'

Jejeune nodded. His relief at his reprieve came first, flooding in, expanding his chest so he could draw in a deep grateful sob of breath. But the pain of his compromise still burned. He lowered his head. 'Is it really all worth it, this life you lead, these lengths you must go to, manipulating lives, destroying people, ignoring crimes, just to get what you want?'

'We don't always get what we want, Domenic, only what others have within their power to give us. But if we are lucky, sometimes that can be enough.'

She saw the defeat in him, the guilt that he had chosen his own fate over that of others, the bitterness, and the anger.

And the relief. And she knew he had accepted. 'You won't be needing an antidote, Domenic, or a trip to the hospital. Your decision has saved you. You may go. But it is still a dangerous world out there, even though you are now no longer unwary. Do please be extremely careful not to touch that door handle with your bare hand on your way out, won't you.'

53

From the front of the King's Landing Incident Room, DCS Marvin Laraby surveyed the assembled officers in silence. Even to someone new to the spectacle, like Lelia Segal, Laraby's displeasure was evident. But to those more familiar with it, this time it seemed to lack its normal fire. This was Laraby following someone else's orders for a change. And however much he may have chafed against them, it was clear that whoever had issued them had left no room for discussion.

'This will be the last time our colleagues from Saltmarsh will be joining us here,' he announced bluntly. 'The chief constable in his wisdom has decided we won't be moving forward with the investigations into the murders of Sampson Lee and Katie Fairfax. He has cited the unlikelihood of a successful prosecution in either case at this time.' He seemed to remember his duty to support the decisions of the upper echelons, and replaced his disgusted look with one of reluctant resignation. 'Hard to argue, I suppose, since we were never able to find even one viable suspect.'

Maik looked across at Jejeune, but he seemed reluctant to meet his sergeant's eye. 'We can build a case, sir,' said Danny. 'If this is about supporting the DCI's approach towards gathering his evidence, I'd be prepared to do that. Unreservedly.'

Laraby shot Jejeune a glance. 'Evidence? What evidence? As far as I am aware, we have no credible evidence against anybody. Even this redaction reversing program you seemed so convinced about has never surfaced. If you have anything you'd like to share, Inspector Jejeune, now would be the time to do so. Well past time, in fact.'

'It's not really evidence,' he said, still unwilling to meet Maik's eye. 'More just a series of conjectures. They amount to nothing in the end.'

Maik continued staring in Jejeune's direction. Laraby took it as a sign that he needed to press. 'We're entitled to hear them, Inspector. Just because you couldn't get them over the line doesn't mean the rest of us should be denied the chance to have a go.'

He waited, as the room did, all eyes locked on Jejeune. Except for Maik's now. He realised his former DCI would not be following through and, though he didn't know his reasons, he knew enough about the man to accept them. 'Sir, perhaps, if the DCI thinks it's a waste of time—'

'Inspector?' asked Laraby, dismissing Maik's attempted intervention.

'When Katie Fairfax suggested that she might be able to find something in the eDNA samples to identify the killer, I began looking into it. She had talked about a change in the quantity of Lapwing DNA, so I started there.'

'Lapwings? Bloody birds again?' If Laraby had limited himself to eye-rolling, perhaps Jejeune would have been content to let things lie, simply say he had found nothing and close the matter. But the contempt in Laraby's voice seemed to fire something in Jejeune and he drew himself forward in his chair as he continued.

'With her still maintaining that she had a way to prove it even after the samples from the day of the murder were stolen, it was clear she was basing her claims on changes to the eDNA quantities in the samples taken from the day before the murder, and the day after.'

Jejeune paused for a moment and Maik had the impression he was even now deciding whether to continue. In the end, he did.

'So I sent the samples off for analysis, to Canada. The head of research there confirmed that there was a significant increase in the Lapwing DNA collected after the murder compared with that collected the day before it. But Katie Fairfax had mentioned that she'd also found traces of another kind of DNA in that second batch, the one from the day after the murder. The Canadian lab confirmed it was from a dog.' He paused again and looked at the ME. 'With that in mind, I asked Dr Segal if it was possible the leather fragments from the post were not from a glove after all.'

'They weren't,' she confirmed. 'Definitely too coarse. My best guess, and one I'd be prepared to back, is unfinished leather from the inside of a dog's leash.'

Laraby leaned forward onto the balls of his feet. 'You think somebody tied a dog to the post up there? And what, this dog's owner might have seen something? So why haven't they come forward?'

But Danny Maik was already following along in the DCI's wake. Except, as usual, he couldn't make the final connection yet. 'Because the dog might not have belonged to a witness,' he said. 'You think it may have been the murderer that tied the dog to that post, sir?'

Jejeune nodded. 'It would have been a pretty effective way to disguise the reason they were up there. Just another person on a walk with a dog. Not some lone individual lurking with the intent to murder Sampson Lee.'

There was a faint hesitation now, all but indiscernible unless you'd worked as closely with Jejeune as Danny had. The DCI had tiptoed as close to the truth as he dared, Maik realised. Whatever followed now would be consigned to the world of conjecture, whether it had occurred or not.

'The next step would have been to see if that kind of dog DNA was present only in the latter sample. Airborne DNA lingers, you see, so if this type was absent from the earlier sample, you could plausibly argue that you had the DNA of the dog that was tied to the post on the day of the murder. Now obviously, if you can't ID an individual human through eDNA, you wouldn't be able to identify a specific dog. But you would have been able to narrow it down to a breed, like a Labrador, say, or a Border collie.'

To Laraby, the mention of the dog breed held no significance. He was beginning to tire of the conjecture. 'Even if it was the murderer who tied the dog to that post, you'd need the identity of the individual dog to establish any sort of link. And you're saying none of this can get you there?'

'No,' conceded Jejeune. 'Not on its own. You'd need to go back to the increase in Lapwing DNA to do that.' He paused and the others looked around, sharing glances. This was DCI Jejeune closing in on something. 'When we were up there after the discovery of the blood on the post, there was a Lapwing nest near the base of the post with a clutch of four chicks. The first step would have been to establish exactly when those chicks were hatched.'

'A few of us saw those chicks,' said Salter. 'They were pretty young. I'd guess a couple of days at most.'

'I'd agree, but an estimate of their age wouldn't have been enough. I'd have been looking at the eDNA evidence to establish precisely when they were born.' He looked at Lelia. 'Dr Segal?'

She stepped forward to speak. 'The chicks' DNA wouldn't register in the air samples until they had hatched. Given that the samples from the day after the murder revealed a sharp, sustained spike in Lapwing DNA, I'd be happy to make the case that you had proof that the chicks hatched from the eggs on the day of the murder.'

'And where would that get you, exactly?' said Laraby, unable to keep the impatience from his voice now. But others had begun leaning forward in their seats slightly, sensing that Jejeune was inching towards a conclusion of some kind.

'Lapwings chicks are precocious. They imprint on the first thing they see. Their parents usually, but sometimes another animal, like a dog. The thing is, hatching takes time, as does imprinting. If you tied your dog to the post with the intention of keeping it out of the way while you strangled Sampson Lee and moved his body to your car, you'd undoubtedly be back to take the dog away long before all the chicks had hatched and imprinted.'

'But if something went catastrophically wrong,' said Maik, unable to suppress a slight, knowing smile, 'and now you have to move a body somewhere else, say a river, the last thing you want is to have a dog around getting fur and hair and bloody paw prints all over the place...'

'So maybe you leave your dog tied to the post,' finished Holland, 'long enough for these newly hatched chicks to imprint on it.'

'And if we could find a witness who saw those imprinted chicks later interacting with a particular dog,' said Salter, 'it would tell you that this was the same dog that was up there during the period of the murder. It couldn't belong to anybody else but the murderer.'

A silence fell over the room. Jejeune had guided them there, finally. But it was to evidence they didn't have. 'Not to point out the obvious, Inspector,' Laraby said coldly, 'but none of our suspects owns a dog.'

'Maybe relatives do. Or friends,' said Salter. 'Our killer isn't going to buy a dog to take up there, or steal one. But they would borrow one. Once we know the breed of dog we are looking for, if we start looking for one among friends and family of the suspects, we might come up with it. And taking the dog up there as a decoy in the first place proves premeditation. It would be enough to get us an arrest warrant for whoever took it up there and tied it up.'

Maik had finally caught up. He knew where they were and why Jejeune had chosen to end his conjectures before getting here. He recognised, too, that they now all needed to do the same. 'It's a stretch,' he said. 'The only way you'd ever get any of this to stick is if you had a witness who could say they'd seen this dog with the chicks. But even then, all you'd have is some vague description of the interaction between them. It would never hold up in court.'

'We wouldn't need a witness,' insisted Salter. 'That imprinting is for life. If we found the dog, we could take it back up there again. If the chicks showed evidence of having bonded, we could capture it on film and show it to animal behaviour experts. It would be definitive proof. We'd have our killer.'

And, now, Maik realised the reason for the trip up to the hilltop that day. Jejeune had been hoping against hope that those chicks were still alive, so he could have brought Johnno's dog up there and filmed them, imprinted on it. And then he wouldn't have needed to ask Lindy for her footage. But those hopes had been crushed. And perhaps something else had died up on the hill that day, too.

'We might have been able to do that,' said Maik slowly, 'except the DCI and I were up there on that hilltop. We found those four little chicks. They're all dead.'

Laraby nodded slowly. 'So that's it then. Absent any other evidence those little birds bonded with that dog, we have nothing to offer the CPS. Further to the chief constable's directive, this case is closed.'

'One of them is guilty, sir,' said Salter disgustedly. 'Chandra, Ishtara, Huebner, Rowe. They have to be. And whoever it is gets to walk away.' She looked at Jejeune. 'Two people dead, murdered, two families denied justice and you're throwing in the towel? You used to have a bit more fight in you, sir, if you don't my mind my saying so.'

'That's enough, Sergeant,' said Laraby. 'They're not all going to be wins.' He nodded emphatically. 'Granted, this one feels like a particularly bitter loss, and I imagine no one is sensing it more than the DCI.'

At the sound of his title, Jejeune lifted his head. He looked like a man incapable of being wounded any more.

'I'm sure we all expected him to untangle the knots, conjure up some solution out of thin air, as he usually does. But this time, all you could come up with was some unproven theory about a missing software program.' Laraby looked at him significantly. 'If there ever was an algorithm for recreating redacted documents, nobody seems to have found hide nor hair of it. It must be hard for you to take, knowing you were so far off this time, and leaving us all without a case at the end as a result.' He straightened and looked at the rest of them.' The reputation of this department, of both our departments, has taken a hit on this one, I can tell you. I suppose we just ought to be grateful we all still have our jobs, thank God.'

But it was not God Laraby had to thank for his job, Maik knew. It was the man he was blaming for the investigation's failure. From preventing him from pursuing the wrong lines of inquiry, to protecting him from the worst excesses of Kim, Jejeune had saved Laraby's career in ways the DCS would never be aware of. Domenic Jejeune would never mention it himself, so perhaps he should. But like all good spies, Danny Maik knew the value of silence. In the end, he said nothing.

Maik had stayed behind after the others left. Only Jejeune remained with him.

'It occurs to me, sir,' he said as he approached the seated DCI, 'if Lindy did want to send that footage she was talking about over to Max, once it had been shared there would be no need for a court order to produce it. They could use Max's version. At first, anyway, to get their warrants.'

'Yes, Sergeant, I think perhaps they could. But the case is closed. It won't be reopened.'

Maik nodded. 'No, sir.' Because any case that was brought would still need the original footage at some point. And it would highlight the fact that it was taken by Lindy when she was out walking alone on the hilltop with Johnno McBride, a murderer she later invited into her home for an intimate afternoon drinking session before he left to also kill Katie Fairfax. Lindy's reputation would never recover from those associations. Nor would she. Who could blame Jejeune for trying to protect the woman he loved? Would not he, Danny Maik, do exactly the same thing to protect Lauren? The human heart, he thought. Everything was a hostage to its power. Even justice.

54

'Are we okay?'

Lindy had asked the question as she came to sit down beside Jejeune on the rocks overlooking the inlet. From the house behind came the faint strains of music, but it was not anything he recognised; not Leonard Cohen, not Motown, not any vintage CD. Lindy was taking her tastes in a new direction, and perhaps Domenic's along with them.

Were they okay? If she meant did he still love her, did he still ache for her sadnesses and feel the need to protect her and care for her, then yes. But other things had shifted. Parts of their relationship had been damaged during these past few days and they could never be repaired. He suspected Lindy knew that, too. It was the reason for her question. Possibly they could put it behind them, if they chose to, and move forward to somewhere new, but the relationship they had once had, the status quo, that was gone for ever. All that remained was to see what the future looked like. If there was one.

He looked at the water, moving restlessly under a low, fugitive wind. In the trees on the far side of the inlet there was movement, but it was too deep in for him to see any birds with his naked eye. His bins lay beside him, but he didn't bother raising them.

'I believe he killed Lee, Dom. And I believe he killed Katie Fairfax, too.'

Jejeune turned to her and could see it in her eyes, the same terrified truth that Kim had recognised, lurking behind all those earlier denials. Lindy knew. And she knew it now because she had always known it, in the deepest recesses of her heart, in those places she didn't want to go. She had known that Johnno McBride was capable of acts like this. She could say he wasn't this person, try to convince herself that he wouldn't ever take that final step, not even for the story. But she knew he would. For the story. For himself.

'I've never told you before, but once, in uni, I got roofied.' She shook her head. 'It wasn't Johnno. It was a long time before I met him.'

Jejeune had heard other stories that began tentatively like this, too many of them. He knew that waiting was the key; no reaction, just patience. He sat silently looking at the water as Lindy gathered herself.

'Nothing happened. My friends were looking out for me and got me home safely. I passed out in the car on the way home and they put me to bed. I don't remember a thing about it, only that I'd trusted him, that creep. It's so hard to know who to trust when you're young.' She smiled sadly. 'I learned a lot about a lot of things that night. But you know the one thing that stood out to me when I woke up later? The sensitivity to light I had afterwards. I had the same thing when I woke up that afternoon. It was so bad I had to wear sunglasses.'

Jejeune nodded. 'The bottle had been washed. I thought it was to remove his fingerprints in case I tested, but that could have been done with a dry cloth. There was no need to wash the bottle inside and out other than to remove any traces of Rohypnol.'

'He has to go to prison for what he's done. To Lee. To that poor, innocent girl. I'll testify that I was drugged, that I can't give him an alibi for the time of her death.'

'It's too late for that now,' said Jejeune. 'He's cooperating with the intelligence services. He has something they want and in return all charges against him are being stayed.'

'But that's outrageous,' said Lindy, tossing her hair as she recovered some of her former fire. 'He killed people, he can't be allowed to get away with that.'

'He has. He'll never again have any of the independence he seemed to value so much, now that he's put his fate in their hands. I don't know if he's had the chance to consider just how much he's going to be under their control. I suspect it's starting to sink in already. But as far as facing any kind of justice for his actions...' Jejeune shook his head. 'He won't.'

She touched him on the shoulder. He realised with a start that it was the first physical contact they'd had in days. 'But you found out who did it, Dom. You cleared those other suspects of any guilt and set the blame where it deserves to lie. That's a kind of justice in that, surely. Even if it's a compromised kind.'

Compromised. Trust Lindy to hit on the exact word. 'I can't tell anybody else what I know. I can't inform the suspects, I can't assign blame. As a serving police officer, I am bound by the Official Secrets Act even if I didn't sign anything. This agreement they have entered into with Johnno is covered by that Act. Nobody else will ever know the truth, Lindy. They can't.'

Lindy was quiet for a long time. The movement of the water that she always found so mesmerising seemed to hold no magic for her tonight. The gently swaying trees across the water danced their elegant ballet to no one. She simply stared into the middle distance. And then she blinked away tears.

Of frustration? Of regret? Or for the death of something between them? Jejeune couldn't have said but, for the first time he could remember, he felt no urge to reach out and comfort her. Whatever pain she felt, it was hers alone and he couldn't share it.

Were they okay? A spectre from his own past had threatened to break them up once before, but they had united against Ray Hayes and overcome it, together. He was now nothing but a memory, living on a different continent. But this threat, from Lindy's past, was different. It had come from somewhere between them, somewhere far more insidious and destructive. He truly believed it had never been Johnno's intention to break them up. But there were always unintended consequences to bad acts, and perhaps their relationship was just one more casualty of the events Johnno had set in motion the first time he had reappeared on Lindy's horizon.

She leaned in gently and rested her head on his shoulder, still staring out over the water, and in that moment he knew that he still loved her, and that she still loved him. Would that be enough? They were not the same people now. Perhaps they no longer wanted the same things. Were they a couple, or just two separate individuals being spun further and further apart by the centrifugal forces of the events of the past few days? If they were to remain on a path to a shared future it was going to require a level of commitment that hadn't existed between them before, something more demanding, that involved plans and goals and a purpose. The chance to drift along until the time felt right to do otherwise wasn't an option any more. But if he wasn't ready for this new phase, or Lindy wasn't, or they weren't, as a couple, then the other option was to bring things to an end. Now, while there was still a chance they could remain friends and avoid the lasting scars that came from holding on, watching as the space between them grew ever larger and sucked into its void all the positive things they had once shared.

Lindy raised her head. 'That's me done, I'm afraid. I'm off to bed. It's been a long couple of days.' She stood up and turned to him. 'Oh, I've decided against taking out a membership in that hiking club, by the way. You were right, it's not really for me after all.'

For a moment, Jejeune wondered if it might be because she had already decided she may not be staying. But no, it was him having the private doubts. She was the one asking if they were okay, if they were ready to draw a line under everything and consign the past to another life. Only he wasn't sure he could. He had made compromises, chosen to let a killer go free and deny two victims the justice they deserved. Perhaps he could convince himself that he had no choice this time, but what about the next time Kim or somebody like her decided someone else had to go free in the interests of the greater good? Surely, the next concession asked of him would be easier. And the one after that. But where would that leave him, a man without principles or integrity or even a belief that what he was doing truly mattered any more, if everything was always going to be compromised in the name of the bigger picture, the greater good?

Lindy paused at the doorway and looked back at him. 'Don't look so sad, Dom. It's a rotten old world out there, where the innocent get hurt and bad people go unpunished. It's lousy, but it's life. Sometimes all you can do is accept it with resignation and move on.'

He watched her disappear into the bedroom, then stood up to walk back into the house himself. His open laptop sat on the desk in his office and he crossed to it now. Once again,

Lindy had found the right word. There was only one way to answer for the choices he had made, one way to settle his debt with justice. *Resignation.*

THE NORTHERN LAPWING

The Northern Lapwing, or simply, Lapwing, *Vanellus vanellus,* has long held a place in human society. The bird is referenced in Ovid's *Metamorphoses,* and an 1895 photograph of a Lapwing incubating its eggs by R. B. Lodge received the first medal ever presented for nature photography from the Royal Photographic Society. It is recognised as one of the very first photographs of a wild bird ever taken. In Victorian times and later, the birds' so-called 'plovers' eggs' were regarded as a delicacy at the upper-class dining table. Even today, the competition to find the first Lapwing egg of the season is a popular springtime event in the province of Friesland in the Netherlands, although the actual harvesting of Lapwing eggs is now prohibited.

Lapwings can be recognised in flight by their broad, round wingtips and plumage patterning that appears black and white. When at rest on the ground, closer examination reveals the Lapwing's back actually has a stunning iridescent green and purple sheen. Together with its distinctive curving crest, this makes the Lapwing one of the most handsome waders in the northern hemisphere. During the springtime courtship season, males tumble through the air in dramatic aerial displays, issuing a piercing call from which the species derives its other common name: the peewit. The collective noun, 'deceit', comes from Lapwing's behaviour of dragging a wing to feign injury in order to draw a potential predator away from its nest or chicks. This behaviour is familiar to North American birdwatchers in the Kildeer, and has been observed in other plover and ground-nesting species from Greenland to the Antipodes.

In a situation worthy of its collective noun, the current state of the Lapwing population is an example of the how misleading appearances can sometimes mask a true condition. The heart-lifting spectacle of Lapwings wheeling through the skies is still a relatively familiar sight in some parts of Europe, and the bird remains the most common and frequently encountered wader species in the UK. But this belies a population decline that has seen the bird occupy a position on the UK Red List of threatened species since 2009. It is estimated the population in Britain and Ireland had declined by over 60% in the last fifty years and the species now occupies less than half of its former breeding range. It has been largely lost as a breeding species from most of southwest England, west Wales and western mainland Scotland.

In winter, the Lapwing is still widely distributed in lowland Britain, but during the breeding season an eastward shift to coastal wetlands has been attributed in part to birds appearing to feed more on mudflats at low tide. An increase in extensive grazing and the loss of mixed farming systems further inland have resulted in reduced availability of high-quality foraging habitat like unimproved pasture and meadows. A clear connection seems to be exist between these agricultural models and the decline in Lapwing populations. While adapting or mitigating these activities would clearly have some impact on breeding success, whether it would be enough to reverse declines in this handsome, once-common wader is by no means certain. Further information on the Lapwing can be found at: www. bto.org/understanding-birds/birdfacts/lapwing and www.rspb.org.uk/birds-and-wildlife/lapwing

ACKNOWLEDGEMENTS

I am grateful to the team at Oneworld and in particular to my editor Wayne Brookes, Jacqui Lewis, and Paul Nash for their hard work and dedication in bringing this book to publication. At WCA, my agent, Meg Wheeler, provided her customary sound advice and guidance every step of the way. I thank her for her valuable contributions to this project.

One of the many great things about writing this series is the interesting people I meet along the way. In researching this story, I have been fortunate to receive the assistance of a number of experts in their field. All have been generous with their time and knowledge and, in no particular order, I list them here:

Clifford Cocks, former Chief Mathematician at GCHQ, the UK's intelligence, security and cyber agency, graciously consented to my referring to him and his incredible achievements in my story. Entrusted with the confidential title of the forthcoming book, he safeguarded this secret as he has so many others over his remarkable career. For this and his other kindnesses, I thank him most sincerely.

I am indebted also to Dr Roberta Bondar, Canada's first female astronaut, for sharing information on space travel, satellite photography and her own AMASS (Avian Migration

Aerial, Surface, Space) project. Uniquely able to provide a 'view from above', Dr. Bondar offered many valuable observations and insights for which I am deeply grateful.

Len Deighton, a much admired author from my early days of reading spy fiction, was kind enough to grant me permission to make references to himself and his works in my story. If my spies stand up to comparison with his, I will be honoured beyond words.

John Carley, whom I have long been fortunate enough to call a friend, drew upon his work with the Fatal Light Awareness Program (FLAP) Canada to offer invaluable advice on this aspect of the story. I thank him for his friendship, his expertise, and also for his continuing efforts on behalf of the local birdlife. They are indeed fortunate to have such a champion.

Despite the demands of being the world's leading authority on environmental DNA (eDNA), Dr Elizabeth L. Clare at York University's Department of Biology found time on multiple occasions to help me come to terms with this exciting new field of research. It was a privilege to be given an insight into the fascinating work being carried out, and I am profoundly grateful for her generosity and expertise. Not content with conducting ground-breaking studies in her field, Dr Clare also proved adept at developing devious mystery plots, and I look forward to seeing her own promised work of fiction on bookstore shelves sometime in the future.

But most of all, as ever, my love and gratitude go to my wife, Resa. Because I promised her mom that I would finally declare in print what I've been declining to say all these years, let me state without reservation that, throughout the Birder Murder Mystery series, Resa has always been right – here beside me!